Memories

and

Moonbeams

Book 2 of The Chessman series

Averil Reisman

Heartsong Books

Published by Indy Pub imprint,
IngramSparks
ISBN-13: 978-1-0878-9177-4

Please Note

This is a work of fiction. Names, characters, places, and incidents either are the product of the author's imagination or are used fictitiously, and any resemblance to actual persons, living or dead, business establishments, events or locales is entirely coincidental unless specified by the author in her notes.

Cover by The Killion Group, Inc.
Website: thekilliongroupinc.com

Story content edited by Ann Leslie Tuttle
Website: Reedsy.com

Awards

The Chessmen Series

Shadows and Masks, Book 1
Booksellers Best

Memories and Moonbeams, Book 2
Hook, Line and Sinker
The Sheila
Romance Through the Ages

Other Book Awards

The Captain's Temptress (formerly titled *To Cuba With Love*)
Spring Into Romance
The Orange Rose
Touch of Magic
Ignite the Flame
Heart of the West
Cleveland Rocks
Duel of the Delta

Dedication

To Isaac, Tobin, Simon, and Regan

Follow your heart and you'll always be true to yourself

——Grandma

Chapter 1

August, 1893
Colorado City, Colorado

WELL, DAMN! PUSHING HIS NEW Stetson off his forehead, Nicholas Shield peered more closely at the two numbers hanging cockeyed over the swinging doors. Right address, but the place was a damn saloon, not the office of the private investigator he had come all the way from Chicago to hire. He clenched his jaw.

Raucous laughter, tinny piano music, and the stink of stale whiskey drifted out, deepening his already foul mood.

Where the hell had his friend Bart sent him?

When Nick had asked for the name of a good detective in Colorado, Bart, an investigator himself, had suggested a Lee Wilcox and given him an address, among other things. But, clearly, this wasn't right. Not a saloon in a sweltering hellhole of a town where the dust made the saliva in his mouth feel like a sandy beach.

From the looks of things, Colorado City was even worse than Chicago's Levee District where he and his friends occasionally visited. Here, the late afternoon sun bore down like a blazing fireball on the bordellos, saloons, and dilapidated sin cribs lining the streets in a pleasure haven of vice. Scores of miners, mill workers, ranchers, and new gold millionaires crowded the town looking for whiskey, a game, and a roll with one of the town's army of whores.

At one time he might have joined them. But he hadn't traveled so damned far to be distracted by any of that.

Today his top priority was finding his sister, who'd disappeared six weeks ago. Pinkerton agents hired by his father had tracked her to these parts but fled when the altitude got to them. Now he needed the help of a local detective to continue the search. Someone familiar with the area who wouldn't get sick up in the high mountains where she'd last been seen.

Bart had picked Wilcox as the man for the job from a list he kept locked in a drawer. Why all the secrecy, his friend hadn't said. Nor had Nick bothered to ask. Bart didn't like to talk much about his investigative work.

Maybe someone in the saloon knew where to find him.

Adjusting his hat, Nick pushed through the swinging doors. A smoky haze hung about like a dark thundercloud, making him squint before his eyes adapted to the noxious gloom. Gamblers crowding around a dozen gaming tables added to the din and the stench of unwashed bodies and cheap cigars.

After sauntering up to the long oak bar, Nick overheard two men sitting nearby arguing about their favorite whores.

". . . titties like melons and an ass soft enough to swallow my whole cock and balls," said the one closest to him, his hands cupping the air to indicate the size of those breasts.

"So what? Lorine sucks me deep and gets me off in no time, then rides me to beat the band. She earns my coin, and then some, she does," his friend retorted.

Having no interest in their conversation, Nick faced the bar.

The bartender, a big man about his own age of thirty, wiped something vigorously with a towel. Spotting Nick, he set the clean glass on a rack and the cloth on the back shelf. "Whadya have?"

Nick managed to smile despite his headache. "Three fingers of your best, my friend." A fine cognac would be preferable, but he doubted this place stocked any.

"Whiskey all right?" The barkeeper grinned, his gaze tracking down Nick's clothing with undisguised amusement.

Nick drew himself straight. Nothing he wore warranted the smirk on the bartender's face. Nick knew more about apparel than any man here, having worked in his father's dry goods business most of his life. As soon as he arrived in town, he'd purchased new western clothes—hat, string tie, jeans, plaid shirt, black vest, and boots—in a store near the train station to avoid standing out like the city dweller he was.

"That will do." He tossed a coin on the counter, leaned his six-foot two-inch frame against the bar's edge and scanned the murky surroundings.

The noise from the crowded establishment made his ears ring. His head still ached from not having slept during the two-day train ride. And his inner turmoil regarding the safety of his little sister hadn't diminished either.

The bartender slid a drink in front of him, picked up his coin, and returned to washing glasses.

Nick took a gulp. Fire raced down his throat but surprisingly, the whiskey was not half bad. Wiping his mouth with the back of his hand, he asked, "Hey, barkeep. I'm looking for a Lee Wilcox. Know where I can find him?"

"Sure do." Chuckling, the man nodded and whispered to a nearby boy of about twelve who was lugging a box of empty bottles. "He'll get her."

Her?

Wilcox was a *woman?* With offices in a saloon? What respectable woman—

Bart would never send him to a whore, not even as a joke, would he? No, he said he didn't know Lee Wilcox personally, only by reputation. But did his friend know this investigator was a woman? With a name like Lee, maybe not. In fact, Nick would bet on it. Bart had referred to Wilcox as *he.*

A brunette of small stature ambled up to him, a sumptuous display of womanly charms rising above a gaudy red dress. A gold chain around her neck drew his attention downward toward where whatever hung on it lodged between her breasts.

Out of sight.

His eyes lingered there a moment, imagining the bauble's surroundings, before he lifted his gaze to her face.

Large green eyes like those of the woman who'd haunted his dreams for the past seven years captured his gaze. Air whooshed from his lungs as he felt a prickle of electricity zip through his body. Their gazes locked in a silent connection that left his heart slamming against his ribs.

Suddenly she stiffened, and he swore she paled beneath her thick face paint. "I'm Lee Wilcox, and I owe you this." Her hand rose.

Whack! A stinging pain slammed into his cheek.

Stunned, he staggered back, his hand flying to his face. What the hell? Struggling to recover his wits, he bent to retrieve his hat from the floor.

Had a card floated off a table and landed on the wood planks below, it would have thundered in the sudden quiet of the gambling hall. The silence was eerie, charged. Thick as a heavy fog. He had the distinct impression each man had taken stock of him and judged him to be a menace. Even the bartender had flung himself flat across the bar top, ready to come to the lady's aid.

"It's all right, Thad. I'll handle this," she said in a melodic, familiar voice that penetrated deep into his soul. Her green eyes were as cold as the ocean's depths.

Handle what? He was the one on the wrong end of the assault. Who was she, and what did she think he had done to warrant such a vehement payback? His cheek still stung like a hive of bees had attacked.

"I'm sorry. Do I know you?" Dumb, but the only thing that came to his rattled mind.

"Try Lee Wilcox. Or better yet, how about Lilly Kane?" Her voice spat venom.

He stilled. Had he heard right?

Lilly! Lee.

Memories burst into his consciousness. Blood pulsed in his ears like a thousand pounding mallets. Old hurts resurfaced. Tamping back his emotions, Nick assumed a pleasant smile. Through eyes rooted in the past, he studied her features.

Familiar chestnut-colored hair piled in a mass of curls atop her head added at least three inches to the woman's diminutive five-foot height. Beneath the heavy makeup, the delicate heart shape of Lilly's face was barely discernible, the hollows below her high cheekbones having filled in for a more rounded appearance. Her youthful bosom had blossomed into a pleasing handful and her hips were more defined than he remembered.

But it was her eyes peering at him through gobs of shadow and kohl that confirmed her identity. Eyes with an exotic slanted shape, irises of sea green flecked with gold and surrounded by a ring of black.

Eyes now sparking with ire.

He struggled to fill his lungs, his thoughts scattered to the winds.

Lilly!

The woman he couldn't forget no matter how hard he tried.

She was here?

Was this woman standing in front of him an illusion conjured up by lack of sleep and worry over his sister? Or was she real, the embodiment of all his wishes come true?

Nick perused the apparition in red.

She looked like every other lush working girl in the place, and for some reason that didn't sit well with him. Her flamboyant gown exposed more of her impressive bosom than the woman he once loved would have dared allow.

Hell, more than he would have allowed. He wanted to throw his suit jacket around her shoulders, cover her up. But he wasn't wearing a suit. So, he just gawked at the swift rise and fall of her bountiful chest.

The change in her was profound, and his mind scrambled to accept it.

What had happened to the little shop girl he adored, the young lady with the beautiful eyes and the sweetly beckoning smile? What was she doing in a gambling hall in Colorado City dressed as a whore?

Or was she ...?

Refusing to acknowledge the truth of what his eyes were telling him, he cut off his thoughts.

No, she was an investigator. His best friend had vouched for her as a professional. Or rather vouched for Lee Wilcox. Nick was sure Bart had no idea that Lee Wilcox was a woman, let alone that the woman was Nick's former lover, Lilly Kane. Theirs had been a secret relationship.

There must be some other explanation for her appearance.

Lilly glanced about and, without a word, headed for the back of the saloon, her silk skirts swishing as her hips swayed seductively.

Why he followed like a dog seeking a treat, he would never understand. Maybe he was just damn curious. Or maybe the siren call of those hips held him in thrall.

Or maybe seeing Lilly in those clothes, in this setting, scared the shit out of him. Could his sister have disappeared into the underworld of sin never to be found?

As they passed table after table of gamblers, blatant male admiration seemed to be drawn to the sensual swing of her bottom. His insides unexpectedly tightened, as did his jaw.

She'd been his.

Once.

She led him to a room at the far corner of the establishment and disappeared inside. Nick, however, transfixed by the sight before him, halted at the doorway of what could only be described as someone's comfortable front parlor.

Bright afternoon sun streaming through a wide set of open windows reached clear across the room, bringing with it a refreshing breeze. Books, photographs, and bric-a-brac were neatly arranged on a massive wooden desk positioned for a view of the mountains. Flowered wallpaper and furniture, and a thick carpet made it a woman's office in—of all places—a rowdy gambling hall and drinking establishment.

The professional domain of private investigator Lee Wilcox. Known to him as Lilly Kane.

What was she doing here?

~~~~

Dear Lord! Why was Nick here and asking for Lee Wilcox? Nick was the last person Lilly expected to see in this no man's land of Colorado wildness.

She despised him, could barely contain her anger at what he had done to her life. Yet seeing his handsome face, hearing the rumble of his deep baritone gave her an undeniable thrill.

While fighting to control her rioting emotions, she stepped inside and let her eyes feast on him while he surveyed her office.

The years had been good to him, molding him into a magnificent specimen of masculinity.

The boyish appearance of his youth was gone, replaced by a starkly handsome blond-haired Viking with piercing, light blue eyes.

His features were more chiseled than she remembered. A firm, square jaw bisected by a deep cleft, sharply edged cheekbones, and a more defined patrician nose lent him an aura of command she had never known him to possess.

Fine lines of maturity and wisdom were etched into his face. Or at least that's what she wanted to believe those lines represented—the same stuff that had comprised her dreams for so many years. Dreams she finally flung upon the muck heap of life to save her sanity. Dreams she had replaced with steely anger and intense hatred.

More likely, those tiny wrinkles came from an overabundance of self-indulgence. And the more she believed that, the better off she would be.

His wider shoulders, broader chest, and thicker muscles spelled danger to the fragile world she had twice rebuilt.

She'd made a life for herself here, and nothing and nobody—Nicholas included—was going to spoil what she had achieved. She had a job to do, and she was darn good at doing it.

Pushing her disquieting thoughts aside, Lilly sat down at her desk and waved him to sit. There was nothing she could do about the mass of butterflies flitting about in her stomach.

Twisting the rim of his hat, Nick crossed the threshold, but remained standing. *Well, fine.* Maybe he won't be staying long. The faster she dealt with him, the sooner he would be on his way.

She leaned back in her chair and crossed her arms over her chest. His beautiful blue eyes bore into hers, daring her to reveal her secrets.

Damn him. She could fall into those eyes and never find her way out. "You have Lee Wilcox's full attention. Why are you here?"

And why now

Chapter 2

WHAT WOULD BILLY SAY NOW if he was faced with the same situation? Nick absently dug his hand in his pocket expecting to find his brother's small wooden toy he always carried. The soldier was a reminder of the love and admiration he and Billy once shared, of the wisdom, encouragement, and guidance he had conveyed. Before he died a horrific death two days before his fifteenth birthday.

Instead, his fingers brushed the ivory chess piece he'd placed there when he'd changed clothes. The chess piece Bart had given him to give to Wilcox. Another mystery Nick hadn't bothered to question.

He moved closer to the desk.

"So, how long has it been?" The words flew out of his mouth, sounding shallow and trite.

Stupid. Stupid. Stupid.

Couldn't he have thought of anything else? Where was that old Nick Shield reputation for charm and blather when he needed it? This little ball of anger had him grasping for words.

"Seven years," she bit out without hesitation, her eyes challenging him to dispute her answer.

As though she'd been counting the years.

As had he.

His breathing ceased, his gaze caught in her glare of confrontation. *God, Lilly, what happened to us?*

If he held any doubt this woman was Lilly, it no longer existed. Only Lilly would know the answer to his question.

Their clandestine relationship had been kept to dark storerooms and walks on the Chicago lake shore after his father's store closed for the night.

He schooled his voice to be as noncommittal as possible, but the question uppermost in his thoughts all these years slipped off his tongue. "Why did you leave me?"

Cheeks reddening through the mask of cosmetics, Lilly shot off her chair, her hands flying to the desk where her knuckles ground into the wood. "I didn't, you bastard. You left me," she shouted through the straight line of her lips.

Nick cringed. Why did she think that? He'd never left her. He wanted her. Desperately. Still did.

Yet, the volume of her pain-tinged voice revealed the depth of her upset. No matter how rankled she might have been, the young woman he knew had never raised her voice.

Lilly careened around the desk's edge and stalked to the window, her back to him, her arms winging about her middle.

"I hate you, Nick Shield. You left me pregnant and alone." Her clipped words had a hard edge to them.

He sucked in a breath, then failed to release it. Deafening silence filled the space between them as his mind struggled with what he thought he'd heard.

"What did you say?" he asked, his question barely more than a whisper.

Lilly's expressive eyes were ice. "I said, I had a daughter, Celia. Her picture is on the desk. You were her father."

He lifted a large frame off the desk. The face of a small child with blonde hair and cherubic cheeks gazed back at him, a face that looked remarkably like the portrait of his sister when she was four hanging in his mother's bedroom.

A brick plowed into his chest, followed by an unexpected warmth. His mind collided with the undeniable reality he'd run from most of his life—responsibility. His sister's well-being was the only thing that mattered to him.

Until Lilly came into his life seven years ago.

And then something else Lilly had said sank into his brain. "Were?"

"She passed of the fever two years ago."

A fist full of crippling emotions barreled through him, leaving him gasping. To keep his weakened knees from buckling, he gripped the back of a chair. The fact Nick sired a daughter he hadn't known about was bad enough, but that she died without knowing her father was devastating.

Damn, damn, damn! He wanted to hit something. Himself, mostly. He deserved it. How could he have done this?

Lord knows, he had not set out to be a father, but if fate had made him one, he might have stepped up to the challenge. Changed the life he now found lacking.

Might have. He was so young then.

Nick met Lilly's glare through blurry vision. "Why didn't you tell me you carried our child? I would have…." Nick stopped, the words clogging his throat like cotton batting. Try as he might, he couldn't bring himself to say what he thought she wanted to hear.

Green eyes narrowed in fury. "What would you have done? Tell me."

"I… I would have been there for you."

"Would you have? Really? Married me? Given your daughter your name, settled into a normal routine, taken on responsibility for once in your life?"

Another punch to the gut. The truth hurt. He swallowed hard but didn't answer. Like the rest of his friends, he'd shied away from marriage as though it were the plague. He was a hedonist who dabbled in fun, adventure, and the finer things of life. There was no room for responsibility and commitment.

Then.

After Lilly left, that way of life no longer satisfied him, but he couldn't seem to find what would. Days were empty, meaningless. Nights, unbearably lonely.

He hadn't realized how much Lilly had added to his life—the laughter, the sharing, the companionship.

Until she was gone.

He'd taken her for granted.

How stupid he had been.

Lilly continued, her voice sounding thin and choked to his ear. "I tried to tell you about the baby as soon as I was sure. I went to your house, but your father said you'd moved away. He said you were managing a new store somewhere far and I should forget you."

Blast his father. He envisioned a different future for his son. A future more like his own—one that made him a pillar of society but created a private life that was living hell. Familiar bands of frustration tightened around Nick's torso.

He shook his head, anger toward his overbearing parent billowing from his chest like smoke from a fire. "Not true. I never moved anywhere. My father sent me to New York on a long buying trip. When I returned, you were gone. I assumed you left on your own accord."

"Then your father lied to me. For you. To prevent me, as he put it, from 'sinking my teeth' into his precious, wealthy son. Assuming correctly that I was in a family way, he made me a generous offer to move away and start over."

Lilly lowered her head, clenched her arms. "I had no choice but to accept his proposal. My baby's future was more important. I couldn't continue working at your father's store, and no one would hire a pregnant woman. And I couldn't give up my child."

The breath in him drained out in a wheeze. "He never told me you came."

"Then he lied to both of us. I showed up at the store for a whole week hoping to see you, but you weren't there, and no one could tell me where you went. I assumed your father told me the truth."

Damn him! This time his father's interference in his life had cost everyone dearly.

Especially Lilly. Moisture glistened in her eyes. He hated seeing her in pain.

"I was alone and afraid. I had no one. My parents . . .disowned me. I hate you for causing my family to turn against me. You didn't even try to find me."

"I did try. Your leaving didn't make sense, so at first, I thought to go to your home and see if you were there. But you once said Kane was the Americanized version of your parents' last name. You never told me the name they were listed under in the residents' directory."

He paused to swipe his palm across his forehead. "I thought of riffling through my father's private employee records to find your address, but that would have been illegal. Even considered hiring the

Pinks but thought that maybe you might not want to be found. As time went on and you didn't come back, that idea became more believable. So, I condemned you for walking away from me. I'm sorry. So very sorry. Had I known—"

"I don't want to hear your 'would haves.' You would have done what you've done your whole life—shirked responsibility. The only good thing to come out of this was Celia. I enjoyed her for four wonderful years and, when she died...."

Rubbing her arms, Lilly turned to stare out the window, her small figure cloaked in sorrow.

Her caustic barb was deserved, but the husk of pain in her voice burned clear through to his heart.

Yes, he had been irresponsible, but he sensed there was more here than she was telling him. Something else causing her pain.

He moved to gather her close, but she pulled her head up and jerked away. Tears welled in eyes of shimmering emerald.

"Don't touch me, Nicholas. You don't get to touch me ever again."

~~~~

Nick paled, his shoulders slumping as his attention slipped to his feet. He shifted his weight to his other hip, and Lilly's mind wandered. Did ridged muscle still line his chest clear down to his hips?

Memories of his arms around her, of his lips molded to hers, of the press of his youthful frame against her body, resurfaced in a sudden burst of lust.

Mortified at the direction of her thoughts, Lilly stiffened. How could she still feel this way about a man who had left her pregnant and alone?

Granted, he didn't know she carried his child, but the resentment she held against him had sent roots deep in her heart. Indeed, she had used those negative feelings to pull herself out of the dark hole of despair, and she was not about to uproot them anytime soon.

If that was what he wanted.

Come to think of it, what *did* he want? He'd come to see Lee Wilcox, but he had not known who Lee Wilcox really was. That was clear by the confusion on his face when she had slapped him.

No, fate brought him here today as sure as that first day they met in his father's store. Nick's easy smile and devil-may-care attitude attracted her then like no other. She had found him fascinating, charming, and more worldly than any of the other men her parents shoved in her path.

But, with a rule banning fraternization among employees, their budding friendship moved into the shadows of dark stockrooms and moonlit beaches.

Became more intimate.

If she was being truthful, she had as much to do with their indiscretion as he did. She'd been so sure of Nick's honor and integrity.

Oh, how naive she had been.

Since then, she had erected a strong shield to protect her heart.

Or so she thought.

But now she found his magnetic presence still evoked wants and needs she was hard-pressed to deny. If she was not careful, her heart would be exposed and made vulnerable once again.

And that would never do.

Nick was forbidden to her on so many levels.

Besides, she was angry with him.

Needing a moment to pull herself together, she returned to her desk. Settling in her chair, she donned her professional aloofness. "What are you seeking Lee Wilcox for?"

Nick stared at her, the clear blue of his eyes raw, penetrating. A riot of emotions raged through them, making her uncomfortable, making her remember.

Making her ache with need.

Finally, he slid his long frame into a small, upholstered chair across from her, the furrow deep in his forehead drawing her curiosity.

Nick never worried.

About anything.

"Sabrina's missing," he said in a dull, flat tone as he set the tintype of his daughter on the desk facing him.

Lilly tensed. She was acquainted with his sister and liked her immensely. For years, Sabrina Shield and her mother had been her best customers in the millinery department at Shield's Clothing Emporium, the largest retail store in Chicago. Nick clearly loved his younger sibling and doted on her at every turn. In fact, she was the only member of his family he seemed to care about at all.

Which made the look of devastation on Nick's face when he learned of Celia's death even more understandable. Never had she seen him display such emotion, such anguish and yes, even remorse. His emotions were real, of that she was certain. Nothing had fazed him or disturbed his equilibrium before.

Lilly tamped back the sudden rush of sympathy welling from the middle of her chest. "What brings you here?"

Out of all the places in the country, why had he chosen to look for Sabrina in Colorado City, a place of sin and decadence renown throughout the state. Even respectable women built their houses a discreet distance away in the nearby Springs.

Nick lifted a small rock paperweight from her desk and absently rolled it about his palm with long, gifted fingers that once aroused her deepest passions. She watched them closely, almost wishing they played on her skin instead of the inanimate object they grasped with care.

"A Pinkerton agent tracked my sister, or someone who looks like Sabrina, to some gold camp called Cripple Creek, but the altitude got him, and he came home without identifying her. I'm picking up where he left off, and I need an investigator familiar with the mountains."

Curiosity broke through the bitterness permeating her mood.

"How did you get my name?" Locating specific individuals was not her type of case regardless of how much she liked Miss Shield. And why was Sabrina in Cripple Creek, a rough and dirty gold camp up the mountain where respectable women were rare.

"You were recommended by a friend. He gave me something to give to *Mr.* Wilcox." The corner of his mouth tilted in reference to the investigator's mistaken gender.

Nick dug in his jeans pocket with his unoccupied hand, the material drawing snug to an important part of his anatomy. She swallowed over a sudden dryness as memories of dark lusty nights invaded her sanity. Much to her chagrin, her face heated. Again.

Still caught in the past, she blinked stupidly before recognizing the item he pulled from his pocket.

An ivory chess piece. A knight.

Lilly's pulse jumped. Oh, dear God. She held out her suddenly cold hand. "May I see that?"

Nick handed the tiny sculpture over, the slide of his fingers along her palm sending an unexpected tingle up her arm. Blinking, she turned the carving over and thumbed its bottom, found the telltale indented identifier.

Her world abruptly tilted.

The piece was the symbol of referral used by agents of the secret federal crimes fighting unit to which she belonged, an agency where anonymity among operatives was imperative. Nobody knew what the next agent looked like.

Their names were written on cards to be locked away in a safe place and taken out only for referral. Each operative possessed a clandestine area of expertise and managed a network of local informants.

Reaching out as a friend to the area's prostitutes was Lilly's cover job. But her government job was to rescue women from the white slave trade growing at an alarming rate in the mining camps. Not that the government cared one wit for the poor souls she rescued. Information about the men who sold them was the real prize.

After the government was done with these unfortunate witnesses, Lilly helped them settle into new lives. That was her new purpose in life she assumed for herself after Celia's death upended her world.

Lilly stared at the small, elegantly carved knight. The air abruptly grew saturated with apprehension as thick as a suffocating shroud. She struggled to pull in a breath but was overwhelmed with a sense of impending doom that defied explanation. It slid up her spine and hid in a dark, ominous cloud of uncertainty. Anxiety swirled about her mind like a swarm of angry bees.

Recovering a modicum of professional control, she swallowed her unaccountable fear and plowed forward. "Who gave this to you?"

Nick's gaze settled on her lips, and she felt its heat as though he'd touched them. "A friend," he answered, his tone flippant and offhand.

Dismayed, she manipulated the knight with her fingers, her

scrambled thoughts racing in a thousand different directions.

Presentation of the marked chessman was the same as being given a verbal directive. The piece represented a mission deemed important enough by another agent to demand a referral. She received very few chess pieces over the years but had never turned down an assignment when presented with one. Could she do so now?

Lilly settled the object carefully on the desk as she considered her options.

Helping Nick would mean she would be in his constant presence. How was she to maintain her distance emotionally and physically when his handsome countenance reminded her of what they'd once been to each other?

The truth was, she didn't think she could.

"Nick, I—"

Chapter 3

SOMEONE POUNDED ON LILLY'S DOOR, then opened it without waiting for a response. Nick twisted in his chair to see who'd rudely interrupted his meeting.

A man in his forties, of middling height and dark brown hair flecked with silver, peered in. Hazel eyes filled with haunting sadness overwhelmed a face covered with a trim beard. Beneath his facial hair, Nick detected the strong jaw and chiseled features of a man of strength and vitality.

Nick tensed. What was this man to Lilly that a closed office door was no barrier?

"Lee?" A deep base voice boomed from the bottom of the smaller man's chest. "I found a badly beaten young lady crying behind the stables. I think you need to talk to her before I take her to Doc's office. I brought her in the back way."

Some unspoken message passed between Lilly and the man. What was it?

"Bring her in. Nick, can you give me a moment with Jacob, please. He's my assistant."

"Of course." He rose.

Though begrudging the interruption, Nick was not about to stand in the way of someone who needed help. But shouldn't this woman be taken instead to the doctor and the police, or whatever passed for law enforcement in this town?

As he exited, he collided with a girl pulling at the sides of a ripped satin gown. One of her eyes was puffed shut, and the other, nearly so. Blood still oozed from her nose which she wiped with a large, wadded handkerchief. What the blazes happened to her?

"I'm sorry," he murmured, and tipped his hat.

The young woman tensed as she fled past him to Lilly's office. Though murmurs followed in her wake, gamblers soon returned to their cards as though the sight of roughed up women was a common occurrence.

What the hell kind of business was Lilly involved in?

Nick leaned against the back wall of the saloon, his mind reeling.

What were the odds of convincing Lilly to take his case? She hated him, and for good reason. From the condition of the young lady he'd just passed, Lilly had far more important things to do than hunt for the sister of someone she despised. His chances of engaging her services had just slipped to slim, if non-existent.

And what effect, if any, had presenting that silly little chess piece have? She'd seemed startled to see it, and yet Bart had said to be sure to give it to Wilcox. Must be some signal of sorts common among investigators.

What he did know was that seeking her help had been a mistake, one of many he had made where she was concerned.

Nick huffed out a breath as he came to a reluctant decision. As soon as Lilly was free, he would tell her he changed his mind and would seek someone else to track Sabrina. That was probably the wisest thing to do.

Then why did that decision feel so wrong?

The men at the nearest table finished their game and made ready to leave. Before they could rise, Nick acknowledged them with a quick grin, slid into an empty chair near Lilly's door and pulled a deck of cards from his vest pocket. "You gents care to learn an easy card trick to impress the ladies?"

Now here was something he was good at—entertaining. Being the buffoon who made life interesting for other people.

"Sure do, mister. I could use all the help I can get," said a short, rotund man with a bulbous nose and blackened teeth. He laughed, and the stink of garlic and dirty clothes hit Nick in the face.

Good-natured ribbing came from the other three, but they sat as well.

Nick glided through the intricacies of the trick, his mind split between the explanation slipping easily off his tongue and the conversation drifting out the crack of the nearly closed office door.

Sobbing, the battered girl told her story in halting fashion. "I didn't know what he intended to do. I just answered an advertisement for a mail order bride. After we met, he took me prisoner, sold me out to men from the back of his wagon. Tied me up when I wasn't. . .working. He added two other girls after me."

Two others?

Sabrina!

Throwing the cards down amid the complaints of the men, Nick rocketed off his chair and burst through the door.

Startled, Lilly frowned over the woman's head cradled against her shoulder.

"What did these other women look like?" Nick asked, forcing the question out of a suddenly arid mouth.

Lilly's jaw tightened.

The girl squinted through red-rimmed eyes filled with anxiety. "A tall black-haired woman who talks like a southerner, and a tall, thin blonde-haired woman with a peculiar nasal accent."

Cold fear pierced his innards, freezing the blood in his veins.

"Oh, God. I wish I'd never left home." The girl's words trailed off into a terrible wail.

Shite. His mind raced at the same fast clip as his heart. *A tall, thin woman with blonde hair and a peculiar nasal accent.* Sabrina was tall, about four inches shorter than him, and thin, and blonde. And he'd often been told by visitors that Chicagoans speak with a flat nasal accent.

"Sabrina!" His sister's name emerged from his mouth in a ragged plea, despair taking over all rational thought. Lilly had to help him now. She just had to.

Gazes locked, Lilly's eyes widened. In the space of a heartbeat, a kaleidoscope of emotions beginning with horror and ending with tight-jawed determination skated across the beautiful face beneath the makeup. She dipped her head toward him in a barely perceptible nod.

Relief blew through him like a sudden gust of wind. He clearly had no choice.

Lilly was his best chance of finding Sabrina.

~~~~

The last thing Lilly wanted to do was spend another moment in Nick's company.

But the fear consuming his features was more than she could bear. The tight grip on his emotions had slipped twice today—once, after learning of his daughter's death and now, realizing his sister might have been kidnapped for sexual use.

Lilly's concern for the woman escalated tenfold. If Sabrina had been foolish enough to answer an ad for a mail order bride, she could have disappeared into the dark world of sexual slavery, never to be seen or heard from again.

These women either died horrible deaths by diseases or were dumped by their owners when looks and age took their toll.

Though more victims were indigenous, black, Chinese, and French women, some were young white girls like Jenny here, lured to adventure and husbands by unscrupulous recruiters placing ads in city newspapers.

As much as she disliked Nick and his father, she would never wish them the pain of losing Sabrina to the darkness of sin.

Lilly glanced at the woman in her arms. From her detailed description of her kidnapper, Lilly was certain the man was the one she, Jacob and Thad had been seeking for months--Cyrus DuPry.

A particularly vicious criminal who beat his captives unmercifully and farmed their services out to miners for exorbitant prices. Unlike a regular brothel, DuPry put his captives in a wagon and brought them to the smaller gold camps. Men waited in lengthy lines outside DePry's tent for a turn with one of his girls.

Despite the government assignment to locate the man and steal his current captives, his whereabouts had eluded them. Perhaps this was the chance they'd been waiting for. To put into play the plan they had developed and trained for with the help of their boss, Reginald.

Lilly gently wiped the girl's brow with her handkerchief. "Jenny, did this man mention where he was headed?"

The younger woman studied her solemnly, her lips pursed in

remembrance. "Said something about making sure he got to Victor before the snow flies. Planned to spend the winter there, I think."

Bloody hell! Not Victor! Traveling that far up the mountain would add time to the mission. Too long to be in Nick Shield's virile presence.

Could she do this?

If Jacob would be accompanying them, surely he'd be able to keep her thoughts from straying into areas too dangerous to contemplate.

The search would be difficult. With all Victor's secret hiding places, mine tunnels beneath the streets, and lack of lawmen, the gold camp was a known refuge for criminals of all sorts. Her network of informants among the whores and other businesses in town will be put through their paces.

Lilly covered Jenny's trembling hands with her own. "Victor. Makes sense. Best place in the world for the likes of this nasty man. Lots of places to hide. But I've got lots of people to help find them. He'll need to travel to Cripple Creek first, and so will we. We'll find him and save these other women."

Nick shifted, and she could have sworn she heard him release a breath. Her own breathing proved harder to control. Though holding to calm on the outside, inside she had grown ragged and raw.

She pinned him with a stare she hoped masked her emotions. "This will be an arduous journey. The Midland train up Ute Pass to Florissant, followed by a rough eighteen-mile stage up to Cripple Creek. If DuPry's going to Victor, that's another ten miles or so up a narrow, winding trail with a wagon and horses."

She raked over his big, broad frame, and an unexpected shiver ran up her spine. "Victor's elevation is near ten thousand feet, and we could encounter dreadful cold or an early snow this time of the year. Are you up to making the trip?"

The dark expression he gave her left no doubt he thought himself equal to the trek's rigors. Drats. She'd meant to discourage him, but perhaps this was for the best. If the blonde woman was Sabrina, she might be traumatized. Having her brother near might help to calm her.

"Are you sure *you* can manage the journey?" he drawled.

Ignoring her previous premonition of doom and her unsettling feelings toward this man, she pulled her shoulders back.

"You're hiring me because you need someone experienced. I have that training. One other thing, Nick. You will do as I tell you, whatever I tell you. The thin air is nothing to fool with. You'll drink water, lots of it, and nothing else. No spirits, no wine, no ale. Nothing but water. Do you understand?"

His blue eyes narrowed to slits. "Yes, ma'am. I do. Only water."

"And...?"

"I will do whatever you say. Just find my sister." he bit out.

"Good. We have an understanding then. Jacob will be coming with us."

His mouth twitched as amusement settled in his eyes. How perfectly delectable he looked. "Why? Do you think we'll need a chaperon?"

Dang if he hadn't stumbled upon her exact thoughts. Embarrassment heated the fire already raging on her face. Nick's grin widened.

"No. I will require a man's strength for certain things. I don't know if you'll be around when I need it."

The amusement leached from his eyes, replaced by a flash of hurt. She should feel elated with the hit she scored, yet the sense of victory lay shattered about her.

Embarrassed, Lilly turned to her assistant. "Jacob, he'll need warmer clothes. I'm assuming Mr. Shield will pay for them, along with some other things we'll need?"

Nick nodded, his gaze resolute.

"I'm sure Cripple Creek has grown," she said. "But I don't know what supplies might be available up there."

Taking charge felt good. She had a client who needed her help. *Time to stow my emotions and pull in my claws.*

To Jenny, she added, "We'll get you cleaned up and fed. Jacob, can you also have Betty take Jenny to Doc Randolph and then to the boarding house. There's an extra room at the moment. Thad, my bartender, will keep you safe, and Betty, she runs Sally's Silver Spoon, will bring you what you need. You can trust them while I'm gone. We'll be leaving as soon as possible if we're to catch this man."

Confusion registered in Jacob's eyes. "Seeing to the women… you always did that."

He paused, looking between Lilly and Nick.

An interminable minute passed, one fraught with discomfort and tension. Did he sense the animosity thickening the air? Did he suspect that the giant blond Viking staring intensely at her was Celia's father? That she was still attracted to him in a forbidden carnal way? That she didn't trust him, and worse, that she didn't trust herself to be alone with him?

Was this the reason for the sense of impending disaster overpowering her thoughts when she first laid eyes on the chess piece?

Chapter 4

ARMS LOADED WITH PACKAGES, NICK stepped outside the men's clothing store in Colorado Springs later that afternoon and headed toward the horse and wagon hitched to a post in front. Jacob Gould followed, his arms full of Nick's purchases, as well.

"Why didn't you buy anything for yourself?" Nick asked as he neared the wagon.

After swinging his bundles into the back, the older man reached for Nick's. "Don't need to. Got everything I need."

"Been here that long, huh?"

"Long enough. Don't intend to leave any time soon, either." The man's tone sounded defensive. Which aroused Nick's curiosity.

"Why is that?"

"My family is buried here. Don't want to abandon them." Jacob glanced across the street to where Lilly, looking every bit the respectable woman in her simple blue cotton shirtwaist, entered a ladies' emporium. "Don't want to abandon her, either."

A dark emotion Nick couldn't identify pressed against his ribs. Whatever it was hiked his wariness of the man standing before him. "You mean Mrs. Wilcox?"

"I mean Lilly Kane. She buried her daughter a few days before I buried my Maddy. My wife followed the next day. The fever took them all."

Remorse coursed through him. Nick busied himself stacking the packages Jacob haphazardly threw in. "How did you meet her?"

"Saw her weeping near her daughter's grave. We consoled each other."

Consoled, my ass. Nick's jaw tightened as a wave of possessiveness he shouldn't be feeling took hold. He glared at the man beside him whose gaze was still fixed on the emporium door.

"You just buried your wife, and you went sniffing around another woman?"

Oomph! A fist plowed into his chin.

Startled, he stumbled backward, then worked his jaw to test its movement.

"You piece of shit city slicker! Have you no feelings? We wept on each other's shoulder! Several days later, she hired me as her assistant. We both still grieve for our families."

Nick studied the man whose eyes had filled with pain. "I'm sorry," he mumbled.

Jacob was silent for a moment. "My guess is she also mourns the loss of someone else. Celia's father, I'm thinking."

Warmth exploded throughout his body. *She mourns for me? No, he's got it wrong. She said she hates me. I caused her pain and anguish.*

Yet, a tiny bud of hope poked through the barren dirt beneath his boots. The fact he found the feeling pleasant confused him. He had come to find Sabrina, not Lilly, but here she was and what was he going to do about it?

Probably nothing.

Yet, despite his better judgment, he strode around the wagon and headed toward the emporium, eager to be in her company.

Jacob's voice exploded behind him, loud and dangerous. "You hurt her again, and I'll kill you."

"I won't," he yelled back. He had no intention of ever causing her more pain. She had endured more than her share already.

Reaching the store, he peered through the window. The object of their discussion browsed the racks of ready-made dresses while the shopkeeper waited on three women at the counter. He opened the shop door and crept inside, choosing an inconspicuous place near the entrance to observe.

Without her makeup, she was still a beauty. He itched to pull the pins out of the tight heavy bun confining her plaited brown hair and run his fingers through the thick strands. What would she think? What would she do?

"Thank you, Mr. Baxter," one of the women said as the three turned to leave. "You'll let me know when it comes in."

"Sure will, Mrs. Simmons. When it arrives from New York, I'll send Tommy around to tell you."

As they strolled away, Lilly approached the counter. Noticing her, one of the ladies scowled in indignation, a tight expression forming on facial features matching her high necked, starched dress. "Your kind shouldn't be in here today. Your time is Tuesday and Friday mornings. Go on, get. We don't want to sully ourselves with the filth you drag in."

The blood drained from Lilly's face, now as white as the garment she held. "My money is just as green as yours, Mrs. Wentworth. I'll shop when I choose."

Good for her!

"Your money! The kind you gain from the *services* you perform? Did you earn your bastard daughter from those *services*, as well?"

Lilly rocked back, naked pain gripping her expressive green eyes.

And tearing his heart apart.

She didn't deserve the woman's derision. No woman did. Certainly not the kind, goodhearted Lilly Kane he knew.

Without thinking, he stepped forward and grabbed a bolt of puce sateen fabric off a nearby table. Three long steps brought him to Mrs. Pruneface's side.

"Excuse me, I couldn't help noticing how lovely this material would look made up in a dress for you. You have the perfect coloring and... uh... form to wear the latest in high couture. I represent a large Chicago dry goods store searching for the right Colorado clientele to appreciate our imported fashions. Might you be interested?"

Stunned Mrs. Pruneface perused his body as though she were buying a steak at the butcher shop. Reaching his face, her eyes widened, and scarlet infused her cheeks. She smiled coyly, though it did nothing to soften her features.

"Oh, my. Yes, of course. We would prefer not going all the way to Denver, but we can't find a decent ready-made gown in these stores. The dresses here are quite ordinary, aren't they, ladies?"

As the others twittered their reply, he glanced at Lilly whose jaw hung open. He motioned with his head toward Mr. Baxter, who waited dumbfounded behind his counter. Though returning his attention to the rude, fluttering hens, the rustle of Lilly's skirts along the wooden floor told Nick she understood.

Drawing upon the famous Shield charm on which he had made his reputation among Chicago's socially elite, he managed to keep the ladies busy while Lilly finished her shopping.

None of them would ever look exceptional in a high fashion creation. In fact, ordinary seemed well suited to their style and their looks. Now that he thought about it, nothing he had seen in either the men's haberdashery or the lady's emporium could be regarded as remotely fashionable. Surely, the wives of mining millionaires needed somewhere local to buy quality clothing.

From the corner of his eye, he saw Lilly quietly leave the store with a small bundle tucked under her arm. After excusing himself, he slipped outside. Instead of heading toward Jacob and the loaded wagon, though, Lilly moved down the plank sidewalk, her skirts swishing with each roll of her sumptuous hips.

Near the end of the block, she stopped abruptly, and turned to survey the windows of the surrounding buildings as though looking for someone. Then, shaking her head, she continued to an eatery called Sally's Silver Spoon on the next block.

Though curious as to why she seemed to be searching for someone and why she went to the restaurant when dinner was hours away, he crossed the street and stood beside Jacob.

His gut still tied in knots, Nick leaned against the wagon and curled his hat brim before returning it to his head. "Got a little nasty in there."

Leaning to the side, the other man spat at the dirt street. "You referring to the three ladies who followed you out?"

Nick nodded, hoping the man with few words would explain without him having to describe the unpleasant altercation in the emporium.

Jacob sighed, then centered his gaze on Sally's Silver Spoon. "Some women have the strangest notions about respectability."

Nick crossed his arms. "Lilly isn't... I mean... she doesn't..." Did he really want to know?

"Spit it out! You asking if Lilly is a working girl?"

Nick held his breath, hoping his worse fears weren't true.

"No, she isn't, and don't you ever think that again."

An audible sigh left Nick's lips.

"Lilly dresses like one to make those women comfortable enough to approach her for help. Though, sometimes I believe she feels herself just like them. Soiled. Having a child out of wedlock will do that."

Jacob's guilt-laced barb caused the heat of remorse to clamber up Nick's neck, an emotion becoming all too familiar.

Tense, uncomfortable moments passed. "What is she doing in there?"

"At Sally's?"

Nick nodded.

"Checking things, I suppose. Owns the place. That's where her rescued doves learn a skill to start their lives over. Sally was one of them and now Betty manages it."

Something that felt remarkably like pride warmed his insides. "Do others recognize who these women are?"

"Some men might, but they're not about to say anything lest their wives become suspicious. Hell, they built a tunnel between Colorado Springs and Colorado City to hide their actions from their families. Lilly says they're the best tippers. It's one way to acknowledge recognition without the wife knowing."

Nick chuckled, but before he could reply, Lilly, minus the bundle, left the restaurant and headed toward them.

He watched, fascinated by the way her womanly curves swayed as she walked. Not in the exaggerated seductive way of a siren, but in the wholesome way a woman oblivious to her beauty would traverse the space.

She existed between two realms of society—the respectable and the tainted. Part of that was his fault.

For leaving her an unmarried mother.

In the one world, she thrived. In the other, she got hurt. But which world did she really want? If circumstances were different, if he had been different, what would her life been like?

~~~~

Body wet with sweat, the man left his inept whore lying on the rumpled bed, and sauntered to the hotel room's only window, naked as the day he was born.

"Aw, come on! Will I still be paid?" whined the skinny body wrapped in sheets behind him.

Hell no, he wanted to shout. She didn't do her job, didn't make him rise to the occasion. His groin still ached, and his balls felt like twisted grapes on a vine, but his prick was still as soft as a cooked noodle. Inside him a violent storm raged, wild and unpredictable. Like a spring tornado. He curled his hands into fists, the fire under his breastbone about to make him retch.

"Maybe, if you get the hell out of here. Now," he barked through gritted teeth.

What kind of man was he? The good-fer-nuthin' yellow-bellied idiot his pa always called him? Lord knows he tried his best, but he was never good enough in his pa's eyes. Never good enough at anything. And now this. The pain in his chest burned its way up his throat.

The rustle of sheets told him the whore had moved. And damned fast. *Good girl!* She didn't know how lucky she was.

Peering out the lace curtain, he caught sight of someone he instantly recognized even from this distance.

Well, well. If it isn't the Wilcox bitch. His breath hitched.

He would know that woman's walk anywhere. Those squared shoulders, that chin in the air, those seductive hips that swayed each time she took a step. His heartbeat quickened, and for some reason, his cock sprang to life.

He smiled. Perhaps it wasn't dead, after all. Especially when it came to this particular woman, the one he had been itching to get his hands on since he escaped.

Suddenly she stopped in her tracks and scanned the surrounding area. Even from here he recognized the look of fear stalking her face. Excellent! Let her be afraid. Real afraid. She couldn't possibly know it was him. Wanting to keep it that way, at least until he decided what to do about his good fortune, he stepped out of her line of sight.

What *should* he do about her?

It was that damned Wilcox's fault he couldn't get it up no more.

Ever since Mimi left, whoring with other women had left him flat more ways than one. Nobody satisfied him like she had. Riding Mimi had been damn good. He loved her big tits, large ass, her moans and sighs, her dark brown eyes filled with the fire of hatred and fear. Damn, he liked when she looked afraid, maybe even loved her for it.

Whatever love was.

And the money he made selling her to others had more than satisfied his need for the other pleasures in life. Maybe he would keep Wilcox like he'd kept Mimi. Would serve the bitch right.

Wilcox stole his woman right out from under his nose.

One night he came back to his room after a long night of drink and cards to find Mimi's chains broken and his prized possession gone. He'd yelled and cussed and beaten the hotel clerk bloody until the man told him who had taken his beloved pet. Then they sent him to jail. Assault with intent to murder, they said. That Wilcox woman got Mimi to testify against him.

He pounded his fist into his open palm. His pa never allowed no woman of his to hie themselves off, and he shouldn't either.

His daddy taught him good. Used to beat his ma 'til she bled plenty. "Boy," he would say. "This is how you treat women. Like the beasts they are." For a long time he didn't believe him. He spent many nights listening to his ma crying, wantin' to go to her, but afraid pa would hurt him too.

Until he was bigger. On the night ma died, he picked up a pitchfork and threw it at his pa's chest. Killed him, he did. And ran off. Became his own man with his own women. Only, he made money off 'em, unlike his pa. He was smarter. Much smarter.

Now that he found *Mrs.* Wilcox, he intended to make her pay for stealing Mimi.

First, with her body, and then with her life.

Chapter 5

"ALL OFF FOR FLORISSANT, HAYDEN'S DIVIDE, Cripple Creek and Victor!" called a conductor.

Light-headed for some reason, Nick grabbed a side rail for balance and leaned forward to gather his wits. His eyes fell on the waiting coaches. Each of the two stagecoaches were pulled by three teams of powerful horses. Behind the coaches were three freight wagons, presumably for baggage and supplies.

So, this was the great Hundley Stage, ready to take them the last eighteen miles to the Cripple Creek gold camp. The coaches, though much larger than most, hardly looked big enough for the small crowd of about twenty people disembarking the train's four passenger cars. Lilly and Jacob stood off to the side, supervising the unloading of their baggage.

Though an experienced traveler, none of his other trips had been as exciting as this one. For the last hour, he'd claimed a space on the precarious metal platform between the first and second passenger cars, awestruck by the magnificent scenery flying by.

Since leaving this morning, the wide, gently rising valley near Colorado Springs gave way to narrowing canyon walls of Manitou, where autumn gold marked the climbing sea of still green aspens and towering pines. Patches of colorful wildflowers created a canvas of impressionistic art so like the paintings hanging in Bertha Palmer's home gallery.

Nick wished his brother could have seen this. He would have loved the majesty of it.

Beyond Manitou, the train crawled up Ute Pass, a steep serpentine track clinging to the walls of the narrow canyon like an ivy vine. In the valley below, white water against submerged rock telegraphed the power of the flow and the steepness of its descent.

Deer were abundant, and once he caught sight of a black bear fishing in the ribbon of water bubbling through the mountains.

He gingerly stepped off the platform and joined them just as Lilly was being helped into the first coach. Jacob climbed in next and sat to one side. Nick followed, flanking Lilly on the other.

A man in a dusty business suit and bowler hat, another in worn, but clean work clothes, and a third, in a well-tailored, immaculate suit, filed in opposite them. Three more men clambered to the top with the small baggage, and one more pulled himself up to the seat next to the drover.

Two other women and the remainder of the men filled the second coach. Within minutes they were off, the jammed coaches rocking and jouncing over a well-worn trail, up and down rolling hills, around lakes and through dark thick woods.

Over the smell of pine and road dust, horses and sweating humanity, Nick caught the faint scent of lilacs drifting from Lilly's hair. He used to love threading his fingers through her silky chestnut locks as he held her still for a kiss.

Shifting to hide his flourishing erection, his leg came to rest along Lilly's thigh. Though she sat stiffly, feet tightly crossed, hands neatly folded in her lap, eyes focused outside Jacob's window, she didn't protest the location of his limb. As the stage swayed, their shoulders touched, then fell away in a delicate dance of remembrance and retreat.

Did she sense it? The spark of electricity that seemed to ebb and flow like an incoming tide every time they inadvertently touched? He had missed her so—the beauty of her smile, the melodic tones of her voice, the sparkle of life gleaming in her eyes.

Should he attempt to converse with her again? Short of rudeness, she had previously answered all his questions about the train and the scenery with brevity and a terseness that made him cringe.

After a while, he stopped trying.

But the fact was, they *were* working together, and the more comfortable they were with each other, the more successful they would be in finding his sister.

He stretched his long legs to the side of the dandy's, sprawled in a similar pose to his. "Look, Lilly, I know you don't want to be with me, but can't we at least be civil? We need to work together. For Sabrina's sake."

Her gaze drifted to his, and he watched as she grappled with the ramifications of his request. Then, her shoulders relaxed, and irritation slowly gave way to resignation. Her smile, when it came, was tentative and unsure. "No, you're the last person I would wish to travel with, but I will accede to your point. Cordiality would be infinitely better than animosity."

On her other side, Jacob fisted his hands in his lap, re-crossed his stretched legs and gazed out the window, his jaw working beneath his beard.

Shit. When they reached town, he and Jacob needed to talk.

~~~~

No matter how many times Lilly visited Cripple Creek, the final three minutes of the trip always caused her heart to escape the confines of her chest. This time was no exception.

The Hundley stage paused at the top of the hill overlooking the booming gold camp, the gloomy gray skies overhead reflecting her apprehension. Mr. Hundley's idea of giving his passengers a thrill had never been a delight for her.

Far from it.

After lumbering up the ridge, the six horses caught their breaths, and blew and stamped with impatience. They knew they were close to home. And home was at the bottom of the slope.

A very steep slope.

"Hold on tight," yelled the drover.

Her nerves jangling, Lilly grabbed an overhead strap. Knowing what came next was far worse than being surprised.

A sharp crack of a whip over the horses' heads announced the beginning of the end. The animals leaped forward and began their plunge, the heavy coach soon rolling behind on its own momentum.

Without thinking, she caught Nick's wrist with her other hand and squeezed white-knuckle tight as the horses careened down the hill at a wild gallop. Only when he threaded his fingers through hers did she realize what she had done. But it was too late now to withdraw it. His attention remained riveted to the scene flying by the window.

Warmth—his warmth—seeped through her leather glove and offered a comfort of sorts. Her heart slowed its pounding and she leaned into his strength. Memories of another time, another place replaced the terror of the race down the hill. Memories of his warmth, the heat of his mouth, the blaze of his touch, the fire of his—

Another crack drew her abruptly out of the past.

At the city limits, the pell-mell fury of six racing horses sent chickens, burros and dogs scurrying to the side. She shut her eyes and tucked her head to her chest.

Seconds later the stage brake shoe squealed, and the heaving animals slid to an abrupt stop in front of Joe Wolf's Continental Hotel. At least fifty men sat outside on barrels, slapping their knees in enjoyment at the hapless, shaken passengers treated to this senseless version of a joke.

Still clasping her hand, Nick captured her gaze. Blue eyes so clear she could lose herself in them studied her with solemn intensity. She could no more look away than she could stop breathing.

Time ceased.

The familiar fluttering of butterflies returned to her stomach with alacrity. Those unsettling eyes. That endearing blonde lock of overlong hair draping his forehead. No man should possess such fever-inducing features.

He grinned suddenly, breaking the moment. "Thrilling. I thought we might take a spill."

She pulled her hand away. "I don't see anything funny in this stupid spectacle." She turned toward Jacob who had already descended and now extended his hand to help her.

The screech of another carriage brake announced the arrival of the second stage behind them.

The scene soon erupted into chaos. Two dozen horses, two stages, three wagons and scores of passengers, drovers, freight haulers and onlookers filled the air with a cacophony of sounds and smells.

Scanning the street, Lilly noted the changes since last spring's visit.

There were more wooden structures and fewer tents, more hotels and restaurants, more saloons and dance halls, and more businesses selling everything from stoves to hardware to clothes to pianos. In just four months Cripple Creek's population had exploded not only with miners, but with the solid feel of respectability and permanence.

A sudden feeling of someone walking across her grave caused her flesh to pebble and the hair at her nape to rise. It was the same sensation she had in Colorado Springs yesterday when she came out of the Emporium—dark, ominous, dangerous.

Her heart raced at a breathless pace. What was wrong with her? She was letting her imagination run away with her intelligence.

Then, through the tangle of hitched horses and milling people, she spotted the long legs of a ghost swaggering across the street, a ghost with a bowlegged gait like someone she once knew.

And feared.

Rocks replaced the butterflies trapped in her belly.

Noooo! It can't be. He's still in jail.

She reached for the hidden chain circling her neck, the one beneath her jacket. Its intricate gold loops felt warm, comforting as she manipulated them with the tips of her fingers. The chain and its treasure were always there. Always available when she needed it.

What if that man really was him? Had she instinctively felt his presence at the Colorado Springs train station? When she stopped suddenly to search through the crowd and was distracted by Nick's hard body pressing into her backside?

Was this man the reason for the insane eviscerating fear she couldn't set aside? Was he following her?

Was this man even him?

A freight wagon picked that moment to roll in front of her. By the time it passed, the man had disappeared. Lilly swallowed over the ball lodged mid-throat and willed the thudding in her ears to quiet. She couldn't afford to panic now. Too much was at stake.

Surely, she had mistaken the man for someone else.

~~~~

Whiffs of lilac and woman teased Nick's senses as he sat near Lilly in the hotel dining room. To reign in his emotions, he combed his surroundings for something distracting.

And found it—the overstated elegance of the restaurant, so incongruous to the raw newness of bustling Cripple Creek's rough pine buildings and wide unpaved streets.

Potted ferns, white table clothes, and perfectly set china and silver offered a luxurious setting for those with money. And from what he saw during his short walk around town, there appeared to be a lot of it.

Here was the chance to explore a world unknown to him, the world of vibrant creativity. It was alive. In the air he breathed. He could feel it, see it, almost touch it. Cripple Creek was a town being born, a place where a man could be a pauper one day and rich the next. A wild and exciting land of opportunity.

If he ventured out for it.

He fiddled with his silverware, contemplating his situation.

Lilly had arranged for two rooms in the Continental, the town's best hotel. At his expense, he soon realized.

Nick shared a room with Jacob, though he wished his roommate was Lilly. Wished he could see her undress, put his hands all over her and bring her to a rousing climax. At the thought, his body sprang to life, his trousers becoming much too tight. He shifted, adjusted himself, and placed his napkin strategically across his lap.

Unaware of Nick's uncomfortable state, Lilly brushed her hand along the back of her neck and scanned the room, an emotion remarkably like fear flickering through her eyes.

Concerned, he asked, "Is something wrong?"

Her gaze finally settling on him, she pulled in a breath, then visibly relaxed. "No, nothing."

He didn't believe her, but he kept quiet—an awkward silence descending on the table amid the clatter of silverware and the clinking of glass in the large room.

A few minutes later she leaned forward and spoke softly, her tone low and sensual, almost secretive. His skin prickled. "We need to establish the whereabouts of Cyrus Dupry. Jacob, I'd like you to talk to our merchant network in town and find out what they might know. I'll visit the doves."

Startled, Nick ground his teeth. Hell if he was going to let her go to a whorehouse. "No you won't. That's my job."

Their truce unwound like a sprung spring.

A deep frown formed on her forehead and her eyes sparked belligerent fire. "Of course you'd say that. You're a natural with the ladies, aren't you?"

Her barb struck home.

"Unfortunately for you, I'm more suited to this. These ladies know me and are more likely to be truthful to me than you. It's what I do, remember?" she said, her voice now more subdued, less strident.

No, he hadn't remembered.

Lilly didn't look at all like the floozy in the saloon he had met the other day. Though she'd freshened up since arriving, she still wore the well-tailored navy traveling suit and a fashionable hat positioned just off her forehead.

She looked every bit the respectable woman, the kind of lady who could afford to dine in the hotel's oasis of luxury. Except he'd seen the puckered faces and the disapproving glances cast her way by the women of the town since they'd alighted from the stage.

They knew her, or of her. Though their condescension bothered him, Lilly seemed to be oblivious to the snubs cast her way. Or chose not to acknowledge them.

"What do you want me to do?" he asked. She was in charge, after all.

"You? Use your charm and wit to talk to the miners, either in the saloons or wherever they tend to gather. I'll leave that up to you. Some of them might know DuPry. We'll discuss our findings tomorrow night at dinner. Hopefully, we'll have some idea of that man's location."

Tonight's dinner arrived, and Nick ate in silence. How was he going to protect himself from the sting of Lilly's barbs when all he yearned to do was seal her lips with seven years of pent-up passion?

Chapter 6

BREAKFAST AT AN EATERY NEXT TO THE hotel was a solitary affair. Nick had risen late, his night restless and uncomfortable. Jacob had snored so loudly that Lilly must have heard him from the adjacent room. Yet, it was Lilly's proximity that had kept him awake, not Jacob's snoring.

He shoveled the last forkful of surprisingly good, scrambled eggs into his mouth, and pushed his empty plate back. Time to go to work. Lilly wanted him to nose around among the miners, but it was only ten in the morning and the saloons were still relatively empty.

Leaving a nice tip for the waitress, he paid the bill and left. The street was busy, but no one location stood out as being a gathering place for miners.

He strolled along the plank boardwalk for a block or two until he found a group of men congregated in front of two stores—the barber shop and the bath house. The latter had the bigger crowd.

Though he'd bathed in the hotel's claw foot tub earlier, he girded himself for a second bath in decidedly more rugged conditions.

The wait among the crowd of miners was short, but fruitless in terms of information. Maybe someone in the bathhouse could provide a more solid lead on his sister, or this Dupry fellow Lilly sought.

The bath house, or what passed for one, consisted of one large room with a rectangular coal burning stove in the center, and about ten over-sized barrels for aging whiskey lining one wall. The clean scent of soap barely masked the lingering odor of unwashed male bodies.

A short burly man with eyebrows running together, and a small Asian, moved pots of water between the stove and each tub. Mr. Burly took his coin and, with a toss of his arm, invited him to select an empty barrel.

The casks were a far cry from the hotel's modern tub. And vastly different from the elegant bath of his home, and the marble public baths he had visited in Europe. Steam heated water was apparently unavailable in this backwater gold town.

Well, nothing for it. He had a job to do.

After stripping bare, Nick shuddered with disgust and crammed his large body into a barrel with little room to spare. Raising his head out of the water, he caught sight of the pale naked backside of a thin man of average height climbing into the next barrel.

So much for privacy.

"Couldn't decide whether to smoke or bathe first, so I'm doing both." The man shifted in the tub to show Nick a long, thick cigar clenched between his teeth, its aroma pleasant and indicative of expense. "Name's Erwin Dowle. What's yours?" As he spoke, the cigar wiggled below a bushy handlebar mustache.

"Nick Shield." He reached for the bar of soap on the small wooden table between the barrels. "Any luck?"

"I'm not prospectin'. I'm in real estate." With a sigh of pleasure, Dowle settled into the barrel and balanced his head on the edge. "There's nothing like a good hot soak to warm your cockles, except, maybe a good hot woman." His eyelids shut.

"Right you are," Nick said more to himself than Dowle. But this was the opening he sought.

Soaping himself in earnest, Nick remained silent, planning how to approach the subject. Before he could speak, Dowle continued.

"So, have you had any luck?" His eyes still closed, Dowle moved the cigar from one side of his mouth to the other with his teeth and lips.

"Me? No, nothing yet." Nick lowered as much of his body as he could under the water to rinse. The water rose to the top, threatening to spill over the side. "But if you are in the land business, you must know everything that goes on here. I could use a little advice on something of a private nature."

A wide smile slid across Dowle's face. "Shoot. Whad'ya want to know."

Nick leaned back against the barrel's side. "I'm looking for a woman."

"Now that's a question I like. What kind do you have in mind? We've got lots of women here who could fix you up in no time."

"This woman is special. I... I was with her once before, and she really caught my eye and my...uh... well. I heard she'd moved up here somewhere recently. A tall blonde woman with blue eyes, nice body, young. Perhaps with a man and several other women." His face heated. Hell, he was talking about his sister, for Pete's sake.

"Let me think a moment." Dowle removed the cigar from his mouth and examined the burning end. "There's a tall looker at the Gold Dust Saloon, but then she's been there since the beginning. With a man and two other women in the same business, ye think?"

Vomit nearly choked Nick. "Most likely, yes."

"Well, not that I had the pleasure of meetin' with them, but I hear a Frenchy was here about a week ago, with three women, one a tall blonde. Don't know if she had blue eyes, though."

A herd of buffalo thundered through Nick's head. His own spit impeded the gulps of air he had a hard time swallowing.

"That could be them. Do you know where they are now?" He hoped Dowle hadn't noticed the tremor in his voice.

"Not sure, but word is the Frenchy took his wagon on up the trail to Victor. There's lots of new gold camps sproutin' up all over the hills."

He tapped the ash over the side of the barrel on the wet plank floor and squinted at Nick. "Kind of a bad time to go up the mountain what with winter comin', don't ya think? Snow can come early up this high, and Victor is even higher yet."

Nick didn't answer since the question seemed rhetorical. Instead, he shifted his shaking body against the barrel's back wall and leaned his head on the edge as Dowle had done.

Sabrina! Though a curse was on the tip of his tongue, he prayed instead for her safety.

Dowle drew on his cigar and watched the smoke curl. "But if you wait a while here, they'll be back again." He flicked his ash and returned the cigar to his mouth. "She any good?"

"What?" Jolted, Nick forced himself to concentrate.

"Your ladybird. Is she any good? Must be if you're chasin' after her like a randy goat. What does she do that some other workin' girl can't give yah?" Dowle's eyes closed.

Nick tensed, recognizing male interest when he heard it. For his sister? Shit! This conversation was over.

But Dowle had other ideas. "This town could use some really nice women willing to accommodate a man's every need, if you know what I mean." He drew the shape of a voluptuous woman in the air with both hands, his cigar wiggling between his teeth.

"Say, if you're ever interested in property here, I've got a few prime lots perfect for a house. Also have a few empty lots on Bennett Avenue for a business," Dowle continued. He leaned his head back and sighed.

Nick poured hot water into the tub. Leaning against the edge, he turned over Dowle's last comment. Though he had no interest in remaining in Cripple Creek, he did notice that most of the businesses catered to mine workers, and not mine owners.

Yet with all the gold being mined in the district, where did the owners go to buy their goods? Colorado Springs? Denver? A man could make a lot of money catering to the wealthier residents in the area. And some day they would bring their wives and families.

Something to think about anyway. But first he needed to rescue his sister from the clutches of Dupry.

~~~~

Someone was following her. Lilly was sure of it. Heart pounding, she scanned the street of well-maintained homes.

Lilly shivered and picked up her pace. A dark evilness was pursuing her with an intent to do her bodily harm. She knew it as well as she knew her own name.

Reaching her destination, she followed the brick path to the back and scanned the yard before slipping inside the kitchen door. She hoped the high-class brothel would reap greater rewards than the seven other places she'd already visited.

Dressed as a laundry woman in a simple brown skirt and crisp white blouse, Lilly easily slipped in and out of the town's most popular bawdy houses. Thankfully, the towels she carried in the large woven basket were light as her arms now ached.

"Why Mrs. Wilcox. I didn't know you was in town." Dinah's loud booming voice reverberated off the painted brick kitchen walls as if it were a narrow canyon. Wearing a white apron covering her apple-shaped frame, the Regal Pleasure Palace's coveted cook stood across the room with her beefy hands planted solidly on well-rounded hips. A wide friendly smile and twinkling dark eyes lit her nearly coal-black face.

Lilly returned the woman's greeting by lowering her basket to the floor and running into her open arms. "Dinah, I missed you so. Missed your flapjacks, too."

"Well then, child, lemme make you some."

"But I've already eaten."

"Honey, there's always room in everybody's belly for my flapjacks. You come to see the girls?"

Lilly nodded.

"Then you go on up there, and them jacks'll be ready when you come down. They're a'sewin'."

"Thank you, Dinah. I'll be back soon."

From the bottom of the staircase, Lilly caught the low murmurs and giggles of the four girls employed by Mrs. Bridger, the Palace's proprietor. Each morning the girls met to mend hems, repair ripped bodices, sew up ragged seams and to tend to other such necessary chores. It was their time to gossip about clients and discuss other pertinent bits of news. Lilly had timed her visit perfectly.

Within minutes, she was up the stairs, exclaimed over, seated in the best chair, and given a mending job to occupy her hands so her mouth could flap with the rest of them. She knew each girl well, having met with them like this many times in the past few years.

These girls were in the trade to make money for other endeavors. Mrs. Bridger was one of the few madams who respected her employees and gave them a fair deal—room and board for a share of their receipts.

Other more unscrupulous madams bought their girls from slave traders and kept their street clothes locked up while charging exorbitant amounts for the skimpy things they were required to wear to draw business. The meager amount the girls were paid for their services was never enough to cover their clothing bills, and so most lived out their useful lives enslaved by their owners. These were the girls Lilly worked to rescue every day.

Her occasional government assignments were levied against the sellers of these women, men like DuPry, the most vicious of the despicable lot of them.

"If you ask me, men are all alike. They want your body, they want it now, and they want it fast." Suzy knotted a thread close to the black silk stocking she mended. "And they want it free! Well, girls, free it ain't."

She tore the thread with her teeth and examined the tiny stitches she made, her bare feet sharing the footstool below Lilly's rocking chair.

Suzy was a formidable force among the working girls in town. She had it all—youth, beauty, brains, and determination to get what she wanted. Suzy was one of Lilly's best informants. She saw and heard just about everything, having enlisted the eyes and ears of nearly every dove in town for her network. The three other women sitting cross-legged on the wooden floor were devoted to her.

Lilly glanced up from the dress she was hemming and smiled at the scene before her. She welcomed the company of these ladies of the night, who were now clad only in corsets and pantaloons since they weren't working. Though she'd never get used to their bawdy talk about men and the services performed for them, the women provided the female companionship that had eluded her among the more respectable.

"This is one hell-of-a-way to make money," Suzy added, "but it's sure getting me to my goal faster than anything else. Almost got enough saved to open my own bakery. Then won't those bankers who refused to make me a loan be surprised."

"I didn't know you could bake," L'il Nell said, her blue eyes intent upon the intricate black lace pattern she tatted for her purple petticoat. "I just thought you liked men. You're always the busiest. I guess you don't like them any better than the rest of us, do you?"

"It's not that I don't like 'em. I haven't found one good enough for me, like that man you came up here with, Lee."

"You mean Jacob? Why—"

"No, not that one. The big blond, the one I hear can't keep his eyes off you."

Lilly's heart jumped a beat. "Where on earth—"

"Honey, word travels fast among us girls when a gent that handsome blows into town. But I hear you've got him all sewed up."

Much to her mortification, laughter over Suzy's pun filled the room. Lilly's cheeks flamed. "Sorry, but you're mistaken. That man—his name is Nicholas Shield—is a client. He's hired me to help find his sister who has gone missing from their home in Chicago."

Four faces looked up from their projects with interest.

Suzy laughed. "Then he *ain't* taken and there's hope for me yet."

More laughter amid a round of hoots and catcalls. And more than one ribald comment about the parts of Nick's anatomy Lilly knew only too well. A band suddenly tightened around her chest.

Jessie set her work on the floor after tucking her needle safely in the corset she was mending. "Tell us more about this sister of his, Lee. We'll ask around. What does she look like?"

Finally, safer grounds. "Tall, blue eyes, blonde hair like her brother."

"That could be a lot of gals. Anything else to help us?"

"She might be traveling with DuPry."

Fear mirroring her own flooded four sets of eyes.

Molly leaned forward, her face twisting with raw anger. "Saw that bastard down at Pete's Livery about a week ago. Seems his wagon had a broken axle. Saw three women huddled behind him so close they seemed to be sharing the same space. One was a tall blonde, but I ain't never did see her eyes."

Lilly perked up, her unease forgotten for the moment. "Did you overhear anything, Molly?"

"Something about making the rounds on up to Victor."

That was it. Corroboration of Jenny's lead. A positive identification of DuPry from someone who knew him, and a definitive direction of travel. She wanted to shout out her elation, but kept it inside, instead. The only thing she didn't know was whether Nick's sister Sabrina was the tall blonde woman seen with DuPry.

Chapter 7

THEY HAD AGREED TO MEET THAT night in the hotel dining room, but finding a quiet spot was next to impossible. As soon as Nick came within ten feet of the elegant room, the noise level pierced his skull.

Had the entire town decided to eat at the Continental tonight? A line was forming behind him.

The maître d glanced up from his small high desk, his eyes brushing over Nick's longer blond hair before settling on his face. "May I help you, sir."

Nick slapped on his best charming smile and pulled a dollar from his pocket. "Table for three and private, if you please."

The man led him to a table in an oasis of potted palms to the side of the room. Much to Nick's consternation, two other tables in the semi-private location were currently occupied. "This is the best I can do, sir," the man said in an apologetic tone. "We're extremely busy."

Should have added quiet to the description. We'll need to shout over the noise. He handed the bill to the man with some reluctance. "I'm expecting another man and a lady to join me."

A smug smile streaked across the young man's features before he pocketed the money. "I'll watch for them sir." He turned and left.

Nick sank into a chair to wait.

In moments, a vision of loveliness wearing a white lace blouse and a simple green skirt appeared on Jacob's arm, laughing at something the man must have said. Lilly's face was flushed, and Jacob sported a large enough smile to turn the soft glow of the gas-lit room to bright daylight.

An odd sensation curled through Nick's chest as he rose to greet them. It intensified when the older man outmaneuvered him to assist Lilly with her chair. Over her head, Nick met a triumphant grin that irked the hell out of him.

Unaware of the skirmish above her, Lilly unwrapped her serviette and placed it over her lap.

"Did Harry seat you? I asked him to save us a private table, and described you in case you arrived first. He's one of my best informants."

Now she tells me, after I spent the dollar. Who wasn't one of Lilly's people?

The familiar fragrance drifted his way sparking memories of another time. He had never encountered a woman as honest in her response, as giving of her body, and as trusting of his expertise as Lilly. That first frenzy-filled night will forever remain etched in his brain.

He hungered for more, his cock reacting as though, it too, remembered that night.

Lilly glanced at him for his response, her gaze flickering away at first before returning to lock with his. The world of noises drifted away as a silent connection bridged the distance.

He held his breath.

Raw, naked yearning crossed her features before her darkened eyes dropped to his lips. The tip of her tongue came out to wet her lower lip and his erection turned to steel.

Had she also remembered? Was an ember still burning in her heart waiting to be stirred?

After taking his own seat, Jacob turned an expectant face toward them. "I hope you both did better than I. No one knows anything, or at least they're not talking."

"I have a lead...." "I have news...." Lilly and Nick said together.

They smiled awkwardly at each other as the waiter stopped to pour water.

When he left, Nick bowed his head toward Lilly.

A line formed between her eyes. "DuPry is definitely headed up to Victor. He plans to stop in a few mining towns along the way. A blonde-haired woman is with him, but I don't have enough information to determine if she's your sister."

Nick's chest tightened. "I heard the same thing. I described

Sabrina, and the man I was talking with said he remembered a Frenchie, as he called him, with three women, one of whom was tall and blonde. He didn't notice her eyes either or remember how she talked." He plowed his hand through his hair. "We need to go after them. Tomorrow. We can't wait."

Eyebrows still knit together in thought, Lilly sipped her water before replying. "Nick, Victor is much higher up the mountains, and we risk getting caught in an early snowstorm. They've been known to happen up there, especially with clouds like these. Half the miners have already come down for the winter. Those staying are aware they could be snowed in for weeks."

Nick absently rotated the stem of an empty wine glass between his fingers. The thought of Sabrina in the hands of someone like DuPry for one more day turned his insides sour.

"Isn't there a road?"

Jacob shook his head and glared at Nick. "A twisting, turning, steep and narrow route that cuts into the mountainside like the train up Ute Pass. It's dangerous, and snow and ice add to the risk. I won't chance Lilly's life on such a trip. We aren't even sure your sister is with DuPry. We should wait to see what the weather brings before continuing the search."

A strangled sound ripped from Nick's throat. "We can't wait. We must find him. If the woman is Sabrina, she'll be…"

He didn't even want to contemplate the horror his sister might be facing. He sat back in his chair and folded his arms across his chest. "I'll go alone, then."

Lilly studied him, her expression pensive. He could almost hear the gears of her practical mind turning over the pros and cons of continuing the search.

He sucked in a breath, squirmed in his chair. This was her decision, not his, and certainly not Jacob's. She might very well tell him to go alone, and then what? What did he know about these mountains?

An interminably long moment later, her eyes softened. "You can't go up the mountains by yourself, Nick. You need help. That is why you hired me. We'll go, and we'll find her. No matter what."

His breath slipped out in a long, controlled sigh of relief.

~~~~

Nick balanced his wooden chair on two legs against the hotel room wall, contemplating the disquieting scene before him.

Lines of concern and fatigue marking her brow, Lilly sat stiffly in another chair next to one of the room's two narrow beds, clasping one of Jacob's beefy hands in both of hers.

Despite what Jacob said earlier about their relationship, emotions he dared not examine swirled through him.

What was their relationship? Were they more than investigator and assistant? More than friends? Lovers, perhaps? The very idea tore at his insides more than he cared to admit.

No, she is mine. Didn't Jacob say so?

Then another disquieting thought tore through him. The bullet could easily have hit him instead of Jacob. Nick might have been the one drifting off into a drugged sleep after surgery to remove that bullet.

Maybe he should have been. Going for a drink had been his idea. To carve out the truth of the man's interest in Lilly. Two hours ago, they were heading for the closest saloon when two drunk miners celebrating their recent gold strike stumbled out the doors shooting their guns.

A bullet must have ricocheted off something and caught Jacob in the thigh. Nick had carried him over his shoulder back to the hotel where the desk clerk used the recently installed telephone to summon the town doctor.

Shifting on the chair, Nick's gaze slid over the pair. Jacob was still out cold after the doc, who hardly looked old enough to shave, dug out the bullet and bandaged the wound.

"Why don't you go get some rest. I'll be here with him all night if he needs anything."

Lilly lowered Jacob's hand gently to the bed. "I suppose you're right. I can't believe this happened."

He couldn't either. Where were the coppers? The peacekeepers? Can anyone just shoot his gun off in this town without a care for unintended consequences?

Glancing at him as she rose, Lilly's tired eyes reflected wariness and something else... fear?

Of course. A sourness worked its way through his belly and gelled into a solid mass. Jacob was unfit to travel.

Would Nick be able to measure up to Jacob's expertise? Be the assistant Lilly needed? The familiar pangs of doubt penetrated his thoughts. He wasn't much good at anything.

Lilly left, closing the door with a soft snick.

Jacob moaned and brought his hand to his head. "What happened? My head hurts like a son-of-a-gun."

Nick plopped his chair down on four legs, filled a glass with fresh water from a pitcher on the nightstand and held it out to his bed-ridden roommate. "Doc Creighton had to dig a bullet from your thigh, and he gave you something to knock you out."

Jacob struggled to sit but met the unsuccessful attempt with a howl of pain.

"The slug lodged against your leg bone and fractured it. You'll be off your feet and a guest of the hotel for a while."

"Damn! I'm assuming you're going to delay the search until I can go with you."

"No. We're going on without you. We can't wait."

"But DuPry...." He shuddered. "You can't send Lilly out there unprotected with that guy on the loose. He'll..."

Nick bristled. "I may be a city dweller, but I don't lack for defensive skills. I can shoot, box, and fence with the best of them. She'll have protection."

Jacob rolled his eyes. "No doubt, I'm sure. Listen, city boy. If something happens to Lilly, I'll come after you, and not to put a bullet in your thigh, either."

Dismissing Jacob's comment as the ravings of a drugged lunatic, Nick returned to his chair and leaned against the wall on two legs again. "Sounds like a threat. Is it?"

"Take it for what you want." Jacob pressed the glass to his lips and drank like a traveler at a desert oasis.

Nick remained silent for a moment, his thoughts racing. The question of Jacob and Lilly itched in the worst way. He had to know, even if he learned something he might not like.

He softened his tone. "She must mean a great deal to you."

Jacob looked up, his sad, dark eyes locking on his. "She does. I asked her to marry me."

The admission flew like a poison arrow to Nick's heart. Jacob's gaze held his in a belligerent stare.

Nick swallowed hard, his throat constricting like a wet knot. "Has she given you an answer?"

"She said no all three times."

The sweet flow of relief calmed his tense muscles, and the why of it left him reeling.

Jacob's eyes narrowed to slits. "Thad also asked her, and she refused. I think she still has feelings for Celia's daddy. Now, you look a lot like that picture of Celia on her desk, and Lilly seems awfully jumpy when you're nearby. You wouldn't be that man, would you?"

Nick's chair banged to the floor. *How....? Shit!* Had she told him?

Jacob shook his head. "Thought so. She ain't said anything, but I know when she's sad and when she's happy. With you around, she ain't nothing but confused. If you're he, she's been hurt enough by you, and with the two of you alone, she could get hurt again. I'll kill you if that happens." This last came out a snarl, the reaction of an angry wolf protecting his territory.

Nick took the man's measure and determined he meant what he threatened. "I won't hurt her. You can count on that."

"Can I?" Jacob sipped his water while peering over the glass.

The last thing Nick wanted to do was cause Lilly more pain. "Yes."

Jacob closed his eyes and the raucous sounds of nearby saloons crept through the open window overlooking the street.

"Tell me the details about how you met?" Nick said after a long silence.

"Told you before. I buried my wife and child in the cemetery near where Lilly buried Celia. They and others died of the fever. Saw Lilly one day sitting by Celia's grave weeping. Gathered her off the cold ground, led her to a bench, and we both wept together. Been with her ever since, protecting her from the vermin walking about in her world."

Nick swallowed loudly. "I'm sorry."

And he truly was. He knew about loss.

"So am I. Lilly's been waiting for you, though she won't admit it. She's buried her heart behind a thick wall none of us can breach. Just don't hurt her as you're goin' about tearing that wall down. If you want to tear it down, that is."

A long breath escaped Nick's lips as warmth swept through him.

Jacob's gaze was dark and penetrating.

And protective.

Good God, the man was deeply in love with Lilly, and would do anything to make her happy, even give her up to another man if that was what she wanted.

The power of that thought struck him dumb. He had always believed love between a man and a woman didn't exist. Marriages were for family alliances, for appearances, or for social improvement. God knew his parents' marriage had not been a love match. His father dallied with the young neighbor in the house behind them, and his mother spent the season in Europe with her many assorted beaux.

The question now wasn't whether he wanted Lilly.

He did. His need for her spirit, her calm determination, her practical view of life was boundless. His desire for her unquenchable.

The question was whether he would measure up to her ideals.

~~~~

Her heart thumping wildly, Lilly stood by the washstand and ran the brush through her hair, her emotions whirling like a spring tornado. Had her instinctive foreboding been accurate? Had Jacob been shot accidentally, or had someone deliberately aimed at him?

Someone like the ghost?

Was she putting everyone at risk because of a long-forgotten case in which she rescued a woman chained to a bed? Memories of the kidnapper's shouts of vengeance, his hate-filled glare as he was led from the courtroom, and the dozens of angry letters he sent her from his cell erupted in her mind.

No, it couldn't be him. Her imagination was running away with her common sense. He was in jail, locked away for a long, long time.

Still, a fierce shiver rippled through her body.

Jacob could have died, and now he lay on a narrow cot, deathly still, his face as pale as the sheet covering him. His wound was too serious to risk the rigors of the steep mountain trip up to Victor and the tumult of the gold camps in-between.

Oh, he would recover with rest, but in her heart, she knew how disappointed he would be to be left behind. Jacob wanted to steal DuPry's women from under the varmint's nose as much as she. Even more so. He'd talked about nothing else for months.

Well, there was nothing for it. Jacob must stay behind. Tomorrow she would arrange for two of her best Cripple Creek informants to look after him.

Which brought her to another problem she never dreamed she would face. Like it or not, she would be spending time alone with Nick—the very handsome, virile Norse king who had sailed back into her life.

Jacob would have kept her focused on what needed to be done, turned her confused state of mind into rational thought, and rational thought into responsible action.

For a man who proposed to her three times, it would stick in Jacob's craw to leave her alone with the man who had caused her such unhappiness. He must have guessed by now Nick was Celia's father. The resemblance between them was unmistakable.

Lilly sighed, a long, drawn-out breath registering her turmoil.

Once again, Nick's irresponsibility had a negative impact upon everyone's structured life.

How was she to handle this most unpleasant situation? How was she to maintain her feelings of anger for him when congeniality with her clients was the hallmark of her business?

Without thinking, Lilly fingered the chain around her neck, the texture of its delicate links halting her negative thoughts midstream.

As it always did.

Nick, why did you come back?

Tears formed as an unwelcome truth wormed its way into her consciousness.

Nick took her breath away now more than ever. Her heart raced like a train engine when he was near.

He made her want—

The truth was Lilly wanted his hands on her everywhere. Inside and out. Wanted his magic fingers to make love to her, his body to fill her. Just thinking about him made the peaks of her nipples harden and the space at the juncture of her thighs moisten.

Trembling, she lowered her brush to the marble table-top and leaned into the looking glass. Her face glowed in the soft light of the kerosene lamp, her eyes blazed with emotion, and her lips parted, ready for a kiss. She felt alive, wakened from the silent sleep of deep mourning where death and grief ruled with an iron fist.

Who was this woman?

A chill suddenly drifted across her shoulders, the fantasy disappearing in a shroud of reality.

She must never again allow herself to feel anything toward a man. Especially this one. The risk of another painful ending was far too great.

The journey would be a business arrangement. A sharing of mission and goals only.

And nothing else.

Chapter 8

"TOP OF THE MORNIN' TO YE, Mrs. Wilcox. Glad to see ye back in town. Been mighty lonely here without ye." The bear of a man pushed past Nick in McDougall's livery yard as if he were invisible and grabbed both of Lilly's hands with one meaty paw. "What can I get you today?"

Nick frowned. The broad-shouldered blacksmith was as solid as an oak tree, his beard and mustache trim and clean. Unlike the unkempt idle miners hanging about the streets, this man presented well despite the streaked leather apron and soiled hands of his profession.

Yet, it was not what the man had said that bothered Nick as much as the gleam of male interest flickering deep in his silver eyes. The giant's leering grin forewarned Nick of the town's hidden danger—too many men chasing after too few decent women. Despite Nick's initial impression of Lilly's virtue, she was, indeed, a decent woman.

Someone who needed a champion.

Nick straightened to his full height. Not as tall as the smithy, but tall enough. "I'm the one doing the hiring, my good man, and we'll be needing a wagon and a team for a week or so."

The giant snapped his head around and inspected him with narrowed eyes. "Who might you be, sir?" His condescending tone was reminiscent of someone flicking away an annoying bug.

Nick ground his teeth. "Nicholas Shield, Mrs. Wilcox's betrothed," he blurted out without thought, startling all three.

Lilly gasped, her mouth moving like a frog without a sound.

A warmth settled in his belly as the thought took hold in his brain. His parents had made a mockery of their marriage, each breaking their vows for the companionship of another. Vowing not to repeat their mistakes, Nick had decided long ago he would marry only for love.

Judging by her actions of late, Lilly barely tolerated him, despite what Jacob had said.

So why had the words flown so easily off his tongue?

Turbulence blazed in her emerald eyes. Yet, she remained silent.

The blacksmith was the first to find his voice. "Betrothed, ye say?"

Nick nodded before Lilly could respond. "I asked her yesterday and she agreed."

At this, Lilly's cheeks turned a mottled red. Anger bursting into flames, no doubt. Yet the effect was the glorious bloom of a bride to be. Now why did the idea sound so appealing?

The other man's gaze traveled down Lilly's frame and back up with a knowing grin. "Well, I'll be. Tons of men around these parts are gonna be disappointed with ye out of circulation."

Lilly squared her shoulders and smoothed out her clothes with precise movements of her gloved hands. "I doubt that, Sean McDougall. I was never in circulation, and you well know it."

The man had the good sense to look sheepish. "I know, Mrs. Wilcox, but a man can dream, can't he? And I ain't the only one. There are nae many women around here can spark a man's interest besides the sportin' kind, if you know what I mean." He smiled, a show of clean white teeth and laugh lines about his eyes. "Where are ye off to?"

Lilly fiddled with a leather glove, shoving her fingers upward into the soft material. "Victor and the gold camps along the way."

McDougall glanced overhead. Billowing dark clouds now scudded across the overcast sky, hiding what was left of this morning's autumn sun. "Could be an early snow up there. Ye sure ye want to do this? T'aint far to Victor, but that twisty turning road is nae good in bad weather. Some of the boys are already comin' down for the winter. The remainin' ain't movin' around anymore on those mountain paths near the mines."

Lilly scratched the back of her neck, her demeanor pensive and introspective. He could almost see her mind revisiting her decision of yesterday, weighing the risks of continuing versus waiting a few more days.

Nick's fingers curled. Delaying their hunt for even a day might mean the difference between rescuing Sabrina and.... He closed his eyes against the knife of fear butchering his mind. He couldn't take the chance. "We're going. Urgent business compels us to leave now."

He glanced at the bonfire raging beside him. Lilly's jaw had tensed, her hands had rolled into fists. Green daggers glared straight at him.

Ignoring her for the moment, he withdrew a roll of bills from his trouser pocket, peeled off the correct amount and handed it to the giant. "We'll wait here while you hitch the team."

"Suit yerself. Don't say I didn't warn ye." The smithy turned toward the barn.

Before he took a step, Lilly tugged on the man's arm, the anger Nick had seen in her eyes gone. "Wait a moment, Sean. I have a favor to ask of you. Jacob was hit by a stray bullet last night, so he won't be coming with us. Would you mind occasionally looking in on him at the Continental so he's not alone?"

"Sure thing, Mrs. Wilcox. Folks say two miners raised a ruckus with them pistols. Hope Jacob was na hurt bad." The man looked from Lilly to him, lines of concern furrowing his brow.

"No, he'll live, but his leg is in bad shape. Do you think Suzy would be able to bring him food?"

Sean laughed, a low rolling sound reminding Nick of thunder. "Suzy? Yes, ma'am. If I'm guessing right, she has a sweet spot for Jacob and would be more than happy to uh. . .feed him."

Chuckling, he backed into the barn a few steps before turning to prepare a team of horses. Leaving Nick alone with Lilly, whose ramrod back told him he was in for a scold.

She didn't waste time. "*My betrothed?* You big oaf. Why did you tell him that? Betrothed to you is the last thing I'd want to be."

An unexpected pain poked him in the belly. Why? He paused a moment to collect himself and to come up with an explanation for the unexplainable. "You can't go walking around here without an escort. It's too dangerous."

"Ridiculous. I have been coming here every few months for the last two years."

"Alone or with Jacob."

"With Jacob."

"Have you gone anywhere without Jacob?"

"Of course, I visit the girls up here."

"Yes, those in the brothels, where you'd be mistaken for any other working girl."

Her beautiful green eyes narrowed, and she raised her chin. "That's not true. I—"

"Look around, Lilly. How many women do you see?"

"I see lots …."

"Respectable women? Decent women? Women men want to marry, not pay for?"

She lowered her gaze to the ground. "Not many," she whispered, her face paling.

Something about her response bothered him. Was it longing buried beneath the small breath of air he heard?

He pressed his case. "How far do you trust any of the thousands of men milling around this town to leave you alone."

Squaring her shoulders, she looked him in the eye, though she had to tilt her head way back. "That won't be a problem. I blend into the background very well, thank you. That's all the protection I need."

Ah, Lilly.

He stared at her solemn expression. She had no idea how desirable a woman she had become, how her innate sensuality radiated off her small frame like a fine Parisian perfume. How watching her walk enticed any and all to follow and partake. It wasn't something she consciously did. It was part of her, like her exotic green eyes were a part of her face.

Seven years ago, the effect was minimal, her movements that of an awkward girl growing into her body. But now, experience and motherhood changed her forever. She definitely needed someone to keep the male of the species from getting in her way.

Someone like him.

Was he up to it? Could he be what she required? He pictured the toy soldier in his pocket and heard his brother's encouraging words. *You can do anything you set your mind to.*

He softened his tone. "Lilly, I saw what happened in the store in Colorado Springs." He tucked an errant strand of hair behind her ear.

Its texture was soft, silky. Just as he remembered.

She stilled. "What did you think happened, Nick?"

Her eyes were on his lips.

Shit! He tightened his control over his rising response. "Those women snubbed you. They were vile, vicious people with viperous tongues. They had no cause to be rude."

A sheen erupted in her eyes, but she kept them trained on his face. "I've learned to live with it. It happens because of what I do and who I work with. Not who I am."

"And because of how I left you, an unwed mother with no respectable means of support." The admission was hard, but he had to say it.

Her breath caught.

Long moments of awkward silence added to the wall building between them.

His mouth dry, he forged through the stillness. "Being my betrothed, at least for the immediate journey, would give you the level of respectability you deserve. It would stem the gossip that could follow two unmarried people undertaking a mission such as ours."

"But...." She nibbled her lower lip with her top teeth, a sure sign she was considering his words. "Jacob and I traveled together."

"That doesn't count. He's old enough to be your father."

Her head popped up, and her eyes widened. "He's not ...." She stopped, her lips tight as his remark penetrated.

A moment later she found her voice. "All right. Betrothed for now. In name only."

She stared into his eyes, challenging him to agree to this last. So much vulnerability welled within those sea green eddies. It humbled him. He would not fail her.

He glanced at her luscious mouth. "In name only."

~~~~

Jammed against Nick's powerful body on the narrow buckboard seat, Lilly was far too close to her former lover to be anywhere near comfortable. His well-muscled thigh, resting against her leg, burned clear through his denim trousers and her divided skirt. A firestorm of want and need spread quickly through her body to places she thought long dead.

She couldn't think, couldn't breathe, couldn't clear her mind of sensual memories that came flooding back.

The irony of their situation drew tears to her eyes. How often had she lain awake wishing for that very thing? Hoping Nick would come for her on his white horse. Tell her that he loved her more than anything, couldn't live without her, and then make love to her as though they had never parted.

But, that was an impossibility she'd buried long ago for more reasons than she cared to admit. She'd let the anger and frustration propel her forward one step at a time.

Until Nick resurrected everything.

Being alone with him was not how she expected this mission to unfold. Jacob was supposed to be sitting beside him on the seat, while she found a place in the buckboard as far from him as she could get.

Jacob.

Had she made the right decision to leave him with Sean and Suzy? Should she have stayed instead, tried to repay his kindness for being a friend when she was sad, had a problem needing solving, or simply needed someone to stave off her loneliness?

What if the shooting wasn't an accident? What if someone, maybe the elusive ghost she thought she saw, returned to finish the job? The possibility tossed her stomach like a butter churn.

She had not been so unsure of herself in years. Not since the day her parents threw her out of their house, pregnant, with no means of support and no place to go. She didn't like the feeling then, and she certainly didn't like it now.

"What are those?" Nick nodded toward the valley below as they rounded a tight bend in the trail and stopped.

Her tension relaxing a bit, Lilly gazed at the lowland on their right.

A familiar chuckle rumbled over her head. "Looks like a tornado sucked the trees away and left only the stumps and roots. And the piles of stones near those holes resemble giant rainbow-colored anthills."

Her lips twitched. He was right, they did, but damned if she would agree out loud.

Amid a forest of tree stumps protruding from the ground lay a sea of six-to-eight-foot-deep holes and adjacent mounds of rubble. White stakes poked out of the earth everywhere, making it difficult to tell where one claim ended and another began. Along the stream bed running through the middle, abandoned water sluices told the story of hope and ultimate disappointment at not finding easy-to-gather placer gold.

"You're looking at what's left of the '91 rush. Those holes are called 'glory holes.' Prospectors came up here expecting to find gold laying around or just beneath the surface. They staked out their claims and began digging. When nothing turned up, they moved elsewhere."

Nick's gaze landed hot on her cheek. She ignored it, glancing up toward the mountains, instead. "Gold is here if you're willing to work hard. In the last two years they've brought out gold worth near three million from deep, hard rock mines higher up."

As she talked, a mist rose from the valley floor, its tendrils soon wrapping about them, cloaking them in a moist cover of cool thin air. The sky turned dark as the cloud mass rolled together. The wind picked up. Within seconds, the temperature dropped again, and the moisture thickened into a dense, impenetrable fog. The wagon road ahead disappeared in a smothering blanket of gray.

Lilly's heart skipped a beat. *Please, no snow!*

The moisture-laden air grew more difficult to breathe as mining dust mingled with the droplets to create a grit that invaded her nostrils. They were barely two miles into their journey and hemmed in by the fog. If they continued forward, they ran the risk of plunging off the narrow twisting road into the gorge below. If they turned around, the way down was now slick and precarious.

Hazarding a glance at Nick, she found him gazing skyward, his mouth set in a grim line.

She followed his eyes. A giant snowflake fell on her face, then another, and another. The first snow, glorious and treacherous, beautiful, and dangerous. The fall might last a few minutes, or several hours, or, God help them, several days.

Her simmering frustration abruptly boiled over and landed on the most convenient target. "Damn you, Nick Shield! I should have listened to my own counsel and waited. Instead, I let you bamboozle me into heading out. It's snowing, and we're stuck out here in the elements."

He cast her a wry glance, though remorse flickered through his eyes and disappeared in a flash. "What's a little snow, Lilly? It snowed in Chicago, and we didn't melt."

"No, we didn't. We were in our houses warmed by fires and thick afghans. You know nothing about snow in the mountains, so don't try to cajole me into thinking this situation isn't dire. I hoped we would make the hotel in Anaconda, but now that is impossible."

Silence.

Awkward and emotion-laden.

Snowflakes continued to fall like a blanket gently placed on a sleeping child by its loving mother.

When Nick finally spoke, his quiet voice held a note of rarely displayed apprehension. "What's the alternative?"

Alternative? What would Jacob do? Squinting through the gray, she dragged up memories of the trail from previous trips. A plan formed— not an ideal one, but one that would have to do.

"We'll build a shelter. There is a copse of evergreen trees just ahead in a little clearing on the mountain side of the trail. We'll go there. And I expect you to follow my orders."

He flashed her a grin, a wickedly boyish one that caused butterflies to dance in her empty stomach. "Aye, aye, ma'am. You're the boss."

Chapter 9

LIKE A GENERAL BARKING ORDERS to his troops, Lilly took charge of their immediate problem—finding shelter from the rapidly deteriorating weather. And like any good soldier, Nick followed her command.

Not because she skewered him with a sharp tongue only moments before, but because Lilly knew these mountains, knew the climate here.

He did not.

She was right. They should have waited until the ominous clouds disappeared. However, fear for his sister had obliterated all caution, and he had pushed his agenda forward without a thought to the consequences.

His chest tight as a vise, Nick guided the horses and wagon forward about fifty feet, angling toward the mountain. Lily's directions brought them to a narrow clearing close to an outcrop of rock containing a small hollow at its base.

Three young firs, their boughs dragging the ground like giant cornstalk brooms, stood against one end of the exposed stone face.

"We'll build our shelter over there," Lilly said, nodding toward the trees.

Her authoritative tone earned his respect at once. No longer the meek, mild-mannered salesclerk who deferred to others, her command exuded confidence and professionalism. On that alone, he would follow her anywhere.

Not waiting for help, she jumped from the wagon seat, steadying herself against the conveyance's corner. "Secure the team, then bring the ax."

He slid off the other side, unhitched the horses and tied them lightly to the trunk of a lone Aspen amid dormant grass. After tending the animals, Nick retrieved the requested tool and strode toward Lilly, who was examining the chosen campsite like a war strategist surveying a battlefield.

She faced him as he approached, her emerald eyes gleaming with purpose. "This will be better than I thought. If we can crawl through those lower branches, we'll be shielded from the wind by both the mountainside and the trees. We can build a small fire ring into that niche in the rock. The smoke should drift up and away from our hidey-hole in the tree. We need to reinforce the bottom with more boughs, though, to create more of a windbreak."

"You seem to know a lot about these things."

"Jacob taught me last spring when we got stuck in a late snowfall further up the road."

Jacob! So, she had been alone with him. The thought unexpectedly rankled. Especially since her assistant was in love with her.

What the hell! Seven years had passed. She had every right to take another lover. He certainly had. Too many, in fact. But nobody had measured up to the woman standing before him.

Her gaze returned to their prospective shelter. "Where's that ax of yours?"

He hefted the implement above his head.

"See that fir tree on the other side of the clearing?"

He nodded.

"I need about five of those lower branches to weave through these trees near the rock face."

"Your request is my command, General Lilly." He raised the ax handle over his shoulder as a soldier would hold a rifle.

A corner of her mouth twitched, and a spark of amusement glinted in her eyes. She turned away, and he had the distinct impression she was smothering a laugh.

The hint of the old Lilly, small as it was, warmed his insides. Theirs had been a relationship of laughter and fun, of jokes and smiles, of countless hours sharing the humorous moments life often presented.

His spirits buoyed, he turned and gave in to an impulse. Leaning his head back, he opened his mouth and caught several wet snowflakes on his tongue, a ridiculous whim he hadn't indulged in since childhood.

His hand slid to his trouser pocket, his brother's words reverberating in his brain. *If you want something badly enough, take the risk to go after it.*

Yes, but what did he want? Something readily available, or something far beyond his grasp?

Reaching the tree, he loped off five low hanging branches and dragged them back. But his general was nowhere to be seen.

"Lilly?"

"Back here." Her voice emanated from somewhere under the firs. A second or two later, Lilly's delectable back end, clad in divided skirts, emerged from an entrance hole she had fashioned. She glanced at the boughs Nick dragged across the clearing. "Perfect. Give them to me, please."

"You're the builder. Let me know when I can help." He pulled the cut ends of the branches closer to Lilly's outstretched hand.

Their gloved hands touched briefly and a spark of something warm rushed up his arm. Startled, his eyes flew to hers, now wide with equal surprise. A flush brightened her cheeks, and she turned abruptly and headed back to the trees, branches trailing behind.

Had she felt it, too?

One by one, Lilly threaded the new boughs through the existing ones, fortifying the natural windbreaker with a stronger, tighter bond.

"I built a fire ring near the rock, and carved out some head room for you. Now we need leaves. Lots of them. The pine needles are all right, but Aspen leaves are better."

"Leaves, it is." Lifting his hand to his forehead in a mock salute, Nick scanned the area for an obvious supply, and found it not far from the horses.

In a short time, their shelter was ready.

General Lilly, however, wasn't finished issuing orders. "We need the blankets and the food. I tucked small bags of ground coffee and some sugar in the coffee pot. Bring that, and the small cask of water. Oh, and the picnic hamper, too."

After retrieving the items, Nick followed Lilly's lush bottom through the boughs into their makeshift shelter. He itched to touch her, to spread his large hands around her rounded bottom and pull her tight to his groin.

Sitting next to her on the narrow buckboard seat had been pure torture. In stretching his long legs, one had accidentally brushed against Lilly's thigh. He had held himself still, waited for her negative response.

None came. If anything, she had pressed against him.

He wished he had been able to slide his hand to her thigh, or that she had slid hers over his to rest against that part of him standing in readiness. Just thinking about it had darn near cost him his control.

Stopping his reverie, Lilly whisked the blankets from his arms, and spread one over the loose Aspen leaves. The remaining two were stowed neatly in a corner.

Their dwelling was a cozy affair. He had just enough room to stretch his long legs when sleeping, and enough headroom to allow sitting without banging into anything. Plenty of room existed for Lilly, though, who plunked her tiny frame down cross-legged nearby.

The only negative aspect was the trunk which served as a natural divider between them. Well, maybe that was meant to be. Touching her was off limits, no matter how much he wished otherwise.

And he was beginning to wish it more and more.

~~~~

Now what? Lilly wrapped her palms around her hot coffee cup, warming her icy fingers after washing the remaining few beans from the pot with a handful of snow. They'd eaten in silence, the atmosphere so thick with awkwardness she could have dipped her spoon in it.

She'd half expected Nick to be his usual effusive self. That was who he was—the charming pleasure seeker who made a joke of whatever life served up regardless of consequence or whomever might be affected. She was ready for that man. Had steeled herself against getting sucked into his vortex of charisma and enchantment once again.

But the man before her was different. More somber. Contemplative. Something was stewing beneath the stoic facade of pensiveness, something powerful and explosive.

Did she want to know? No. Yes.

She turned away from him, directed her attention to the scene through the branches, to the world outside their makeshift home.

And then laughed at the absurd memory a branch of pine needles brought back with a wallop.

A memory of a ridiculous hat and the customer who insisted upon purchasing it.

"What do you find so funny?"

"Remember that red felt hat with the feathers you placed a Christmas wreath over as a joke one year?"

"You mean the one Mrs. Crowley insisted upon buying?"

"Yes, that one. There's a branch out there looking just like the wreath, complete with red berries and all."

"Where?"

Within seconds, he was beside her, his cheek inches from hers, his scent of bergamot and spice, and the rich musk of male playing havoc with her equilibrium. Oh, how she'd missed this smell, missed brushing her tongue over Nick's broad chest where he'd splashed his cologne, missed the incredible heady feeling of being wrapped in a cocoon of spicy maleness and raw masculine strength.

She turned toward the branch, girding herself against this onslaught of lust and foolishness. "There. To the right."

He leaned closer and peered out. His cheek touched hers, the scrape of fresh whiskers igniting a bonfire against her wind-chafed skin. Yet, he didn't pull away. And, heaven help her, neither did she. She stilled instead, letting memories of happier nights drift through her mind like billowy clouds on a warm summer day.

She knew it wasn't right, wasn't sensible, yet the electricity zipping to her nerve endings left her longing for more. Using every ounce of her mental fortitude, she pulled away.

"I see it now. And you're right. It does resemble the wreath. The fact Mrs. Crowley bought it as her Christmas hat was astounding." He laughed, a deep throaty sound that rumbled through her.

"Well, the store's motto was 'give the lady what she wants,' so I did." She giggled. "Do you remember the hat with the three dead green parakeets?"

He nodded.

She wrinkled her nose. "That was the most hideous hat I've ever seen."

Nick turned and sat cross legged in front of her, his eyes alight with humor. "But somebody bought it, because I came back the next day and it had been sold."

"To Mrs. Cramdon. The elder Mrs. Cramdon. She didn't like big hats, and that one was small brimmed."

Nick grinned, laughter sparkling in his deep blue eyes, creating lines around his glorious lips. Lips now drawing her attention as he spoke. "Dead birds seemed to be big that year. There was another hat with white doves, and another with big black plumes which made the wearer look like she was sprouting wings."

Caught in the frivolity of the moment, Lilly leaned forward and laid her hand on Nick's knee. "Oh, do you remember a spring hat resembling the bouquet sitting on the round table as you entered the department? I once mistook that hat for a vase of flowers. It should have been worn by a tall woman, but instead a short woman no taller than I am purchased it. It weighed six pounds if it weighed an ounce. I wonder how the poor woman's neck handled all the weight."

Nick leaned back on his elbows. "But the most ridiculous one of all was the monstrosity Mrs. Grey commissioned. Remember it? It was nearly three feet tall with about a foot of white material done up to look like bows on a green hat base. On top of it was this fluffy stuff that looked like giant cotton balls with black things sprinkled all over. It reminded me of vanilla ice cream with whipped cream and nuts."

Lilly laughed. "I remember that one too. Oh, and there was another one I remember I laughed at nearly every time I went by it. It was black felt and tall, but the front was covered by a mass of white feathers. From a distance it looked like a chicken had been artfully displayed. We called it the Chicken Hat, and someone bought that as well."

"Whoever was buying Paris creations for my father that year was being paid way too much for what he did. You could have done a better job than the buyer."

The fun died an abrupt death "Yes, well. That would never have happened, Nick," she said in a dull tone that sounded flat even to her own ears.

The reason why never reached her lips. It was more than the pregnancy, more than their forbidden relationship. And it hurt far greater than anything she had ever experienced. The hurt went to the soul of who and what she was.

Something she should have told him years ago but failed.

And now it didn't matter.

Nick's charming grin vanished, his gaze sweeping her face.

Afraid her eyes would betray her emotions, she peered through the branches again. Snow had covered the ground in white, and moonlight created a path of sparkling brilliance much like it had on the soft waves of Lake Michigan long ago.

Tears formed behind her eyelids. For a while she had forgotten her anger, had let herself be carried away by the humor and the quiet companionship they once shared.

And in that glorious moment, she experienced the pain of knowing what once had existed no longer could. She dare not allow memories to seep into her reality. The past was gone.

And it was for the better.

Chapter 10

WHAT HAD HE SAID TO PRODUCE such sadness in the woman sitting across from him? She looked so forlorn and wistful, so achingly lonely and irresistible that Nick found it hard to keep from reaching out to her. And he'd wanted to.

Badly.

The touch of their cheeks had ignited a physical need for Lilly his body couldn't deny. Seven years without touching her, without hearing her sighs, without kissing her had taken a toll on his restraint.

Glad her attention was elsewhere, he shifted his legs to make his embarrassing physical reaction less obvious.

He'd come looking for his sister.

And found Lilly.

What did he want to happen next? Did he deserve to have her again?

Though he'd never expressed it—not to her or even to himself— she'd been his once. But like a fool, he let her slip away, and she'd vanished with a part of his heart he hadn't realized he'd given her. And now that they were together again, each moment without her regard was torture of the worst kind. He felt the desperate emptiness clear down to the bottom of his feet.

She turned from her peephole and pulled the collar of her sheepskin-lined jacket up around her neck.

"How did you become an investigator?" he asked, breaking the deadly silence.

Her startled look told him she hadn't anticipated his question. She lowered her eyes and her shoulders rounded. "I stumbled into it."

"How?"

She raised her head and scrutinized his face. "I'll tell you a story, but you can't interrupt."

He nodded. Story telling had been one of their favorite pastimes.

She picked up a stick and traced circles with it in the dirt. "Once upon a time there was a little woman who sat upon a park bench crying. Thinking she heard the rustle of leaves and the sigh of the wind, she looked up, right into the eyes of a kindly fairy godfather standing before her. He wore perfectly tailored clothing, and his perfectly shaped handlebar mustache hid a perfectly wonderful smile and perfectly straight white teeth."

Enchanted, Nick sat back and listened.

"'Why are you crying,' the man asked. 'Because I have nowhere to live, no work to attend to,' she replied. 'What work did you do?' he asked. 'I sold hats to ladies at the grandest store in Chicago,' she said. 'Well then,' he replied, 'we need to find you a job so you can rent a place to live,' he said. The woman placed her hand over her belly and looked up hopefully at the man. 'But who would hire a woman who....'"

Suddenly rocks rained down upon Nick's head. His chest squeezed. *Who would hire a woman who was with child?* He had done this to her. Fire raced to his cheeks.

"The fairy godfather looked pensive for a moment, then smiled. 'I know some people who would welcome your skills, but they're extremely far away.' 'But I have no skills,' the woman said. And he replied, 'Oh, but you do, my dear. You know how to talk to ladies, how to get them to buy what your store has to offer. The ladies I have in mind are desperate for help, but they have no idea how to ask for it. You could help them,' he said, 'if you have a mind to mix among the unfortunates.'

"And because the woman was also an unfortunate, she accepted the fairy godfather's offer, took what money she had, and with the fairy godfather's letters of introduction and signature on a loan, bought first a saloon in a far-away town, and later a restaurant, and much later a boarding house, and lived...and lived....' The light suddenly left Lilly's eyes and her voice cracked.

He didn't have to hear the rest. Lilly's eyes flashed the emotions clogging her throat. The truth sat naked and raw in her charming tale. He was to blame for her unfortunate circumstances.

With the help of her fairy godfather, whoever he was, she rose from her despair like the phoenix she embodied. Strong and able and professional.

And responsible.

He couldn't help but admire her accomplishments in the face of such hardship. But helping soiled doves seemed to be only part of her job. Going after this DuPry fellow didn't quite fit. The search for Sabrina seemed to dovetail right into something set in motion by Jenny's appearance.

And, for a woman, was far more dangerous.

And that didn't sit well with him.

"Isn't what you're doing now risky? Something bad could happen."

Her chin came up and her eyes narrowed. "You think I can't handle this because I'm a woman?"

"I didn't say that."

"But you thought it. Pinkerton used women as spies during the war, and every minute behind those lines was just as dangerous. They hung spies, you know. Besides, I'm rarely alone. Jacob or Thad, sometimes both, come with me on every mission. Sometimes they're needed, and sometimes I'm the only one that can get the job done.

"I see. Thank you for telling me."

Except, now he wanted to know who this godfather person was who put her life in danger. And what did he expect from her in return?

~~~~

Lilly lay on her side of the tree, going over the story she'd told Nick. She'd told him the gist of what happened. But she hadn't shared the details of her contract with Reginald Griffith, that he'd asked her to join his secret government agency as a specialist in vice, in prostitution and sex slavery, to be specific.

It was difficult enough for someone to understand the nature of her cover job, let alone that of her government work. Of convincing enslaved women to follow her to freedom and turn against their abductors in a court of law. The newspapers in Chicago had been filled with advertisements warning young girls about meeting unscrupulous men in ice cream parlors and train stations, men who promised them riches and a life of luxury but instead, abducted and sold them like cattle into a life of prostitution.

She shivered and pulled her blanket close to her chin.

She could have been one of those unfortunate women, meeting Reginald as she had, alone in the park with no one about. But he appeared genuinely interested in her plight and in helping her and her unborn child.

One thing Lilly had always taken pride in was her ability to size up people accurately, to take their measure and give them what they wanted. And Reginald, with his well-tailored clothes, his soft-spoken manner and eyes that twinkled in the sunlight, rang true to her sense of trustworthiness.

Or maybe she had been too desperate to think straight.

But she hadn't been mistaken about him, unlike her misjudgment of Nick's character.

He'd never cared a whit about anyone but himself. The fact that he had shown up in Colorado with such passion for finding his sister had surprised her. That passion was probably the single most important reason she had agreed to help him.

A wind blew through the tree boughs. Closing her eyes, she curled into a ball to keep warm, but the cold penetrated deep into her bones and her teeth began to chatter. Then she imagined floating in a hot bath, blessed heat penetrating her body, especially her back side. She moved closer to the heat and found herself enveloped in its blissful warmth, comfortable and snug. Her limbs relaxed, her world becoming a soft blanket of blessed contentment.

Until she heard the pathetic whimper of a suffering animal. Her eyes flew open. Shock struck her numb. For she lay within the circle of Nick's arms, the source of her precious heat. Mortified, she rolled away and scrambled to her knees.

"What…" he asked in a sleep-laden voice.

"You were to stay on your side of the tree. Why are you here?"

"Because your teeth were chattering so loud, I couldn't sleep."

Scouting back an inch or two, he muttered, "You should be thanking me, not berating me."

"My teeth were not chattering."

Nick looked like he was about to respond, but the howl of wolves startled them both.

"I heard a hurt animal out there before. I'm going to check before the wolves find it." She rose on all fours, but Nick, fully awake now, rose faster, his wrist grabbing hers in a vice-like grip.

"No, you're not. The wolves may have been drawn by whatever animal is injured."

Lilly peered through the branches. An animal with the markings of a wolf lay on its side not ten feet from their tree house. "The poor thing is injured. I can't just leave it there."

"Leave it, Lilly. An injured animal, especially a wolf, is dangerous." His commanding tone brooked no argument.

Her heart tugged between her desire to help an animal in distress and the wisdom of Nick's command. She looked again. The moon bathed the snow in a gleam of radiance, the sparkling shimmering jewels of moisture floating like a sea of purity. She thought she saw a ring of sparkles around the animal's neck. She squinted and studied the prone animal more carefully.

"Dear lord! That's not a wolf. It's a wolfdog, and it belongs to someone. See the beaded harness, the glittery lines around its neck and belly. Wolves have bigger, broader skulls than that animal, and longer muzzles and bigger teeth. They also have bigger paws. That's a dog and it needs help before the wolves get it. I'm going."

She pushed through the bough opening and rushed toward the animal. The horses, tied nearby, shuffled uneasily. The howl of wolves broke the silence again. The frightened horses pulled away from their tether and ran off.

Blasted horses! Now they would have to chase after them or be stranded without them.

Behind her she heard Nick run to the wagon.

She knelt in the snow about two feet from the wounded dog. Its soulful brown eyes mirrored its pain. Slender quills stuck out from its muzzle and its paws. "Looks like you met a porcupine in your travels, huh boy?"

She reached out to touch it when a growl came from her side. She turned her head slowly and found herself staring into the startling blue eyes of a snarling wolf, lips curled backwards, fangs bared. She froze, her heart thundering. The animal snarled again and crouched backwards, ready to spring.

Five more wolves appeared out of the darkness, their glowing gold eyes focused on her. And on the wounded dog in front of her. She looked away. Afraid to meet their eyes. Three of the wolves moved closer.

~~~~

Heart pounding, Nick struggled to breathe. Shards of cold air punctured his throat, but he gave it no thought. Raising his Winchester bootleg shotgun, he aimed and pulled the trigger.

The shot flew over the head of the wolf closest to Lilly. The pack of six fled in a whirl of snow. Trembling all over, he lowered the weapon and buried the smoking barrel in the whiteness covering the ground. His wits scattered, his hands shook like leaves in a stiff fall wind.

She could have died!

Breathe, breathe. She needs you able-bodied.

Repositioning the rifle over the crook of his arm, Nick rushed to her side. "Are you all right?"

Still kneeling, she stared at him, shock registering on her ashen face. Widened pupils nearly obliterated the emerald of her eyes, and her chest rose and fell with rapid irregularity beneath her jacket.

Needing to get her to a warm place, he lifted her and headed toward their refuge.

She twisted in his arms, her gaze flying back to the wounded animal laying still in the snow. "No, please. We must save him. He belongs to someone."

Nick halted. Knowing Lilly, she would never return to safety without the creature. Her compassion, even seven years ago, was limitless, her readiness to give of herself boundless.

He set her on her feet, scooped up the wounded dog and took off for their shelter. As he passed her, he discovered tears glittering in her eyes and a look of gratitude spreading across her face. The sun breaking from behind a cloud. The mask of indifference shielding his heart melted under its warmth.

"Looks like you ran into a porcupine, dog. Lucky for you, I know how to fix things."

The animal lay quietly in his arms, its brown eyes reflecting an emotion that was anything but aggressive. Lilly's instincts were right. As sure as he knew his own name, Nick knew this dog was someone's well-loved pet. It deserved nothing less than loving care from its rescuers.

Nick wiggled himself and his charge through the tree boughs and sat on the makeshift bed of leaves and blankets with the animal's head inches from his folded legs. Lilly followed, the fright in her eyes easing into tenderness.

She glanced at him, and he smiled. "Don't worry. I know what I'm doing."

Though her hands still trembled, she scrambled to the small fire pit and stoked the embers. Grabbing the pot she used for their dinner of ham and beans, she scooped up some snow to melt.

Nick dug out his Swiss Army knife from his jacket and opened it to the tweezers. The dog's watchful eyes followed him as he dragged a flask of whiskey from an inside pocket.

"All right, my friend. I'm going to take these quills out, but it's going to hurt some."

Making sure he extracted the shaft in the exact direction it entered to avoid it breaking prematurely, Nick pulled each quill with care.

"How did you learn to do that?"

"When I was a boy, my brother and I used to go hunting with our dogs when we visited the country. Dogs are curious creatures, and porcupines are not particularly amenable to being the subject of scrutiny. Billy taught me how to deal with them in the woods."

After relieving the animal of all the quills around its muzzle, Nick did the same for each of its front paws before opening the flask. "I'll need some of this blanket."

When Lilly nodded, he folded a corner of the blanket and soaked it with whiskey. Cupping his hand, he poured a small amount in his palm and allowed the dog to lap it dry. Seconds later, he gently wiped the soaked material over the sores on the animal's muzzle and paws. The dog whimpered while Lilly hissed in empathy.

"Sorry. That was necessary. Now we sleep. He'll be fine in the morning."

"Sleep?" Lilly scanned the small space for room to stretch out. "Where?"

A glib answer rose to his tongue, but he never got to say it. His patient stood, circled on top of the whiskey-soaked cover, and plopped down in its dry center.

Leaving the two of them to share the one remaining blanket.

Fate. The gods were either on his side, or he had been handed the greatest torture ever—to be this close to Lilly, yet unable to touch her.

And the urge to touch her, to verify her continued existence after encountering a hungry wolf pack, surged within.

Chapter 11

LILLY WOKE WITH A START, the warmth of her cocoon both compelling and abhorrent. Sometime during the night, the dog had stretched out beside her. Despite the strong odor of animal, the dog's fur protected her from the wintry drafts still seeping through the branches.

Nick, however, lay spooned to her back, his long body molded behind her knees, his muscled arm resting across her waist. The sensation was familiar, and strangely comforting. How often had they slept that way on the beach after an evening of loving each other? It seemed natural and right.

Then.

But now?

As comfortable physically as it might feel, his proximity, his extreme closeness played havoc with her emotions.

As well as her body.

The desire to turn toward him, to encourage his hands to caress her aching breasts, to press herself against his morning erection, coursed through her veins.

Somehow, he still possessed the power to seduce her, to weaken all her good intentions.

Her opinion of Nick was changing, and that made her afraid she was heading for a fall. And more pain.

The dog raised its head, its ears twisting forward as though listening. Lilly listened as well but heard nothing. Whimpering, it rose, and Lilly followed, her movements waking Nick, whose sleep-filled eyes fell on her mouth.

The dog barked, then bounded through the boughs. Lilly, and a now fully awake Nick, trailed.

With newfound energy, their patient charged across the clearing straight for a Ute girl of about eight, kneeling in the snow with open arms. Tail wagging furiously, the animal leaped into her lap and bathed her face with his long pink tongue. The girl fell backwards, laughing and hugging her beloved pet.

Lilly studied them silently with mixed emotions. Though she was happy they were united, the girl reminded her of Celia. A bit of melancholy entered her heart. After a moment, the warmth of Nick's presence at her side penetrated her emotions. She glanced up to find a quiet understanding filling his eyes.

Nick had never had a chance to be Celia's father, never held her, never played with her. Never heard her laugh or seen her eyes light with joy. Her throat clogged on an emotion as big as her fist.

At last the child stood, the dog by her side, and stared at them.

Lilly blinked. The girl was beautiful, destined to grow into an even more stunning young woman. There was no other way to describe her.

Unlike other Ute natives, this little girl had an oval face with a strong chin, lighter complexion, and hauntingly sad brown eyes. Her brown hair was parted down the center and braided into two long plaits which hung over a thick buffalo hide flowing from her shoulders to her knees.

Deerskin boots encased her feet, and white leggings with beaded designs poked out from below a deerskin dress under the buffalo robe.

After a moment, she smiled shyly and pointed to herself. "Willow."

Then to Lilly.

Afraid their visitor would run away, Lilly eased forward, knelt to look directly in the girl's eyes, and brought her finger to her chest. "Lilly."

The girl laughed and pointed at Nick.

"Nick," Lilly answered, and turned to offer a tentative smile. Nick grinned in return and squatted, pointing to the dog.

"*Saridj*, dog." She grinned back. "I call him Dog."

"You speak English." Lilly smiled at the child, delighted they would be able to converse.

"Mama taught me, but now there's only Grandmama." Unexpected tears rose in Willow's round expressive eyes, and the sadness deepened into grief.

"Come. Get warm. Grandmama waits for me." The girl looked around, caught sight of the wagon, and scanned the area for the horses.

Lilly glanced at Nick, asking the same question with her eyes.

He shook his head. "I'm afraid they got spooked by the wolves. They're probably halfway back to the livery by now."

The girl patted her pet's head. "Dog will help with your things."

"How?"

"You will see." Willow pulled a pouch from under her robe and emptied its contents—a wide strip of buffalo hide and several leather cords of various sizes. "We will need two fir branches. What do you want to take with you?"

Nick extracted two of the spruce boughs from their tree shelter while Lilly crawled in to retrieve the basket and blankets.

"Nick, we'll need the rest of the food, the ax, the rifle and ammunition. The water barrels can stay. I'm sure Willow and her Grandmama have access to water."

Fascinated, Lilly watched Willow, a mere child, fashion a makeshift travois out of the boughs and leather thongs, and attach it to Dog's belly straps. Lilly loaded the finished travois with their blankets, spare clothes, and most of their meager food supply.

After stuffing his pockets with shotgun cartridges, Nick hefted the gun and the ax to his shoulder while Lilly grabbed the basket. The wagon would have to remain behind. Someone would surely recognize it as belonging to the livery and bring it back.

As they left their tree shelter to follow an eight-year-old native girl, Lilly had the unsettling feeling her life was about to change.

~~~~

Lilly inched closer to Willow in the small miner's shack, awed by her grandmother's nimble fingers as she sewed beads on a whitened deerskin garment.

Despite a table and chairs near a black potbellied stove, the woman sat cross-legged on buffalo hides on the floor, small bowls arranged in two rows before her. An opaque white film covered her eyes, yet the old woman reached for beads as though sighted.

Willow laughed and ran to hug the woman. "Grandmama, we have visitors. They saved Dog from a porcupine last night."

The old woman smiled. "You found him. I knew you would," she said in English in the lilting, sing song fashion of her native language. Only, her words were drawn out in the slow drawl common in the South.

Dog flopped down beside her and laid his head on her folded thigh. She ruffled the animal's fir with a gnarled hand in welcome.

The woman looked up in Willow's direction, and Lilly sucked in a breath.

The smile on the woman's leathery face was the same as her own grandmother's—one of pride and indulgence granted to a granddaughter by the true matriarch of the house. A smile Lilly would never witness again.

Theirs had been a special bond. Her grandmother had cared for her while her mother worked in the family grocery store with her father. She had wiped away Lilly's tears, told her stories of the old country, and sang to her when she couldn't sleep. The heartbreak of loss suddenly filled her eyes. Her grandmother had died nearly ten years ago, yet the memories of her love remained vivid.

Here in this ramshackle excuse for a house, beneath the ravages of a long, hard life written deep into the woman's face, beauty radiated from both inside and out. A perfect symmetry of facial features, a strong jaw, straight nose, and high cheekbones suggested the woman most likely had caught the eye of dozens of braves in her time.

Even sitting, her regal bearing marked her as someone important, someone used to garnering respect and devotion.

And not just from her granddaughter.

In her presence, Lilly felt humbled, as she had in the presence of her own grandmother.

Grandmama placed her fingers on Willow's cheeks. "My child, I am glad you found Dog. He brings you much joy. Now, let me meet your friends."

Willow glanced at Lilly and Nick. "Grandmama wants to touch

your face, so she can see you."

"I would love to meet your Grandmama." Nick's deep voice rumbled past Lilly's ear, his delight evident in his tone. If she glanced his way, she would likely see a charming smile to match his voice. It was his way.

Nick stepped forward and knelt, careful not to upset the bowls. "I am Nick."

Grandmama lifted her hands, and Nick placed them on his face. Slowly, softly, with the tentative touch of a stranger, the woman ran her fingers down his cheeks, along his chin, across his forehead, and down his nose.

"You are tall, and strong, and proud, and compassionate. You laugh a lot, but you also worry. There are lines deep in your forehead. You are looking for someone, or something?"

Nick pulled in a breath. "You are very perceptive. Willow calls you Grandmama. What should I call you?"

"You turn from my question with one of your own, but unlike you, I will answer. I am Gray Dove, widow of a great Ute leader. Willow is my daughter's daughter. And your woman? I can sense her presence."

Lilly's heart stuttered before racing on. *I am not his woman, nor will I ever be.* But, to blurt out the truth would be rude. Cheeks flaming, Lilly knelt beside Nick, unsure how best to answer Grandmama's question.

Then she remembered what they'd agreed upon after Jacob's injury. "I am Lilly, and Nick and I will be wed soon. I am happy to meet you." She raised the woman's hands to her face and hoped the woman wouldn't detect her lie.

Gray Dove moved her fingers across Lilly's face in the same manner as she had Nick's. "You are small, with large eyes and lips many braves would seek, but you don't laugh enough. Sadness covers your head."

Lilly stilled. How could she know?

The old woman leaned over and traced the line of Lilly's jaw with long, gnarled fingers. "We will talk later. We have much to say to each other. Now I rest, for I am old and not well."

Despite her curiosity about what Grandmama had meant, Lilly realized within a short time that Willow had been taking care of her grandmother whose health was fast failing. Judging from the adeptness with which the child made them a breakfast of fry bread, honey and berries, the girl had taken over the household chores long ago.

She clearly needed help.

~~~~

Nick popped the last of his breakfast in his mouth with gusto and glanced across the table at Lilly whose slow perusal of the small cabin spoke volumes. She was appraising Willow's ability to care for her blind grandmother by herself.

Earlier, he had made the same assessment as Willow expertly handled the heavy fry pan despite the hot sputtering grease. And now, he ate in silence, his desperation to continue searching for Sabrina colliding with the indisputable urgency before him.

This child needed help.

The wood pile in the basket was low, there seemed to be no meat available, and the water barrel was near empty. How had Willow kept herself and her ailing grandmother alive?

Did he dare stop his search for even a day? Sabrina could be held captive somewhere, or lying out in the snow freezing, or be servicing—

Nick cut the direction of his thoughts. What should he do? He already committed one unwise action by insisting they start up the mountain even though the weather was deteriorating.

And where had that led?

To spending a night shivering beneath tree boughs. Though being close to Lilly had its benefits, they risked freezing. Who would rescue Sabrina if that happened?

As dire as his sister's situation might be however, it was an unknown while Willow and her grandmother's circumstance was obvious. They both might perish if no one helped them. Judging from the old woman's gray pallor this morning, death hovered nearby.

His mind made up, Nick finished the last of his coffee and lowered his cup. "An extra day here to help restock shouldn't set us back too far. What do you say, Lilly?"

Startled, she gaped at him at first, a slow smile soon spreading over her features as her emerald eyes sparkled. "I was hoping you'd say that. If you can help with the outdoor chores, I'll start in here with Gray Dove."

Picking up her grandmother's plate from her pallet, Willow offered a shy smile, the lines on her forehead smoothing. "Thank you. I think firewood first. I'll take Dog and collect small branches. You go bring down a tree."

Bring down a tree? He peered at the child. She waited expectantly as though felling a tree was the most natural thing for a man to do.

Maybe it was, but not for him.

He shoved his hand in his pocket, felt Billy's toy soldier solid beneath his fingers. His brother's encouraging words reached out to him. *You can do whatever you set your mind to, Nicky.*

He stared into the child's dark brown eyes, eyes reflecting a life of hardship and resignation. Rising, he slipped into his sheepskin jacket and picked up the ax. "Where is this tree you need me to chop down?"

Chapter 12

HAVING CONVINCED NICK AND Willow to wait until she took care of personal needs, Lilly plodded through the snow toward the bushes the child described. A light flurry blew around her, and in the distance, the burble of swiftly moving water filtered through the magnificent silence. Overhead, gray skies mirrored the murky confusion of the thoughts now tumbling about in her head.

Nick was showing a side she had never seen. Had he changed or was this the man he seldom revealed beneath his amusing, fun-loving facade. Had she really known him all those years ago?

Turning over that thought, she continued walking, mindless of how far she'd gone.

Until she stumbled.

Her breath caught as she struggled to remain upright. To no avail.

Pitching forward, she tumbled down a steep slope, her body weight adding to the forward momentum. She came to a stop face down near a swollen icy stream, the breath knocked clean out of her lungs. After gulping in the cold, thin air, Lilly pushed to a sitting position.

Glory be, where was she? Obviously not where Willow said she should be. Why hadn't she been paying more attention? Forcing herself to stand, she assessed her surroundings.

Nothing looked familiar. She must have gone beyond her destination. How far beyond, she couldn't tell. The stream followed a deep ravine, about twenty feet high on either side and continuing in both directions for some distance.

An ache in her lower abdomen reminded her of the urgent nature of her trip outside. Lilly glanced around for privacy, but none existed. Well, so much for it.

A few minutes later and feeling far more comfortable, she cast about for a way out of her predicament. Along the gully's wall from where she had fallen, several clumps of small saplings struggled to maintain a grip on life. Maybe she could use them to pull herself up.

Shifting, she trudged through the snow to the first group of trees, mere sticks. Hauling herself up with the use of the trunks, she climbed gingerly toward the second clump of saplings, her breathing labored.

Needing to rest, Lilly grasped a small tree and pulled herself up intending to lean on it.

Metal snapped with a shrill, grating noise. A sharp pain bit into her ankle.

She shrieked. Waves of nausea rolled through her belly as she sank to the ground sideways.

Something clung to her boot impeding her movement.

Oh, God. A snake? She hated snakes. Heart pounding, she peered down.

No, not a snake.

A trap. Gah! A curse worked its way to her throat but failed to erupt.

An old rusty snare had engulfed her foot, its bite swallowing her entire ankle boot. Pain radiated up her leg. Another scream formed but her constricted throat cut it off.

Rusty traps brought lockjaw, and lockjaw often led to death. Fear slithered its way through veins beginning to freeze.

Pulling her wits about her, she examined the trap. The contraption, meant for small animals like fox or squirrel, was tethered to the ground by a chain and iron stake. Using all her strength, Lilly pulled up on the chain to loosen the stake.

But no matter how old and rusty the thing had become, or how much the ground had heaved and fallen during the years, the metal spike remained solidly implanted.

Before the intense pain further addled her brain, she identified two options. Yell for help, only the roar of the stream and the distance to the cabin were too great for anyone to hear. Or try to wedge the trap open herself and extract her foot.

The last seemed the best, and the sooner the better. She wasn't sure how long she would be able to endure the pain without fainting dead away.

Having determined a plan, she instantly calmed. She'd first find a useful wedge, which turned out to be a branch half buried in the snow. Its thickness and length made it the perfect lever.

Lilly strained against the stake, but the log remained a few inches beyond her reach. Desperation crawled through her pores. Despite the cold air, sweat formed on her brow. She tried again. Her fingers touched the branch. Barely.

Grunting, she stretched further, the torment of separating joints adding to the agony of the steel jaws. This time though, her fingernails dug into the bark.

Elated, she yanked.

Hard.

The branch shifted. Determined, she tugged again, and this time it rolled toward her, its end now within easy reach of her palm.

Lilly grabbed it and sat up, relief easing the tension tying her muscles into tight knots. The world about her began to sway. She needed to get more oxygen into her lungs, or for sure she would pass out.

Closing her mouth, she drew in a deep breath of the thin mountain air, then exhaled until there was nothing left to expel, repeating the effort several more times. Her head gradually cleared.

Returning to her task, Lilly worked the small log between the trap's metal jaws, then pushed down as hard as she could.

Snap! She fell to her back, a small piece of the branch still in her hands, the trap remaining tight around her ankle.

Hope disappeared like smoke from a chimney.

Furious, she yelled in frustration and then lay on the cold ravine wall and vented her self-directed anger, tears flowing down her icy cheeks.

After a while, sanity returned, and she summoned what was left of her shattered determination. Lilly rose on her elbow and searched for another log. Spying a long, rounded ridge not far from her head, she frantically dug until she touched the rough surface of bark. Brushing the snow away with great sweeping heaves, she exposed a branch thicker and longer than the first.

Though unwieldy, she managed to pull the log out of its white blanket, position it through the opening next to her boot-covered ankle and push down as hard as she could. The metal jaws creaked open a fraction.

Lilly jerked her foot out. The trap snapped shut, landing upside down.

She screamed, which instantly turned to hysterical laughter followed by a short bout of tears of relief.

The sharp pain disappeared, but a pulsing throb took its place. Examining her boot, Lilly found tiny indentations made by the trap lining the leather, one nearly piercing all the way through. Where the boot ended higher up her ankle, blood oozed from two small puncture wounds.

Her breath hitched. Would lockjaw set in? Oh, God!

Grabbing a handful of fresh snow, Lilly wiped away the blood, then clambered the remaining distance up the incline as fast as she could. At the top, she swiped her frozen fingers across her tear-stained face.

Nobody must know of her lapse in judgment.

Least of all Nick.

~~~~

Every muscle, every tendon in Nick's body ached as he lowered himself to his pallet of buffalo skins after the surprisingly tasty dinner of rabbit stew. It had been a long time since he felt this much satisfaction in good, old-fashioned physical labor.

He had completed all of Willow's tasks, from felling a sizable tree, to checking the traps, to learning to skin a rabbit. All without the need to seek his brother's encouragement.

The day's activities had given him a deep respect for Willow's tenacity and industriousness in making a comfortable life for her grandmother. The girl shirked nothing hard yet accepted help with gratitude and appreciation.

She barked orders like a true leader, instructed him with the patience of a teacher, conversed with him like an old friend, and queried him like an experienced investigator.

Willow reminded him of a younger Lilly. The two presented impressive examples for him to follow. Could he measure up? Nick chewed his lower lip contemplating an answer.

One thing he did know.

Nothing—neither man nor animal—was going to separate him from Lilly ever again. He found her by chance and was not about to let chance take her away.

He breathed in deeply. He had been there when she needed him to save her from the wolves. Could he continue to be the man she could count on? He tossed another log in the stove and returned to his buffalo skin nest.

Heat soon enveloped the tiny one-room cabin, home now to four people and Dog, who lay at his feet. Settling his back against the wall, Nick watched Gray Dove unravel Willow's braid and draw a wooden comb through the long dark strands.

The girl, whose tall, thin frame reflected her name, sat on the floor between Grey Dove's spread deerskin clad legs talking to her grandmama in their native language. Considering they both spoke English, he assumed she was describing her day with the strange white man who'd accompanied her.

Though he couldn't understand a word, their love for each other was more than evident in the intimate scene unfolding.

Fascinated, he studied the old woman as she drew the comb slowly down Willow's hair with one hand and followed it immediately with a caress of her other hand. Again and again, she plied the comb and her bare hand until Willow's shimmering tresses spread like a fan across her back.

A memory of performing a similar service for Lilly flew into his mind. She had complained of a headache and, while they rested on a blanket under stars at the lake, he suggested she release her tightly coiled hair. When she complied, he ran his fingers through the silky strands, caressing the heavy lengths with reverence.

Despite the fact they both had remained clothed, the scene held an intimacy all its own. The rush of waves upon the shore had failed to drown the sound of her moans and his stifled groans of pleasure as he played with her hair in an erotic fantasy. He had itched to undress her, to touch her all over, but their relationship had been new, and he was afraid he would scare her.

He hazarded a glance at Lilly sitting nearby, her attention drawn to Gray Dove and Willow, her fingers idly playing with the chain about her neck. A look of wistfulness had settled across her features and her sad eyes shimmered in the flickering glow of the stove. Minutes later, her hand rose abruptly to brush something off her cheek. A tear?

An iron band tightened about his chest.

Was Lilly thinking of Celia, a remembrance awakened by the scene before her? As had his of their time at the shore.

His gaze returned to the pair. They were silent now.

Nick clasped his fingers across his belly. "What was she like?"

Startled, Lilly peered at him as though searching for something in his features. Then, the faint tinges of a smile tipped one corner of her mouth. "She was beautiful. Her blonde, curly hair and big blue eyes drew people like flowers draw bees. Celia looked like you."

A warm glow spread like honey through his veins.

She regarded him a moment. "Everyone went out of their way to answer the million questions she asked about everything. She was charming. She made people laugh." Lilly paused. "She was like you."

The warmth spread to his fingers, to his toes, and brought tears to his eyes.

Lilly turned to face him, crossing her legs in front of her. The smile was fully developed now, and a light flickered in her lovely eyes.

"When we went to the general store, she wanted to know everything about the canned goods. Who put the food in the cans, how they came to be in the store, how long the contents could stay in the cans before spoiling? People were happy to give her an answer."

"Go on." His throat tightened.

Lilly's gaze shifted to the wall behind him, her soft eyes unfocused. "Celia didn't walk. She ran or skipped. Her curiosity was boundless and her impatience sometimes a curse. I had a hard time keeping up with both her and her questions."

She peered down at her hands. "We went for picnics in the meadow and she would pick dandelions and dance in circles, plucking off petals when they first flowered, and later blowing the seed heads to 'decorate' the grass. Thad took her riding on a pony as often as he could. She adored the animal, treated it as her own."

Thad? The bartender? The other man who had asked Lilly to marry him?

A small chuckle emerged from her lips. "And she sang, but, unfortunately, there's where I had a problem. She somehow learned the words to a few bawdy songs she heard in the saloon. We had to discuss which songs were appropriate and which ones were not."

Nick frowned. "You brought her to the saloon?"

Her head popped up, and her eyes narrowed.

"Yes, there were times I had to bring her there during the day because I had no one to watch her. I did what I had to do to put food in our mouths and a roof over our heads. The men were very protective of her. They were all her 'fathers.'" She emphasized this last. "But most often, Celia went to stay with the ladies in the restaurant."

An awkward silence descended, thick with disapproval, but then who was he to judge how she raised Celia?

"I didn't mean to criticize you, Lilly. I'm sorry I wasn't part of her life. She sounded like someone I would have been proud to have as a daughter. You must have been a wonderful mother."

She could be a mother again. The thought slipped in unbidden, the truth of it slamming into his heart. Lilly was born to raise children.

His children.

"I'm sorry you weren't there," was all the response he received, an arrow flying straight to its target. Hope died.

Lilly stretched out on her pallet of buffalo hides with her back to him.

Though Willow and Grandmama soon settled for the night, Nick found himself wide awake.

His mind sifted through their earlier conversation for nuggets that would turn his daughter into more than just a name on a gravestone. The need to be Celia's father, even in death, to know her through the eyes of her mother, was strong, vibrant. A part of him he yearned for as much as the extraordinary bond he had once shared with Lilly.

Much later that night, a four-year-old girl with blond hair and blue eyes danced in a field of dandelions. He awoke, shivering, and discovered the fire practically non-existent. Rising, he pulled a log off a small stack near the wall and placed it in the stove.

As he turned toward his pallet, he caught sight of Lilly's chain spilling to the bed of buffalo skins, her half-opened hand holding whatever object hung on its length. Curious, he shifted to see it more clearly.

And drew in a breath.

Firelight sparkled across a large piece of amber, the flat jewel secured in a heart-shaped gold setting by intricately carved, tail feathers of a bird.

It was the locket he'd given Lilly on her twenty-first birthday.

Had she worn it beneath her clothes close to her heart all this time? Was the pendant Lilly's remembrance of him, the gift she refused to part with because she still loved him? Like he did with his brother's toy soldier.

Hope, bright and shiny, rose from the ashes of despair.

Was this a sign of her true feelings for him no matter what she might have said?

He had to find out, had to take the risk.

Chapter 13

THE NEXT DAY, WHILE PINE NEEDLE tea steeped on the stove top, Lilly cut the last of the unfamiliar dried roots for a stew and tossed them in the black iron pot. Arching her stiff back, her gaze fell on the breathtaking scene outside the tiny cabin's only window.

The snow had stopped. Bright sunlight made the thick white blanket sparkle like millions of tiny diamonds. Fir trees wearing heavy coats of white on feathery branches dotted the landscape, lone reminders of the green of summer among the naked Aspens.

Only the footprints of a human with large feet, a small child, and the paw prints of Dog dragging an empty travois disturbed the bright and cheery fairyland. Nick and Willow were once again outside handling chores not completed yesterday.

Finished with her cooking task, Lilly turned to Gray Dove, sitting on the floor near the stove's heat, working on her beaded dress as diligently as if sighted.

Did she dare apply more of Nick's whiskey to her ankle? Though it no longer hurt after several surreptitious applications yesterday and last night, only diligent care would stem the danger wrought by the rusty trap.

But could Lilly risk discovery?

Gray Dove might not see her actions, but she would surely hear them. Better to hold off. No one must know how distracted she'd become in Nick's presence.

"You love him. Why does that make you sad?"

Lilly gasped. Gray Dove's question caught her off guard. "I... I... don't know what you mean?"

"I listen to your hearts through your voices. They tell me more than the words you speak. He loves you but is afraid to tell you. He hesitates. Your man is unsure of himself, yet he belongs to you. I hear longing in *your* voice and sense a sadness in your spirit. He is your strength, yet you push him away." She stopped, waiting for Lilly's response.

Shock blocked her reply, but her pulse throbbed with marked speed. If Gray Dove's awareness of Lilly's own feelings rang true, was her version of Nick's emotions also accurate?

Grandmama's incredible perception deserved an answer, and only the truth would do.

Pulling in a deep breath, she seated herself on the floor beside Gray Dove and, for the first time, lowered the gates sheltering her raw and bleeding wounds. "Once many years ago I loved him, but...."

Had she? Was it love, or lust? Or the excitement of being with someone so different from her? Her head ached with confusion. She would rather be anywhere else but in the presence of this sightless old woman who possessed the power to see into her soul.

"But what, my child. What pains you so?"

Her breath hitched. Her mind struggled, then abruptly cleared.

Shame, uncovered and lying naked, sliced through her heart. "We...lay together without marriage and I bore his daughter. I tried to tell him about the baby, but his father... sent me away and I came here. My daughter died of the fever when she was four, and—"

"You blame your man."

Another gasp. How did Gray Dove know about a belief she rarely admitted, even to herself?

"He's not my man, Gray Dove. I haven't seen him for seven years. He didn't know I carried his child."

Why was she defending him?

"You are together now. Why?"

"We travel together for a common purpose. We are not really promised to each other. I'm helping him find his sister. I am..." How could she explain what she was? "... a tracker. I find women who may have been kidnapped and sold."

A sound left Gray Dove's mouth, her sightless eyes reflecting the soft light of the potbelly stove.

A chill passed through Lilly, though it had nothing to do with the weather or the temperature in the cabin.

Gray Dove broke the awkward silence moments later.

"I think your thoughts are confused. Your head tells you one thing, and your heart says something else. You must listen to this warrior not with your ears, but with your heart." She drew her hand to the middle of her chest. "The words in your ears go straight to your head, where you think, but love lives here in your heart where you feel. The truth will come when you listen to it."

Unbidden, a memory flooded her mind of a dark night on the beach, the night they first made love. When she lay with her head on Nick's naked chest listening to the thudding of his heart and the rumble of his voice beneath her ear.

The night she fell in love with Nicholas Shield.

Did she still love him after everything that happened?

"What happened to Willow's parents?" she asked, wanting to change the painful subject.

Gray Dove paused, her needle still, her head dipping. She shrugged. "Willow's father was a white man with a smooth voice and words that flow like honey. He hunt for rocks. He said he would be rich someday. He leave here when his pockets grow empty after Singing Bird . . .. I do not like him. He is no good for anything except teaching us to speak the white man's tongue."

"Do you know where he went?"

"No. I hear he live with the Natchez now."

"And Willow's mother?"

The dress slipped from Gray Doves hands with a soft rustle, and a tear rolled down her leathery face.

"My daughter gone. Two years now." Her answer was but a whispered lament of a mother for her daughter.

After a moment, she shrugged, and returned to her beading, her pained silence leaving a host of unanswered questions.

Willow was as close to becoming an orphan as one could be. Judging from Grandmama's gray pallor, the child may soon lose her only other relative as well. What would happen to her then?

From her closed expression, it was obvious Gray Dove didn't want to talk about her daughter and Lilly had to respect her wishes. She leaned forward and grasped the woman's hand, the bond of motherhood strong between them, defined by searing pain from daughters lost.

The old woman must be worried about Willow's future when she passes on. Her granddaughter was so young, so vulnerable. If only Lilly could reassure her everything would turn out well, that her daughter would return soon, and Gray Dove could die in peace.

But she couldn't. She had no idea whether the woman was even alive.

And the future held no guarantees. Lilly understood that only too well.

~~~~

Legs apart and shoulders lined up as Willow instructed, Nick swung the ax high and brought it down hard. The log split cleanly in half, the pieces toppling to the ground with a clunk. Lining one of the halves on the stump like before, he repeated the action, then repeated it again with the second half.

Taking a step back, he admired his handiwork—four pieces of wood perfectly sized for the pot-belly stove.

The snow had stopped by mid-morning, and the afternoon was bright and sunny. Far warmer than the day before. Already the path from the cabin to yesterday's felled tree had turned to slush. They had better finish their chores before the night air froze the melting snow and made walking treacherous.

As he reached for another log, he surveyed the pile yet to be split. He could do this. If he were to complete the task today, he and Lilly might be able to leave tomorrow. He was anxious to continue his search for his Sabrina.

From the black depths of buried memories, his father's parting advice rose loud and blunt. *"If you fail to bring your sister back, boy, don't bother coming home. This is a job for someone who knows what he's doing. You don't and never will."*

The words had stung. Even thinking about them tightened his

chest. So, he pushed them away, buried his emotions in a walled section of his heart filled with a lifetime of his father's disdainful comments.

Nick might not know what he was doing, but Lilly did. She wanted to find this DuPry fellow in the worse way, and DuPry was their best lead on the whereabouts of Sabrina.

But they had delayed their search again this morning when it became obvious Grandmama had weakened during the night. The old woman's coloring had taken on the blue hue of death. Today she lacked the strength to even sit.

Leaving Lilly with the ill woman, he and Willow set off to check traps, and feed and care for the two livery horses discovered this morning at their door, cold and hungry. That left gathering winter berries and filling the water casks to Willow, while Nick split the remaining tree trunk into firewood before the sun sank.

He raised his Stetson and wiped his brow with the back of his gloved hand. Oblivious to his surroundings, he established a rhythm— place a log on the stump, position his body, swing the ax, repeat. With time, the cut pile grew while the original shrank.

The afternoon wore on until the frantic barking of Dog, followed by the faint screams of a child, broke through his mindlessness, chilling his marrow.

He dropped the ax and ran toward the animal pacing near the stream. A few hours of snow melt had turned the picturesque mountain brook into a swollen roaring river. Its fast descent down the rocky ravine bed to the valley below whipped the current into giant clouds of frothy white foam.

He glanced at the path Willow usually took to the stream's edge. The slippery slush revealed the outline her body made as she slid on her back into the raging fury.

His breath hitched. Why hadn't he filled the casks himself?

A faint child's scream came from downstream where the torrent spilled over a five-foot fall. Dog rushed past in a blur of dark fur. Nick's chest seized with horror. Nothing but large boulders lay below the drop, and despite its lack of height, the landing was deadly.

Willow!

In less than two days she had become the embodiment of the daughter he might have had, of the life he might have enjoyed, had he made other choices, been more of a man. He cared deeply what happened to her.

In the few seconds fear had him rooted to the ground, he knew he couldn't let her down. He had failed Celia, but damned if he would fail Willow as well.

He took off through the trees along the bank, tramping his way through heavy wet snow untouched by the sun, Dog by his side barking wildly. The thunder of the roiling water and the roar of the small waterfall grew louder and more ominous the closer he got. His heart pounded and sweat trickled down the sides of his face.

He had to reach her in time.

Dog made a sudden turn toward the stream through a heavy copse of trees. A low hanging branch dragged across Nick's cheek as he followed, letting Dog's instincts have free rein. Suddenly he was at the water's edge, a sloped bank overlooking the fall.

In the middle of the raging stream, not more than ten feet from the drop-off, Willow clung to the side of a slippery boulder protruding above the foam.

Dog barked, and Willow turned in their direction, her widened, terror-filled eyes piercing Nick's heart.

"Hang on. I'm coming to get you," he puffed through his constricted throat.

"My foot is caught," she screamed.

His heart seized. Even if he managed to reach her in the swirling vortex, he couldn't just grab her and haul them both back to shore. He needed to pry her loose under the water without breaking a bone first or being dragged to his own death over the jagged rocks.

"Dog, go bring Lilly." He flung his arm in the direction of the cabin.

Dog hesitated, then took off.

Nick threw his hat and gloves on the snow and shed his heavy sheepskin jacket before wading into the icy water. He gasped, the shock instant. His breathing quickened. He felt as though he'd run smack into a brick wall, yet he knew he had to work fast before his hands froze and became useless.

Carefully picking his way across the rocky stream bed, Nick struggled to maintain balance. The force of the racing waters buffeted him first one way, then the other. The normally three-foot deep flow was now at least five feet, with another six to ten inches of white-water foam above.

Finally reaching her, he placed his wet hand on her cheek and shouted above the deafening sound, "Which foot is stuck?"

"Left," she yelled back.

"At the ankle, or higher up?"

Her mouth barely opened. "Ankle."

"I'm going down to see."

Now over the first shock of the freezing water, he pulled in a deep breath and plunged beneath the surface. Every square inch of his skin screamed with icy fire. The burn numbed his face, his hands, his feet with pinpricks of pain. He forced himself to focus.

Her foot had snagged at the ankle between the boulder she clung to and a second slightly smaller one submerged beside it. His heart plummeted to the depths of the stream. There was no way in hell he would be able to move either mass.

He popped up and swallowed a gulp of the cold, thin air, gagging as water and air fought for the same space in his throat. When the coughing stopped, he found Willow's lips blue, and her whole body wracked with shivers. Action was needed now, before they both lost consciousness.

As she hugged the rock, he assessed the situation and then an idea struck him.

"Willow, we're going to try something, but I need your full cooperation." She nodded, though the movement of her head might have been just a shiver. "I want you to turn and lean your back against the rock."

Her eyes widened to the size of saucers. "I can't let go. I'll drown."

"I won't let you. You have to trust me."

She hesitated a moment, then nodded. Slowly she turned, her arm twisting behind her to maintain physical contact with the rock for as long as possible. Squeezing her eyes shut, she released her hand and backed up solidly against the boulder.

Pulling in another deep breath, he ducked into the icy flow. Her foot had twisted back to a normal position with her toes pointing forward in line with her knee and the rest of her leg. With a gentle tug, he wiggled her foot free from its prison and popped to the surface.

Willow's abrupt cry of relief filled his soul with something warm and bright.

But his fingers were numb, painfully so. Lifting the child in his arms, Nick took a few awkward steps toward the bank, the weight of her soaked buffalo skin coat impeding his progress.

Ahead, he heard Dog barking. He glanced up and found Lilly, her face nearly as white as the snow, her teeth pulling on her lower lip.

His coordination failing, he reached dry ground in eight more excruciatingly slow steps. First to greet them was Dog, who stood on two legs against them and licked Willow's limp hand. She giggled, and he knew she'd be all right. His tight muscles loosened somewhat.

When he finally reached Lilly at the top of the slushy slope, beautiful verdant eyes filled with gratitude and approval met his. Something deep within him shifted.

Then lightheadedness and nausea shook his world. He took off, his steps clumsy and drunken. At the cabin, he threw open the door and set Willow in one of the chairs.

Then fainted dead away.

Chapter 14

GASPING FOR AIR THROUGH A CONSTRICTED chest, Lilly rushed to Nick's side.

With surprising strength, Gray Dove pushed herself up from the floor with a loud grunt and shuffled to Willow slumped over the table. Lifting the girl's head off her arm, she gently slapped Willow's check to get her attention. "You must shed these wet clothes. I will help you."

If not for the beads of sweat illustrating her exertion, no one would have guessed how frail and ill the old woman was.

Acknowledging the order, Willow nodded and sat back in the chair, letting her grandmother work the tightened knot holding the buffalo robe jacket together at her neck.

As Gray Dove's gnarled but still nimble fingers pulled the tangle loose, she nodded toward Lilly. "Undress your man and warm him under the skins with your naked body. Wake him first. He'll need to help."

My naked body against his? Shock opened, then closed Lilly's mouth. Erotic memories exploded in her mind, memories of wantonness, entangled bodies, cries of passion, his groans, and her sighs. She trembled with the remembered feel of his hardness pressed against her belly, seeking her, then filling her. His stomach muscles flat, his torso beginning to develop ridges, his—

No, it was too much to ask.

She peered down at Nick's deathly pale face. His eyes were now open but unfocused, his breathing rapid and shallow. His violent shiver, his abject vulnerability, shredded her heart.

How many years had she fantasized about the night she and Nick would be together again, bare skin touching, hands and lips seeking?

Too many to count.

He wrapped his arms about himself, his entire body quivering violently. Dear Lord, he was freezing to death, and she was ruminating over how she might react to their nakedness. Her chest filled as she sucked in air. She had to do this.

Lifting his chin with her forefinger, Lilly addressed him. "Listen to me, Nick. You need to get out of these wet clothes."

Eyes unfocused, he nodded and shifted his hands to his shirt buttons. She pushed them away. "Let me."

The buttons were slippery, his shirt stiff with cold. Each thrust of a fastener through its opening brought her fingers in contact with his chest. Her breathing quickened. His feathered gently across her face.

A few torturous minutes later, his shirt gaped open to the waist. Before yanking the garment out, she peered up at his face. His clear eyes were fastened on hers with an enigmatic blue gaze that said everything, yet nothing. What was he thinking?

As she lowered her eyes, she couldn't help but notice the deep washboard ridges of his torso bared to her view, more delineated, more defined, more achingly fascinating. Nor could she help but notice the dark blond tufts of hair spiraling down the middle on their long run to what lay between his legs.

The place where her hands once roamed freely.

Dear Lord, what was she thinking?

Pushing her inappropriate thoughts away, she unbuttoned the last button, yanked his cold wet shirt free, and drew it off his arms and shoulders with some difficulty. "I'll get your boots."

Still shaking uncontrollably, Nick straightened his limbs and she knelt at his feet. Lilly struggled with his boots to no avail. Without thinking, she rose and sat between his open legs with her back facing him.

Gripping the boot's toe with one hand and the heel with the other, she jerked back and found herself sprawled against his privates and a hard wall of chest muscle. Strong arms surrounded her. *Damn!* Her heart fluttered despite her best efforts to control her response.

Scrambling out of his hold, she dispatched the other boot with less force, and less consequence.

Rising, Lilly held her hand out and helped him up to a standing position. "Now your trousers and small clothes."

She presented her back. "Off with all of them."

"But—"

"All."

"Um…my buttons." His voice sounded almost amused.

Heat flooding her cheeks, she turned, and with her head down, unbuttoned his trouser plaque, though now her hands trembled as much as he shivered. Accomplishing her task, she turned her back to him once again, and thought she heard a soft chuckle behind her and the rasp of wet cloth sliding down damp flesh. Oh, heavens!

"Now what?" The sound came out almost a stutter.

"Under the buffalo robes." *And fast.*

Lilly glanced at Grandmama, who was in the process of lowering her naked body beside Willow. When she was flat, she tugged the skins over them both before pulling her granddaughter spoon fashion into the warmth of her arms, tucking her knees behind Willow's.

Lilly peered again at Nick, now safely beneath the furs. Considering their height disparity, warming him the way Grandmama warmed Willow would never be effective.

Her back to him, she shrugged out of her clothes and folded them across the chair back. After carefully lifting the locket he gave her over her head, she dropped it into her half-boot.

When she turned back, his beautiful eyes were slowly traveling the length of her body. The body that had borne a child and grown fuller and rounder over the years. Struggling against the urge to cover herself, she slid under the furs next to him.

"Your plans?" This time there was no mistaking the male interest exhibited by the man who was supposed to be freezing to death.

She gritted her teeth. "This is Gray Dove's idea of how to warm you, not mine. I just need to figure out how best to do it. Her way will not work for us."

"How about spread across me like a blanket?"

Nick *would* suggest that position. An image of her laying naked atop him flooded her mind. A position of control, of undeniable pleasure. It had been their favorite and they had chosen it often. Much to her chagrin, dampness flooded the juncture of her thighs.

Well, there was nothing for it.

He was too pale, his lips too blue, his shivering still visible. He needed her. Lord have mercy, she must do this to save his wretched hide. She couldn't let him die of hypothermia. He was still her client, and she was responsible for his safety.

Or so she told herself.

Lifting the robe, she slipped her small body spread eagle across his larger one, her lips in line with his neck, her hip bones at his waist. Every part of her ached for his touch, for the brush of his fingers on her sensitive skin.

Nick's arms wrapped tightly about her, his violent shivering propelling the chill clear through to her bones. Pressing closer, she brought her arms around his back to heat them both, encountering corded muscle where only skin and bone existed before.

His heart thudded beneath her ear—or was it her own—as the familiar musky scent of his maleness, denuded of aftershave, conquered her senses. Made her want. His chest rose and fell, swiftly at first, gradually settling into the smooth rhythm of normalcy.

If she closed her eyes, she might hear the waves of Lake Michigan, feel the soft breeze of the warm summer nights, believe nothing had changed. She drifted with the current, her mind surprisingly at peace.

~~~~

Clinging to Lilly's soft, comforting body, Nick stared at the clumps of drying herbs and grasses hanging from the knotty wood ceiling, afraid to speak. Afraid to break the temporary bond fate had thrust on them.

Too many feelings clogged his constricted throat. Sorrow, remorse, anger, guilt, and hope were all there in vast amounts. Yet, it was another thought that plagued his mind, a thought he was reluctant to examine because of his own culpability.

Lilly didn't trust him.

The trust she once gave him unconditionally even though he never believed he deserved it.

What a blasted mess he'd made of things.

Could he ever earn it again? The question threw him into the dark waters of self-doubt plaguing him for years. The never-ending cycle of blossoming hope and painful disappointment perpetuated by an uninterested father. Could he go through it all again?

Locked within his arms, Lilly sighed, her breath feathering across his torso, her fingers playing in his chest hair as though it was the most natural thing for her to do.

He kissed the top of her head.

Could he be the man she said she needed that first day in her saloon office? He didn't really know.

One thing was certain, though. If he wanted to win her trust, he had to take a risk.

Tell her the truth.

Nick shifted uncomfortably.

Lilly lifted her head, and he caught her gaze through watery eyes.

She stilled.

"I have a story to tell you, something I should have shared years ago. Except I hadn't the courage then." He heard the plea in his voice, and he paused.

He never pleaded for anything. Never even shared his deepest thoughts, not even with Sabrina. That he was now willing to do so with Lilly scared him silly.

Nick raised his gaze to the ceiling and sought divine guidance, his swallow audible in the quiet room. "Once there were two brothers. The oldest was perfect. Did everything right. Accomplished everything he set out to do. The younger idolized his older sibling, loved him more than any playmate his own age. He strove to be just like him."

Lilly's fingers moved on his chest in an oddly calming circular motion.

He paused, scanning her face as she placed her head against his chest. "But the boy was small and clumsy and didn't know as much about things as his elder sibling. They played together often, the older one helping the smaller one with things he couldn't do, encouraging him, teaching him."

Nick covered her hand with his, gliding his thumb along the

webbing between her thumb and index finger. Air moved in and out of his chest in short, irregular bursts.

"One day when the little boy was nine, his brother, who was visiting a friend, died in a terrible fire—the Great Chicago Fire. His death devastated the younger brother. There was no one he loved more than his big brother. Overcome with grief, he hid in the carriage house among the horses and cried for hours on end."

Nick's voice broke. He seldom talked about his brother. Lilly squeezed his hand. It was all the encouragement he needed.

His voice broke on a hoarse whisper. "Finally out of tears, his beloved brother's words came to him in his head, and told him to carry on, that he could accomplish anything he set his mind to. That he would be with him always."

Despite his effort at control, despair leaked out with the expulsion of his ragged breaths.

"The younger brother went to his father and asked if there was anything he could do to help his father with his grief. His father barely looked at his youngest son, and muttered, 'You should have been the one to die in that fire instead of Billy.'"

Lilly gasped.

"The boy heard his father's words, and they hurt so bad he crawled beneath Billy's bed and wept again. When he stopped, he resolved to be more like his brother so his father would love him the same."

He swallowed thickly as all the remembered hurts resurfaced. Yet, he pushed forward, propelled by a need to unburden his heart.

"The little brother tried and tried, but he never received a kind word or words of encouragement from his father. He simply was not good enough. His father told him at every opportunity he could."

His breath caught.

He paused again, the silence as loud as thunder.

"To hide his feelings of inadequacy, he fell back on the one thing he *was* good at—making people laugh—so they would laugh with him and not at him. For he continuously failed in everything he did."

Fire logs shifted sending a blaze of embers dancing around the inside of the stove.

"As he grew and the negative comments from his father

accumulated, the boy, now a young man, came to believe he would never please his father. He stopped trying, and consciously or unconsciously became the charming, happy-go-lucky man everyone liked and wanted to be with. The man who sought pleasure without a care for anything or anyone else."

Nick stopped playing with her fingers. "He used the pleasures money could buy to cover the fact he was incompetent at most everything he attempted."

"But you're—"

"Then the man met a woman who took his breath away, who liked him for who *he* was and not who his father happened to be. Only, by then, he didn't know how to be someone who could keep her safe and comfortable."

He cupped her cheek, turning her face until their gazes collided. Green eyes filled with emotion caused moisture to well again in his own. "When my father sent you away, I couldn't find you. Or rather I didn't know *how* to find you. So, I gave up . . . and my life was never the same. My ineptness kept us apart."

He paused and swallowed several times, his fingers trembling against her flesh.

"Nick, you were never inept. Maybe a little self-absorbed, but never inept. And now I know that this part of you was only a shield to hide your true self. There was someone else lurking behind the facade, someone who only ventured out in small steps because of a heavy mantle of vulnerability. I see the man you've become, and I like that man very much."

"Thank you. I needed to hear that."

"Truth be told, I like both men. The one you were and the one you are now. Your charm and your zest for life was what attracted me originally. I loved your laugh, enjoyed the stories of your escapades and in participating in your exciting world of secret pleasures. Even the sensual ones."

He smiled and raised her hand to his lips, his mind conjuring up images of the sensual ones.

"Thank you for telling me, Nick. I know it couldn't have been easy."

No, it wasn't, but for the first time in years, he felt at peace.

Although he'd prefer to plunge deep into her moist heat, holding her naked body in his arms, her soft fleshy curves evoking visions of what once was, would have to be enough.

For now.

~~~~

Gray Dove died that night.

Her passing was peaceful, going unnoticed by everyone in the small cabin until Willow rose to add wood to the stove. Dawn had crept through the dirty window to underscore the immutable fact the child was now an orphan.

Heedless of her nakedness, Lily rushed to the wailing child's side and pulled her into her arms. Dog padded to Lilly's side, lowered his head across Willow's legs and gazed at her with sad, sorrowful eyes.

Memories of her own grandmother's death cut through Lilly like the slash of a sword. Memories of her soothing callused hands, her judiciously imparted advice, her beautiful lilting voice laced with the heavy accents of the old country.

Abruptly, the melody of a lullaby came to mind, with words as familiar to Lilly as the children's rhymes she had read to Celia. Hugging the sobbing Willow, she hummed the haunting melody her *bubbe* used to sing to her, softly at first, and then a little louder. A little bolder.

The plaintive song, rich with the sound of her ancient heritage, filled Lilly's heart with longing for the family she'd lost—her grandmother, Celia, and though they still lived, her parents. Tears welled as sorrow and grief clawed their way to her consciousness from long-buried corners of her memories.

Desperate for composure, Lilly lowered her head to Willow's and swallowed hard. "Hush, my daughter. Listen to my song."

She began to sing, the words of the lullaby imprinted on her brain, words she now fought to bring through the narrows of her throat.

Unter Yideles vigele
Shteyt a klor-vays tsigele

Dos tsigele iz geforn handlen,
Dos vet zayn dayn baruf,
Rozhinkes mit mandlen
Shlof zhe, Yidele, shlof.

Lilly's voice cracked. Her beloved grandmother's face swam before her, the English words ringing in her head.

Under Yidele's cradle,
Stands a small white goat,
The goat traveled to sell his wares
This will be Yidele's calling, too.
Trading in raisins and almonds,
Sleep, Yidele, sleep.

Nonsense really, but in the language of the old country, the poetry and waltz rhythm fascinated her as a little girl. As they did now.

Blessed warmth landed about her shoulders in the form of a buffalo robe, placed there by Nick whose fingers on her bare skin sent prickles of awareness skittering along her flesh. Glancing up, she caught a suspicious shimmer in his eyes as he settled cross-legged beside her, his presence bringing unexpected comfort and support.

"That's beautiful. What language is that?" His breath whispered lightly across her ear as he peered at Willow.

"Russian," she lied, hoping to keep the truth from him a little while longer.

Pulling the robe tighter to cover the child, Lilly began the second stanza, the thought of Nick's broad expanse of naked chest so close disturbing her concentration. She closed her eyes and pushed the image of his virility to a corner of her mind.

In an instant, it was Celia's cherubic face before her, the lids of her beautiful eyes fluttering as she fought the forces of sleep.

Celia, I miss you terribly.

Lilly gazed at the girl in her lap. Straight dark brown hair instead of curly blonde, chocolate-colored eyes instead of blue, lean and lanky instead of round and cuddly.

Unsettling maternal feelings swept over her like a tidal wave, bringing with it a yearning so intense she nearly collapsed from its force.

Hugging Willow tighter, Lilly rocked and finished the second stanza, and the third, repeating the three until the grieving angel quieted and lay peacefully in her arms. When Lilly glanced down, the shocked, exhausted child lay asleep at her breast, her hand curled near her face with her thumb a hair's breadth from her lips.

Sighing, Lilly considered the future. Tall, competent, a child in years but an adult in bearing and action, Willow had no one to love her, no one to care for her. With both her mother and grandmother gone, what would happen to her?

The sudden weight of Nick's hand on her shoulder startled her. "She will come with us," he whispered as though reading her thoughts. His voice quivered with banked emotion, and moisture still clung to his eyes.

He cared what happened to Willow as much as she! Of course, he did. He risked his life to save her.

The revelation forged another crack in the wall protecting her heart.

"I imagine Celia was proud to call you mother. Someday, Willow will, as well. I will see that it happens." The promise in his voice and the determination in the firm set of his jaw were clear and potent.

And nearly her undoing. Her hands shook as she stroked the long strands of the girl's hair. Did she dare take him at his word? Nick hadn't demonstrated responsibility for Celia, so why should she trust him with Willow's care?

Because he risked his life to save this child.

Perhaps it was time for Lilly to do the same. To take a step toward a life where nothing was guaranteed, and happiness came to those who chose to embrace it.

She would take the risk.

For Willow's sake.

Chapter 15

"WE ARE BORN OF THE EARTH. We live our life. Then we die, are buried, and thus return to the earth. Then ascend and join the creator."

Willow's flat, unemotional recitation of the benediction made the hair on the back of Nick's neck stand on end.

Coming from the mouth of one so young, her rote prayer lent a macabre quality to the interment ceremony. It sounded as though she had learned it at an early age and had been expected to regurgitate the words at the appropriate time. Indeed, Willow had taken charge of the entire burial preparation, delegating few tasks to the two remaining capable adults.

After crying herself to sleep during Lilly's lullaby, the child woke a short time later and, without a word, bathed her grandmother's body by herself. The only assistance she accepted was dressing Grandmama in the beaded deerskin dress she had been working on, a thick buffalo robe and, finally, a white cloth.

Nick had carried Grandmama's remains to the shallow grave he had been instructed to dig next to Willow's grandfather in the nearby woods. They'd all helped construct the stone mound to the girl's satisfaction before she spoke. To Nick waiting quietly beside her; Willow suddenly seemed older and wiser far beyond her years. Lilly flanked Willow's other side, while Dog sat at her feet, his eyes riveted to his owner's stoic face.

Glancing at Lilly over Willow's head, he noticed tears falling from Lilly's eyes as she watched Willow place the last rock over the remains of her only remaining relative.

The girl was alone now, with no one to feed her, put a roof over her head, protect her from harm.

He would give her all that.

With Lilly's help.

The idea of the three of them together lit a fire in his belly, fanned a need he just recently realized he craved—a family to love, to call his own.

The weight of responsibility settled evenly across his shoulders, and he found himself welcoming it. It gave him purpose, direction, and determination, all the things his foolish past failed to provide. It grounded him, forced him to plan, set priorities.

Priorities with Lilly, and now Willow, at its center.

The young native turned and, as though in a trance, trudged through the melting snow to a Ponderosa Pine sapling about twenty yards away. Pulling a knife from somewhere under her buffalo skin robe, she carved a small chunk from the sapling's thin trunk about a foot above the ground.

Inspecting the remainder of the tree from the opposite side, she asked, "Can you lift me, Mr. Nick?"

When he complied, she dug another shallow piece from the trunk before asking him to lower her to the ground.

"May I ask what you were doing?"

"Creating a memorial for my grandmother. She was a great healer for The People." She pointed to the base of the sapling. "As the tree grows, the first cut will make the pine bend horizontal indicating a life. The second will make the bent trunk grow upright again indicating her ascent to the creator."

Dog trailing at her heels, she searched among the nearby copse and found an older tree with two ninety degree turns in its trunk. "My grandfather's."

Odd that she hadn't shown them a memorial tree for her mother.

"What a splendid way to honor your family." Lilly's comment was directed toward Willow, but her gaze lit upon Nick before she glanced away.

A twinge of contriteness pierced Nick's conscience. Did her observation have anything to do with Celia?

The wind shifted and nearby naked Aspen branches swayed in the swift breeze. Yet, the sudden chill sweeping through him had nothing to do with the weather.

It was the same disquieting sense of unease that had sent tingles up his spine yesterday. Someone, or something, was watching them.

Nick's quick perusal of the landscape produced nothing out of the ordinary. Nevertheless, a tightness gripped his chest. "We must leave now, Willow. Pack whatever you want to keep. We most likely won't be coming back."

The child swiveled sharply, a scowl shrouding her red-rimmed eyes. "I will return here to tend Grandmama's tree," she said through gritted teeth. Her back stiff, she turned and stomped toward the cabin.

Lilly stepped to his side, her fisted hands planted on her hips. "Wonderful. You told a child who just lost her last relative she might not ever return to the only home she's ever known. Get the horses, Nick. We need to reach Anaconda before the sun sets." She stalked after Willow, her lovely back end swaying beneath her fur-lined jacket.

Her admonition, however, took root in his thoughts.

The weight of responsibility grew heavier, suffocating. All his best intentions had been obliterated by his thoughtless words. It seemed the burden he eagerly accepted included more than just physical care; it encompassed emotional regard, as well.

He had much to learn about this responsibility business.

~~~~

Lilly breathed in the clean scent of Willow sitting bareback in front of her and eased the child closer to her chest as Willow expertly led them toward Anaconda, the closest gold camp in the Cripple Creek mining district. Nick trailed on the second horse, followed by Dog pulling the travois with Willow's meager possessions and what was left of their supplies.

A small intricately carved box Willow called her "heritage," which she'd retrieved from under a cabin floorboard, was among them. The container raised Lilly's curiosity, but she knew now was not the time to inquire as to its contents and their significance.

Or to ask why there had been no grave or memorial tree for her mother.

Though the distance to town was short, travel over the mountain was difficult. Sparkling white snow lay like a blanket of minuscule precious stones winking in the bright sun, its shimmering glaze producing a near staggering blindness.

Their horse soon showed signs of weariness as it obediently slogged through the dips and rises, drifts and flats of the unseen path Willow followed. The animal's withers were shiny with sweat and its heaving sides from breathing oxygen-poor air were not lost on Lilly. She hoped the journey would end soon, both for the horses' sakes, and her own. The plain fact was she didn't know how much longer she would be able to maintain her seat.

The closer they came to what passed for a town, the more her insides twisted. Try as she might, Lilly couldn't quell the peculiar sensation of being followed. Her arms tightened around Willow.

At last, a few rooftops nearly buried in the snow became visible. Sighing with relief, Lilly knew at least one of the buildings was a hotel. The town, supporting the Anaconda, the Mary McKinny, the Doctor Jack Pot, and the Morning Glory gold mines, also contained a drug store, a grocery store, and doctor's and lawyer's offices.

Nick slid neatly off his horse and tied it to the post in front of the hotel before turning to help both Willow and Lilly to the ground.

Though the child landed solidly on two feet, Lilly didn't fare as well. Much to her chagrin, her legs buckled, and she found herself wrapped within the steadying confines of strong arms and a solid chest. The musky scent of man mixed with the smell of animal and the freshness of the outdoors engulfed her. She breathed it in as if she were starving for air.

Or starving for something else.

Appalled at the direction of her thoughts, she recovered her balance and stepped back, but it was too late. Heat flooded her face and below her waist. Glancing up, she caught Nick's gaze fixed on her mouth, his blue eyes dark with desire. His lips had fallen open, and part of her wanted to step back into his embrace and take what he plainly wanted to give. The other part stopped her in her tracks.

Damn him for mirroring her wayward imaginings.

She lowered her head to Willow, who had followed their non-verbal interplay with interest. "You wait here with Nick. I'll see to our rooms."

"That is my job. I'll do it." Nick turned and walked into the hotel.

Lilly followed him in, careful to control the limp from her now stiff leg. Willow's soft footsteps crunched in the snow behind her.

"I have only one room left, sir," the clerk murmured to Nick.

Reaching the desk in time to catch the clerk's comment, Lilly's heart sank. Lordy, she didn't want to be anywhere near Nick, not when his mere scent did strange things to her senses.

"One room? Impossible. Nobody comes up here this time of year."

"All the rooms are taken, ma'am."

"Are you sure," Nick asked, and pushed a dollar toward the man.

The bald clerk eyed the bill with a look of regret. "Look, mister. I would love to take your money, but only two minutes ago I gave the only other vacancy I had to another guest. Do you want the remaining room or not?"

Nick glanced at Lilly, who nodded reluctantly. At least they would have a roof over their heads, though how they would manage was beyond her.

Willow tugged on her sleeve. "Dog, too." A statement.

Her mouth set with determination, the child raised her chin. She wanted Dog to sleep with her. Poor thing. The animal was the only family she had left.

"A dog will be staying with us."

"Uh, no ma'am. No pets aloud."

Lilly clenched her teeth. "I said, a dog will be staying with us."

The clerk opened his mouth, but Nick pushed the dollar back in his direction. "You heard the woman. A dog will be staying with us."

With an audible sigh, the man picked up the offering and turned to retrieve the key.

A sudden flash of movement to the side caused Lilly's skin to prickle like a thousand tiny insect bites. She glanced toward the stairs, at the profile of a hauntingly familiar figure—the ghost she thought she saw in Cripple Creek. Her breath seized and long talons of fear ripped through her.

It can't be him.

Beads of perspiration formed and rolled between her breasts. Echoes of the devil's oath delivered years ago in a harsh venomous screech reverberated in her brain. A mottled red face, eyes as dark as night, a mouth contorted in rage ravaged her inner mind's eye.

Her gaze flew to Nick, so tall and straight.

Then to Willow.

Why now? Why, when she had so much to live for?

When she turned back, the ghost had disappeared.

~~~~

Lilly's quick intake of breath pulled Nick's attention away from the desk clerk like a gunshot in a closed room. In an instant, her face transformed from the ruddy flush of cold to bloodless white.

The temperature of the liquid pulsing in his own veins plummeted at the sight. Fearing she might faint, he wrapped his arm around her shoulders and followed her transfixed eyes to the stairs.

To the empty stairs.

What the …?

Suddenly, Lilly sagged against him, and his gaze flew to her face. Her eyes were the size of saucers.

His breath hitched. She feared nothing and nobody, or at least the Lilly she had been did, the assured, self-possessed woman who never let anything ruffle her.

Nick's heart twisted at her anguish. He longed to hold her tight, whisper words of comfort in her ear. Do anything to eliminate her fear. But he knew she'd have none of it.

He glanced at the staircase again. "Who were you looking at?"

"Wha…what did you say?" Lilly pulled her gaze from the stairs and stared into Nick's face, her breath coming in short, irregular pants, sweat beading her brow.

Shit! An ache settled deep in his chest as a rush of protectiveness swept over him. What the hell had scared her, or should he ask *who*?

While he hesitated, she took a step toward the hotel door.

Blast it! She intended to flee. Alone, and vulnerable to any horny man walking the street.

Pulling her back, he whispered into her hair. "I'm here beside you. I won't let anything happen to you. Whatever it is, we'll get through it together."

"Together," she echoed faintly, her mind clearly elsewhere. Somewhere safe, he would guess.

Willow slipped her hand into Lilly's and leaned her head against Lilly's arm. The action seemed to steady Lilly, for she straightened and shook her head as if to shake off the emotion. Her eyes cleared, and she leveled a serene gaze at him, the fear banked for the moment.

"I don't know what I saw. Can we discuss this later?" Her eyes shifted to Willow and back, a plea stamped all over her face.

Fair enough, if she talked to him eventually.

"Lilly, if there was another hotel, I'd take us there, but this is the only one in town. We must stay here for the night. I'll be right near you."

Willow gazed up at him, frown lines furrowed between her eyes. "So will I, and so will Dog. I will get him."

"No, wait. I want you all where I can see you. You will have to come with me while I tend to the horses and unhitch the travois from Dog." Better with him than alone in some room with whatever had scared Lilly only doors away.

For once, Lilly didn't object. Something was wrong. Terribly wrong.

At the livery, the craggy-faced owner greeted them, or rather Lilly, with a warm, friendly face reminiscent of crinkled leather. "Well, if it ain't Mrs. Wilcox. Now, you're a sight for sore eyes. What brings you up here this time of year?"

Lilly's smile of acknowledgment barely reached her eyes, but her voice was all business, her fear masked for the moment. "Hello Frank. Nice to see you, too. We're looking for a tall, blonde woman who might have been traveling with Cyrus DuPry. They're supposed to be heading up to Victor. Have you seen them?"

The weather-wizened old man stroked his scraggly beard. "DuPry? Ya missed him by a few days. Probably up ta Victor by now." He glanced at Nick, then back to Lilly. "Heard there was a blonde with him, but I ain't seen her myself. Others did, though. Yessireee." Male interest flared in the man's watery blue eyes.

Vomit propelled up Nick's throat but stopped short of erupting. *Rina!!! I shouldn't have delayed.*

Willow chose that moment to step into their circle. Her quiver was slung across her back, her arms filled with buffalo skins and her bow. Rina would have approved his reason for staying.

Nick raised an eyebrow at the girl but said nothing.

"Well, hello, Willow. Two lovely surprises in one day. How is your grandmother?" Frank reached a wrinkled hand out and tweaked one of the child's braids.

Tears shimmering in Willow's dark brown eyes were the only sign of emotion on an otherwise stoic face. "She died last night. We buried her this morning and now I go with Miss Lilly and Mr. Nick."

"Aw, gee. I'm sorry to hear that, child."

"I am guarding them, now." She peered up at Nick. "You have a rifle. I have my bow and arrows. We are safe."

Nick felt a corner of his mouth twitch as he suppressed a laugh. Not that an arrow would have much space to fly in a cramped hotel room, but if Willow wanted it with her to protect them, he had no quarrel.

After making arrangements for their horses and the travois, Nick led Lilly, Willow and Dog to the hotel.

Toward whomever it was that scared Lilly half to death.

Chapter 16

ᡐ

THE CLOSER THEY CAME TO THE hotel the less Lilly was able to keep her fear from overwhelming her sanity. Strangled lungs trapped her breath, cold sweat froze on her forehead, and numbness claimed her extremities.

Had she really seen him, or was her overactive imagination conjuring up the strange gait of a man she thought she'd sent to jail for life. She had not thought of him in years, so why was she now searching for him in every person walking the streets?

The epitaphs he threw her way when they led him from the courthouse had made her skin crawl. His promise of cruel punishment and unspeakable acts had sent terror streaking through her then, and tormented her now.

Lilly never attended trials of the men she helped bring to justice. If Mimi hadn't refused to testify against her captor unless Lilly accompanied her, Lilly's role in his arrest might never have been exposed.

And now she was being stalked by a man who not only knew her name but knew what she looked like.

Fear making mincemeat of her insides, she slipped her hand into her pocket, felt the cold hard metal of the tiny pearl-handled derringer she carried since. Its presence, however, did nothing to quell the feeling of impending doom.

She couldn't tell Nick about this man, couldn't tell anyone. Shame for how wrong she had been, for how naively she had embraced a life of danger in the name of making a difference, kept her silent. In the last few years, disrespect and life-threatening close calls were as much a part of her life as brushing her hair.

And now she was bringing her unsavory world to Willow, to Nick, if he meant what he said about helping to care for the child.

Dear Lord! What kind of life was she asking them to share?

By the time she reached their room, Lilly's pounding heart thrummed mercilessly.

Restraining them with one arm, Nick used the other to shove the door open with a loud bang. Cautiously, he stuck his head in and checked the interior, waving them in when satisfied the room was empty. Once inside, Nick locked the door.

Lilly surveyed the clean, but spartan accommodations with dismay. Only three items graced the tiny space—a washstand, a pot-belly stove, and a narrow wrought-iron bed pushed against one wall. Hooks for clothing graced the wall near the door.

Despite the unsettling issue of their sleeping arrangements, the band of steel around Lilly's chest loosened. Nick's large, imposing presence in the confined space was oddly comforting.

"We need to talk, Lilly." The rumble of his low, soothing baritone slid over her skin like silk, yet she didn't mistake the note of command his voice held.

Nick wanted answers. How could she tell him her world had become more dangerous with each passing year? That it brought her in contact with undesirable people far more often than she had anticipated.

That, although she thrived in its risks, its challenges, and its rewards, respectability remained beyond her grasp. She was as undesirable as the criminals she sought, shunned by the very society she'd risked her life to protect.

Ignoring his request, she removed her jacket and hung it on a hook. Willow and Nick followed suit while she moved further into the room. Rats, it was even smaller than she first thought. Five steps brought her to the far wall.

Who would sleep where? Or rather, where would Nick sleep?

Willow should sleep in the bed, she and Nick, on the floor.

Far apart. In separate corners.

Nick waved his arm toward the bed. "Willow, you sleep there. Lilly and I will take the floor."

"No, Mr. Nick. I always sleep on the floor. It is the way of my People. I am more comfortable there. My things are right here." She lifted her arm full of buffalo skin blankets, the bow balanced carefully on top. A sheepish grin spread across her face. "Besides, I have never slept in a bed."

"All right, Willow. For now. Someday you will learn to sleep in a bed. Lilly, you take the bed. I'll take the floor with Willow."

"But ...." *Oh, dang.* Too tired to argue, she nodded.

As did Willow.

"Hungry?" Darkened blue pools reflected a different need Nick tried to hide with a quick glance around the room.

"Yes, but—" she murmured, dropping her own gaze for the same reason. *Dear Lord, Lilly, stop that!*

"You don't want to leave the room, do you?" He broke in, misreading her thoughts.

Lilly shook her head, her eyes drawn to Willow arranging her buffalo rugs near the stove.

Nick poked his head out the door and, after giving the houseboy waiting in the hallway a coin, arranged for a meal for the three of them with enough scraps for Dog.

Later, after hot thick stew, hearty bread, and apple pie, after warmth from the potbelly radiated through the room, Willow fell asleep in her nest of fur, her arm hugging her pet. Nick leaned against the wall, his long legs sprawled on the floor in front of him.

Silence filled the small room with a tension that drained the energy from her muscles.

"What frightened you, Lilly? You don't scare easily." His voice was soft, concerned.

In the warm glow of the stove, his penetrating eyes reflected barely banked emotions. Fathomless blue held her gaze a moment, then slid to her lips. She gripped the edges of the bed with both hands to keep them still.

Oh, how she wanted to snuggle into his arms, cocoon herself within the safety of his powerful body, away from the realities of a world she had embraced without thought.

Was she ready to tell him about her work world, about its

unexpected twists and turns? About the harmful consequences of the real reason his father had sent her away? And the dangers she unwittingly dragged Celia into, what might lay ahead for Willow and for him, if he stayed with her?

For she did want him to stay.

Lilly jerked mentally, amazed at where her thoughts had led. How had he managed to worm his way back into her heart, her good graces? Even her body craved him. She finally recognized those strange, vague feelings plaguing her since the first day he'd walked into her office. Lust, pure and simple. A wanting. A hunger she had not experienced in a long time.

She was heading toward the abyss of painful rejection yet again, and to save herself, she needed to pull away.

But how?

Lowering her body to the floor, Lilly wrapped her arms around her knees. Nick moved closer and leaned back on his hands, crossing his stretched-out legs at the ankle. Heat emanated from the shoulder touching hers.

She relished his closeness. Wished he were further away.

"Talk to me, Lilly," he whispered.

She heard the plea and was sure he wanted to know more about what was frightening her.

It was time to tell him the truth.

Or at least the part of the truth she felt comfortable sharing.

~~~~

Nick watched Lilly struggle with her thoughts, knowing the last thing she wanted to do was reveal anything about her new life. Waiting was going to kill him.

At last, she spoke. "It's a long story that started years ago, but I need to tell you something first, something you may not know."

The snapping sound of moisture escaping a burning piece of wood punctuated her sentence.

"I told you before I help women who want to leave the working world."

Nick nodded, his eyes on her whitened knuckles.

"What you don't know is that I also work for the government. I track down men who force women into prostitution or sell them as sex slaves to someone else."

His body tensed. "Are you crazy, Lilly. That's a dangerous business." Appalled, he sprang to a sitting position and crossed his legs under each other. Why hadn't he asked before about her other reasons for pursuing DePry? Perhaps on some level he didn't want to know.

"I'm careful. Most of these men don't realize I've been there until they find their women missing. Though I'm not sure, I believe one of those slavers is following us." Lilly's voice slid off into a whisper and a shudder ripped through her. "John Baylor is a slimy snake who did violent, indescribable things to a woman I rescued, including selling her services to others."

Baylor. Not this DuPry they were tracking.

God, how he wanted to pull Lilly into his arms, protect her. But, fearing she would take any such action the wrong way, Nick grazed the top of her fingers lightly with his hand instead. Seconds later, she threaded them through his and squeezed, and a current of fire zipped up his arm and settled in his groin.

Her gaze turned downward as she studied their clasped hands. "I was given the assignment of finding Baylor and rescuing the woman he held, which I eventually did."

Nick's fingers involuntarily tightened around hers. He didn't like this at all—the dangers she continually faced—yet he hung on her every word.

"I found his last slave, Mimi, chained to his bed in a hotel room while he was in the saloon downstairs drumming up business for her favors. Her clothes, what little she wore, were little more than dirty rags. Her eyes were nearly swollen shut, and she was hanging on to consciousness by sheer force of will." Lilly paused, closing her own eyes for a moment as a shudder rolled through her body.

When her eyes opened, they were distant, unfocused. "I asked her if she wanted to leave, and she spit before breathing out, 'Hell, yes.' I used my tool to pick the lock on the chains, and we crept down the hotel's back stairs. Though it was difficult for her to remain upright, we managed to get to a wagon I'd tied nearby, and we left. Thad was with me, but I didn't want him in the hotel because his size would be too intimidating to the woman."

Nick let his breath slide from the prison of his lungs. At least someone had been with her. Though he still didn't like it.

"Two weeks later, the sheriff arrested Baylor and brought him in to stand trial. The rescued woman testified against him, but she insisted I accompany her to the courtroom. Baylor must have figured out the role I played in all this, and after he was sentenced, he vowed to get me when he got out of jail. His sentence was lengthy, and I never expected him to be released."

Lilly glanced at Willow on the other side of the stove. "Though I haven't seen him full face, I think he's here, endangering everyone. You, me, and her."

Nick brought their clasped hands up to his lips and kissed her fingers. "Baylor will never get to you, not if there is a breath left in me."

Lilly pulled her hand away. "Don't promise something you can't keep, Nick."

The sting of her words wounded him.

Not *might not be able* to keep, but *can't* keep. She still didn't trust him.

Dejected, he stretched out on the floor and turned to face her profile. Her arms circled her knees again and her teeth worked her lower lip, the very lip he longed to pull into his mouth. Deep lines sank across her forehead and she rocked on her bottom with increasing speed.

How was he to protect her, keep her safe, if she refused to believe him capable? And keeping her safe was now his most fervent desire. Something he had failed to do before and didn't want to repeat.

"I wish I could have been Celia's papa." The words slid out from nowhere, formed from thoughts rattling in his brain since first learning he sired a child.

They were met with silence.

Until. . ..

"You'll marry one day and have another." Her gaze flicked to his, an unreadable emotion showing in her eyes.

Maybe, but only a small woman with green eyes would do as his wife.

Willow stirred and Lilly's gaze turned toward the child. Long moments passed as she studied the lithe sleeping form.

"You have a second chance to be a father, you know." Lilly's huff of breath was scarcely a murmur, but it carried over the pop and crackle of the small stove fire. "She has no one except us."

His heart stopped. *Us?* Was this her olive branch? Unspoken possibilities whirled through his mind. He mentioned it before but had not received a response.

"Lilly, does this mean we can start over?"

~~~~

Start over? Startled by his question, Lilly stared at the dancing flame through the grate. Her deepest thoughts must have slipped out before she had the sense to reign in her tongue.

Of course, they couldn't start over. Too many obstacles stood in their path, not the least of which was the increasing danger of her secret life. Danger she had brought to both Nick and Willow.

Each government mission drew her deeper into the bowels of vice and sin, to the depravity and cruelties of man. If Celia had been alive, she might have left the service long ago. Before Baylor and his threats darkened her path.

No one doubted Willow needed a family. Lilly had planned to raise Celia on her own with the help of Thad and Jacob. But, based on comments she had heard them both make in the past, she doubted either would welcome a half-breed child.

Which brought her back to the real reason his father had split them apart.

Once he knew, would Nick hate her as his father had?

She would like to believe Nick didn't harbor the same prejudices. The fact that Willow was half native didn't appear to matter to him. Indeed, he was more than willing to learn mountain living, and sounded genuinely interested in understanding her culture, two things Lilly intended to foster.

Judging from the anguish written across his face when he learned he'd sired a child who died, Nick may have wanted to be a father after all. Perhaps being Willow's father would give him another chance.

But did he deserve another chance?

He told her previously he'd tried to find her all those years ago but had been confused by her last name. Not disclosing her parents' real surname had been her fault. Was it Nick's fault his father lied to her about his son's whereabouts?

No, Nick was not to blame.

His father compounded the issue by not telling him of her pregnancy. Had Nick known the truth, would he have made a more concerted effort to find her? Did she even want him if his only reason for coming after her was because of the baby?

The myriad reasons why they could never be together rotated through her thoughts like juggler's pins. The confusion made her head ache.

She jumped when the tumble of resettling logs sent sparks flying inside the stove's grate.

Listen to your heart.

The whisper could have come from someone in the room, so real and lifelike was its tone and timber. The image of sightless Gray Dove sewing beads on her burial dress flew in her mind.

If Lilly were truthful with herself, she feared her own feelings for this charming man who once swept her off her feet and made love to her so tenderly. Every time she looked at him, she was reminded of what they had once shared, what they had missed all those years.

Heaven help her, more than anything she wanted to feel the strength of his arms around her again, wanted to lean into his solidness and forget the fears Baylor provoked. The outcast she had become.

The danger all around her.

She slid a sidelong glance in his direction. His eyes reflected hope and something else she'd seen of late but hadn't wanted to investigate. She swallowed hard. Something about the light in his clear blue eyes made her not want to see it dim.

Yet, she didn't want to lead him on either. "Willow needs both of us. Let's start from there."

Suddenly, Nick tugged her head toward him, his eyes filled with desperate need.

Oh, God! He was going to kiss her. Was she ready for this? Her pulse raced. Her lips opened of their own accord, and she leaned forward. He covered her mouth in a sweet, chaste brush, his lips as soft and tender as she remembered, his scent of bergamot and spice, oh so enticing.

He pulled back all too soon, his widened eyes now dark pools of sapphire, his features stark with want, with a deep yearning making her heart beat faster and her breathing erratic. Behind his kiss had been tightly controlled passion she felt as keenly as the soft pressure upon her flesh. Tension crackled. Liquid heat spread to her womb.

His gaze settled on her lips. Hers settled on his.

And then his mouth crushed hers in a hard, hungry kiss meant to reestablish his claim. His tongue forged in, exploring, touching, laying siege to her senses. She surrendered eagerly, overcome by her own need to touch, to taste. Loving the feel of him, she sighed with joy.

The years separating them dissolved.

And in her heart, she acknowledged she would always hunger for this man.

Chapter 17

A SLIGHT SHAKE DREW LILLY out of a deep, peaceful sleep, the first she'd experienced since Nick walked into the saloon and upset her orderly world. The rosy fingers of dawn crept across the eastern sky through the flimsy curtain covering the room's only window.

Reluctant to leave the comfort of the soft, narrow bed, Lilly turned toward the owner of the hand, and peered into the heat of Nick's smiling eyes. Flame engulfed her cheeks as she remembered the kiss from the night before.

Crouched beside the bed, he quickly banked his sleepy grin of morning desire, leaned close to her ear, and whispered, "We need to get moving before Baylor sees us."

The warm glow changed to clammy cold in an instant.

Baylor!

How could she have forgotten he was staying at the same hotel? Perhaps even on the same floor. For a few glorious hours of sleep, her heart had been wrapped in a bubble of frothy dreamless serenity.

Until reality broke through. She cleared her throat.

"Wake Willow and gather your things. I'm going to the livery to arrange our transportation. You stay here with Dog until I come for you. Under no circumstances are you to go outside alone."

She opened her mouth to object, but his finger against her lips stopped her.

"No time for arguing. The two of you are my responsibility now, and from what you told me, Baylor is a danger to us all. The sooner we get out of here, the better."

Lilly scanned his handsome face. From the determined set of his jaw and his direct and commanding gaze, he appeared unlikely to agree to anything she suggested.

Yet, she couldn't keep her hand from cupping his face. "You'll be careful?"

Nick nodded, though she could have sworn he leaned his cheek into her hand before halting the movement.

He rose, adjusting the clothes he had slept in, and took care of his morning ablutions at the washstand. After pulling on his boots, he shoved his arms into his sheepskin jacket and reached for his hat.

The intimidating specimen of masculinity before her couldn't possibly be the finicky city dweller she knew before. Several day's beard growth contributed to his aura of danger, as did the thick outerwear which broadened his shoulders into mammoth proportions.

He had turned into someone she hardly recognized. A man more willing to take charge of his actions. Surer, more confident. She liked this man, but she also liked the smiling, fun-loving man he had once been before.

He adjusted his hat on his head and left.

Dog stirred and nudged the sleeping Willow with his nose.

"Sleep, Dog. The sun is not yet up," the child murmured into the fur next to her head.

Lilly threw back her warm covers. "I'm afraid he's right, sweetheart. We must leave soon. A long day lies ahead." No sense in alarming the girl if Lilly couldn't be sure she hadn't imagined Baylor's presence.

Willow sat up abruptly and rubbed her eyes. "Yes, ma'am."

An unexpected sting sent moisture to Lilly's eyes. She didn't want to be Willow's 'ma'am.' She wanted to be her "mama."

The thought struck her dumb.

Unlike Celia, who explored her world with a child's laughter and delight, Willow's stoic practical demeanor tore Lilly's heart apart. The only time the girl laughed was when she was with Dog. Robbed of her childhood by circumstance, for Willow survival had been paramount.

The differences were stark.

And sad.

Lilly wanted to scoop the child up and tickle her until laughter made them both cry. Wanted to hug her and tell her everything would be all right.

Keeping her face turned while she composed herself, Lilly folded Nick's buffalo hides while Willow brushed her teeth at the washstand.

A few minutes later, Dog whined, then parked himself at the door, his amber eyes darting from the child to the door and back.

Willow sighed and laid her towel beside the basin. "I'll take you out in a minute, after I gather my things."

Despite Lilly's desire to heed Nick's warning, it was obvious the dog had to go out. If Baylor was indeed, in town, he wanted her, not the child. Besides, Dog was quite capable of guarding his owner. "You go on, Willow. I'll take care of your things. Come right back when Dog finishes. No dawdling. Promise me."

Willow nodded as she tugged on her leather moccasin boots. "I promise. We'll be quick."

Willow's "quick" turned out to be not quick enough. Ten minutes turned into twenty. Lilly's patience was ebbing. It shouldn't be taking Willow and Dog this long, should it?

Their belongings long since folded and ready, Lilly tightened her boot laces, slipped into her sheepskin jacket, and left to find the child. A tightness in her chest now accompanied the tumult in her belly.

A trail of animal tracks in the snow brought Lilly to the side of the livery a few buildings down from the hotel.

"Well, lookie here!" An arm snaked tight about her waist from behind, lifting her off the ground and up against the unyielding hardness of a man's chest. Shock held her immobilized. As did his arms.

Baylor? A desert invaded her throat, drying out the scream that clamored for release. Oh, Lord! How stupid had she been?

The pistol. Where was it? In her jacket. Unreachable. His arm covered the pocket's opening. Her pulse throbbed a staccato beat of impotence.

Hot fetid breath brushed her cheek. "I been following ya. Seen ya go in the back door of them bawdy houses in Cripple Creek and I says to meself, that's a fine piece of woman. I want me some of that. Before I got me coin collected, ya up and left. I done found yer trail and followed ya to that squaw's place. You being a whore and all, I thought we can do a little business back here. Waddya say, girlie?"

For some reason, the bands of panic loosened around her chest. Though Lilly couldn't see him clearly in the dusky haze of dawn, the man was not the ghost she thought she had seen. She would recognize Baylor's voice anywhere, its high-pitched screech having haunted her dreams for years.

Then something he had said entered her consciousness.

This man thinks I'm a prostitute!

A hand slammed across her mouth as she opened it to yell, and she was shoved farther down the wall to the rear of the livery.

Bloody hell! I'm going to be raped.

Lilly's shock shifted to rage in an instant. The hell she would allow a man to touch her without her permission. Instinct took over. She twisted, and turned, and kicked. Pounded, and scraped her nails into skin. Desperate, she clamped her teeth on the hand under her nose. Anything to escape.

"You bit me," her attacker whined in astonishment. "Alls I wanted was a little poke." He tightened his grip around her middle. "Do that again, girlie and I'll make ya pay." The menace in his voice cut through her outrage like the slash of a sharp steel blade.

Lilly stilled.

Vomit rose in her constricted throat, propelled by her fear of rape as much as the stench of stale beer, garlic and unwashed teeth assaulting her nostrils. She jerked her head away, but the motion wasn't enough to stop her stomach from turning into a fomenting ocean of foulness.

Before she could move again, her assailant shoved her against the wall and pressed into her back side. An unmistakable male hardness poked into her bottom through her divided skirt, and ground against her. Fingers came between her thighs, searching for the juncture of her legs among the folds of her voluminous skirt.

Blood rushed from her head, and a dense gray fog obscured her vision. Panic, dark and terrifying, once again descended, grabbing at her insides, and tearing her heart. The gun remained deep in her pocket, buried and inaccessible.

Lilly's face collided with the rough wooden wall. For an instant, the hand on her mouth loosened, and she gulped in air like a fish pulled from the water. Her pulse throbbed without mercy. Beneath the odor of his body, his breath, new pine planking and manure, she could smell the stink of her own fear.

Her assailant's hand disappeared from between them, and he ground his pelvis against her back side again. Seconds later he turned her around, one hand still tight to her lips. Lust filled gray eyes of a young miner, a man who may have been without a woman for months.

Her blood froze.

Using every bit of strength she had, she struggled again to break free only to be slammed a second time against the wall. Blackness threatened. No, no! She must remain conscious no matter what.

Still covering her mouth, he pulled a kerchief from his overcoat pocket and tied it around her head and between her lips. The cloth smelled of soured sweat and trail dust and tasted worse.

The contents of last night's dinner rose once again. She swallowed hard, her throat parched, the lump lodged there massive and immovable. Lilly twisted again.

"Woooeee! You're quite the spitfire, ain't ye?" A malicious grin exposed broken teeth stained by tobacco and neglect. Rampant male lust glittered in dark eyes set too close together.

Struggling to breathe, Lilly fought to remain vertical, ruing the day she had said yes to Reginald. This was all her fault . . .this life . . .this world.

Her would-be rapist seized her hands and flung them over her head, his grip tight around her wrists. She screamed, but the scarf muffled the sound.

As her assailant leaned forward to kiss her face, Lilly turned her head at the last moment. His lips landed on her hair. Anger flared in his eyes. Sneering, he pulled back his fisted hand.

Lilly tensed, her eyes closing for the expected blow.

The punch never came. Instead, the man reached through her jacket which had opened during the struggle and grabbed the white shirt tucked into her skirt. Buttons flew to the mushy ground.

Frigid mountain air stung her exposed skin. Startled, she trembled violently.

The miner studied his handiwork while her galloping heart pounded in her ears. *Please no.*

Whistling softly through his darkened teeth, the man grinned. "Would ya look at all the fancy lace!" His voice was filled with admiration.

Try as she might, Lilly couldn't stop her chest from heaving. The man's eyes rose to her face. With another lust-filled smile, he ripped her camisole in two and spread the halves wide, exposing her breasts.

Her muscles tightened, as her fear turned to anger.

And anger shifted to rage.

Red, hot, violent rage.

Nobody, but nobody was going to touch her and get away with it.

Lilly positioned her leg between his thighs and, with a guttural shout more animal than human, jerked her knee up hard into his groin. The man screamed and bent at the waist.

From out of nowhere, a mass of flying fur lunged at him with jaws bared, saliva dripping. The man flung his arm up in defense. Dog gripped it and shook with the fury of a hungry beast bringing down its prized meal.

Then searing heat covered her breast from behind and she was yanked away from the violence at her feet. The soft rumbling of a familiar voice broke through her fright. She caught the scent of wood smoke and horses.

And Nick.

Seconds later, a shot exploded.

~~~~

At the sharp crack of a gun, Nick shoved Lilly to the ground and fell on top of her. A whoosh of air passed over his head and a bullet slammed into the plank wall, sending tiny wood shards flying.

What the hell! Were there two of them? His breath all but stopped. Not knowing what had happened, he lay there waiting, listening.

Aware of the commotion raised by Dog and Lilly's attacker.

Aware of the soft texture of her breast cupped in his hand.

Of her heaving breaths inadvertently pushing her flesh deeper into his palm, her nipple, hard from the cold, right where he had longed for it to be. Nick struggled against the urge to tighten his fingers. She wouldn't like it, though he sure would.

The next thing to register was the locket he had given her, its heart shape trapped sideways between his fingers. He made a mental note to ask her about it later.

Dog's feral growls broke his distraction. Where was the shooter? The animal needed to be dragged off the man soon before it tore a limb from his body. Not that the miner didn't deserve his fate.

Nick raised up on his elbows and cast about for someone with a gun. Seeing no one, he scrambled up and waded into the frenzy of man and beast.

Grabbing Dog's beaded leather collar, he yelled, "Dog, stop."

Dog shifted, the man's arm still tight in his jaws.

"Dog!" Willow's voice was loud and shrill in the early morning silence.

The animal gave one last growl and released his prey, leaving Lilly's attacker lying ignobly in the muddied snow. Emitting his own growl, Nick hauled the filthy man up by his coat collar and slammed his fist into the attacker's jaw. The man crumpled to the ground unconscious, blood from his nose dripping to the dirty snow.

Dog trotted back to Willow, tail tucked between his legs.

The girl crouched and encased the animal's head in her hands. "Good boy, Dog. You rescued Miss Lilly." The dog's ears perked up and a long pink tongue washed the girl's face.

At the sound of Willow's laugh, Nick glanced at Lilly now leaning against the unpainted wood wall. Her colorless face blank, she attempted to pull the edges of her camisole together. Failing that, she tried to button her jacket, but her fingers shook so badly, she couldn't work the fasteners through the holes.

Running to her, he drew her tight to his chest. Smothered sobs rose from her shuddering body as she buried her head against his jacket. Behind him, the crunch of snow told him her assailant had awakened and was getting away.

He glanced behind him. The guy looked like a miner. A frightened one, judging from the size of his eyes and the puddle of piss beneath him when Dog's wolf instincts took over. Hopefully, Dog had scared the shit out of him as well. He would describe him to the authorities later. Lilly needed him.

He pulled her closer, whispered words of comfort, his own fury barely contained.

Obviously, there were two assailants.

But why?

Baylor!

After a few minutes, Lilly stopped crying, yet she made no move to leave. He leaned his cheek against the top of her head and heard her sigh.

She lifted her chin, revealing red and swollen eyes. "You could have been killed."

His heart beating wildly, he stared at her for a moment. She spoke not about her near rape, but the bullet that flew over his head. "Would you have cared?"

"Of course, I would." His chest expanded. "You're my client. I'm supposed to protect *you*. Not the other way around."

Nick swallowed over a ball of disappointment, then perused her ashen face. Her gaze was fixed on his lips, her own slightly apart. Her tongue slipped out and wet her lower lip. He tipped her chin up. Her green eyes were dark with desire.

Without further thought, he lowered his head and brushed her mouth. Once. Twice. Then her hand snaked up, and she pulled his head down for a third kiss that was far more than a brush of soft flesh. She foraged through his mouth, hungry and seeking, her fingers tightening on his shoulders in a strong grip.

This he could offer—safety for her battered and shocked sanity. A validation of her humanity, of her personal worth.

Nick let her take what she wanted, what she seemed to need. Reveling in the unexpected return—the soft, surrender of her lips, the lure of her lilac-scented hair, the desperation of her need.

Tongues tangled in the hot, wet recesses of their mouths. Breath mingled. Sighs, and groans and moans erupted as passion exploded. His. Hers. So great was his need, his want of her, his control was in danger of crumbling.

Lord a mighty, they had much to talk about.

She was the first to pull away, her face now suffused with color. "I … I—"

"Later," he mouthed.

Away from the interested eyes of Willow.

After they found Baylor or whoever fired that shot.

After they found Rina.

Chapter 18

LILLY BARELY FELT NICK'S STRONG HANDS around her waist as she landed on the narrow wooden seat. Biting cold winds caught her breath and kept the few words of thanks lodged in her throat. Her world still a gray fog, she scarcely noticed Willow beneath a pile of buffalo skins, huddled against Dog in the wagon bed.

Though Nick arranged a fur around Lilly's tightly buttoned sheepskin jacket, her bone-deep chill rapidly progressed to a violent shudder, her thoughts settling on one indisputable fact.

Nick had saved her.

Put his life in jeopardy for her.

That bullet might have killed him, and the thought of his death shook her more than her own narrow escape. More, even, than the shocking heat of his hand on her breast.

Shoving the startling insight aside, she swallowed over the boulder lodged in her parched throat. "I was nearly raped."

The admission was a whisper, more to herself than for anyone else, yet Nick, sitting beside her, answered. "You weren't. Dog saved you."

She glanced up. Eyes of vivid cerulean blue studied her from beneath a Stetson hat, eyes that never failed to melt her insides. What did they see? The fear clinging to her each time she encountered the world of sin as of late? The panic still gripping her from her near violation only hours before?

Or the fact she cared whether he lived or died more than she was willing to admit?

"If Dog hadn't been there. . .."

Nick's hands flexed on the reins and his lips formed a tight line. "I would have."

"How would you have known? His hand covered my mouth."

Nick stared ahead. "I heard you, Lilly. It was not a shout, but somehow I knew you needed help." His voice held a terse edge to it.

"And you came," she whispered, still amazed by his selfless act.

"Of course, I came. Why would you think I wouldn't?"

A heartbeat passed.

Raising his head to the sky, Nick shut his eyes, but not before she noted pain flickering through them.

Oh, dear. She had made a terrible mistake. She'd hurt him, and he didn't deserve it. Regret turned the air between them into a thick miasma of awkwardness. They sat without speaking, the crunching clop of horse hooves against the slushy trail beating a mesmeric rhythm of discomfort.

The minutes passed slowly. Then, "I'm sorry," they both said simultaneously into the silence.

Lilly's gaze snapped to Nick whose eyes were trained on the team of horses. A bone worked in his jaw as though he were grinding his teeth.

"I am sorry I was not around for you."

Lilly didn't mistake his reference.

"I deeply regret my actions, or lack of them. You needed me and I failed you . . .failed my daughter . . .failed myself. I would give anything to make it up to you, but I know that's impossible now."

He glanced sideways at her. The morning sun glistened off something in Nick's eyes, something she strongly suspected might be moisture. Despite her vow, his few words, his honest expression of remorse settled close to her heart.

Lilly placed her gloved hand on his jacket sleeve. "You already have, Nick. You saved me from being raped."

The bone in his jaw worked faster. His mouth tightened, as did his grip on the reins.

Several minutes later, he switched the leathers to his left hand and flexed the fingers of his right. "Frank and I got the sheriff out of bed and we found the miner but lost the shooter. We checked all over, but whoever shot at me disappeared."

A sudden thought streaked through her mind with alarming clarity.

She shivered.

"It's Baylor. I know it was him. He followed us up here, Nick. I wasn't imagining anything. And if he aimed at you and not me, he may have shot Jacob, as well."

To get to me.

Nick's eyes narrowed. "You think Jacob was shot intentionally?"

"The possibility can't be ignored."

"So, now we have two men to watch out for, DuPry and Baylor." Worry seeped into his silver baritone which rumbled over her like smooth river rock rolling down a slow-moving stream.

Dear Lord! With everything that happened this morning, Lilly had forgotten about Sabrina. Nick must be frantic not knowing if she was with DuPry.

She fell silent, her thoughts drawn to his sister's plight and the possibilities too horrid to mention aloud.

Sometime later, she placed her hand on his arm. "You might have died back there. What you did for me is way beyond a simple thank you."

The tension in Nick's jaw relaxed a bit and the edges along his mouth moved upwards in a tiny curve. His breath released in a puff of cold air, and her heart beat a little faster. But his next words jolted her.

"Some day when you are ready, I'd like to know why you chose such a dangerous job."

She pulled her hand away. She couldn't tell him why; she didn't know herself and didn't care to examine her motivation any time soon. It was a compulsion. A need.

Once.

But now?

Lilly glanced at Willow in the back. "Someday I'll tell you, but not now."

He seemed to accept her excuse without comment. For the present.

As the morning wore on and the road climbed, the snow began to melt. A good sign.

They stopped for lunch close to some trees near a high mountain meadow shielded from the sun's brightest rays by an imposing peak.

Though several trails of animal tracks ran through it, the field still sparkled white.

Dog jumped from the wagon and, after sniffing each trail with enthusiasm, took off after the life form hitting his nostrils. Nick handed Willow down and rounded the bed to help Lilly.

Lilly's breath caught as her body slid along his to the ground. Heat radiating off him like a stoked fire, he held her entirely too close, and for far too long. Her eyes flew to his, which were focused on her lips. He was going to kiss her, and by all the heavens, she wanted him to. Even ached for the press of his mouth on hers. Her lips parted and she leaned forward.

But, at the last moment he stepped back and walked toward the horses.

Disappointment and a small bit of humiliation worked its way to the middle of her chest. Lord, what was she thinking? Or was she thinking at all? She narrowly escaped being raped this morning, and Nick had almost been killed. Yet want and need seemed to replace all reason, or at least whatever sense she might have had before his reappearance in her life.

There could never be a future for them. Too many obstacles stood in their way.

So why had she been so eager to accept another of his kisses? To yearn for it, even?

~~~~

Nick unhitched the horses and tied them to a tree branch. What the hell was he thinking? Only a few hours ago Lilly escaped from being raped and killed.

And he had kissed her right afterward.

What kind of man would exploit a traumatized woman?

From the moment he recognized Lilly's muffled cries outside the stable, fear rampaged through his body, spiraling to his head with a forceful thrust that burned every rational thought to a crisp. He had rushed out of the barn, his heart all but bursting from his chest.

Though his rifle remained in the hotel, he had his fists, and he damn well knew how to use them. Many a club prize had come his way for his skills as a boxer in the heaviest of weight classes. He had wanted to beat the crap out of the guy, pound him into bloody pulp. Assuage the anger streaking unimpeded through his veins. Anger born of fear.

Nobody gets away with hurting his family.

But her assailant wasn't Baylor, and he didn't have to lift a damn finger. Dog did it for him.

His unrequited fury was still fomenting, still flowing hot and wild, along with a deep fear for Lilly's safety, for Willow's. It took him hours to cool his emotions, to not let Lilly know how scared he had been for her.

How much her well-being mattered to him.

Pale and silent all morning, Lilly's only sign of continued agitation were her hands, alternately gripping and flexing against her jacket. He'd wanted to pull her against him. Offer her comfort, but he held back with as much restraint as he could muster. She was too damn vulnerable. He wanted her trust above all else, but first he needed to control his own rampant impulse to hold her.

Lifting her out of the wagon just now proved to be more temptation than he could handle. Despite himself, he had drawn her close. Too close. His body had reacted strongly, and now he had to hide among the horses until his considerable arousal subsided.

A few minutes later, Willow and Lilly returned from the bushes and climbed into the buckboard to prepare the lunch purchased from the eatery. With both females more subdued than normal, they ate their meal in relative silence, speaking only when necessary. Willow seemed to understand this morning's occurrence and sat closer to Lilly than before. Almost as if she were protecting her.

His erection now under control, Nick studied the two. He should be the one offering Lilly comfort, yet he would never begrudge the two females the opportunity to support each other.

A cloud passed over the sun and cast them in shade. He glanced up. Dark, moisture-laden clouds were blowing from the north.

"Looks like we're in for some snow again. We might not make it all the way to Victor tonight." Tension knotted his throat as he spoke.

Sabrina was out there somewhere, and he had to find her. He had spent far too much time away from the search. She could be—

Don't think that way.

Lilly dipped her hand over the wagon's side and dropped a torn bit of bread to Dog. "If we can get to Lawrence, we'll be all right. Though the town doesn't have a hotel, there are many houses. Hopefully, we'll find one still occupied."

Then what? Another night of torment?

~~~~

Cold winds buffeted Lilly's face as an avalanche of white fell from the sky at a slant. She sat stiff on the seat, the rapidly disappearing rutted trail sending her careening back and forth against Nick's side in a sensual dance of intense awareness and colliding bodies.

The altercation with the would-be rapist and the shooting this morning unnerved her, cutting a wide swath through the vulnerability she so carefully hid from the world. Her core lay open and bleeding, fear and anxiety exposed like never before.

She had avoided her informants in town, avoided asking anyone other than Frank yesterday about DuPry's whereabouts for fear they would see the damaged person she was.

Lilly slipped her hand in her jacket pocket, her fingers sliding over the cold, tiny pistol Reginald insisted she learn to shoot. A woman alone … he had said. Yet when the time had come, the weapon hadn't kept her safe.

Nick had saved her, and she was grateful for his presence. Though her body now screamed to be held, to be calmed in the way only he could do, he had turned away from her.

The afternoon drew on, the sky gray with low, moisture-laden clouds. "At this rate we won't even reach Lawrence by nightfall. So close, yet so far with all this snow. Any deeper and the wagon won't be able to roll through it," she lamented, her patience and composure worn to shreds.

Dog yawned, a small whine drifting over the sound of the wind.

Lilly glanced behind her. Buffalo skins topped by a light dusting of white nearly buried Willow and her pet, huddled together for warmth.

"We need to get this little one out of the cold. When we get to Lawrence, we'll see if we can find someone to take us in."

Nick grunted an approval, his first utterance since lunch.

She glanced sideways at him. Set tight, his hardened jaw made his face more chiseled, more determined. He sat tall in his seat, long fingers beneath his gloves wrapped tense around the reins.

Had he seen her make a cake of herself earlier? Had he known she was eager for his mouth upon hers. That she needed his comfort?

As they rounded a turn, a grand vista of ranch land covered in white opened to their view. Lilly pointed. "Lawrence."

In a flat area near a frozen creek, several newly built cabins sat scattered along a rough L-shaped grid of snow-packed streets. The main street had a post office, a general merchandise store, a laundry, and a restaurant, but no hotel. Out of the dozen or so houses, smoke curled out of only two chimneys.

Nick turned the horses in the direction of the closest, a small structure with an outhouse and shed behind it.

Lilly combed the town for other signs of life. "Looks like most of the miners are gone for the winter. Only the hardy and the well-stocked remained."

The large man beside her shifted the reins to his left hand and flexed his right fingers. "Suits me as long as someone takes us in."

Stopping in front of the house, Lilly wiggled her frozen digits while Nick walked the short distance to the door and knocked. Seconds later, the door swung open and a rather rumpled-looking miner with a ragged, full beard poked his head out.

"My fiancée and I are traveling these parts and couldn't quite make it to Victor. Might we impose upon your kindness for a place to stay the night?" Nick asked, shoving his Stetson off his forehead.

The man scanned Nick from hat to boots, then settled on Lilly before squinting at Willow who had climbed off the wagon with Dog.

The wary look on his face softened. "That there youngin' ought not be out in this weather. Me and my misses can take care of ya, if ya don't mind her cookin'. T'aint too great, but it's hot, and there's plenty of it."

He smiled and opened the door wide.

"Thank you, sir. We're grateful," said Nick, who turned and waved them forward.

Relieved, Lilly gathered Willow and Dog and slogged through the heavy slush to the cabin. As they entered, a savory aroma of something cooking in a cast iron kettle atop a potbellied cook stove hit her nose. Much to her embarrassment, her stomach growled loudly.

Upon seeing visitors at her door, a sturdy-looking woman of middling age and twinkling dark eyes wiped her hands on a calico apron and came forward. A friendly smile turned her rough, weathered features into a mass of tiny laugh lines.

"Welcome. Please come in and make yourselves t'home. Don't get many visitors this time of the year. I'm Daisy Fuekes, and this man here is my husband, John. And who are you?"

Blunt and to the point. Lilly liked her immediately.

Nick slipped out of his jacket and hung it on the peg John had indicated. "I'm Nick Shield, and this is my fiancée Lilly Kane, and that's Willow and her pet Dog."

No matter how many times Nick referred to her as his fiancée, the title startled her.

"What brings you folks up this way?" John grabbed Lilly's jacket and hung it on a peg next to Nick's, then eyed Willow who had already pulled her buffalo robe off and was laying it out in a corner to dry.

A faint smile turned the corners of their host's mouth up. "Industrious little imp, that one."

At Daisy's direction, Lilly lowered herself to a bench at the table and answered the last question first.

"Willow is quite a busy little person, sometimes more than she should be. And as to your other question, we're looking for Nick's sister and we have reason to believe she might be up here somewhere."

Daisy set several mismatched plates on the table. "Oh, my. Is she lost?"

Nick spoke before Lilly could answer. "Truth is we don't know. A Pinkerton tracked her up to Cripple Creek, but altitude sickness claimed the agent before he could identify my sister." He glanced at Lilly, then continued. "We're following someone who might have kidnapped her."

Talk of DuPry, no matter how subtle, reminded Lilly of the hazards of her work, especially her near rape. Though she was safe now, her shoulder muscles had tightened into knots and her hands still trembled.

"Kidnapped! Gracious! I hope not." Daisy returned to the stove, dipped a spoon in the pot and tasted her creation. Satisfied, she announced that dinner was ready.

With a sigh, Lilly turned herself around on the bench, thankful the woman hadn't asked any more about kidnapping. The less Willow knew of that subject, the better.

Nick and Willow settled on each side of her, and John and Daisy took the other bench. The meal—a venison stew loaded with potatoes and carrots, along with freshly baked biscuits—was surprisingly good. Whatever John had said about his wife's cooking was obviously false. Daisy would fare well against any restaurant chef in Colorado Springs, including the one at Sally's Silver Spoon.

For a few minutes nobody talked as they dug into their dinner with gusto. Especially Willow, who ate as though she'd been starving.

John tore a biscuit in half and slathered it with butter. "There are three kinds of women here—women with families, mail order brides, and whores. Women like my Daisy come with their families looking for gold. The mail orders are a breed unto themselves, willing to take a risk when there ain't no guarantee they'll get a good man. And the third, the whores are here for a while and then gone. Tend to leave for newer, fresher pickin's."

Nick stiffened. "My sister isn't a whore."

"I'm not saying she is," John said.

"Then what are you saying?"

Lilly recognized the hint of belligerence edging into Nick's tone.

"Did she come with a family?"

"I'm her family, and no," came the sharp reply.

"Mail-order bride, then. Daisy, here, knows most of the women in these parts. Not many respectable women up here and they flock together like birds—old marrieds and new marrieds like them mail-order ones."

Despite her discomfort with the term *respectable* and all that entailed, Lilly's interest was piqued.

"What's she look like, your sister?" their host went on.

"Tall and thin, with blonde hair and blue eyes." An odd light flickered in Nick's eyes and Lilly heard the note of hope in his voice.

Daisy regarded him for a moment, her forehead crinkled in thought. "What's her name?"

"Sabrina Shield, but she also goes by the name of Rina."

Startled, Daisy glanced at John in silent communication. "Rina Murphy," they both exclaimed at the same time, their faces beaming.

Willow stopped petting Dog, her eyes riveted to Daisy's.

Nick's eyes widened to the size of saucers. "Rina *Murphy?* My sister isn't married."

Lilly placed her hand on his arm. "But she might be now. Listen to what they have to say, Nick. No leads can be cut off at this point."

"Tell me about her?" Nick asked.

The woman perused Nick's face as though looking for similarities. "Well, you look like her. Even talk like her. That flat nasally tone, you know."

Nick fidgeted in his chair. "About when did she come here."

Lilly held her breath.

"Not long ago. Maybe six weeks or so."

Lilly wanted to shout for joy, and from the waves of electricity flowing from Nick, so did he.

Daisy continued, oblivious to the excitement growing across the table. "She is one of them mail order brides. Tim's mine panned out, and he got himself a wife as soon as he could afford it. Risky business, mail order brides. Ya never know what you're gonna get. He spent months writing to her and building that house of his."

Nick thrust his fingers through his hair. "She never told me, never gave even a hint she was unhappy."

"Well, she's happy now. Comes here every Tuesday for the sewing bee. A little shy at first, but she's since made friends with just about every woman around these parts. And the way Tim looks at her, I'd guess her marriage is right nice. Ah, to be young and in love." Daisy sighed, her gaze landing on her crimson-faced husband.

"Is their house close by, Daisy?" Nick asked, hope permeating his voice and flaring in his eyes.

"Not far. Over in Independence. The town ain't much. Just a few houses. The Murphys might be the only ones still up there this time of year. Follow this road through Victor past Goldfield. Snow should be over by mid-day. Maybe you can set out after lunch."

If Nick could wait that long. He seemed fairly jumping with unspent energy.

It looked like finding DuPry would have to wait. This lead seemed far more promising.

Chapter 19

THAT NIGHT, AFTER SETTLING IN AN empty miner's shack the Fuekes had opened for their convenience, Nick shoved another log in the stove and waited until it caught.

Still reeling from discovering his sister might be close by and safe, he plunked himself on the floor near Lilly on his pile of buffalo skins and leaned against the bed frame. Willow, tired and full of Daisy's cooking, lay sound asleep on the floor on the other side curled next to Dog. No one seemed interested in sleeping in the bed.

For now.

Sitting cross-legged beside him, Lilly's gaze rested on the small flickering light radiating from the stove's grate. She had been quiet since retiring to the cabin, dark shadows hiding her expression from view.

"I hope it's her," Lilly murmured.

"So do I."

Sparks erupted behind the grate in a flash of light. Lilly drew her knees to her chest and rocked gently on her bottom, her lower lip drawn tight between her teeth.

The day's events, especially this morning, were clearly upsetting her. He wished she would talk to him, unburden herself of what had to be painful memories. Until she did, though, he would remain her quiet support.

Time passed. Two souls deep in thought, sitting in silence so close their heat blended. Together, yet alone.

Until a sound slipped from Lilly's mouth. He glanced her way. Her body shook as her long wavy hair fell to cover her bowed head.

He heard a sniffle.

"Lilly?"

She started, turning to him at last, her face decimated by emotion. "Hold me, Nick. Please hold—"

He didn't wait. Reaching out, he pulled her across his lap, folding her tight to his chest. She didn't resist, but came willingly, her head landing against his shirt.

The silky texture of her hair beneath his chin, the roundness of her flesh pressing into his ribs, the weight of her across his legs all added to a profound sense of possession. Her delicate scent of lilac and woman reached his nostrils, wrapping him in her heady, but emotional presence.

The fact she had turned to him of her own accord, needy and vulnerable, affected him deeply. His heart ached for her, wished he could take away her pain, make her feel whole. For once, he was there when she needed him. The day's events were too much for anyone to deal with alone.

He rocked her for a while, whispering nonsense in her ear. Then, rolling with her to the furs, he lined up their bodies, and held her in his arms.

He kept his breathing slow and steady, willing her to accept his comfort with the sheer power of his mind. Soon she quieted, laying still in his arms, her breaths like soft feathers rustling across his neck.

At first, he barely felt it. The brush of her lips against the underside of his chin, the tightening of her fingers around his shoulders. Surprised, he loosened his grip and lowered his gaze. Dark pools of green desire stared back at him.

"Make love to me, Nick."

He stilled, the wind knocked out of him by her request. No, not a request. A demand. Every muscle tightened with burgeoning need. Every breath battled for completion. Questions darted to his tongue. "But—"

"I need you. Please, make new memories for me. I want you. I have always wanted you, and I can't hide it anymore. From you or from myself. I have never been with anyone since you. Make me forget . . .."

Her whispered confession and request coursed through him like a healing balm. He needed her as well. Now, more than ever.

Despite the years of separation, Lilly had remained his.

And now, she was offering him a second chance. Not only in mind, but in body. Something he could give her as well.

"Lilly …."

Her gaze fell to his lips. Invitation enough.

Dog shifted position. Nick pulled in a breath, listened. Lilly did the same. Willow's soft snore told him she remained asleep on the floor in her nest of buffalo skins, the bed shielding her from view.

Swiveling over the rest of Lilly, he cupped her cheeks. With utmost care, he covered her mouth, brushing it with feather touches that tested his control.

Her lips were soft, searching, and her taste sweet. Memories of other kisses on other nights crowded his mind. Of her lovely mouth touching him everywhere. He wanted her like that again. Craved her.

She leaned into him, her hard nipples pressing his chest like tiny seductive pebbles beneath her blouse. Nick lingered on her lips, savoring her essence, then traced kisses down her pert nose and high cheekbones. He longed to glide his fingers elsewhere, to explore her curves and bewitching sensuality. But he must go slow. He didn't want to overwhelm her with the strength of his long-buried need.

Her chest heaving, Lilly pushed away for air, her lips moist and swollen, her eyes dark and heavy-lidded. He thought he saw moisture in them, but he wasn't sure. "Don't go slowly, Nick. Seven years is a long time to wait."

Oh, God! Fast was just what he yearned for but never acted upon with her. In every dream he'd had since they parted, he rode her with wild, feral lust, with a possessiveness and fierceness that scared the hell out of him.

He had always controlled this side of himself, loving her with all the tenderness and gentleness he could muster. But now, she wanted him to not only make love to her but take her the way he had dreamed.

With no further thought, he crushed her mouth, demanding entry. She opened on a soft sigh, and he swept in, dancing with her tongue in a tangle of thrusts and parries, exploring every part of her, leaving nothing untouched. His ragged breathing turned to a tremble, and soon his entire body shook with emotion.

"Please," she implored on a whisper, struggling to unbuckle the belt on her divided skirt.

Impatient, he pushed to his knees and helped her. In a flurry of hands, together they managed to pull off her blouse, a corset of some sort and a waist-length chemise.

Stunned, Nick sat back and stared. Lilly's breasts were much larger than he remembered. Round and shapely, fuller from childbearing, and far more enticing. He couldn't wait to touch them, to love them with his hands and mouth, to stoke their sensitive nerve endings into a wild uncontrollable passion.

A flush rose to Lilly's cheeks and, like a modest maiden, she crossed her arms over her nakedness. "I'm not the twenty-year-old girl you once knew, Nick. I've borne a child." Her voice was small, almost embarrassed, yet the desire in her eyes couldn't be dismissed.

He slid his tongue over his suddenly dry lips. "I don't want that Lilly. I want the woman you are now—every beautiful inch of you." He wanted her so badly he feared he would spill like an untried boy.

A timid smile played upon her face, and she relaxed.

Reaching out, Nick cupped a breast in his hand. It was a perfect fit for his palm. So plump, so lush, her nipple hard and ready for him. He bent and sucked the tip into his mouth. Seven years of dreaming about this woman erupted in a frenzied need, and he licked her flesh like a thirsty man drawn to a well.

Lilly arched her back. As he switched to her other breast, a low moan escaped her lips, and he rejoiced. Never had he thought to hear passion from her again. His trembling hands glided over her torso, felt the rise and fall of her breaths, the smooth surface of her skin, the curves defining her waist and hips beneath her skirt.

Reluctant to stop his worship of her body, he sat back, and Lilly uttered a faint mew of disappointment.

"We are both wearing too damn many clothes." He tugged at her boots.

"Yes, we are." She leaned forward and did the same for him.

After helping her stand, in a mad scramble of hands and legs, they managed to shed the rest of their clothing without waking Willow or Dog.

They stood there naked, he hard and ready, and she.... she was magnificent. The years had added pleasing contours to her slim girlish figure, pillowy flesh to the hollow between her hipbones, and ripe firmness to her charming bottom. He couldn't wait to touch her, feast on her.

His gaze rose to her eyes which were assessing him with similar appreciation and a hunger he couldn't wait to satisfy. A painful throb pulsed to the end of his rod, now straining toward her with blatant eagerness.

Take me fast. Her words echoed in his head.

Nick pulled her tight to his chest, her taut peaks pressing against him. As he slid his hands to her buttocks, hers circled his waist. Lifting her, he settled them both on the furs.

"You sure you want this? Because once I begin, I won't be stopping," he gasped.

"Don't you dare stop, Nicholas Shield. I want this as much as you do."

Why? The question was uppermost in his mind, but he held it.

His pulse streaking, he knelt above her, resting his weight on his forearms, his hands cupping her face. She gazed up at him. Need filled her eyes. Her lips beckoned.

And he claimed them. Took her mouth with forceful possession. She was his. Always had been. Always will be. She accepted him with greed, reciprocating in kind. Claiming him as hers. As he had been since the first day they'd met.

Aww, God! Thank you for bringing her back to me.

He trailed kisses along her throat to her breasts, over her belly, and down to where he had dreamed of being. Her opening was ready for him, her moist flesh glistening in the firelight. Placing her legs over his shoulders, he raised her bottom.

"What are you do—"

He lowered his head and licked the nub of her passion.

"Oh, God." Her fingers threaded through his hair. "Whatever this is, don't stop."

He didn't plan to. Not until she came. Not until he had wrung every scream, and moan and shudder from her soul. This is what he had fantasized about. Hungered for. Giving her everything he had in him to give.

Her sweet salty flavor pushed him forward. Her quiet moans were his encouragement, her sighs, his reward. He couldn't stop now even if he'd wanted to. Her muscles tensed as she neared her release.

"Don't fight it, Lilly. Let go."

Seconds later, she convulsed, her teeth clenching to smother a cry that might wake Willow. His heart soared with her. As did his erection. He couldn't hang on any longer.

He positioned himself at her entrance, ready to sink into her glorious body. But her small hand reached out and touched the sensitive tip of his engorged shaft. More memories rose from the ash heap. His gaze flew to her face. A smile curved the edges of her mouth as she used her thumb to spread a bead of moisture she'd found around the responsive nerve endings of the head. He groaned. His erection turned to stone.

Then she wrapped her fingers around him and stroked. Her caress was as he remembered—tight, yet gentle. And arousing beyond measure. He could have continued in her hand forever, but he would never last, and she wanted more.

"Now, Lilly."

Opening her eyes, she guided him to her and rubbed him against the moisture of her cleft. Her flesh remained swollen and lustrous in readiness, beckoning him to drive home. Dark as the bottomless seas, her eyes brimmed with a yearning that touched his soul. She needed him inside her as much as he needed to be there.

Nick kissed her as he plunged through her slickness, only stopping when a small grunt escaped her lips. Had he hurt her? Summoning every ounce of control he could muster, he withdrew.

But she would have none of it. "Don't stop. Hard and fast, Nick."

Elated, he thrust into her again, and she clamped her scalding heat around him. Breath left him. Heaven welcomed him home, and he could have cried with joy. Nothing was more important than loving her the way she wanted, the way he wanted.

Nick withdrew and sank into her again, and this time her hips rose to meet his.

It was all too much.

"Lilly," he hissed out in a strangled whisper.

The hard coil of passion burgeoning inside him snapped. Sheer ecstasy engulfed him, the caress of her moist heat, the motion of her body, the rush of her breath across his cheek. His world faded. Nothing existed except the two of them straining toward their goal, their bodies molding together, his hips grinding into her pelvis with desperate hunger. He rode her hard, pumping into her heat at a frenzied pace, aware she matched him thrust for thrust.

Lilly's sighs and murmured words warmed his insides and propelled him forward. Her ragged breathing thrilled his soul, and the slick noises of their lovemaking intensified his long-buried need for the woman lying beneath him.

When she tensed, he knew her climax was near. Struggling to withhold his own, he felt her quake and her mouth opened in a silent scream.

Only then did he let go. Plunged deep inside her once, twice more, straining toward release until he exploded. He shuddered as he filled her with his seed, wave upon wave of pleasure spilling over him. Not since their last time together had he experienced such contentment.

Still joined, she clutched him about his waist, her contractions still wracking her frame. When the last vestiges of her orgasm were gone, she lay facing him on the fur, her face pressed to his chest, arms still around him.

Not until he regained his full senses did he feel Lilly's deep quivering against his body. His breath caught, for he feared it had nothing to do with her sexual release.

She was crying. Silently. Her arms tight about him in a vice-like grip.

~~~~

Swamped by emotions, Lilly clung to the only thing of substance in her whirling, teetering world—Nicholas.

What had she done! Giving in to the wants and needs she harbored for years, knowing a future together could never be. Positioning herself for heartbreak yet again.

One she might never recover from.

Perhaps, even conceiving another child.

Had she stabbed herself in the heart with her own womanly need?

She had wanted validation, an elusive something to make her whole again after this morning's brutal assault. Wanted … what? Comfort? Solace? Safety? Yes, but that wasn't all.

She wanted something she knew she might never have.

Love. Respectability.

Family.

But what now? What would he do after he found his sister? Would he help her find DuPry? Would he return to Chicago with Rina in tow?

What would he do if he knew her secret? Would he be accepting? Would he turn from her in disgust?

One thing she did know.

This couldn't go on.

She couldn't go on.

Not when she brought the dangers of her life— the randy men, the rapists, the killers, the vile slave traders—to everyone around her.

Not when she kept such a weighty secret from him—one that would surely turn Nick away as it had his father.

The impossibility of a future with Nick tore at her fragile heart. For despite her vow to protect it from this man, he had stolen it clean away.

Lilly tightened her hold on him and gave vent to her anguish.

If nothing else, she owed him the truth.

The real reason his father had sent her away.

Chapter 20

AS THEY APPROACHED THE ONLY house in Independence that seemed occupied the next afternoon, Lilly scrutinized it carefully. "A woman lives here. See those boxes under the windows. They're flower boxes, newly built if I'm not mistaken, waiting for spring. What miner would hang those on his house if he didn't have a woman living there? And I see curtains. Nick, these are all good signs."

Nick pulled the horses to a stop and glanced about. All morning long, he'd paced across the Fuekes' floor like a caged animal, waiting for the snow to let up. And now that they were at the moment of truth, Lilly detected a tension drifting across his shoulders and framing his mouth.

"Stay here. Let me check first. I hope this isn't a dead lead." As he passed the reins, Nick's gloved hand closed over hers, its warmth seeping through to her frozen fingers. Without thought, she caressed the underside of his palm with her thumb.

He lingered a moment staring at their clasped hands. When his gaze finally lifted, she struggled to swallow a gasp. Raw emotion inhabited their brilliant blue depths, an emotion she dared not name for fear of losing her heart to it.

One she wasn't ready to acknowledge. In him, or in herself.

He released her hand and jumped off the wagon. She watched as this Viking god tramped through the pristine snow to the structure's front door and knocked.

The door opened, swinging wide a second later. A tall blonde woman emerged. Lilly's breath caught as recognition exploded in her head.

"Rina!" Nick's excited shout reached Lilly's ears seconds before the woman disappeared in his long arms.

Lilly clambered down and helped Willow and Dog to the ground. As she turned to face the house, Nick lifted his sister and twirled her around to the sound of squeals and laughter.

"Get your hands off my wife, mister, before I plug you."

A mountain of a man a full head taller than Nick and half again his width, pushed out the door and ripped Miss Shield from Nick's arms. Nick scowled, his hands rolling into fists ready to use.

Knots tightened across Lilly's shoulders as anxiety supplanted joy at finding Sabrina alive and well. Nick was a large man, but not as big as this stranger. The probability of her Viking getting hurt grew with each second.

"Miss Shield, we've found you at last," she yelled before picking her way toward them.

Not exactly an enlightened comment, but it served its purpose. All three turned in her direction.

Nick's sister's eyes widened. "Miss Kane? Is that you?"

Stopping close enough for Nick's heat to penetrate her clothing, Lilly answered, "It is. Your brother hired me to help find you."

"He hired you? Why on ear—"

"Sabrina Shield, now that we've found you, you have some explaining to do." Though his tension had relaxed, Nick's blue eyes now blazed with sibling irritation.

Sabrina's face paled. "Uh, yes. Of course." She tugged the giant to her side. "This is Timothy Murphy, my husband. Tim, meet my brother, Nick, and Lilly Kane."

"My fiancée." Nick slid an arm around her waist and pulled her close.

Nick had no reason to continue the ruse now. Not in front of his sister. Nonetheless, warmth tracked through her veins like heated molasses. Which was unsettling. Not because she abhorred Nick's use of the word *fiancée*, but because this time she didn't.

Turning bright red, the man called Timothy found something interesting to study at his feet. Then his head popped up, and he shot his hand out to Nick. "I'm sorry, sir. You see—"

"No need. I'm as surprised to see you as you are to see me." Nick shook the man's hand, but his eyes remained cool as he took measure of his new brother-in-law.

Protective older brother and possessive new husband stared at each other. Eyes hardened and jaws clenched.

Sabrina's gaze flitted from one to the other before her eyebrows knit into a straight line. "Gentlemen, please. Do come in." Stepping back, she ushered them in.

Beckoning Willow, who stood with an arrow notched in her bow, Lilly followed Nick inside.

With an impatience only a sister would dare exhibit, Sabrina pushed Nick's jacket off his considerable shoulders and hung it on a peg. "I knew in my heart you wouldn't stop looking until you found her. You've been such a bear since she left."

Startled, Lilly's gaze swung to Nick's and held. A shy blush worked its way up his neck to his cheeks. Fascinating!

The moment ended when the woman wrapped a long arm around her and glanced at Willow and Dog with curiosity. "And who do we have here?"

Lilly pulled her gaze from Nick and made the introductions while removing her coat and hanging it on a peg. "The child is Willow and her friend Dog. Her grandmother died recently and so Willow will be coming with us. Willow, this lady is Mr. Nick's sister, the woman we've been searching for."

Tweaking Willow's braid, Miss Shield smiled warmly at the child before turning her attention to Lilly. "Please call me Sabrina, or Rina, and now that you found me, I hope you'll join us for dinner. Our meal is simple, but there is plenty of it." She slid a glance at her husband. "Timothy's appetite is. . .well, extremely healthy."

Intended or not, the innuendo didn't pass Lilly unnoticed. She smiled. Married life must be agreeable to Nick's little sister. Or at least certain aspects of it.

Lilly at once wanted to know what made the woman risk her life to become a mail-order bride. So many unsuspecting women answered these ads only to end up like Jenny, enslaved into a life of prostitution.

While the woman's gaze rested lovingly on Timothy, Dog flopped close to the warmth of a cook stove, and Willow, having removed her buffalo robe, lowered herself beside him. After rummaging through her things, she drew out a small doll made of leather and glass beads and began to play. A sign she deemed Tim Murphy friend rather than foe.

Lilly perused the cabin's interior, amazed at how warm and cheery Sabrina had made it. Green gingham curtains hung on the windows, and cushions of the same material covered the seats of the plain wooden chairs. A massive handmade bed took up the back half of the one-room cabin. Savory smells rose from a sizable black stew pot on a cast iron stove. The pleasant aroma of freshly baked biscuits made her stomach rumble with hunger.

It was a home, as cozy and comfortable as any house could get up in the mountains.

Turning, she hazardrf a glance at Nick in the process.

A scowl now marked his features.

"So, tell me, how did you find me, and why you, Miss Shield?" asked Sabrina as she motioned Lilly to one of the chairs surrounding a sturdy wooden table.

Though the question had been asked of Lilly, Nick fairly shouted an answer. "Father hired the Pinks to find you. You left behind a newspaper article on the gold strike near Pike's Peak. Their agent got as far as Cripple Creek before he got sick. I got the name of a local investigator who turned out to be Lilly. We've been following a white slave trader up to Victor because one of his captives fit your description. The Fuekes took us in last night and they diverted us here. Does that answer your question?"

Lowering herself to a chair opposite Lilly, Sabrina's blue eyes, identical to Nick's, narrowed. Belligerent sister stared at an equally belligerent brother.

The air crackled with tension.

Her chin raised, Sabrina ignored her brother and flicked her gaze to Lilly. "Let's try this again. I'm curious about you as an investigator. It sounds absolutely fascinating."

Sabrina's question smacked of being a stalling tactic, but it sent Lilly's heart racing, nonetheless. How she had become an investigator wasn't a topic she cared to explore with anyone besides Nick. Fumbling for an answer, she spoke the first words that popped into her head.

"I needed a job, and my boss thought my skills would fit the opening he had. To put it bluntly, I help ladies of the night change their lives to one of respectability. My boss said my sales skills would make me an excellent candidate for the job."

"But that's a far cry from searching for me."

Lilly squared her shoulders. "Nick came to Colorado City with my professional name in hand. About the same time, I received word that someone of your description might be held captive by a slave trader pimping women to the miners up here. We were following that lead."

Sabrina's face lost its color again.

"The Fuekes told us you were a mail-order bride. You must know you took a great risk following a blind ad. Some ads are perfectly legitimate. But others just lure unsuspecting women into the underworld of murder, theft, fraud, and forceful seduction. I see more of these cases than I care to."

Sabrina glanced at Tim, her eyebrows disappearing beneath her the short blonde fringe ringing her forehead. "Then I guess I'm one of the lucky ones."

"Why did you choose that path?" Lilly shuddered to think how desperate the shy, sweet woman must have been to take such a drastic step.

Sabrina leaned toward the giant, who in the light of the kerosene lamp, was quite handsome in a rugged sort of way. Tim placed a hand on the chair back, a possessive measure that didn't escape Lilly's notice.

The soft smile forming across the man's features highlighted the classic beauty of his square face, strong nose, and warm, brown eyes. "I placed an ad for a bride in a Chicago paper and Sabrina answered it. I can afford a wife now that I found a promising vein to work. But with few women here of the marryin' kind, I needed to search somewhere else. Advertising for one was the best way because I couldn't leave my mine alone or someone would claim jump it."

Nick's sister nodded and slipped her fingers through her husband's. "I know I took a chance, but Tim and I had been writing each other for about four months before I left Chicago to join him. His letters were sent to my friend Catherine's house. She and Ramsey, her butler, swore to keep them secret."

Hurt registered in Nick's eyes. "Why didn't you write and tell us you were all right? Do you have any idea what hell you've put us through?"

"I did write, Nicky! I wired Father that I had eloped and was safe."

"You what?"

"I wir—"

"When?"

"Four days after I left home. Two days train to Colorado Springs and one day up to Cripple Creek. We married there, and I wired the next day before we left to come up here." Bright red bloomed on the cheeks of the newly wed woman.

"If that's true, then why did Father hire the Pinks?"

Silence. Lilly could almost see Sabrina's mind working on Nick's question.

Then her mouth pursed into a straight line. "Were you aware Father had arranged a marriage for me?"

Nick's eyes widened, and he slid into a chair. "What? No, I wasn't. Why that conniving. . ... He did the same to me. Arranged for me to marry Tessa Brownly, of Brownly Shoes."

Lilly started. What?

Sabrina continued. "He sent the Pinks because he didn't want me to be married. At least not to someone of my own choosing. I was supposed to marry William Sears. He had just moved his retail business back to Chicago from Minnesota and told Father he was looking for a wife. The marriage was arranged, not for my sake, but for Father's. He wanted to keep the competition in the family. No amount of arguing could change his mind. Under those circumstances, I couldn't stay in Chicago."

"But why didn't you tell me, trust me? I would have kept your secret. I was half out of my mind with worry. We used to be so close, you and me. If you had confided in me, somehow I would have found a way to get you out of it." Nick's baritone was filled with pain, and Lilly ached for him.

Sabrina took his hand and held it between her own, her voice now soft. "We *used to be* is exactly right, Nicky. When Lilly left, you changed.

You had no time for me. It seemed you were always out with your friends. I lost my big brother, my champion. I learned to rely wholly upon myself, and I did what was right for me. Please understand."

Tears formed in Lilly's eyes. So many people had been affected by Nick's father's actions.

Nick leaned back and threaded his fingers through his hair, his shoulders slumping. "So, Father wanted to break you two apart? So you could marry Mr. Sears?"

Grabbing her husband's hand, she nodded at her older brother.

For a second, Lilly felt sympathy for the woman. But she'd hurt Nick. And that rankled.

"I didn't tell you for fear Father would discover the truth. But then you weren't around so my fear was groundless. Nicky, Mr. Sears is a nice man, but he doesn't stir my blood the way Tim does."

Sabrina turned to her husband and there was no mistaking the passion flowing between them. It was a living, tangible thing weaving them together, covering them with the electricity of intimacy, and with the hope and promise of the future.

Theirs was a display of love so intimate, Lilly had to turn away.

Watching Rina and Tim love each other with their eyes, their smiles, their small caresses, revealed how dead her world had become by contrast. How barren of warmth and feeling and sharing and caring. How devoid of the emotions making one human.

It was also a painful reminder of what she had lost—the opportunity to be loved completely and unconditionally. A hole opened in her already wounded heart, a cavern so deep it took her breath away.

Rina had taken a huge risk, found a man in a way that reeked of danger, accepted a life that ripped her away from her family. Yet Lilly couldn't deny the sweet reward that had come with the risk.

Her gaze swept to Nick, whose attention was riveted on his sister and her new husband.

Now that Nick had found Sabrina, would he return to Chicago? Or would he stay to help her find DuPry? They were so close to finding him.

Would he forget his pledge to care for Willow? To be a family.

Uncertainty claimed her tongue, held her in silence as conversation swirled around her.

And then, like the passing of clouds, clarity emerged.

She had committed the same sin as Sabrina.

She had failed to trust him with the truth.

Was he worth the risk?

Whatever he had done before, he was now a different man. Someone she could respect.

Someone she could trust.

Someone totally, and utterly forbidden.

~~~~

"I'm not going back, Nick. I'm quite happy here."

Jolted, Nick lowered his glass to the table with a clatter. Sabrina's comment seemed to come out of nowhere, preceded by nothing remotely resembling their current conversation. The last few hours had been spent in friendly banter over a rather tasty meal, their conversation devoid of all controversy. In a few minutes they planned to move to a nearby cabin his sister said she would open for the night.

Nick stared into Sabrina's warm blue eyes, the mirror of his own. Seconds later, her gaze switched to the hulk standing next to her, who grinned and squeezed her hand. The heat in the man's eyes telegraphed an intent Nick would rather not contemplate.

"He's my husband...," his sister's cheeks turned an answering shade of pink, "...and I love him. We may not have much now, but we have each other."

Sabrina married!

The thought still boggled his mind.

She seemed happy.

More than happy.

Overjoyed, really.

How had he not seen her desperation, her unhappiness? How had the fact his father arranged a marriage for her completely escape his notice? Especially since he, himself, had barely escaped a similar fate.

Had he been that blind to what was going on around him? That consumed by his own unhappiness? The thought squeezed his insides.

Despite the risk she took, despite the worry she might have caused her family, Sabrina had overcome her shy submissive ways and boldly grabbed the life she wanted.

Envy stabbed his chest.

He wanted what Rina had risked everything for.

The elusive something he had gone from woman to woman to find.

Love. Passion. Friendship for life.

His gaze flashed to Lilly sitting quietly beside him. Riveted on Sabrina and her husband, Lilly's eyes were filled with a painful emotion tearing at his heart ...an emotion he could only describe as yearning.

So engrossed in Lilly's reaction was he that he almost missed the import of Rina's words. "You're not going back?"

Rina shook her head.

Of course, she wasn't going back, and he understood her reasons why. She had run away to a life as different from his father's as she could make it. Being a mail-order bride had offered freedom, and peace, and a future of her own choosing, despite the risks that came with it.

And now it was his turn to grab the life he wanted.

With Lilly.

Later that night, after Willow had fallen asleep on her pile of buffalo skins, after the fire in the small pot belly stove of the miner's cabin had been stoked, Nick and Lilly chose the floor rather than a pair of rickety chairs to while away a few hours of quiet.

But not this quiet.

Lilly had stopped talking, stopped responding to the idle chatter that began the evening.

Her arms drawing her knees tight to her chest, she seemed caught in an internal struggle. Her teeth gnawed her lower lip until he thought it would bleed, and once or twice she opened her mouth, then closed it again.

What was she thinking?

Was she as moved by seeing Rina and Tim as he was?

His sister had poked a giant hole in the belief that had ruled Nick's actions for decades. His parents hated each other and never bothered to hide it.

But Rina—

The log spit with a loud pop, shattering his introspection.

Unable to stand the silence anymore, Nick pulled one knee up. "Did you see the way he looked at her? As though she was the air he breathed and the water he drank. As though he wanted to devour her."

Silence. The atmosphere in the room thickened, grew uncomfortable.

"The way you look at me sometimes." The murmur beside him was so low he knew he wasn't supposed to have caught it.

But he had.

Nick's gaze edged to her face. Did he? Look at her with the same naked yearning he found in Timothy's eyes.

She glanced up then, her face emerging into a dim patch of shifting light. Dark pools of blatant desire drew his rapt attention. Warmth swept through his body, becoming a fiery torch by the time it reached his neck. His privates stirred. Lust and need burst into flames.

He changed the subject.

"My father and I argued about my going to find her." Nick paused. His next words took a long time to make their way out of his mouth. "He said if I didn't bring her home, I shouldn't bother coming back myself."

Lilly gasped, her hand landing on his arm, its presence a welcome comfort. "What an awful thing to say. What do you plan to do?"

Nick swallowed as old emotions rolled through him like ghostly specters. All he ever wanted from his father was a word of encouragement. And now once again, the gray specter of disapproval lay before him.

Another loud pop erupted from the stove.

He gazed unseeing into the deep shadows of the room. "Rina deserves to be happy. If she wants to make her life with this man, I won't interfere, my father be damned."

The strong words belied the turmoil claiming his thoughts. He had never defied his father openly. Not really. Not on things that mattered, anyway.

Dog shifted.

"Are you planning to go back to Chicago?" An odd quality tinged Lilly's voice, one he couldn't identify. Her hand on his arm tightened.

"I don't know. I can never forgive my father for what he did to us." Her fingers crept down to his hand, and he clutched them tight. An avalanche of unwanted feelings threatened to engulf him. "If my father had not interfered, we might have—"

She released his hand, and it grew cold without her warmth.

"And besides, those women in DuPry's wagon need rescuing, and you can't do that alone," he added.

More silence.

Talk to me, Lilly. Tell me what's bothering you.

Straightening her back, Lilly finally spoke.

"There's something I need to tell you. Something I omitted about my conversation with your father. . .."

She stopped, pulled in a breath. "I'm Jewish, Nicholas, and that's why your father sent me away."

Chapter 21

LIKE THE SLICE OF A SWORD, Nick's intake of breath cut through the deafening silence following her confession. Despair pierced Lilly's heart as the very life ebbed from the room.

Despite the pain, she summoned the strength to continue.

"My parents are Russian Jewish immigrants who came to America soon after they married. Although they might have used an Americanized version of their name in public, they never legally changed their original name. Because they found persecution here as well, they chose to keep their Jewishness from the outside world. I did the same. My real name is Lillian Kanefsky, Lilly Kane to you. Lee Wilcox is my work name."

Nick's hands rolled into fists.

She wavered, quashing a sob. "Your father must have discovered the truth, because when I went to your house to tell you about the pregnancy, he turned me away. His exact words were, 'I'll not have a dirty kike baby as a grandson, nor will I have my own son play father to one.'"

His jaw tightening, Nick's brilliant blue eyes turned stormy and cold. He vaulted off the floor and strode to the curtain-less window. She shivered, yet continued, the need to tell him the truth both painful and restorative.

"I went numb with shock at his words. I was born in this country, thought myself the same as any other person born here. Though I experienced many hurtful slights growing up, no one ever spewed such hatred and venom in my direction as he did. He made me feel like I didn't belong, like I was some hated enemy, a rag he couldn't be bothered with."

She silently cursed the quiver in her voice, but her frayed emotions were close to imploding.

"I went home and told my parents about my condition. My mother and father immediately disowned me. They expected me to marry someone Jewish, someone picked by the *shadchan*, a matchmaker. When I become pregnant by you, a *shegitz*, a non-Jewish boy, my family sat *Shiva* for me. They said the prayers of the dead as though I no longer existed."

The image of her beloved *bubbe*, her grandmother, flooded her mind, and this time she couldn't keep the sob from escaping her lips.

"Why didn't you tell me when we first met?" His voice thundered across the room waking Willow.

Rubbing her eyes, the child sat up. "Is something wrong?"

Glaring at Nick, Lilly frowned. Turning to Willow, she said, "No, sweet. Go back to sleep."

Willow flopped back on her furs and closed her eyes, but the tension in the miner's cabin had turned thick and cold.

Why hadn't she told him the truth? She'd asked herself that questions hundreds of times since the horrible day his father had shouted those words of hatred.

The truth, Lilly. Tell him the truth no matter how ugly.

"I didn't mean to keep my Jewishness from you, Nick. It just never came up. We liked each other, we spent time together, and then we were to go our separate ways. You promised nothing, and I accepted that. I just wanted to be with someone who …swept me away before I fulfilled a life of duty and dullness married to someone of my parents' choosing."

Lilly closed her eyes and swallowed over the hard ball of reality. "Then Celia happened."

Her daughter changed everything. Life with Celia was joyous and hopeful. But after Celia died, Lilly's world turned gray and empty.

Until Nick re-entered it.

And now that he knew the truth, he'd react the same way as his father.

Hate her.

Want nothing to do with her.

And her heart would shatter yet another time.

A quick glance at Nick leaning against the window frame confirmed his disgust. Soft moonlight highlighted the dark anger tightening his features, the cold and disapproving glare of his eyes, the grimness of his tightly closed mouth.

He turned. "Answer me, Lilly, were you ever going to tell me?"

No. Never.

In the beginning there hadn't been a need to tell him, but by the time her heart had become fully engaged, it had been too late. Fear of losing him had held her back.

Suddenly she couldn't breathe, couldn't pull air into her paralyzed lungs.

Emotions tangling her sanity, she bolted for the door.

With lightning reflexes, Nick grabbed her wrist, his grasp firm and unyielding. He pulled her back to face him. "Where are you going?"

The heat of his body within inches of hers penetrated her clothes as though they didn't exist. Fire raced along her arm, scorching her from head to toe. The tears she struggled to contain spilled down her cheeks.

"I couldn't bear—"

"*You* couldn't bear. Did you ever think about what I couldn't bear? You deceived me, Lilly. About something that was extremely important to both of us."

She struggled to pull her arm away to no avail. "Because I knew how you would react."

"Did you? You know nothing about how I would react. You didn't trust me with the truth. And that is something I can't forgive."

"Forgive? You can forgive Sabrina for not trusting you with her truth, but not me?"

"Sabrina isn't you."

"What does that have to do with this?"

"In case you haven't realized, *this*, as you put it, is about us. About two people who were supposed to trust each other. While you were keeping your secret from me, did you once think about what I might think, what I might want, what I might need?"

Stunned, Lilly stared off into the darkness. Was he right? Had she been selfish in her secrecy?

"I thought. . .I assumed. . .."

"Don't assume anything, Lilly." His lips formed a flat line.

"But your father—"

"I am not my father!"

Willow turned fitfully at Nick's loud assertion.

His hand on Lilly's wrist tightened like an iron manacle.

"How can I not think you would react the same. Life for Jews, especially new immigrants, is not easy. That's why we live in our own communities. Outside is hatred, resentment, cruelty. Marry your own kind is the mantra every Jewish mother instills into their children. I didn't know how you would react, and I wanted desperately to be with you."

"And I wanted to be with you just as desperately." His whispered admission brimmed with reluctance, as though he hadn't wanted to admit it.

"You did?"

"Lilly, do you think I care what religion you practice? My father and I don't agree on most things, his prejudices included. I see the woman you are, and I don't care whether you are Jewish, Protestant, Catholic or believe in faeries. I still want you. Yes, I'm livid, but not because you're Jewish, but because you didn't trust me enough to tell me from the day we first met. You didn't see me for who I am. And that hurts, Lilly. More than you'll ever know."

What have I done!

He set her away from him. "Take the bed, Lilly. I'll sleep on the floor."

And it ended as she had feared all along.

With Nick pushing her away.

~~~~

Dawn streaked through the unshielded window as Nick woke the next morning after a long restless night. Dog was already lying near the door, nose to the threshold, hind legs straight behind.

Nick sighed. Reluctant to leave the pleasant warmth of the buffalo skin blankets, he gazed at Lilly still asleep on the bed. She lay on her stomach, one slender, well-formed leg poking out from beneath a disheveled pile of thick blankets.

How could he have missed the physical hints of her heritage—her olive coloring, her thick dark hair, the slight bump on her nose? Things he'd noticed but hadn't thought twice about.

Maybe because he hadn't been looking for them.

Hadn't given her background much thought.

Because it never mattered to him.

Still didn't.

Though her admission last night had surprised him, her lack of trust in him had wounded him deeply.

Ever since finding her again, he'd been intent upon winning back her trust. But her confession told him she had *never* trusted him. The pain of that knowledge cut deep into raw wounds he'd thought long healed.

Though he'd talked about creating a family for Willow, that idea had died last night like flowers after a hard frost. He wanted a marriage based upon trust, something his parents never had. And the likelihood of that happening between he and Lilly seemed highly unlikely.

Tightness squeezed his chest as he contemplated his next step.

Sabrina wasn't going back to Chicago and, if he were truthful, he didn't care to go back either.

Lilly still needed to complete her mission of finding DuPry. As much as he abhorred the dangerous aspect of her life, he knew she would never abandon her search when she was so close to rescuing the bastard's women.

He would continue on with her then—to protect her, keep her safe while she completed her objective, bringing both Lilly and Willow safely back to Cripple Creek as fast as possible.

And after that?

Dog picked that moment to whine. Nick forked his fingers through his hair.

Duty called in the form of a long-haired wolf dog he didn't plan to anger anytime soon. The animal may be Willow's pet, but Nick had no intention of ending up on the wrong side of his vicious jaw.

Slowly extracting himself from his pile of buffalo skins, he pulled on his clothes, boots, jacket, and hat and left the cabin with Dog. The air was cold, but the day promised to be bright. Not a cloud existed as the sun rose like a giant orange ball over the rim of Pike's Peak on the eastern horizon.

The sharp crack of a gun rent the still air.

A gust of wind blasted across his ear knocking his Stetson to the slush. Instinct sent his body slamming to the wetness. Icy shock froze his face.

What the...?

While lying flat, he retrieved his hat, wiped it against his denims, and inspected it for damage.

What he saw made his breath hitch. Bullet holes rent the felt about two inches above the trim band in two places—front and back. An inch or two lower and his head would have been blown off.

He was the intended victim, not Lilly. No doubt about it. This second shot in his direction confirmed Lilly's suspicions.

Nick scanned the area for signs of the shooter. The dawn was calm, peaceful. Even the wind had eased. Everything appeared quiet and undisturbed. Yet, Dog growled, his attention riveted to the woods on the left. Did he sense someone, or was he merely reacting to another animal?

The door behind him flew open with a bang. Wrapped in a buffalo hide, her hair tangled about her shoulders in sensual disarray, Lilly peered across the threshold, the whites of her eyes nearly crowding out the green.

Shoving his hat atop his head, Nick scrambled to his feet and headed back toward the cabin to get his weapon.

"Was that a gunshot?" Her question slid out in a slur through a tight smile resembling a grin.

Willow appeared at Lilly's side, her dark eyes a mirror of Lilly's.

Shit! He couldn't leave them unprotected to go after his would-be assassin.

Nick pushed them back inside, holding the door for Dog who whined in protest. When they were all in, he shed his jacket and hat and grabbed his rifle.

"What . . .what happened out there?" Willow lowered herself beside a silent Lilly who had already sunk to the floor near his pile of buffalo furs.

"Someone shot at me."

While Lilly's hands rolled into fists, the child spoke again. "You? I thought they were after Miss Lilly."

He shook his head. "The shooting in Anaconda wasn't meant for Miss Lilly. It was me they were after." He glanced at Lilly, grinning now, a wholly unnatural expression.

"But why?" Willow grabbed Lilly's hand and stroked it gently. Shouldn't Lilly be asking these questions?

He hesitated. Lilly's business was danger personified, but he wasn't about to voice his concern to this child.

"I think someone wants to harm me."

Lilly's eyebrows flew up, but she said nothing.

"So they could grab you, Lilly. I'm afraid you were right. A bullet downed Jacob and now someone has me in their sights."

"Baylor," Nick and Lilly both said at once, only Lilly's came out slurred, the word sounding more like Maylor.

What was wrong with her?

Lilly shivered, pulled the skins tighter around her neck. Her teeth began to chatter, yet a bead of sweat rolled from her temple down her cheek to her chin.

"You need to dress."

No response. Her expression remained unchanged—an unnatural smile with fear reflected deep in her eyes.

Nick frowned, squatting in front of her. "Lilly?"

"I think she is sick, Mr. Nick. Very sick."

Talons tightened around his chest. Nick thrust his fingers through his hair and peered at Willow in disbelief.

Lilly swayed, her body shifting sideways on the pile of buffalo skins. As she fainted, he caught her before she hit the floor.

Shit! He needed help. A doctor, or at the very least, Rina and Timothy. He'd send Willow for them. No, he couldn't do that. Baylor was still out there somewhere. He couldn't chance it. He needed to go himself.

Nick stood. "I'm going to get my sister, and I want you and Dog to stay here and guard Miss Lilly. Do you have your bow and arrow?"

She nodded.

"Good. Keep it near you." He shoved his jacket and hat back on, grabbed his rifle, then carefully opened the door, and peered out. All seemed quiet. He exploded on a run, zigzagging from shack to shack to anything he found large enough to provide cover until he reached Rina's front porch down the road.

Crazed with fear for Lilly, he bent over to fill his oxygen-starved lungs and banged on the door. Blackness ringed his vision, and he clung to the frame to keep his legs from buckling. Hell, to keep himself from passing out in the thin mountain air.

As he waited, one thing became crystal clear—the hell if he'd allow Lilly to continue her search for DuPry in her condition.

~~~~

Nick shoved the door open with his boot and entered the office. Why the hell didn't Victor have a real doctor?

Holding Lilly in his arms, he stood a moment until his eyes adjusted from the bright light of the snow to the darker aspect of the room.

Tending a patient in his dental chair, a rather rotund Dr. Harris looked up, a frown furrowing deep lines on his fleshy forehead. "T'ain't no way to get on my good side, son. Pullin' teeth can be mighty painful, and I can dispense the gas at will, young man."

"We're not here about a tooth ache, Doc. Tim Murphy over in Lawrence said you're the only doctor in town, and my. . . fiancée is sick."

Harris craned his neck in Nick's direction, then motioned to a room at the back. "Put her in there. I'll be over shortly."

A muffled objection rose from his patient.

"Oh quiet, Horace. I'll be done with you in a minute, anyway."

Nick brought Lilly into the back office and laid her on an examining table. Though her face bore a grimacing smile, fear and pain radiated from her eyes. Heart pounding, Nick unwrapped the buffalo skin from Lilly's now clothed frame and grasped her hand which had tightened into a fist.

"You'll be all right. The doc will fix this, whatever it is." He kissed her knuckles before massaging her stiff fingers one at a time.

It seemed like hours ago when he almost collapsed at his sister's front door, desperate for help. The three had raced toward the miner's cabin, aware they might have been picked off with a bullet at any time. He tried not to hover as both Rina and Timothy scanned Lilly's tormented face.

After a moment, his new brother-in-law rose and pulled Nick aside. "Lockjaw is my guess. Seen it before, but Dr. Harris will know for sure. I won't spare you, Nick. This disease is a killer, but many manage to survive. It depends upon how bad it is. You need to get her to the doc's office immediately. Take my sleigh and horses. We'll keep Willow and Dog safe, and your rig and team as well. Go!"

Nick wasn't a praying man as such, but on the short ride to Victor from Lawrence, he prayed like he'd never prayed before. *Please, please let her live. She's loving and caring and devoted to all your people, especially the lost ones. If anyone deserves your mercy, it is Lilly.*

Nick had just started to work Lilly's other hand when the dentist-turned-doctor entered and moved to Lilly's side.

"Let's see what we have here."

Nick shifted, but he felt a small tug on the hand flexing her stiff fingers. Lilly's eyes registered a plea that speared him in the gut. "I won't leave you."

And the realization that he meant it, sent him reeling.

The doctor felt her forehead, asked her to turn her neck, felt around her jawline and studied her tightened limbs. Removing her shoes, he examined her feet carefully.

One foot revealed two small puncture holes above the edge of her boots an inch or so above her ankle.

"Definitely lockjaw. I can clean these two wounds on her leg, but little can be done . . ."

Something walloped Nick's gut at the same time Lilly squeezed his fingers until they hurt. *Little can be done.* The hell if he'd accept that.

". . . take her someplace quiet. Keep the room dark and free of drafts. No visitors except for whoever cares for her. In some cases, drafts, light and being physically disturbed will cause full body spasms, but that might not happen here. She seems to have a milder case."

Mild or not, she could still die!

". . .warm compresses and massage might help loosen her tight muscles and keep them toned. I'll give you some laudanum for the pain. Let's see if she can fight this. Some do, you know, and lead normal lives when fully recovered."

But how many die? He shuddered and pushed the question from his mind. Lilly will be among those who survived. She had to. Willow needed her.

Hell, he did too, more than he ever thought possible.

Twenty minutes later, with Lilly tucked safely in his arms, Nick climbed the long staircase to the top floor of The Palace. An older woman in a garish striped dress baring more of her bosom than he cared to regard sat behind a desk reading a newspaper.

Why the hell had Doc Harris recommended this place?

Nick hadn't expected a hospital, but a decent hotel would have been fine. Hell, even the smallest spit of a town on the way up here boosted a place to stay. When Harris assured him the Palace had access to the best nurses in Victor, he never imagined a whorehouse over the most raucous saloon he had seen yet.

Damn! How was he supposed to nurse Lilly back to health here?

As he reached the landing the woman looked up, her lively brown eyes raking down his body with female interest before acknowledging the woman in his arms. Her demeanor promptly changed.

Popping out of her chair, the woman rushed to his side for a better look at his charge. Her face paled as her hand flew to her mouth. "Mrs. Wilcox! Aw, hell."

A concerned gaze filled with questions met his.

"Doc Harris sent us over here. She needs rest and quiet, but—"

"She'll get it here. He sends all his sick folks to me. The hotel won't open until spring, so me and my girls will nurse her. Follow me."

The woman turned. Her black and yellow skirts swished behind her as she headed down a long dark corridor to a door near the end of the hall.

Opening the door, she ushered him in. The room appeared small but comfortable. And spartan. He laid Lilly on the blue spread covering a wrought iron bed and glanced about. Two wooden chairs, one a rocker with flowered cushions and the other a simple straight-backed chair, flanked the bed near two small end tables. Across the room, a porcelain bowl and pitcher and a pile of folded towels sat atop a washstand with a large oval mirror.

Nick glanced at Lilly. Despite the awkward smile suffusing her face, her beautiful green eyes were wide with fear. His breath caught as his heart seized. Pulling the straight chair around, he lowered his body, and with great care, uncurled her rigid fingers.

"I'll bring you through this, Lilly. I promise." He kissed her knuckles and her hand tightened slightly around his. Lilly's eyes lost some of their terror, and though her muscles remained tense, she seemed to be calmed by his presence.

The woman stepped to the other side of the bed and pulled the buffalo skin away from Lilly. "I'm Hazel, mister. Me and my girls are the closest thing this town has to a hospital." She glanced at him a moment while she expertly loosened the buttons on Lilly's heavy sheepskin jacket. "Who might you be?"

"Name's Nick Shield, Mrs. Wilcox's fiancée." Each time he disclosed his fake relationship to someone, it sounded closer to the truth than before. Or was that wishful thinking on his part? He caught Lilly's gaze, and despite her illness, a softness had settled around her eyes.

Hazel's head shot up and a grin slowly played across her once lovely features. She peered down at her charge. "Well, well. I knew one day someone would claim your heart." To Nick, she added, "We love her, you know, and want the best for her. But fiancée or no, it ain't proper for you to be here while I change her to a night gown."

At that, Lilly flushed a charming shade of pink and a genuine smile filled with hope appeared in her eyes. His heart leaped. Oh, to see her smile for real. He would do anything to make her well again.

Anything.

Leaning close to her ear, he whispered, "I'll be back."

Chapter 22

A CRAMP SEIZED LILLY'S LEG sending it into violent spasms. She cried out and twisted to the side as if a change in position would relieve the pain.

Lockjaw! How had she been so stupid?

And now here she was in a room at a brothel with Hazel, its madam, hovering over her like a hen with a wounded chick. The woman's heavy arms wobbled as she deftly maneuvered Lilly's clothing off her stiff, tight limbs. The slippery silk of a night shift slid down her body just as easily.

Oh bollocks, this hurts.

The madam, renowned for her healing skills as well as her stable of clean working girls, threw a light blanket over Lilly and took her hand. "There, there, Lee. Me and the girls will nurse you back to health. This ain't gonna be easy, but with that big strappin' fella of yours, we'll take right good care of you. You'll see. You done plenty for us over the years. It's time we pay ya back."

Her jaw immobilized, Lilly only nodded.

Would he return? He'd been so upset last night, so hurt she doubted he'd ever want to see her again. Not because she was Jewish, but because she hadn't told him from the beginning, hadn't trusted him with the truth.

The sharp, biting pain of a thigh spasm wiped away her thoughts. She opened her mouth in a silent scream as the rest of her muscles tensed under the onslaught. Tears leaked down her cheeks as she waited for the spasm to subside.

Long, excruciating moments passed before she felt her muscles relax.

Nick returned and sat near her on the bed. Her gaze roved across his magnificent shoulders as she remembered how he carried her effortlessly from Rina's to Doc Harris' office and now here.

Sinewed forearms poked out of rolled shirt sleeves as though he had prepared for hard work. "The doctor said you need rest and quiet, as well as hot compresses and massage for your muscles. Let me do this for you, Lilly. Please."

Despite the pain, Nick's soft rumble flowed over her flesh smooth as honey and wrapped her in a cocoon of comfort. Yet, anxiety filled his eyes, concern registered in his voice, and a plea shaped his words. She closed her eyes and nodded, hoping he hadn't noticed her longing for him to stay.

"I'm not going to sugarcoat this, Lilly. The doc says this disease will worsen before getting better. We have laudanum for the pain. I'll be here with you, taking care of you. Always." This last word came out choked, almost unintelligible.

Yet she heard it, and her racing heart stuttered.

~~~~

Baylor leaned against the corner of one of a dozen saloons in Victor and scanned the street for a gunsmith. He had missed his shot—again—and the guy was the size of a wagon.

Damn gun. Something was wrong with it and he needed to get it fixed. Fast. He spat into the dirty slush at his feet, irritation seeping up from his toes to his belly. God almighty, what had he done to deserve this?

Lifting his head to a cloudless sky, he found solace in the pleasing warmth on his face. Funny how he had always taken the sun for granted. Prison changed all that. Now, he took nothing for granted, enjoyed life's little pleasures when and where he happened to find them.

Scanning the street in the other direction, he recognized the familiar hip jerk gait of his biggest competitor—Cyrus DuPry. Walked as though one leg was shorter than the other. The gimp.

Dark, putrid hatred rumbled through his veins, and his jaw

tightened. The man was bad. Mean bad, and dumber than horse shit. Kept his women tied to his wagon in all kinds of weather. Starved 'em. Beat 'em to hell until they died on him.

Or sold them for top dollar to the highest bidder. He had been to a few of DuPry's slave auctions. His merchandise was always dirty, diseased, and crawling with lice. Made him want to puke. Yet they went like hotcakes to horny miners willing to offer a bath to any whore with open legs.

Hell, he could have gotten a fiver a toss for Mimi up here if she hadn't been stolen by that Wilcox woman. His merchandise was always nice and clean, though it didn't pay to dress 'em in fancy duds when they ended up peeling them off anyhow. Hell, Mimi looked so pretty he plowed her himself whenever he got the urge.

Which brought him back to his problem. How to grab the small, dark-haired woman who both earned his hatred and raised his dick.

Extracting a pouch from his coat pocket, he pulled out a paper and a small bag of tobacco and rolled himself a smoke as he sifted through his options. None seemed workable.

Except one.

Of course! Why hadn't he thought of it before?

After several more puffs, he tossed his cigarette into the street and followed DuPry into the Gold Coin Saloon. The place was busy for mid-day, the bar crowded and the tables full. In the corner, a skinny black piano player banged a lively tune in a rhythm he had never heard before.

Peering through the dimness, he spotted DuPry leaning on the makeshift counter a few feet away. After elbowing his way through the three-deep crowd to the man's side, he slapped him on the back. "Well, well, DuPry. You turn up at the most predictable places."

Startled, DuPry jerked out of his study of some dark rotgut in a glass before him. "Baylor. Didn't know you were out."

"About two weeks ago. Been travelin' about. Seeing what's what."

DuPry smiled, the scar down his right cheek twisting his mouth into a grotesque grimace. Jesus, the man was an ugly son-of-a-bitch.

"What brings you to Victor?" Baylor asked, as though he didn't know. Winter in Victor and Cripple Creek was peak season for flesh-peddlers.

"Mines are closed for the winter, money is still plentiful, and men want women anyway they can get them. Business, Baylor. Business." DuPry took a long swig of his drink. "Hey, you better not be stepping on my territory. I've got three prime bitches, and they're making me lots of coin."

"Got rid of Mimi five years ago, but I'm startin' clean. Got my eye on someone else. Someone *you* might even be interested in."

Curiosity filled DuPry's beady eyes and his tongue slid out over his bottom lip like a snake's. "Oh yeah? What she like?"

"She's not your average. This one's a spitfire. She'll give your customers quite the ride of their lives."

DuPry's eyes narrowed beneath his bushy brows. "Yeah? You plan on workin' her?"

Baylor hesitated, then reeled in the line. "First rights, but then I'll loan her to ya until I can get my shit together."

DuPry's eyes lit. "Loan her, ya say? I ain't sharing. I get everythin' while she works for me." Not a question. A demand.

Baylor nodded. The dumb ass.

"What's the catch?"

"You have to help me . . .ah, convince her."

DuPry gulped the last of his whiskey, set the glass down with a bang and wiped his mouth with his sleeve. "Have ya got a plan?"

"We're going to kidnap her. I'll tell you more when I figure it out." And figure out what hole she crawled into.

He dropped a coin on the counter for a drink he never ordered, shook DuPry's pudgy hand and left.

Stupid idiot. May he rot in hell.

After he proved his usefulness.

~~~~

Blessed heat. The sun beating down on her face. Onto her jaw. Softening. Melting the tightness keeping her silent.

Then coolness.

Strong fingers moved in circles down her face to her chin. Then up to her ears and back to her cheek.

Nick.

The fresh manly smell of him. Close. His minty breath flowing over her face. His touch so smooth, so gentle. Soothing. She relaxed into the sensation. The pain lessened.

Then oblivion.

The cold metal edge of a spoon touched her lips. Someone murmured. Her mouth opened like a bird. She swallowed. Repeated again.

Something blessedly cold landed on her forehead.

Blackness claimed her.

~~~~

Heat again. Glorious warmth.

Seeping into the muscles, tendons, skin, and bones of her left hand, the one pain kept her from straightening. Her fingers relaxed. A washing cloth, damp from hot water, its texture rough against her skin.

She sighed with pleasure anyway.

A rumble.

Nick. Close again. The spicy scent of his after shave. The masculine undercurrent of musk.

The cloth disappeared. Warm fingers spread her clawed hand out. Manipulated the tight muscles. Gentle, yet firm. The pain decreased. Her hand relaxed.

Now her other one. In his.

Open your eyes.

Too much effort. The blackness came again.

~~~~

For what seemed like the hundredth time that day, Nick rang the excess water from the cloth and brought it to the bed. Lilly's right leg had seized in spasm, the muscles of her thigh outlined beneath her flesh like the drawings in an anatomy book. Though firmly under the influence of laudanum, her eyebrows knit, and her eyelids clenched with pain. Moisture gathered in their corners, tiny dewdrops of agony he prayed would disappear soon.

His gaze drifted lower, to the amber and gold locket lying askew against her chest. The irregular rise and fall of her breaths made the stone seem almost animate.

"I will always wear it," she had said.

Without thinking, he lifted the locket, his thumb gliding over the gold filigree that kept the flat, heart-shaped amber stone secure to the pendant's front cover.

He had been nervous when he had given it to her. Afraid she wouldn't like it. The pendant wasn't new, although the jeweler had polished it until it gleamed. Nor was the bauble expensive. He had spotted it in a jewelry store, banished by its lesser value to an obscure corner of a back showcase.

Its Old-World charm had drawn his attention, reminding him of Lilly, a first-generation American who straddled two worlds—the old country of her parents and the new country that was her own.

He flipped the locket to its back side.

To Lilly, the woman I adore.

Not *love.*

Adore.

A long sigh left his throat. He had been so damn young then. Too young to realize the real treasure he held until it had slipped through his fingers. That was the first time she had allowed him to make love to her, and the experience had left him shaken and confused. And forever changed.

If Lilly had been disappointed the inscription hadn't said more that night, she'd never mentioned it. The fact that she kept it all these years and wore it over her heart, even when she hated him, was humbling.

He reached under the hem of her nightgown and laid the hot cloth along her thigh, his fingers grazing her soft skin. Sparks flew up his arm. Startled, he almost withdrew his hand, but instead inexplicably brought it down upon the compress to add his warmth to its healing heat.

Lilly! You must survive. I am nothing without you.

~~~~

Lilly struggled to open her eyes. Though her sight was blurry, she found the room dark. The shade on the only window had been pulled and the drapes drawn.

A light snore drew her attention across the room, and she squinted into the darkness.

Nick.

Stretched out in a rocking chair, his Stetson perched at an angle on his head, his feet crossed at the ankles.

What time was it? How long had he been here? For that matter, how long had she?

The long muscle in her back suddenly spasmed and a scream tore from her mouth.

Nick flew to her side. A scraggly blond beard covered his face, and his beautiful blue eyes had sunk within deep, black circles.

"Where does it hurt?" His soothing rumble sounded tired. Dead tired.

Her body pitched up as her entire back knotted. She cried out. She couldn't help it.

"I'll get you some laudanum."

"No, no more."

Despite her objection, he reached for the blue bottle on the table, poured a spoonful, then pinned her with a commanding stare. "Take this." Concern and something else filtered through his eyes. Fear?

Abruptly her resistance disappeared, as did her thoughts. Pain gripped her back and thrust her rigid torso forward in an arch. She opened her lips and accepted the blessed oblivion the opiate brought.

Nick moved to the basin and wrung out another cloth.

And that was the last thing she saw.

~~~~

Cool air swept across Lilly's limbs. She shivered. Was it time to wake up?

Open your eyes.

She fought to clear the laudanum-induced fog shrouding her muddled brain.

Rough hands pulled her to a sitting position. Her head lolled forward, and her chin hit her collarbone.

Oooff. She fell over something solid. And surprisingly warm. A man's shoulder.

The murky haze drifted like smoke, clearing for seconds before clouding over.

Nick? But . . .

The wretched stench of an unwashed body and rotting teeth stormed her nostrils, causing the meager contents of her belly to threaten to erupt. She swallowed. Hard.

Not Nick. Then who?

Her insides cramped into a gnarly mass.

Open your eyes, Lilly. Open them now.

She did. But wished she hadn't.

The wooden floor pitched like a raft adrift on a stormy sea. *Don't get sick. Don't you dare get sick.* Her kidnapper's odd, lurching gait was more than her stomach could bear, however. She vomited. Over the floor, over the man's backside.

A hand squeezed her bottom so tightly that tears formed in her eyes. "Do that again and I'll kill you," came a harsh whisper.

Blood rushed to her head and her vision faded. Who was that? And what was happening?

They passed Hazel asleep in a chair, gagged. At some point, she must have come to relieve Nick.

Dear Lord. I'm being kidnapped.

Scream!

She did.

Or thought she did.

Silence careened off the walls like the yell of a banshee. Her heart thundered, its noise a raging pulse in her ears.

She bounced on her bony perch as they descended an endless staircase. Her thigh muscles cramped and her back twisted like a pretzel.

Oh, damn, it hurts!

Someone make it stop.

Breathe, breathe.

Don't fight it.

Working from her scalp to her toes, she pictured each coiled sinew of muscle in turn and willed it to relax. Soon her body lay loose and pliant.

The pain, however, remained jagged and unrelenting.

Scream.

But her jaw refused to move, and her cry remained locked in her throat.

A door flicked open, and they stepped outside, her thin nightgown no match for the frigid air now assailing her bones. Something scraped her hip as she felt herself lifted over a hard edge and dumped like a sack of potatoes on a rough surface. A wagon bed?

Blessed warmth unexpectedly sheathed her—a wool blanket smelling of mustiness and use, and the sweet comfort of human body heat, feminine body heat.

What ...?

The world turned black.

Chapter 23

BAYLOR SMILED AS THE WARMTH of satisfaction seeped into his bones. Grabbing Wilcox turned out to be as easy as plowing a well-used whore! The long years of planning his revenge were finally over. His prized bitch lay chained in DuPry's wagon, unable to do a damn thing. She was completely at his mercy. And he couldn't wait.

Lust, raw and wild, roared through his body. His prick sprang to life, filling his trousers with the tool failing him with all other women as of late. Shit if the old boy wasn't impatient to slide into her sweet wet tightness. He planned to do other things to her, as well. Like whip that plump ass of hers until it turned beet red, and bite those ripe tits until she screamed with pleasure and begged for more.

Then he would kill her, slow and painful like, letting her blood drip until the life drained out of her.

After he killed her, maybe he would bang the hell out of her carcass one last time before he fed her body to the wolves. Baylor smiled. On second thought, maybe he would let her live and sell her out to the highest bidder. Now, wouldn't that beat all—the woman who saved whores becoming one herself.

The wagon jostled over a particularly deep rut, tipping him perilously close to the seat's edge.

Where the blazes were they? Baylor searched across the dawn horizon, but not a blasted thing looked familiar. Twisting in his seat, he scanned the road behind them.

Wheel tracks as far back as he could see marked his direction like beacon lights at sea. The melted snow had turned the high mountain trail into a muddy mess. Should have worked out the escape himself instead of leaving it to DuPry. The damn Frenchie was good for nothing. Totally useless.

Except for their getaway, Baylor had planned the kidnapping to the last detail. Ferreting out where she was hiding and paying good money for the hookers so the two of them wouldn't look out of place. It took only a few minutes of snooping into each room to locate the bitch.

Lucky for them, the person guarding her was some old slut asleep in a chair, not the blond behemoth who stuck to Wilcox like flypaper. A little chloroform he kept in his bag of useful stuff did the trick. The old whore never knew what hit her.

Now that he had claimed his prize, the whole plan might unravel because of the ineptness of the foul-smelling excuse for a man sitting next to him. He had to act soon or his fun with his prize might end before it begins.

Baylor slipped his hand into his jacket pocket, wrapped his fingers around the cold, metal handle, and fired through the material. A crack fractured the silence.

Eyes widening, DuPry twisted toward him before slumping to the side. Seconds later, he bounced off the wagon, deader than a downed deer. Buzzard bait. Let the animals deal with him.

Picking up the reins, Baylor continued. An abandoned mine in the back hills of Battle Mountain shouldn't be that hard to find. Especially if he was the one doing the lookin'. He would smooth over their tracks later.

~~~~

"Mr. Shield, Mr. Shield. Come quickly."

The high-pitched screech of a woman jarred Nick out of a deep sleep. Shooting up to a sitting position, he discovered Blanche, one of Hazel's girls, standing beside his bed wringing her hands. Her normally dark complexion had taken on a pasty cast nearly as white as the frilly underclothes she wore.

A sense of foreboding sank into his chest. "What—"

"I come in to relieve Hazel, and Mrs. Wilcox, she gone, and Hazel, she bound in a chair with a gag in her mouth, out cold."

Nick's vision narrowed and beads of sweat erupted on his

forehead. Lilly had been kidnapped right under his nose while he slept no more than a few feet away. He should have never taken Hazel's advice. He should have been guarding Lilly.

Cycling in his brain, his father's words taunted him as though the man stood before him instead of Blanche. Nick swallowed over the ball of clay clogging his throat.

Still dressed except for his boots, he jumped off the bed and flew across the hall to Lilly's room, his heart thudding. Blanche followed close behind.

Hazel sat in a straight-backed chair, her hands tied behind her back, her head bent forward, gagged. Out cold.

Puke barreled up his throat as his knees turned rubbery. *I will not fail her again.* Nick pulled himself together. "Blanche, get the others. I don't care what they're doing, Hazel will need their help."

As he untied the knots behind the older woman's head and pulled away the material, a sweet alcohol-like odor hit his nose.

Chloroform.

Damn!

After loosening Hazel's bonds, he lifted the unconscious woman and placed her on the empty bed. Six of the brothel's girls gathered around her, one waving a bottle of smelling salts under her nose. Outside the room, men in various stages of undress peered curiously through the opened door.

Ignoring them, Nick forced down his fears and focused on what was important.

Getting Lilly back.

The kidnapping had been well-planned and well executed. Men paying for an hour's tumble could climb the bordello's front stairs and roam the hall at will. Anyone could have taken Lilly down the nearby back staircase without notice. The same drug could have been used to keep Lilly quiet.

Had the kidnapper been Baylor? Or someone else?

Uncertainty crawled through his mind. His trembling hand moved toward his pocket, toward the symbol of his brother he always carried with him.

He stopped mid-air.

Did he really need to seek his dead brother's advice? He wasn't the dolt his father had deemed him to be, nor the reckless, carefree fribble he had pretended to be. The real Nicholas Shield, the responsible, adept, and able person he had once been, still lived beneath the layers of hurt and longing buried deep in his heart.

Time to drag that being into the light, let him breathe, and feel, and participate in life. Admitting he needed help, that he couldn't save Lilly by himself, was the first step. The stakes were too damn high. "Is there a sheriff in Victor?"

The scowling faces of six females skewered him to the wall, their frowns clearly telling him what they thought of his request.

A girl of about sixteen stepped forward. "Don't need one. Leastwise, none of us wants one. We'll spread the word ourselves. Surely someone must have seen somethin' with all these people around here."

He scratched the nape of his neck as a pounding ache stormed through his head. In her current laudanum-induced state, Lilly was defenseless and sick as hell. Most likely in terrible pain. He had to find her and bring her back to safety.

And to health. Soon.

He needed her. Without her, he would forever remain an empty, lonely shell of a man. He knew that now.

He straightened, grim determination sweeping away self-doubt and recrimination. Lilly would expect him to be strong and focused. Where should he search? The saloons? Other brothels? He knew nothing about Victor.

"Did anyone see them leave?"

Her eyes filled with questions, Blanche glanced behind him. "Will?"

A burly man towering over the men in the hall shook his head. "No, ma'am. I woulda seen 'em if they'd come by me."

Blanche returned her gaze to Nick. "Will usually sits at the top of the front stairs to keep things orderly like. If he didn't see the kidnappers, they must have gone down them back stairs."

"Thanks." Adrenaline surging, Nick returned to his room, tugged on his boots, grabbed his jacket and Stetson, and bounded down the back stairway three steps at a time.

Every bone in his body ached, but his heart ached more. He would not fail her again.

Outside, the melted slush had created numerous puddles, but the muddy ground miraculously gave up a bountiful treasure.

Wagon tracks.

Nick lifted his head skyward and thanked the power above.

~~~~

The crack of a gun jolted Lilly awake. Ear-splitting feminine screams ripped away the remainder of Lilly's laudanum-induced fog. Her eyes popped open as the blood in her veins pulsed like a kettle drum in her ears.

Where was she?

Overhead, the blush of first light rose in hues of blue, pink, and gray. Instead of the softness of a down comforter, wintry winds slapped against her fevered cheeks. Cool physical relief blending with a heart pounding sense of danger heightened her confusion.

As Lilly turned her head, the muscles and ligaments in her neck spasmed and her jaw dropped into a painful open position. She heard a moan. Her own?

Something warm shifted beside her and the coal dark eyes of a native woman of undetermined age peered at her through black lank hair dangling about a gaunt face. Though fear dwelt in the depths of those eyes, determination burned beneath the emotion. Inexplicably, Lilly relaxed, or at least as much as her body would let her.

Holding a finger to her lips, the woman cast a furtive glance over her shoulder.

After struggling to lift her head, Lilly followed the woman's gaze to a man on a wagon seat not more than a foot away.

DuPry? How ...? What ...?

Then she remembered. Trembling, she flopped back, her strength spent.

He had kidnapped her.

But why? DuPry didn't know she was looking for him.

Unless someone told him. But who?

Focus, Lilly. Focus.

She'd found the native woman said to be traveling with DuPry. But what of the blonde-haired woman they'd been tracking, and the third woman?

Squinting, Lilly discovered two females huddled under blankets against the wagon's back side staring at her with blank expressions. Lilly cringed. One of them was not much older than Willow. A black girl of about twelve years with a puffed, bleeding lip and missing front teeth, an innocent pulled into a life of misery and humiliation.

And the other?

A pale-haired woman sporting a blackened eye and purple and orange bruises on her jaw.

Hell's bells! This woman could have been Sabrina. Lilly swallowed convulsively. If this woman had been Nick's sister, how would he have reacted to her physical condition, or her state of mind? Both females seemed lost in a world of their own, one far more pleasant than life in DuPry's wagon.

Her pulse bellowing in her ears, Lilly lay back and gazed unseeing at the pastel sky. These women needed rescuing. But how? In her present state, she was useless, and unless the opiate wore off soon, her mind was in similar shape.

The native woman's penetrating gaze hovered over her. Kind eyes, bright with intelligence, examined her like a doctor might peruse a patent.

Minutes later, the woman's eyes softened, and she smiled, a timid upturn of her lips that brightened her features like spring sunshine. Before Lilly knew what was happening, the woman's warm hand slid into Lilly's seizing claw, forcing her fingers apart. In a pattern like Nick's, the woman massaged the disease-afflicted limb, bringing a small measure of blessed relief.

Lilly's heart leaped and tears fell unfettered down her chilled cheeks. She knows! Lilly closed her eyes, content for the moment to let the woman knead the painful rigidity out of her hand.

After what seemed like hours on an uphill course, the wagon stopped. Lilly forced her eyes open. The woman frowned, her magic fingers halting their rhythmic dance upon Lilly's hand.

DuPry leaped from his perch and his face became visible.

Lilly gasped.

Baylor!

In DuPry's wagon.

Though still feeling the effects of laudanum, she forced herself to think professionally.

What were the facts so far?

Baylor wanted revenge for her freeing Mimi and sending him to jail. To accomplish his objective, he needed to separate her from Jacob and Nick. So, he shot Jacob, then shot and missed Nick not once, but twice. Changing tactics, he hired Dupry and his wagon to help kidnap her. As soon as Baylor had her in his possession, however, DuPry became a liability, so he shot him, leaving his body to rot in the snow.

Oh, dear God! They were all liabilities.

Baylor would kill these ladies in an instant, and when he was done doing terrible things to her, she would end up dead as well. He'd said so as he was carted off to prison. Memories of his high-pitched screech of venom exploded in her mind. Talons of fear abruptly dug into her chest.

She had to do something soon. Something that would get Baylor to release these women unharmed.

Think, Lilly, think.

Wisps of fog drifted through her brain, dragging her awareness behind a shimmering curtain of gauze. Eyelids growing heavy, she grabbed at the edges of consciousness with the remaining strength she possessed.

Her fingers fell upon the icy links of the chain around her neck. Nick's amber and gold locket lay safely against her breast, giving her hope. Abruptly, a glorious calmness penetrated the empty spaces of her mind.

He would come for her. She knew it as well as she knew her own name.

Until he found them, however, she had to keep these women alive, give them a chance for a future.

And she knew just how she would have to do it.

~~~~

Nick raced back up the stairs to his room. Nobody was going to take his woman and get away with it.

Digging through his things parked in a corner, he grabbed his Winchester, loaded it with cartridges, and stuck the extras in his jacket pocket. Turning to leave, he discovered Hazel, arms out to each side of the door jamb, the expression of a mad bull drawn on her jowly face.

"Glad to see you up and about. Do you have a pistol you might lend me? I have a rifle, but I might need a close-range weapon as well."

She nodded, though the action produced an unsteady sway. "You bet I do."

She left, leaning against the wall for support as she went. A minute later Hazel returned with box of ammunition and a small .32 caliber Smith & Wesson revolver meant to be concealed in a lady's reticule. That would do.

Handing the pistol to Nick, she said, "You find her, you hear? She ain't well yet, and I'm guessing it was that monster DuPry who took her. He'll use and abuse her something horrible. I seen what he does with his girls." Her face crinkled in disgust.

Nick's hand tightened around the weapon. "I will, Hazel. I will if I have to die doing it."

Stuffing the gun and bullets in his other jacket pocket, he loped down the stairs and raced to the livery for a horse.

DuPry?

Nick shuddered. He knew damn well how the bastard used his women. An image of a savagely beaten Jenny surged through his mind, the young girl so frightened she could barely speak. The thought of the prig hurting Lilly walloped him in the chest.

Concentrate, man.

Struggling to keep his emotions in check, he shoved the thought aside. Reaching the stable minutes later, he steadied himself against the barn's open door and bent to catch his breath. "Somebody kidnapped Mrs. Wilcox, Amos."

The jaw of Amos Jackson, one of Victor's two blacksmiths, flew south, his dark brown eyes widening to the size of silver dollars. "Lawd, Mister Nick!"

"Whoever took her had a wagon, and there might be other women with her. Where would a man hide with that kind of cargo? I plan to follow the tracks, but I'd like to know what to expect."

The tall man stroked his whiskered chin in thought. "Maybe the *Anaconda* up Battle Mountain. Richest mine around. There ain't nobody working it this time a year." He paused. "Naw, they gotta guard there. Probably one of them abandoned shafts up that way, though. There are plenty of 'em. If'n you go, take an extra lantern. Got one here some miner left."

The blacksmith pulled some items off a shelf—a cloth cap with a leather brim and metal bracket, and a small oil lantern resembling a kettle with a wick and a hook.

"When you know you're goin' in, light the wick and hang it like so." He demonstrated how to attach the lamp to the cap before giving it to Nick. "It'll give you enough light to see just beyond yer feet but watch out for the smoke."

"Thanks, Amos. Hopefully, I won't have to use it. Hey, I've got Tim Murphy's sleigh and horses here. Can you see they're returned?"

The man's gap-toothed grin split his dark face. "Yes, sur. Built himself a right nice house for his missus over in Independence. His mine paid off—"

"Can you bring him a message as well?"

Amos's smile evaporated, but he nodded.

"Tell him, Lilly's been kidnapped, and I need him to follow the wagon tracks out behind the Pleasure Palace. I'm going ahead, but I might need someone to back me up. And I'll need a horse right away."

"Sure will, sur. Anything to help. Miz Wilcox, she a real fine lady."

"Yes, she is. Real fine."

And when this thing is over, he planned to marry her.

If she would have him.

Chapter 24

LILLY HELD HER BREATH AS BAYLOR, dressed in his signature black, charged around the backside of the wagon like a warlock readying to fire a blast of energy.

Except for his omnipresent vicious sneer beneath a derby set low on his forehead, his chiseled square jaw, dark with stubble, and intense brown eyes might have drawn a second look from most women.

Not her, though. She was well aware of the depth of the depravity underpinning his pitiful nature.

"You whores, git to the mine there." He nodded over his shoulder to indicate the direction. "All except you, Wilcox. I want that pleasure of bringing you there myself."

Baylor smiled, the coldness in his eyes a stark contrast to the feigned welcome on his face. Lilly's fingers turned to ice.

The native woman popped her head up, her gaze colliding with Lilly's. Though fear and resignation inhabited her eyes, that spark of determination Lilly noticed previously still lingered, a dying ember yet to be extinguished by the hard cruelty of her situation.

Wouldn't it be something if Willow's mother hadn't died? What was the name Grandmama had mentioned?

Embracing the woman's spirit, Lilly forced her lips to move, though pain caused the edges of her vision to fade. "Whatever happens, keep yourself alive," she murmured.

The woman nodded. "You, too." Her perfect English spoken with an elongated cadence sounded oddly familiar. But sorting it out would have to wait.

Baylor leaned against the wagon and hung his arms over the edge close to Lilly, his soulless eyes trained on the other woman.

"Come on, squaw. Git." His menacing tone allowed no argument.

Grimacing, the woman crawled over the side and landed on unsteady legs near their captor. The blonde woman went next. The black girl followed, her face a mask of pain.

Lilly remained, the moisture in her mouth evaporating until her tongue felt glued to its roof. Memories of Baylor shouting at her in court pummeled her confidence. *I'll get you for this, Wilcox, and you'll damn wish you were dead.*

She knew what the future held for her.

For them all.

Pulling in a deep breath, Lilly let it out slowly, aware of the tremor in its release. *Stay alert. Stay focused.*

Something hard and cold pressed against her temple, and the smell of rotten eggs drifted up her nose.

The muzzle of a recently fired gun.

Lilly's pulse bolted like a spooked horse. Damnation, the man planned to shoot her now. Nick's image flooded her mind, as did thoughts of a life together lost to death, of Willow without a mother once again.

Instead, Baylor raised the pistol to the sky and pulled the trigger. The explosion near her ear shot new pain through her body, the sound echoing off the hills like a thunderbolt and rendering her temporarily deaf. A startled flock of turkey vultures lifted their large wings and flew off.

The vile man climbed in and crouched beside her. "Now you, Wilcox. I've been waitin' for this day for years."

Undisguised male lust burned in the dark eyes sweeping languidly over her blanket-clad body. The kind of hunger that threatened violence instead of tenderness, cruelty instead of kindness, pain instead of pleasure. A slow shudder of revulsion spiraled down the length of her body. How had she gotten herself into this mess?

Forcing his hand under her, he heaved her up over his shoulder like a sack of flour and climbed down. Despite the fastidiousness of his clothes, the stench of stale liquor, cigar smoke and horse hit her nostrils. Fighting both the nausea and her body's accursed weakness, she pushed against him, but failed to loosen his grip.

A cry of agony tore through her disease-laden jaw as a painful cramp gripped her upper thigh.

Baylor's hand fell upon her gnarled muscle, his fingers creeping close to the juncture of her legs. "Steady there, Wilcox. I'll be glad to lay both hands on that creamy flesh of yours soon enough."

Her fingers clenched with more than disease. Sweat beaded on her forehead, formed between her breasts. Breath came in pants through lungs no longer able to expand.

He carried her about twenty feet into a mine where the bright light of day faded to the gloom of evening. As her eyes adjusted to the dimness, she spied the three other women huddled together like frightened children on the dirt floor.

Dumping her near them with a thud, he set about lighting several oil lamps hanging from hooks on the timbers. Like Valkyries, the flickering glow danced along the rough rock walls and wooden frames as though waiting to take them to Valhalla. Lilly's belly erupted into thousands of tiny pinpricks of pain.

Baylor turned, his pistol drawn and cocked.

And pointed at the head of the youngest and most vulnerable of them.

"You'll stay right where you are, or this one here will meet her maker. I'm going to wipe away some tracks that damn wagon made," he said. His voice was hard and edgy, his eyes cold as ice.

He disappeared, leaving Lilly with no reason to doubt the truth in his warning.

Breathe in. Breathe out. Think.

Forcing logical thoughts through her still foggy brain while enduring unbearable pain seemed like an impossible task, but she had to do it.

For the sake of these unfortunate women who had faced so much.

Glancing at them, she found the native woman sitting cross-legged mumbling something, her body rocking unceasingly. Arms wrapped tightly about herself, the light-haired woman trembled fiercely, her eyes as wide as saucers. A vacant stare marked the face of the traumatized young girl. The mother instinct in her wanted to hug the child close, to soothe her, protect her, but her own severe pain prevented her from moving.

Her body was useless, her brain nearly so. The time had come to seize the only option available. One which would force her to retreat to a dark place in her soul to endure.

Could she do it?

Baylor returned sometime later, his physical presence appearing like a specter from hell.

Taking a deep breath, Lilly inched her shoulders off the ground, pain grinding away in every joint and muscle, blood pulsing through her veins in powerful bursts. "You want me, Baylor. Not these women. Let them go."

"Not on your life, bitch. They're goin' to make me money, just like you will." He hung the last lamp on its hook and turned around, lust glittering in his eyes.

A lump of something rose in her throat, putrid and vile. Swallowing with difficulty, Lilly's mind raced. "They won't do you any good. They're used up, dry. Nobody will pay you anything for them. Leave them be."

He squatted before her, the bulge in his trousers a stark reminder of the path she had chosen. "They'll bring in money. You'll see. Besides, I'll be sellin' their services until I put you out there in their place. Then I'll get rid of them."

He chucked his finger under her chin and examined both sides of her face as he would a horse he planned to buy. Lilly shivered at his touch, his long, callused fingers scraping her cheek as he inspected her.

"Yep, you'll fetch me top dollar, you will. After I get my time with you, too. Maybe I'll teach you a few new tricks to offer them gents. Sort of spice things up a bit."

Breath deserted her. Imagining this man putting his hands on her made her ill. Yet, saving these women was more important than anything he might do to her.

"Listen Baylor, they are excess baggage not worth wasting food on. Let them go. Besides, they'll only be witnesses to what you want to do to me."

"Shut up, bitch." He slapped her with the back of his hand, and her head hit the cold, hard ground. The copper taste of blood flooded her mouth.

He stood and unbuckled his belt, the heat in his eyes betraying his impatience. "I've waited five damn years to spread those thighs of yours. Give you a sample of what a real man is like shoved up every hole in your whoring body. Makes no difference to me who watches."

Pain and fear merged, plunging her body and brain into twisted masses of tissue and water. *Stall.* "But you said you wanted to kill me."

"I plan to do that, too. After I get my fill of you and you make me some money. My ma taught me to never let anything go to waste if it can be used, and you sure as hell have lots of uses." The devil laughed, the savage sound bouncing off the narrow mine walls like the squeal of a pig about to be slaughtered.

Only she was the one about to be destroyed.

Dear God! How had she believed herself capable of saving prostitutes, of stepping into their world, enduring the danger and the heartbreak they faced, and . . .and the abuses of men like Baylor. She would give anything for a life of normalcy, a life filled with children, perhaps a house, and a respectable livelihood.

A life without shame or ridicule.

A life with Nick.

Her beleaguered lips caught a sob clamoring for escape. "You don't want an audience, Baylor. You want me alone. If you let these women leave, I'll come to you willingly. Besides, they'll probably freeze to death in the cold."

"Don't do it," murmured the blonde lady beside her, a voice which surprised her since the woman hadn't spoken a word before.

Lilly glanced at the native woman on her other side. Understanding, and something else shone in her fathomless dark eyes. Gratitude? Understanding? The woman nodded and shifted her attention back to their captor.

After glowering at Lilly through squinted eyes for another moment, Baylor's gaze swept over each woman in turn, his nose crinkling into an even uglier mass. "Aw, shit. Go. You're all disgusting excuses for women DuPry picked up from the slops anyway. I don't want to feed ya, or waste my bullets on ya, and I sure as hell don't want to be haulin' ya around these camps."

His attention returned to Lilly. "I want this one. After I'm through with her, I'll be bringin' her around and charging plenty for a roll with a fancy city lady."

The native stood, an unspoken message of gratitude visible in her gaze. The blonde woman turned to the young girl and helped her rise. All three scurried out the entrance.

Lilly remained, alone with the man who would make whatever life she had left unbearable. She closed her eyes, tears forming behind her lids. Had she made a mistake?

"Well now. It's just you and me, lady. I got somethin' for ya that will make ya scream to the bloody skies."

Baylor pulled her feet toward him and Lilly's head hit the rocky floor again. Pain shot through her skull and the edges of her vision turned black.

No, Lilly. Remain conscious.

Vicious cramps attacked her back as a hard, male body settled on top of her. Her struggle to push him away only succeeded in sending his turgid arousal up against the cleft between her thighs. Dear, God!

"Calm down, Wilcox. You're gonna like what I have to give ya."

Night breezes rustled Lake Michigan's tall marsh grasses as though they were leaves on a tree, their sound a musical backdrop to the relentless rush of water over pebble. A moonbeam cast a magical reflection of light, expanding in width as it reached the beach where she lay.

Nick would be here soon.

~~~~

Nick had found her!

An odd combination of dread and relief poured through his veins as he studied the mine opening. Sliding off his horse, he flexed his clammy hands to remove the kinks developed from hours of gripping the reins.

His back and shoulders screamed with tension as a vision of terror-filled eyes infiltrated his thoughts. Was Lilly safe? Had DuPry hurt her? How was she enduring the terrible pain of lockjaw?

If the bastard so much as touched a hair on her head, he would kill the prick.

He was damned lucky to have discovered the right shaft. After losing the wagon ruts on the gravel trail above Battle Mountain's tree line, he had wasted hours following every turnoff he'd come upon. Some led to working mines, others to abandoned claims, all empty. If a horse hadn't whinnied further up the mountain, he might have missed this shaft's hidden entrance altogether.

A considerable distance off the main trail, the opening looked like all the other discarded mines he'd scouted, except for one thing—DuPry had failed to adequately hide the empty wagon behind a nearby tool shed still hitched to a team of horses.

The bands constricting his chest tightened. He had to save her.

He wanted her.

Needed her.

Loved her.

Love?

By God, he did love her. More than he ever thought possible.

And no offense, no matter how egregious on her part it might be, was going to diminish that fact.

But first he had to get her out of there.

Sprinting to a tall mound of tailings about fifty feet from the mine, he slid around the discarded rocks and aimed his rifle at the entrance.

"DuPry, come on out," Nick shouted.

"Not DuPry," came a woman's voice from behind a second pile of rock debris close by, a voice with a slow drawl sounding vaguely familiar. "DuPry's dead."

Nick snapped his head around. A native woman who looked like she hadn't bathed in weeks showed herself. Fear and pain lingered in dark resolute eyes. Not the face he expected to accompany the lilting drawl.

"There's another man. She called him Baylor. He let us go a few minutes ago."

Suddenly, what she had said registered. DuPry dead? That bloody mess down the gulch was human? Though turkey vultures had damn near obliterated his view, what he glimpsed looked like the remains of a deer or a bear. He shuddered, his jaw tightening.

A string of expletives flew from his mouth.

Baylor must have followed them to Victor and talked DuPry into helping kidnap Lilly. When no longer of use, he must have murdered him.

And he'll kill Lilly, too.

After using her, damn him.

Nick's fingers turned to ice.

He focused his remaining wits on the nearby woman. "Is there anyone else with you?" *Like Lilly. Out here safe with you.*

The woman pulled a light-haired woman and a black girl to her side. The blonde woman's wild hazel eyes loomed like dinner plates over a swollen battered jaw. The child's vacant, haunted stare left him reeling. She was so young, only a few years older than Willow.

Struggling to hide his shock, he covered his lips with his forefinger. Drawing a knife from his belt, he tossed the weapon to the ground in front of the native woman. At least they would have some protection until he could get them all to safety.

Comprehension dawned in her brown eyes. Retrieving the knife, she drew the others back behind the mound to wait.

Lilly was alone with the bastard. Had she sacrificed herself for their safety?

Of course she had. That was exactly what she would do.

Anguish, raw and all consuming, ripped through Nick like a breached dam. It filled his mind, clogged his pores, and laid bare his violent need for retribution and revenge.

"Baylor! Come out here and face me like a man."

Silence. The air grew thick with the strange calm, its presence rolling from the mine on a giant wave of nothingness.

Blood pounded in his ears. "Don't make me come in and get you."

Baylor's answer boomed out the entrance like a horn of Jericho. "Think you scare me, city slicker? Think again. I have something you want, and if you want to see her alive, drop your weapons. Including that damn pistol you got shoved in your pocket."

How did he. . .?

He had no choice. There was only one way to get her out safely.

Tossing his weapon to the ground, he withdrew Hazel's from his jacket. He dropped it beside the rifle. Maybe he shouldn't have given away his knife. Damn.

"All right, Baylor. I'm unarmed. Come out with her. And she damn well better be unharmed. I'll let you go providing you leave her here. Your wagon's ready. You can escape to wherever hole you crawled out from. Just let her go."

Silence.

Then, "You dumb piece of shit. You think you're in charge? Hell, no. I got her, and I'm not leaving here without her. We have unfinished business, her and me."

Nick curled his fingers into a tight fist.

Even though he itched to kill the bastard with his bare hands, reason won out. He was no killer. And he needed to be clear-headed.

He shoved his emotions into a dark corner where he hoped they would remain.

Seconds later, an ungodly screech resembling a wild cat erupted from the shaft. *Lilly!* Legs threatening to buckle, Nick leaned against the pile of tailings.

Shadows moved within the darkened entrance. A tall middle-aged man dressed in black emerged holding Lilly in front of him as a shield, a pistol to her neck. Nick's heart skipped a beat, then burst into a breakneck gallop.

Lilly was slumped over Baylor's arm like a rag doll.

What had the son-of-a-bitch done to her?

Nick fought for control.

Suddenly, Lilly lifted her head. The movement grabbed his attention. Clear eyes stared at him with what? Relief?

No, more than that. An emotion arced across the distance, sending hope rampaging through his heart. Love swirled between them like an ethereal river, a wanting, a yearning so deep it took his breath away. A relief so sharp it cut through his fear like a steel épée.

Baylor shifted, resettling Lilly tight to his side. "You want her, don't ya? So do I. Well, I ain't giving her up," he shouted.

The noon sun slid to the corner of Baylor's derby.

An idea took shape in Nick's mind.

He was not without weapons.

He had his fists.

And he was damn good with those.

He just needed to stall.

"Or what, Baylor? I know you don't want to kill her. You won't have your fun with her if you do that."

A ball of despair barreled up his throat at the thought of Baylor hurting his sweet Lilly. She raised her head slightly, enough to expose the terror now filling her eyes.

His heart constricted in response. He prayed his plan would work.

Chapter 25

BAYLOR COCKED HIS WEAPON. "Already did, and she was nice and tight. Just the way I like it."

The bastard licked his lips as though relishing a tasty morsel.

Lilly gasped.

Nick's heart stuttered. A knot of emotions stampeded through him as waves of anguish smothered him in a black haze. He sought confirmation from Lilly, but her head was down, her dark hair cloaking her face.

Breathless, Nick struggled for control, his insides screaming to act.

To kill the bastard who hurt his love.

Feeling totally impotent, he held himself in check, remaining rooted to the ground instead.

Wait. . .wait.

There!

Blazing sunshine hit Baylor's eyes.

Barely able to contain his rage, Nick sprang toward his target, his feet flying as though winged. Time escaped him, distance escaped him. Nothing mattered but the desire to destroy the man who dared to violate his beloved.

Lilly must have heard him. She pulled away from her captor an instant before Nick fell upon him like a panther after its prey. The gun clattered to the rocky terrain in front of the mine.

Despite the loose gravel tearing skin, they rolled on the muddy ground landing significant blows to each other. Dirt and blood covered their faces, invaded their eyes.

Nick fought hard, but he was not a street fighter, nor a wrestler, and Lilly's freedom was in jeopardy. If he was going to win, he had to bring Baylor to his feet.

"Get up," Nick taunted, as he scrambled to his feet. "Fight like you mean it."

The exertion in the high mountain air made him lightheaded. He filled his lungs with deep breaths and pushed past it.

Beneath a battery of Nick's light blows to his shoulder, Baylor rose to one knee. "You're dead! I'll pound you into the ground," he growled, his voice low and deadly.

"Try me, old man." Giving him time to rise, Nick danced back, his left fist protecting his jaw.

Baylor stumbled to his feet. Assuming a more aggressive fighter's stance, he shielded his face with his left and jabbed with his right.

Striking nothing.

Using the fancy footwork he was noted for, Nick bobbed about, letting Baylor throw punches as he analyzed the man's technique.

Baylor possessed some skill, but he was not the trained pugilist Nick was. Baylor's swings were wild. Poorly aimed. Badly timed. And his balance was off.

Nick's confidence soared.

Protecting his face with his fists, Nick maneuvered Baylor around to where he wanted him.

A ray of sunlight flashed, momentarily blinding Baylor. He squinted.

Nick threw a solid right-hand, square to the man's jaw, forcing his head and shoulders sideways.

Baylor turned back, blood flowing from his mouth and dribbling down his chin. Enraged, he grunted, returning a barrage of blows to Nick's chest.

Lilly cried out, breaking Nick's concentration.

Though none of Baylor's punches landed with much force, he dared not acknowledge her.

Left leg forward, right fist protecting his face, Baylor returned to his fighting stance. "Come on city man," he bellowed. "Let's see what you got."

This time Nick was faster. Rotating his feet and hips, Nick threw a straight cross into Baylor's cheek. The force of the blow knocked the man to the ground. Rolling to a sitting position, he spat out a bloody tooth.

"Give up yet, Baylor?"

"Hell, no. I'm just gettin' started." He pushed to his feet, his grin exposing blood-soaked teeth.

Nick glared at Lilly's kidnapper. A menacing glint radiated from the man's swelling right eye. A cut above it opened and dribbled blood down his cheek like clown's paint. Pustules of embedded gravel marked his skin.

Why in the hell am I fighting honorably? Why not just beat the crap out of him and leave him for the buzzards? Like the bastard had left DuPry.

Because Nick *was* honorable.

Because he always fought fair.

Rules regarding honor and integrity had been pounded into him with as much muscle as the techniques of boxing.

And because Lilly was watching him. She would never approve of murder even to save herself.

Unfortunately, his momentary distraction cost him.

A fist came out of nowhere, knocking Nick off his feet. His jaw exploded with pain. Breath left his lungs. Failed to return. Darkness curled at the edges of his vision.

"Get up, Nick!" Lilly's horrified yell broke through the shadows.

Hell, Nicholas. Get up. Lilly's counting on you.

Despite his wooziness, Nick scrambled to his feet.

This must end.

Dancing a few steps closer to Baylor, he swung hard.

The punch landed square on the man's nose. The unmistakable crunch of bones told Nick he'd connected. A fountain of blood spurted forth, spraying Nick. Baylor took a step back, his eyes filled with startled confusion. Then he crumpled to the ground with a loud thud.

Out cold.

Hauling in a breath of relief, Nick raced to Lilly's side.

Blank emerald green eyes stared up at him.

His heart stopped.

Then she blinked.

And the tightness in his chest eased.

Lowering himself to the ground, Nick sat cross-legged and pulled Lilly into his lap. Wrapping his unbuttoned jacket about her scantily clad body, he hugged her to his chest.

Seconds later, the clattering of gravel to his side drew his attention. Baylor was nearly up on his feet.

Before Nick could shift Lilly and rise, a piercing yell like nothing he had ever heard reached his ears.

A swish of something flying ended with a dull *thwop*.

Now on his feet, Baylor pitched forward with a grunt, Nick's knife protruding from his chest.

How. . .?

Shocked, Nick combed the area for answers.

The woman he had given his knife to earlier rounded a mound of rock debris and ran toward Baylor. She must have thrown the knife some fifty feet with deadly accuracy. Even he couldn't accomplish a stick at such a distance.

Bending, she felt under Baylor's chin for signs of life. "He can no longer hurt you. That man had no soul. He was evil. Like the man he killed." Hatred burned in eyes once filled with fear.

Words left him. Nick had given her his knife for her own protection, yet she had used it instead to protect him.

And Lilly.

The only thing to emerge from his mouth was a quick 'thank you' which failed to portray the depth of his awe and gratitude.

Footsteps at a run halted beside him, breaking his thought.

Tim Murphy shifted his rifle over his shoulder, a grin forming on his face. What the hell was he smiling about?

"Looks like between the two of you, I wasn't needed." Eyes filled with respect, he glanced at the native woman.

"Nick?" Lilly's voice sounded weak, as though she hadn't enough air to force the sound from her throat.

Nick whipped his head in her direction.

Her face paled.

And she slumped across him in a dead faint.

~~~~

Soothing heat seeped into Lilly's compromised tissues and beleaguered bones.

Next came Nick's familiar, comfortable scent, like a favorite robe she wanted to curl up in on a cold winter day.

He came for her. She never doubted he would.

Opening her eyes, she found herself wrapped in his arms, her back to his chest, cradled between his legs. The wagon rocked them gently as it made its way down the mountainside through a sea of mud and gravel. Each jostle brought waves of nausea to Lilly's pain-wracked body.

Seeking their own warmth, DuPry's three women huddled in a sisterhood only they could form.

Think about something else, anything to distract from this excruciating pain.

Baylor was dead. There was satisfaction in that.

Nick had saved them all.

With the assistance of a very capable woman whom Lilly had come to admire and respect.

Nick leaned forward to adjust the blanket around her legs and his face came into view. Dark circles beneath his eyes signaled his weariness. She wanted to reach up and caress his stubbly chin only inches away, but she couldn't summon the strength. Full recovery remained weeks away.

"Thank you," she murmured through her tightened jaw.

Furrows deepened in his forehead, the sun reflecting a sheen in his eyes that made her heart flutter.

He cupped her cheek. "I'll have the truth, Lilly. Did he hurt you?"

Please don't ask.

Walling off the memory was hard enough. Speaking about it was more than she could handle. Tears formed, but she willed them not to fall.

He saw them anyway. Anguish and rage erupted in his magnificent blue eyes. He lowered his head and drew in a long, shuddering breath.

"Lilly," he breathed out, the word a sigh filled with pent up emotion.

She forced the words through frozen lips, the sound slurred to her ears. "He lied. You came just in time."

She'd told him the truth, but not how close she had come to losing her sanity when Baylor's fingers explored her body.

Tears shimmering in his eyes, Nick turned his head to kiss her palm. The soft caress sent sparks flying up her arm, its tender message of regret and sorrow reaching clear to her soul.

An unexpected liquid dampness suddenly warmed her female flesh.

For a moment, she wished they were alone and able to act on the wild impulses running within her. To be touched and to touch this man, to moan and to hear his response, to be filled and to give herself to him to fill.

Dear lord, how she wanted Nick, her need for him so great she almost expressed it. But then a horse snorted, and the reality of their surroundings returned full force.

Her gaze fell on the two horses tied to the back of the wagon—Nick's, and Tim's, which carried the body of her kidnapper.

Baylor had sought revenge, and damned if he hadn't achieved it.

Lilly had taken his Mimi.

And he had taken something she hadn't realized until now she cherished—her peace of mind. Her outlook on the world and her place in it had been forever changed.

~~~~

The regular rhythm of Lilly's soft snore penetrated deep into Nick's heart. For the first time since her kidnapping, she had finally found peace. Relief from long nights and endless days of painful contractions and spasms that would make even a strong man cry.

A loud exhale left his lips on a prayer of thanks.

Lilly had been asleep now for twelve hours, the dark shadows around her eyes evidence of her battle against the nightmarish ravages of her disease. Since their return to the Pleasure Palace two weeks ago, every disturbance—noise, visitors, nursing care, and his own ministrations—had set her muscles into spasm. Sleep had been impossible.

As soon as they were back at Hazel's, he had continued his routine of warm compresses and light massage.

During Lilly's brief periods of lucidity, Nick distracted her with questions about her religion, her family, her customs and traditions. Questions he'd asked long ago that had only been answered with vagaries and ambiguities.

In return, he told her about his visits to Chicago's Maxwell Street, the bustling retail district of Jewish immigrants. Of his fascination with the sights, the scents, the hustle of pushcart vendors and shop keepers. Of the interesting but unfamiliar items for sale, the savory scent of foods he'd never tasted, the language he thought was German or Polish but wasn't.

Theirs was a companionable discussion, even laughter.

Like the ones they used to have many years ago.

Session by session, the tension ebbed from Lilly's rigid sinews and stiff limbs, and her fever abated, leaving her weak and thin. He doubted he could have been as brave as his Lilly in her fight against the disease.

He settled his aching body deeper in the chair and leaned his head against the wall.

She'd smiled yesterday, the first one in a long time that wasn't the ghoulish grimace of lockjaw. He had wanted to shout his joy to the world but, instead, had only grinned like an idiot, struck dumb for words.

This morning Hazel pronounced her well enough for visitors. Tomorrow, if Lilly was up to it, he would bring Willow for a visit.

He had missed her sorely.

The little girl, stoic and wise, had somehow managed to steal his heart. He looked forward to raising her, watching her turn into the lovely woman she promised to become, walking her down the aisle, playing with her children.

She and Lilly were similar in so many ways. Intelligent and resourceful, practical and flexible. Survivors, both. Maybe that was why he had felt an instant connection to the girl.

"Nick?" Lilly's hoarse whisper broke into his thoughts.

His heartbeat escalated. He rushed to her side and sat on the bed. "I'm here, sweet. How are you feeling?"

Frown lines furrowed deep in her forehead, she scanned his face with what felt like a soft caress. "Pardon me for saying, but you look terrible. You need to sleep. And to shave."

He started.

Smiling, he lifted his hand and felt the stiff bristles of a considerable beard gracing his face. When was the last time he shaved? He couldn't remember. Which startled him even more. As someone who mingled with Chicago's elite, his appearance had always been of great importance.

Until now. "I had more important things on my mind."

Her eyes softened, and she cupped his face. The heat of her palm on his bearded cheek spread through his body.

"Oh Nick," she said on a sigh. "You've taken great care of me, and I'm feeling better now. It's time you took care of yourself. I order you to bed."

A wicked image popped into his head and his body reacted.

"You bet." Grinning, he lay down beside her.

She giggled, a sound from the past he would forever cherish. "Not here, you goose. Your own room. Neither of us would get any sleep if you stayed here."

A promise of things to come?

"Aw, that's no fun." He straightened but couldn't stop his grin from widening into a smile. She was flirting with him, and he loved it. "All right. I'll go."

Her hand landed on his arm, its weight light, almost ethereal. "Promise me you'll sleep."

Someone knocked, saving him from promising her the world.

Lilly reached for her pink bed jacket at the foot of her bed. He grabbed it first and slid it around her shoulders.

"Come in," she called as she pushed her arms through the sleeves and tied the ribbons at her neck.

The door opened and three women peered in, all wearing the modest clothing of respectability, and not the gaudy dresses of Hazel's working girls. The women from DuPry's wagon—rested, fed, and properly groomed.

"Well, well," he said in appreciation as he stood and waved them in. "Lilly's awake, but your visit must be short."

The tall, thin woman with flaxen hair they had mistakenly assumed to be Sabrina entered with small tentative steps. Her hazel eyes, wary and tired, darted around the room. Aside from her hair color, she looked nothing like his sister. Her lined face spoke of hard living rather than age, a life of drudgery and ill use, a life no woman should have to endure to survive.

Next came the young girl clutching the arm of the blonde woman, a blank expression upon a fragile face dominated by wide dark eyes. She was only a few years older than Willow. He shuddered, unable to imagine what someone so young must have endured as DuPry's captive. No wonder she chose to hide in her own mind.

The last to cross the threshold was the woman who had aided him in rescuing Lilly. However, instead of long stringy hair, tattered dirty rags, and smelling of sex and unwashed flesh, the woman standing before him was stunning.

Not like Lilly's petite green-eyed beauty. This woman's allure was different. Regal, self-possessed, she exuded quiet determination, a sense of purpose reflecting confidence and an iron will. Tall and thin, she seemed to command the space she was in. Like a princess. The only hint of her inner turmoil was the wariness and fear that lurked in her dark expressive eyes.

The woman swept past him to Lilly's bedside. "Forgive our intrusion. We heard voices and thought you might be awake. My name is Birdie," she tilted her head toward the light-haired lady, "and that's Rosa, and the child is Flora. We wanted to thank you for what you did for us."

What Lilly did?

Lilly's face turned a bright crimson, and she glanced at her hands upon the coverlet. "It's nice to finally know all your names, but I didn't do much. Mr. Shield, here, rescued us. And if it weren't for your skill with a knife, none of us would be alive today."

Lilly shifted her gaze to Nick and nodded, her smile, a normal one. Warmth rippled through his body.

Birdie didn't acknowledge him, nor her part in the rescue. Instead, she lowered herself to the bed where Nick had been moments before and grasped Lilly's hand.

"You did much more than you think. You gave us hope. None of us would have survived DuPry much longer. Especially Flora who escaped into her mind and remains trapped there. As for the man who shot him, this Baylor, his eyes had the same dark look of evil."

The longer she talked the more she sounded like Willow, the drawling cadence of the south combined with the sing song pattern of her native language.

Could this be...?

No, Grandmama told Lilly Willow's mother was dead.

He shoved his suspicions aside. He and Lilly would raise Willow as their own.

Wouldn't they?

Their searches were over.

Tim had buried Baylor in Victor. With Sabrina's whereabouts discovered, and the women rescued from DuPry's wagon, the only thing remaining was to collect Jacob in Cripple Creek and bring him home to Colorado City.

Home.

Why did the thought leave a dull ache near his heart?

Because Colorado City wasn't his home. He didn't even know where his home was.

He moved toward the women. "Lilly needs her rest now. Tomorrow you can spend more time with her."

And tomorrow . . ..

What?

An unsettling sensation seeped into his pores and filled his lungs with smothering anxiety.

Worse, he couldn't shake the impression of impending disaster.

Chapter 26

FROM HER SEAT ON A CHINTZ-COVERED chair the next morning, Lilly surveyed the interesting array of womanhood taking up every available space on the floor. Hazel's girls sat cross-legged in their white corselets and pantaloons tending to assorted mending. One of them, far too young to be in the business in Lilly's opinion, tatted cream-colored lace in an intricate pattern attempted by only the most experienced weavers.

"Come on, Rosa," said one of the girls in white. "Hazel could use another girl, or maybe two or three." She nodded at Flora and Birdie.

Panic racing across her world-weary features, Rosa stiffened and glanced at her two silent friends. Tears had formed in Birdie's eyes. She shook her head in a movement so slight, Lilly wasn't sure she had seen it.

"Thanks, but no thanks. We don't want any part of this business anymore."

"What will you do?"

"I can cook some. Maybe open me a restaurant. There's lots of money to be made here in Victor with so many men lookin' for good home cooking. Gonna teach Flora here, coax her mind back t'order." Rosa patted Flora's arm. The girl looked up, her blank expression fixed in place. "She's my responsibility now."

Lilly leaned forward. "If you need a loan, I might be able to help you. With a lease as well, and whatever other things you might need. It's what I do. I own a diner in Colorado Springs where girls can learn the restaurant business. And if you ever need to talk. . . I'm a good listener."

"Right nice of you, Mrs. Wilcox. Might take you up on your offers.

Me and Flora could use all the help we can get," Rosa said.

From her tone, Lilly knew her unspoken message had been received. Recovering from their ordeal was going to take these women time and patience. And someone to help them sort their feelings.

Funny how she could do this for others, but not for herself. Her own emotions were a jumbled mess, tangled in a knot by the man who had come to her aid. She could assist all these women on their journeys to respectability, but she couldn't seem to find the path for her own journey.

Her life had become increasingly tawdrier and more sordid. Not ideal for raising a child, by any means. Or for keeping a man like Nick, for that matter. Why had she ever consented to Reginald's offer all those years ago? Had she been that naive?

No, not naive. Just desperate.

Then.

And now?

Nearly raped, kidnapped, scorned by society. What kind of a life was she living? A chill rattled her bones.

Maybe she should consider making a change.

"And Birdie, what plans to you have?" asked the same woman in white.

Birdie shrugged, a small smile on her lips that never reached her eyes. "I haven't thought much about the future, but I'll be fine."

No you won't.

Lilly had seen it before. The desire to block the traumatic event from their minds, go on with their lives as though it hadn't happened. Not trusting anyone, not even themselves.

Someone knocked, interrupting Lilly's train of thought. Before she could answer, Hazel walked in. "Your man's bringing a young'en up here, Mrs. Wilcox."

Willow! Lilly had missed her greatly these past three weeks. Sabrina had taken her in while Lilly recovered, and she would be forever grateful.

Hazel turned her attention to the women on the floor. "You gals ain't dressed fit to be in the presence of a child. Now git." She clapped her hands and six ladies in white rose amid a flurry of laughter, teasing, and mending projects, and left

"Last door on the right, honey." Nick's deep rumble echoed down the long hallway from the front of the building. Tim's voice followed at a softer level.

Birdie, Rosa, and Flora inched to the back wall.

Away from the door.

Safe.

The light sounds of soft boots on a run and the click of an animal's paws on the wood floor came next. Lilly's heartbeat picked up its pace.

"Miss Lilly!" The door swung open with a bang.

Spotting Lilly, Willow flung herself into her outstretched arms. Dog leapt forward with a soft *woof* and barged into the fray with wet licks. Both females giggled, happy to include their pet in their reunion.

A muffled sob ebbed from the back wall. Too eager to embrace Willow to consider its source, Lilly ignored it.

Laughter, and crying, and kisses marked their reunion. Tears flowed down Lilly's cheeks, or maybe they were Willow's. She didn't know and didn't care. The girl had wormed her way into Lilly's heart, filling empty spaces created by Celia's death two years ago. She hugged Willow tight, afraid to let her go.

Eventually, Willow pulled back and grasped Lilly's face between her hands. "You are well now?"

The drawl and the sing song pattern of Willow's voice triggered a memory.

A startling one.

"Yes. I'm all better," Lilly answered, her gaze falling on Birdie over Willow's head.

No, it couldn't be. Willow's mother was dead.

The woman's eyes were wide, their dark depths swimming with moisture. She took a tentative step forward. "Willow?"

Both Lilly and Willow tensed. The child turned, her eyes round as saucers. Something inside Lilly's chest twisted, then knotted.

Tears rolling down her cheeks, Birdie sank to her knees. "Is that really you, daughter?"

Willow studied Birdie through narrowed eyes. "My mama is dead."

Birdie hesitated a beat. "No, I'm not. I just went away for a while, and now I'm back."

Tears flooded Willows eyes. "You look a little like my mama, but you aren't her. She is dead. My grandmama told me so."

Silence.

Lilly sat stiff in her seat, her heart pounding with each exchange of words. The air was thick, unbreathable.

Birdie leaned back on her heels. "She must have told you that because she didn't want you to worry."

No, no, no, no, no!

Willow mulled Birdie's answer a moment, her intelligent eyes sweeping the woman's face. She took a tentative step forward. "Why should I have been worried? Where were you? Why didn't you come home? Didn't you want me?"

Hope filtered through Birdie's moisture-laden eyes. "Oh, Willow. I wanted you very much, but a bad man wouldn't let me go home. Someday I will tell you the whole story, but not today. Today I just want to hold you."

She opened her arms. Pausing a moment, Willow flew into them with a cry.

Birdie wrapped the girl in a tight hug, and rocked them both, sobs of unexpected joy marking their reunion.

Shock hit Lilly like a jagged rock.

There was no doubt they were mother and daughter. They shared the same smile and the same strange drawling lilt of their speech influenced by Birdie's husband, Willow's father.

Birdie must have disappeared two years ago, and her mother assumed her dead. She even told Willow she had died. But DuPry must have kidnapped her and forced her into his living hell.

Now she was free.

United with her daughter.

Lilly should be happy for her, and she was. But her own dream—of a family, of motherhood, of a life other than what she had—lay crumbled at her feet. Celia was long dead. Willow will soon go with her mother.

While Lilly's arms remained empty.

The pain of loss engulfed her. Tears of happiness quickly turned to tears of sorrow. In a small part of her heart, she had embraced Nick's idea of a family built around the care of Willow.

And now it was gone.

Nick! What must he be thinking? His arm tightened around her waist, strong but trembling.

Lilly glanced up, straight into Nick's watery eyes filled with emotion. Was it happiness for Willow, or sorrow for the loss of the child he longed to father? Her heart reached out to him, but her hand remained at her side. She yearned to lean into his strength, to comfort and be comforted, but something held her back.

His steady gaze imprisoned her, his emotions naked and raw in his piercing blue eyes.

His lips lowered to her ear. "Marry me, Lilly. Be the mother of my children."

Her world caved in. She became keenly aware the only thing holding her upright was Nick's arm tight about her waist.

With Willow lacking a family, Lilly had embraced raising her with Nick. She had accepted her responsibility, her fate. But now that Willow was no longer hers to raise, she had a choice.

He turned her to face him. "Lilly?"

"I can't." Her whispered words left her mouth as the reality of her life forced its way into her hopes and dreams like a sharp knife. She couldn't marry him. Her world was too dangerous. She dare not bring him into it.

Now that there was no reason to.

Not until she figured out a way to extract herself.

She loved him too much to bring trouble to his doorstep.

Anguish flickered across his handsome face as the impact of her response hit him. His hold on her waist loosened.

Doubt bubbled up from deep in her chest. Was she making the right decision?

"Can't or won't?"

"Does it matter?"

His eyes narrowed, and his blue irises turned dark and stormy. "If you think I'm going to let you walk out of my life a second time, you have another thing coming. This isn't over. We are not over." He turned stiffly and left.

Her heart thundered as the import of his words hit her. It wasn't only the impending loss of Willow motivating his proposal. He was claiming his future, the one they should have had.

One now far too dangerous to live.

~~~~

Hands behind his head, Nick lay on his bed that night oblivious to the sounds of a whorehouse ricocheting down the long hall.

His world was in tatters. Willow had found her mother. He had found Sabrina. Lilly had found DuPry and rescued his women. Baylor was dead. And Lilly didn't want to marry him.

Where did all this leave him?

The thought of going back to his father and asking for a job curdled his stomach.

He wanted Lilly as his wife.

He loved her. Always had.

Memories of the night he had made love to her slammed full force into his brain. He could almost smell her scent, feel the texture of her skin, hear the soft sighs and sounds of her passion.

Damned if that evening would be the last time he touched her.

Suddenly an epiphany exploded through his brain like a thousand gas lights flicking on.

The reason Lilly had turned him down.

He was expecting her to live his life. He should be asking if he could live hers.

A marriage to him meant a move to Chicago, away from the life she had made for herself—her business, her associates, and the women she protected. She had worked hard to get where she was, and she most likely didn't want to leave it.

But neither could he accept the dangers that came along with her work. Nearly raped, then kidnapped and nearly raped again. No wife of his would ever take those risks again.

Was there a compromise that could be made here? Some solution that would work for both of them? Something that would entice Lilly to accept less hazardous cases?

What would he do? Where should he start? He had no means to provide for her if they stayed here.

Not unless . . ..

For the rest of the night, amid laughter and the sounds of sex filtering through the thin walls, a plan to combine their lives took shape, detail by minute detail.

~~~~

A hollow ache formed in Lilly's chest as they rounded the final bend of the trail from Victor two days later. The crosshatch pattern of Cripple Creek's streets rose from the floor of the ancient volcano's crater like the webbing of a fisherman's net.

Riding astride a blanketed mare, Willow and Birdie, whose real name was Singing Bird, followed behind with Dog and the travois bringing up the rear. Rosa had chosen to stay in Victor with Flora and open an eatery with Lilly's notes of reference.

With Nick's arms around her on the horse they shared, the journey had been uncomfortable. Not because she had refused his offer of marriage, but because his nearness caused her to question her decision.

Soon after they'd left Victor, he pulled her tight to his hard-muscled chest, and his scent of male musk, bergamot and spice aftershave, and the outdoors enveloped her in a blanket of familiarity and contentment. Each time he spoke, his warm breath feathered across her cheek and goosebumps rose on her skin.

Memories of their last lovemaking surfaced, and a sob made its way up her throat before she caught it with a fake cough. She wanted Nick just as much as he seemed to want her.

Regret became a constant presence, its existence a thick mixture of confusion and indecision.

What, exactly, did she want?

Afraid she would say something she shouldn't, Lilly forced her attention back to the town.

At first glance, nothing had changed. There were the same old saloons, the same old stores, the same old bawdy houses. Nothing seemed to have changed in the three weeks they'd been gone. On closer inspection, however, she spotted several new residential homes nearing completion. Piles of lumber laying on empty lots marked an intent to build a few more.

As they rode past the residential structures, a sudden intense longing bowled through her, knocking the air from her lungs. A yearning for a place of her own instead of rooms in a boarding house, a home with a bright kitchen, warm stove, and a newfangled icebox. A cozy front parlor and inviting bedroom, or three or four would be nice as well.

In short, a house screaming of respectability. A new life far from the dark world of saloons and bordellos, of sex peddlers and danger.

A house with children, and a husband to beget them.

Pain as sharp as a knife abruptly sawed through her chest. She had a daughter once, and she died. Then she had Willow, but now she, too, would leave. Lilly never had a man to call her own, but Nick wanted to be that special someone.

If he died because she brought her world to his doorstep, she would never forgive herself.

She had made the right decision.

Now she had to learn to live with it.

After settling in two rooms at the Continental Hotel—one for herself and the other for Birdie and Willow—Lilly and Nick walked down the hall to the room he shared with Jacob.

Peals of laughter, one male, the other female, greeted them through the closed door.

A smirk ripened across Nick's features. "Sounds like Jacob is enjoying his recovery. I have a key, but maybe we should leave them alone for a while." His eyes twinkled with amusement.

Lilly couldn't keep her own smile from forming. "Not on your life. He'll want to know what happened in his absence."

"Maybe yes, maybe no. Any idea who's in there?"

"Suzy is my guess. Before we left, I asked Sean McDougall to see if she would bring him food. Sean said Suzy was a little sweet on him."

"Well then, the man deserves to be interrupted." Nick knocked.

"It's open. And whoever you are, we're decent." Jacob's bass voice boomed out.

Nick thrust the door open and ushered Lilly in ahead of him. Jacob and Suzy, indeed, were decent. Fully clothed, they sat at a small table, their eyes on a chess board. Strapped into a long stick by three lengths of leather ties, Jacob's leg hung out to the side like an oar in a boat.

Jacob looked up at the intrusion. "Well, well. Look who's back. I'd get up, but I'm all tied up here."

His eyes strayed to Suzy, a slim red-haired woman in a prim green and white shirtwaist. Crimson crept up his neck as she returned his stare with a bold one of her own.

Behind Lilly, Nick chuckled and murmured something she didn't quite hear.

She ignored him. "Jacob, you look well. I see Suzy has taken good care of you."

Jacob flashed a smile at Suzy that lit the room. "She sure has. Quite the chess player."

Nick stifled a bark of laughter with a cough. "Probably not the only thing she's good at."

The comment was another soft murmur Lilly heard.

This time she reacted with a light punch to his shoulder. "Nick! Be nice."

Jacob and Suzy both laughed.

"Sorry. Lilly wants to bring you up to date on what happened."

Suzy glanced from Nick to Jacob and then to Lilly. "You probably need a little privacy, so I'll leave now."

She rose, but Jacob grabbed her hand. "Meet me later in the lobby? Please?"

Suzy studied him silently before flashing him a brilliant smile. "Of course."

And for the first time in years, happiness glowed in Jacob's dark eyes.

Lilly felt Nick's hand on her shoulder. "Uh, I'll follow her out. I need to take care of the horses and file a report on Baylor's death with the sheriff. Besides, you and Jacob have plenty to talk about."

Lilly nodded, lowering herself to the chair Suzy had vacated, grateful for a private moment with Jacob. For the next ten minutes,

Lilly relayed the events of the past three weeks, including her near rape in Anaconda, her recovery from lockjaw, being kidnapped and then rescued. She told him about DuPry and the rescue of his captives, and about Baylor and his demise.

Jacob asked a few questions of his own, expressed his regret about not being with her, and then fell silent. There were so many other things she wanted to discuss with him, but before she could gather her thoughts, he spoke.

"Things are different between the two of you." A statement, not a question.

Startled, Lilly leaned her forearms on the table, bringing her head closer to his. "Oh, Jacob. Is it that obvious?"

"That man can't keep his eyes off you. Nor his hands, for that matter. And as far as I can see, it's mutual."

"Yes, it's mutual," she admitted on a sigh.

"Has he asked you to marry him?"

"Yes, and I turned him down."

He grabbed her hands. "Aw Lilly. You shouldn't have done that. You love him. And you have for years."

"I have not."

Jacob leaned back in his chair, his hands still gripping hers. "Don't think for one moment that every time you turned me down I didn't know you loved someone else. I just didn't know who it was until Celia's father showed up." He leaned forward again. "Lilly, you deserve some happiness in your life for a change. Why did you turn him down, if I may ask?"

Tears formed in her eyes, and she swallowed over the sudden constriction of her throat. "How could I bring him into my life, as dangerous as it is? I'd die if anything happened to him because of what I do."

"Your life doesn't have to be dangerous. You can choose a new one."

"But how?"

A key rattled in the door.

Nick!

Jacob squeezed her hands. "Lilly, as soon as we get home, we need to talk about our lives. Make some changes."

Nick opened the door, his gaze immediately going to their clasped hands.

Chapter 27

AS SOON AS WE GET HOME, WE NEED TO TALK about our lives. Make some changes.

Nick's heart tightened. It was one thing to be rejected by the woman you love. Entirely another thing to stand before the reason for the rejection.

He removed his Stetson.

"Excuse me. I didn't mean to intrude." Though he'd tried hard to keep his emotions in check, he couldn't help the sarcasm from flowing from his lips.

Lilly rose. A flush had turned her cheeks pink. "You didn't, Nick. I was just leaving. See you at dinner?"

He perused her face, unsure of what he'd find. The fading afternoon sun bathed her eyes in a shimmer of sparkling green.

Tears?

Unsure of what they meant, he nodded silently.

Lilly quit the room, closing the door softly behind.

As soon as he was sure she was out of hearing, he flung his hat on one of the beds and faced his competition.

"What the hell, Jacob. You can't be satisfied with one woman? You have to have two?"

Jacob shifted his leg under the table. "Ya know, Nick. You're the biggest goddamn idiot I know. The woman is in love with you and has been for years. She doesn't want me, or Thad, or any other man who's sniffed around her skirts. She only wants you."

A bead of hope pulsed through his veins. "Then why the hell did she turn me down when I asked her to marry me?"

Jacob opened his mouth and gaped at him. "You honestly don't know, do you? It's as plain as the nose on your face. Because she doesn't want you anywhere near her dangerous world. Baylor shot at you twice. Do you think she could stand to lose anyone else she loves?"

The kernel of hope suffusing his heart suddenly disappeared, leaving him confused. "She never told me. She loves her work. And as much as I hate the danger she puts herself in, I'd never take her work away from her, if that is what she wants."

"She doesn't know what the hell she wants. I'm going to help her figure that out when we get back."

"Is that why you made arrangements to meet with her? To discuss work?"

"Yes. Hell, I feel the same way she does about the nasty business we're in. If I want to marry Suzy, I can't go bringing every scumbag I come across into her life. Not after I convinced her to leave her rotten world behind. Besides, my leg's all busted up and not good for this type of work anymore."

"You want to marry Suzy?"

Jacob glared at him. "Not only are you an idiot, but you're a blind one at that. Because we're older, me and Suzy knew what we wanted almost immediately. The bullet I took made me rethink a lot of things. Life is short. You must grab what you want while the grabbing is good. You know what I mean?"

Nick plunked himself on a chair. "Yeah, I know what you mean." He leaned his elbow on the table and thrust his fingers through his hair. He was far from grabbing what he wanted in life.

"Give her some time to sort herself out. Decide what she wants, and how to get it. Meanwhile, get your own life in order while you're waiting."

Get his own life in order.

Without Lilly?

Damned if he'd be able to live without her sharing it.

Yet for his own sake, he had to set down roots, create a life that would bring him peace. Make him happy.

And trust that Lilly would want to be a part of it.

~~~~

So, this was goodbye! A dull ache quickly escalated to a throbbing pain with each breath Lilly forced through tightened lungs. Or was it the roar of her pulse surging through her ears like a raging river that caused her distress.

With Jacob, Singing Bird, Willow and Dog already aboard the Hundley Stage the next morning, she turned and met Nick's intense gaze studying her as though memorizing her features. Equal measures of hope and sadness lived in the clear blue eyes sunk deep into his smooth ashen face.

Leaving him tore her to pieces. Yet she fought the urge to rush into his arms and accept his offer.

Nick told her this morning he planned to remain in Cripple Creek. For what, he didn't say. Nor for how long. Maybe forever, for all she knew.

"I'm sorry, Nick," she whispered through an arid throat.

He raised her chin with shaking hands, tucked a stray strand of hair behind her ear. "Sorry about what?"

"For allowing you to believe there was hope for us." Letting the unspoken drift on the mountain winds, Lilly clamped down her yearning to kiss his beloved mouth.

His strong jaw tightening, Nick's eyes darkened. He leaned forward, his fingers reaching for the locket chain visible from the neck of her brown travel suit. "Sweetheart, don't think for one minute this is over. This time I'm not letting you leave me. I'll be coming after you in a few days, and we'll talk."

Sucking in a breath, Lilly struggled to hold back the flood of tears threatening to fall.

Nick was not saying goodbye.

Elation ran headlong into fear that the inevitable end had only been postponed. She'd never let him get close to her world. She'd never survive another loss. She swallowed convulsively, her mouth turning to sand.

"Pullin' out!" The stage driver's yell, however, gave her no time to reply.

Or react.

But Nick did.

He hauled her into his arms and slammed his mouth hard upon hers in a possessive, electrifying kiss that sent her senses flying.

When he finally broke away, they fought for breath. Then she felt his lips on her forehead before he gently pushed her toward the big stagecoach, his eyes filled with loss.

And tears.

"Go. I'll meet you later in the Springs." With those words, the despair in his eyes vanished, replaced by the twinkle of a rare boyish grin making him appear years younger. She loved that look.

Loved him.

But this was goodbye. There was nothing more he could say to change her mind.

Afraid of her emotions, she pivoted, climbed into the coach, and settled herself on the only seat available. The one next to the window where she could still see Nick standing, looking dapper in his expensive suit she recognized from Shield Clothing Emporium of Chicago.

Their gazes locked like magnets.

The stage pulled away.

And a hole opened in her heart miles deep, threatening to suck her down to a swirling maelstrom of nothingness.

~~~~

Nick shifted closer to the map of Cripple Creek hanging on the wall of Erwin Dowle's land office and peered at the street names. Blood rampaged through his veins, and clamminess claimed his hands. He was about to plunge into one of the most important decisions of his life, and his nerves were getting the better of him.

Confidence, man. Own it. Show it.

Nick pulled himself tall and shoved his doubts where they belonged—atop the trash heap of negative thoughts he had harbored his entire life. He knew what he wanted. Knew how to get it.

Put your life in order, Jacob had said. Well, he was about to do just that.

Pointing to an unmarked square on the map on Bennett Avenue, the town's main street, Nick asked, "What surrounds this lot?"

Dowle shifted his omnipresent cigar to the other side of his mouth. "Not much yet. Here's Charlie's Chow House, and next to him is the local barber and sometimes dentist."

As he spoke, his index finger swung from rectangle to rectangle near the space Nick indicated. "Over here is a butcher, didn't quite catch his name. Some foreigner. Across the street, this guy here plans a big hotel. On the next block is a mercantile. They sell to the miners and such. Saloons are two blocks down this way, and the whore—"

"What's the terrain like?"

"The south side has a steep slope which allows you to build another floor down that would be invisible from the street. Some like it. Some don't. Depends upon what you plan. What, may I ask, *are* you planning?" The realtor pulled the thick stogie out of his mouth and flicked the ashes in one of a dozen glass trays littering every surface of the tiny office.

Nick hesitated as he groped for words to explain his outrageous idea, one growing on him for some time. Well, here might be the first test of his concept.

"I'm planning to sell expensive, fashionable clothing to all the millionaires and their families this town is going to see. If I have to, I'll go all the way to Paris to obtain these fashions."

The other man's eyes widened, but he nodded. "Go on."

Encouraged, Nick felt his muscles relax. "There is money here, Erwin. Soon enough, there will be a whole lot more. Why should those who strike a payload go all the way to Denver to find fashionable clothes. Why can't someone offer them here?"

Dowle smoothed his hand down the back of his neck, the cigar once again swinging to one side of his mouth. "Well, you have a point there. T'ain't nothin' to buy here but work pants and miner's shirts. Go to Denver myself for suits. Not that they're the expensive kind, mind you. But nice. What are you calling this fancy store of yours?"

Nick hadn't thought much of the name, but one dribbled off his tongue anyway. "The Chicago Store."

Dowle chuckled.

"Well, why not? The name's good enough." He certainly would not call it Shield's Clothing Emporium.

"You bet, Mr. Shield."

Well, well. His idea passed its first test. A bunch of tightened nerve strings loosened across his shoulders.

"It's Nick." He stuck his hand out. "First names, if we're going to do business together, Erwin. I want the whole damn block."

This time the salesman's eyes bugged out. "Whewy. The entire block? Gonna be some store."

"Plan to build on only a quarter of it at first, then expand as demand dictates. I can always sell the extra lots later if I don't need them."

"Sounds like you gave this idea of yours some thought."

"I have." *More than you'll ever know.* Settling down, establishing roots, doing something useful with his life. Those thoughts had consumed him all night and half the morning.

All he needed to do now was convince his love to marry him.

~~~~

Lilly gazed unseeing outside her office window in Colorado City, reflecting upon her future.

Or lack thereof.

Since returning last night, concentrating on the few tasks before her posed a monumental challenge. Beyond settling Birdie and Willow at the boarding house and arranging several days of mother and daughter activities so they could reconnect, she'd accomplished little.

Over the years she had helped over sixty women escape prostitution, sent dozens of slave traders to jail with evidence she had gathered, and investigated hundreds of cases of theft, claim jumping, murder, and other forms of mayhem for whatever forms of law enforcement requested her services.

However, her work no longer brought her a sense of fulfillment, no longer brought her joy.

Her thoughts kept returning to Nick's kiss. Its banked hunger. Its quiet demand. Its gentle possession. Soft and hard at the same time, his lips both caressed and ravished her, leaving her breathless and wanting more. She yearned for his touch with a craving she could no longer deny. No longer wished to deny.

In their weeks together, he had marked her as his, made the emotion between them impossible to forget. He had shown her how different her life could be. Full of respectability, decency, love, and joy. And though she longed for parts of it—well maybe, more than just parts—it was a life she knew would never be hers.

And she mourned its loss.

Mourned Nick's loss.

But what now?

She felt mired on a road she no longer wished to travel, its brambles and challenges pulling her deep into a forest of death and destruction, danger and terror.

More and more, both her heart and her head told her to change course. Doing so would be the most practical solution. But that decision posed its own set of problems. As half owner of a saloon, a restaurant and a boarding house for ladies, her enterprises provided rooms and jobs for scores of women. She couldn't just leave them out in the cold.

If she only knew what to do.

A light rap on the door broke into her thoughts. She swiveled her chair around and called, "Come in."

Easily maneuvering his crutches as if they were part of his body, Jacob swung into her office and headed for one of her cushioned chairs. Thad followed with two mugs of coffee.

"Here you go. I'll see you later."

"Thanks," Lilly said as Thad closed the door behind him.

Early morning coffee with Jacob had become a routine started years ago. In the beginning, their meetings were a way of supporting each other as they mourned the loss of their loved ones. But later, when Jacob became her assistant, business matters became part of their daily discussions.

And this morning, the state of their business was the very thing she wanted to discuss.

Before she lost her courage, she blurted her thoughts. "Jacob, would you be interested in buying my business?"

Jacob's thick black eyebrows rose as he reached for his mug. "You're giving it up after you worked so hard to grow it?"

Sighing, Lilly nodded. "Believe me, this was the last thing I thought I would ever do, but the comment you made the other night about choosing another life kept rattling around in my brain. The more I thought about it the more it made sense. I should be doing something else, Jacob. Something less dangerous. I don't know what yet, but I'll think of something. Eventually."

Something more respectable.

"Does your decision have anything to do with Nick?"

Lilly drew in a breath. His question had hit on the truth with stunning accuracy.

A sob rose she couldn't suppress. "Yes, but. . . I'm afraid I burnt that bridge. Besides, I need to make this change for me. Not for Nick."

"Make your changes, but don't count him out," Jacob mumbled.

He studied her through the serious eyes of an experienced investigator, a man who had the uncanny ability to read people accurately. What did he see? A confused woman trying to set a new course? A woman deeply in love with a man who didn't love her back? A jaded investigator who wanted out of the business?

Or all those people?

Jacob leaned across the desk and took her hands. "Lilly, I don't think I'm the right person to ask. My leg has made me unfit for this job. I'll never be able to do the things I once did with any degree of agility. And that's a requirement of the job. I had planned to tell you this morning that I wanted to resign."

Panic caused her stomach to tighten. "But in time, your leg will mend, and a little exercise will make it as good as new."

Then he dropped the other shoe.

"It's not only my leg I'm thinking about. I've asked Suzy to marry me."

A smile pulled the corners of her mouth up. "That's wonderful, Jacob. I am not surprised. She's a wonderful woman, and she's lucky to have you. I'm assuming she's said yes?"

"She has, but that's another reason why I have to resign. Like you, I can't bring any of this business close to Suzy. Not after I've convinced her to leave it all behind."

Lilly's smile faltered. The door on the only way out had just closed.

Jacob shifted his leg. "A better idea would be to close both the investigation business and the agency work. Shut them both down completely."

Not the solution she was looking for, but she wasn't about to dismiss it without consideration. Lilly took a long sip of her coffee and mulled the idea.

Drinking his own, Jacob gave her time to think the idea through.

A few minutes later, she set her cup on the desk and leaned back in her chair. "Your idea has merit. But what about the saloon, the boarding house, and the restaurant? I don't hold those partnerships personally. The business does. If I close the whole operation, many women would be out of work. They depend upon that income to support themselves, and I wouldn't want them to go back into prostitution. And there's also a small outstanding balance on Reginald's loan to consider."

"Are these enterprises profitable on their own?"

"The saloon is, but the other two aren't quite."

He took another sip. "I could buy out the interest in the saloon, assuming Thad agrees. You could use the money to pay off the remainder of Reginald's loan. With a little legal assistance and the guidance of a banker, you can operate the Silver Spoon and the boarding house on your own. Or sell your shares in those businesses, if you want to."

Lilly took a deep breath, then another, and then euphoria descended like a light rain shower on a hot summer day. The world had just opened, and she stood in its doorway ready to embrace it.

Respectability.

Hers for the taking.

A life of uncharted paths and unidentified goals. Risky as hell.

Did she dare?

Chapter 28

ᔕ

TAKING A BREAK FROM PAPERWORK, Lilly stood before the picture window mesmerized by the long shadows creeping slowly down the northeastern slope of Pike's Peak in the distance. The remaining sunlight to the west painted the gathering clouds atop the mount in brilliant hues of oranges, reds, yellows, and mauves. She pulled her arms about her and sighed. Autumn was especially beautiful. The sky seemed to meld with the yellows and golds of the fall Aspens below in a riot of colors.

How she loved this view.

But this will be Thad and Jacob's office soon.

Not hers.

She was taking a big step, one of the biggest in her life, and she needed a clear head to embrace its host of consequences.

Since her conversation with Jacob this morning, her day had been filled with meetings. With Thad, with Betty, with her lawyer, and with her banker.

Their plan had been set in motion. Jacob had purchased the business's share of the saloon. She had only to sign the papers and half ownership of the saloon would be his. Her lawyer and banker were drawing up the papers for Lilly to personally buy out the business share of the restaurant and the boarding house.

And then the investigation business she had started seven years ago would be folded, its dangerous and unsavory aspects gone from her life. The only remaining detail was informing Reginald of her decision.

A soft knock on the door halted her scenic musings.

Birdie, followed by Willow and Dog, entered. The door closed with a snick.

Lilly gasped.

The pair were stunning in their matching yellow and white dresses and dark hair. No one could mistake them for anything but mother and daughter. Envy gnawed at her belly, but she pushed it aside and smiled.

Birdie's hair was coiled in a neat bun at the nape of her long neck while Willow's thick braid hung down her back. The yellow color of their dresses highlighted their darker complexions, though her father's parentage was noticeable in the girl's paler skin tone and more oval-shaped face.

Chin level with the floor, Birdie stood like a queen, her regal bearing and radiant beauty belying the two years of horrific sexual slavery she had endured. The only hint of it was the sadness flitting through her large brown eyes, eyes now gazing at Lilly hesitantly.

Lilly studied her carefully. How was she coping with her experience? There were none of the usual signs other trafficked victims had exhibited—depression, panic, shame, or guilt. Was she hiding her emotions, or was she in denial, attempting to go on with her life as though nothing had happened?

"You look well rested, Birdie."

The woman smiled, but it failed to reach her eyes.

"Come sit with me." Lilly led them to the davenport where they settled into its flowery cushioned comfort while she took a nearby chair.

"What can I do for you?" she asked, her eyes darting to Willow who looked well. Happy even.

Birdie's hands flowed restlessly down the skirts of her dress. "You and your friends have been most kind to us. The women at the restaurant helped me pick out suitable clothes at the mercantile. Thad said to put them on your bill. Willow bought some new things as well, and we thank you."

Lilly got the distinct impression the woman would have preferred a beaded deerskin dress, but practicality may have overruled desire in this case.

"Getting you both a wardrobe is the first step in helping you create a new life." Lilly paused, then her hand flew to her mouth. "Goodness, I never even asked if you wanted to return to your cabin in the mountains."

Birdie shook her head. "No, I don't. Willow doesn't either, though she wants to return occasionally to care for my parents' burial trees."

Willow shifted to the edge of the davenport, and with a frown etched between her eyes, laboriously rearranged her skirts. Every few seconds she glanced longingly at the floor. For a child who had worn doeskin leggings beneath a beaded tunic most of her life, she seemed discomfited in her longer, skirted dress and crinoline petticoats.

"There is something else I hope you can help me with," Birdie continued.

"I'll do what I can. What is it?"

"I was hoping you could give me the name of a good lawyer in Mississippi. Somewhere near where the Natchez People live."

Confused, Lilly hesitated. Until understanding dawned. "Oh, you mean the town of Natchez along the Mississippi River? Your mother mentioned your husband might have gone there, but I don't think the Natchez People exist anymore."

Birdie frowned. "Willow told me Mama said Antoine went to live with the Natchez soon after I was kidnapped. They assumed he meant with another People. He said he would come back for them when he was settled, but he never returned."

"So, you want to find him." Why did the thought of Willow living so far cause so much pain?

Sparks erupted in Birdie's narrowed eyes. "Find him, yes. Share my bed, no. He was not a good husband. An acceptable father, yes, but not a man for me. He owned a gold mine, but he never wanted to work it. He said it was worthless. Antoine was too lazy; he drank instead."

Her hands worked restlessly through the folds of her dress. "He thought it would be easy to find gold, and when it wasn't, he stopped working his claim. Started drinking. Whenever he was drunk, Willow and I went out to the hole in the ground and dug some more. We found rock containing gold ore, and it is ours. Mine and Willow's. My name is on the claim record, and I want to buy his half. It is my daughter's heritage."

"Inheritance, you mean?

"Yes. Her future. Her education so she can live in the white man's world if she chooses. I sold the rocks in our bag for enough money to go to this Natchez place and hire a lawyer to help me with the papers. But I don't know anybody. Do you?"

Definitely in denial. Not a word about what happened to her in those two years she was gone. Not a word of anger against her kidnapper, or losing two years of being Willow's mother, or not being present for her mother's last days. Birdie seemed to have pushed her trauma deep, wiping out all vestiges of memory that would cause her pain.

Someday something will trigger Birdie's emotions, and she will need someone to help guide her through the resulting turmoil. Lilly wished she could be that someone, but it seemed Birdie had no plans to stay.

Lilly moved to her desk, seated herself in the chair and opened a box on its top. "Well, let me see."

Taking out a key, she unlocked the bottom draw and pulled out a stack of cards containing information on the other members of the secret government agency. Not that any of these would be appropriate, but they were the only people she could safely recommend. Reginald had scrutinized their backgrounds and character with a fine-tooth comb before he had hired them. As he had done with her.

Her finger flowed over the names and stopped at the second to the last. "We're in luck. There's a man in Natchez, a Mr. Jack Mason. I don't know if he can help you, but if he can't, he might be able to recommend someone who can."

After writing the name and location on a blank sheet of paper, she rose and walked toward to the sofa. Almost as an afterthought, Lilly grabbed a white queen chess piece as she passed a small game table and handed it to Birdie.

"Here is his information, and if you determine he is the right one for you, give him this. It should convince him to help you." As Nick's presentation of another such piece had persuaded her. "Tell him a friend gave it to you to give to him, but don't give him my name."

"Thank you, Mrs. Wilcox. I owe you much more than I could ever repay." She rose.

Lilly did as well and was quickly enveloped in the taller woman's arms.

Patting her back, Lilly said, "I hope everything works out for you. You've been through enough."

"Thank you. My daughter and I have a lot of catching up to do." She held out her hand to help Willow rise. "I hope everything goes well for you, too. Your man loves you and wants you. It was more than my man did."

Heat crawled up Lilly's neck to her cheeks. She tried to smile, but the effort was too much. Tears came to her eyes instead.

Willow gazed up at Lilly solemnly. "I will never forget you, Miss Lilly. Never. Please don't forget me."

Her heart breaking, Lilly knelt and pulled Willow into her arms, her tears beyond the point of control. She inhaled the child's sweet scent of wildflowers, memorizing its fragrance, the essence of the girl herself. "I could never do that, daughter of my heart. You'll come visit me?"

Willow nodded. "I will, when I come back to tend Grandmama's tree."

Seconds later, Dog, Birdie and Willow—the daughter she thought she would raise—left via the back door to begin their new lives together.

One she hoped they could survive when Birdie's period of denial came to an end.

~~~~

Seated the next day at Sally's Silver Spoon in nearby Colorado Springs, Lilly ate her lunch with gusto. The hearty beef barley soup more than satisfied her craving for something warm and filling.

And comforting.

A crowd filled the restaurant and a line had formed outside. Business was good.

Jenny, the young woman who'd escaped Cyrus Depry's lecherous hands a month ago, was adapting nicely as a waitress. Her smile came far more easily now. She fairly glowed with happiness.

"Lee?"

Thad's baritone broke into her thoughts, and she quickly slid her business smile into place. "I'm sorry. I didn't realize you were there."

Expectation marked his handsome face. Thad once asked her to marry him, but she turned him down for the same reason she refused Jacob's proposal.

Though she liked him immensely, she didn't love him.

"I just walked in. An older gentleman in a suit is asking after you in your office. Says to tell you his name is Reginald. *Your* Reginald?"

Startled, Lilly's heart raced. Her boss here? "Goodness. I just posted my resignation letter yesterday. Why would he be here so soon? I better go."

Though she had until the end of the week to clear up outstanding business, she had started packing a few personal items in crates, and her office was in some disarray. She never expected a face-to-face conversation with Reginald so soon.

Lilly waved at Jenny serving apple pie at a nearby table. "When you have time, I'll take my bill."

Instead of looking at Lilly, however, Jenny's gaze landed on the man standing at her table. A cherry red flush appeared on her cheeks. "Why Thad. I didn't see you come in."

Lilly gaped at her former partner whose face also bore a rosy stain and a look that could only be described as yearning.

In less than a second, the man's bowler came off, and he nervously fingered the rolled felt brim. "Hello, Miss Jenny. Nice to see you today. I came in right behind those gentlemen over there." He nodded in the direction of a table full of men perusing menus.

Oblivious to the rush of life around them, the two continued a stilted flirtation like too lovebirds out together for the first time. Not wanting to interfere, Lilly rose and left them, pushing through the maze of crowded tables to the front where Betty worked a new cash register.

"Seems Thad and Jenny share an interest in each other," Lilly said, leaning over the counter.

"You bet, Mrs. Wilcox. He comes in here to see her couple times a day. Wonder when he's going to get his nerve up to ask her to step out with him? The kitchen already posted a betting chart for the big event." Using both hands, Betty shoved a paper check down over a long spike.

"I would love to stay and watch the entertainment, but I'm needed back at the office. What do I owe you for a bowl of that wonderful new soup of yours and a cup of coffee?"

The other woman scratched the items on a piece of paper and showed it to Lilly.

After paying the bill, Lilly left and strode the short distance to the Golden Nugget saloon in Colorado City, her disquiet ratcheting up with every step. Why was Reginald here so soon? Surely, he couldn't have gotten her letter already.

Opening the office door, she discovered a tall trim man with a shock of white hair staring out the window at the blaze of yellow Aspens. His shoulders were as wide and as imposing as the mountains beyond.

It seemed like yesterday when they had met in the park near her home in Chicago. She was a different woman then—desperate and alone—and he had offered her a way out. For that she would be eternally grateful.

But she had changed. The lifeline he had presented no longer appeared desirable.

Would he understand?

"Reginald?"

He turned, and a welcoming smile glided across his face.

Lilly's lips parted in a silent gasp. The man who was like a father to her looked weary. Dark shadows underlined his bright blue eyes, a furrow etched his forehead, and the laugh lines around his eyes and mouth seemed deeper than she remembered. However, his back was still straight and his waist, though a little thicker, would still be considered trim by anyone's standard.

Yet, he didn't look well.

Opening his arms, she rushed into them, the scent of after shave and pipe tobacco enveloping her.

"I should have come sooner, Lilly. I have been incredibly remiss. Letters certainly don't do you justice." Reginald loosened his grip and, still holding her hands, pushed her away to inspect her from head to toe. "You are becoming more lovely with each passing year. I'm surprised some young buck hasn't claimed you for a wife by now. Why, if I were thirty years younger, I would marry you myself."

The joy at seeing her beloved mentor dimmed.

"Pshaw, Reginald. I don't need another man in my life when I have you."

Her mentor pinked, the telling hue crawling up his neck and settling in his cheeks. In his sixties and still possessed of an impressive form, he was far from a doddering old curmudgeon. Any number of mature ladies would find him an attractive companion or even a husband.

Lilly ushered him to the davenport. "What brings you to Colorado City? You're not checking up on me, are you? I just sent you a report of our latest case. It probably crossed paths in the mail, but I'll tell you anyway."

She settled herself on a nearby chair. "While searching for a missing person, we ran into Cyrus DuPry. He's now dead and his captives rescued. And, our old nemesis John Baylor must have been released from prison early, because he came after me. He's dead, too. We found the missing person, but unfortunately, Jacob took a bullet in his leg and is no longer able to be my assistant. The details are in my report."

She knew she was babbling, but she couldn't quite control her nerves. How could she tell the man who had given her a chance that she no longer wanted the job he'd offered?

His frown lines deepened. "We? Jacob?"

"Yes, and. . . ." She hesitated, heat flowing to her cheeks. "My client."

She looked away before her eyes gave away her emotions. Tears formed.

"Lilly…." Reginald cupped her cheek, forced her to look at him. His voice softened. "I'm a former copper. I can tell when there is more. Are these tears for Jacob?"

"They should be, but. . .." *Please don't ask me anything else.*

His kind blue eyes searched her face. "Then, tell me about your client."

With that single directive, something bubbled up from deep in her heart. It came unexpectedly, like a geyser releasing pressure.

"It was Nick, Celia's father, but before we discuss that, there's something I need to tell you. Reginald, I'm grateful to you for giving me a life, for allowing me and my baby an opportunity to thrive, for providing a purpose—"

"But now you want something different."

How did he know?

"Yes. I've decided to close the business. As for its assets, I've sold the half interest in the saloon to Jacob, and I'll be personally buying out the business's half-interest in the restaurant and the boarding house."

"Ah, so that's the reason for the crates. That's quite a big step." He didn't seem at all surprised.

"Yes. I. . . This last case . . .it was dangerous. I was almost raped. I was also kidnapped, and I had a bout with lockjaw. I might have died if not for. . . "

"Your young man, this Nick."

"Yes," she said, softly.

"Lilly, you're a lovely woman and I knew some day your heart would turn again toward the future. When we met in the park, I found you desperate and unhappy, and terribly guilt-ridden."

He covered her hand with his. "No amount of my telling you the guilt was not yours to bear would have changed how you saw yourself. You believed you deserved every hardship life could bring. I've long thought you accepted my offer not just for the financial security it brought, but as atonement for what you perceived as your sin."

Lilly's jaw dropped. "What?"

"Isn't that why you thought you would be capable of walking in the underworld of working girls? Because you thought you were one of them? I'm not judging you here, just stating what I saw all those years ago. A woman who gave herself to the man she thought loved her, only to have his child out of wedlock?"

Too struck by the truth in his words, Lilly rose, wrapped her arms about herself and walked to the window on shaky legs. Was he right? Had her desire to help these women been a cover for a deeper hidden motivation?

To punish herself for surrendering to her baser needs?

The heat of Reginald's hand fell to her shoulder. "I knew some day you would want more out of life. I had hoped Celia's father would come looking for you one day. And now I see that he has."

"He came looking for his sister, Reginald, not me. Seems he had my professional name and a chess piece in his possession. As much as I fought taking him on as a client, I couldn't turn him down after seeing the chessman."

"Of course not. Has this young man asked you to marry him?"

She turned to face him. "Yes, but—"

"But what?" He peered into her eyes, his own growing soft and filling with understanding.

"I turned him down before I made the decision to close the business. He was shot at twice and faced great danger in rescuing me from Baylor. I couldn't bring him into my dangerous life. If something had happened to him, I'd never forgive myself."

"You must love him very much."

Lilly slumped, her hands flying to her blurry eyes. "Yes, I still love him, but closing the business was for my own peace of mind, not because of Nick. Right now, I'd settle for a healthy dose of respectability and a great deal of boredom."

She wasn't going to be a watering pot. Just wasn't. The tears fell anyway. Reginald handed her a clean handkerchief which she eagerly accepted.

"Perhaps what I came to tell you will help ease your mind. At least in one area."

Lilly tensed. So, there *was* a reason for his visit. Reginald led her back to the sofa and settled beside her.

"The government is going to be changing the way it goes after people who commit federal crimes. They are no longer going to employ outside agents like you who work for themselves or other organizations. Plans are being made to establish a Bureau of Investigation using internal people to staff it."

What was he saying? That her services would have no longer been needed anyway?

Her mentor took a swift breath in and let it out in a grunt.

"Not that they'll get the same level of expertise as my employees, but that, I suppose, will come with training." He shifted, his brows knitting together in a straight line. "You would have been out of a job, or at least a part of it on December 31. The decision to close your business was most fortuitous."

As Lilly absorbed this information, an awkward silence fell between them. Would closing the business have been necessary if the government planned to eliminate the most dangerous part of it anyway? Had she made the right decision?

Or acted prematurely?

Don't question your decision.

In her heart she knew she'd done the right thing. Right for her. Right for Jacob. Right for everyone else connected to her network. The nature of the work had changed in seven years. Murders, beatings, drugs, slave trafficking, and gun violence, among other things, had become far more commonplace.

"Pardon the questioning of an old bachelor, but if you've forgiven Nick, and you love him, what's keeping you from telling him you've reconsidered his proposal?"

The question caught her by surprise. "He may no longer want me."

"You don't know that for a fact. Where is he now?"

"Still up in Cripple Creek." Probably taking advantage of all the pleasures the town provided—the gambling, the pleasure houses— without Lilly as an encumbrance. The sting of that thought was too painful to ignore.

Reginald's gaze turned speculative. "Don't you think he deserves some time to see what he's up to? Frankly, if it were me, I would think long and hard about your man. It sounds like he loves you. He did you wrong before, but some men take longer to figure out what they want. Looks like your life will be changing faster than I expected. You should leave all your options open."

Dear, dear Reginald. Always there when she needed him the most. A mentor who preferred to look on the bright side of life. Too choked to speak, she placed her hand over his and squeezed, grateful to have him in her life.

"Lilly, while you're thinking about things, make sure you're running toward something you want, and not away from something you don't. Follow your heart, not your head."

Similar advice to what grandmama had given.

But could she?

Chapter 29

LILLY'S DARKENED BOARDING HOUSE loomed before Nick like a ghostly silhouette against the clear night sky. Halting his run, he pulled in deep gulps of early fall air. A strange mix of anticipation and dread added fuel to his heart's already erratic pace.

How would she react to his news? He'd created a future for them without her having a say.

Creeping around the side of the building, he selected a few small pebbles and tossed each one against her bedroom window on the second floor. The one she had mentioned in passing once before.

Ribs quaking with the thunder of his heartbeat, Nick waited.

Nothing happened.

He threw several more. *Wake up, Lilly.*

Seconds later, the glass pane lifted, and Lilly's head popped out, ropes of her long hair flowing down like Rapunzel in the fairy tale. "What on earth?"

"The train just arrived, and I have something to tell you that can't wait."

"Well, it *is* sort of late." Lilly pulled her head part way in, and his pulse faltered. "The front door has a bell that will alarm the whole house. Come to the kitchen at the back."

Releasing the breath he hadn't noticed he held, Nick strode to the rear.

She appeared in the doorway. The dark-colored robe she wore hung open to reveal a voluminous white nightdress that reflected the moonbeams like a beacon in a storm.

Disheveled from sleep, she looked like she had been thoroughly bedded. The hard peaks of her round, full breasts pressed against the flimsy lawn fabric, causing his groin to come alive with instant need. Reluctantly, he lifted his eyes and discovered emerald green pools filled with a yearning that made his knees quake.

Lilly's gaze slipped to his lips.

Groaning, he hauled her against him and slammed his mouth over hers. The clean taste of peppermint merged with the sweet scent of lilacs to inflame his desire. Plunging his fingers through her still damp tresses, he held her head tight, the tips of her breasts against his chest erotic and beckoning.

He prayed she would say yes.

~~~~

Good Lord, she would miss this!

Nick took Lilly's mouth as though he owned it, the hard pressure of his lips on hers demanding, his tongue seeking.

Thirsting for his touch, she opened for him, want and need nearly bringing her to her knees. Accepting her invitation, he swept in, touched gently, then thrust forcefully, bathing her mouth with the sweet caress of his passion. The intoxicating scent of him, his commanding possession, his restrained desire turned her world on end. She would forever hunger for this man.

Yet in her heart she knew this would be the last time.

Savor it, Lilly. Hold it dear. Remember it.

Her nipples hardened, her breasts firmed, and liquid heat rushed to the place where her legs joined. Lost in carnal pleasure, Lilly surrendered, happy to have one more taste of him before he walked out of her life forever.

The hands holding her face trembled as Nick deepened the pressure, plundering her mouth as though starving. Breathing heavily, he gasped for air before sliding his tongue along the ridge of jaw to a sensitive spot below her ear.

In that moment, she realized she would never say no to this man. Not even when the sad vestiges of their past surfaced to take away her peace.

It was Nick who broke the moment.

Lifting his head, he stepped back, her body crying out at the loss. Though dark desire had turned his eyes a midnight blue, another emotion shimmered in their depths. "Marry me, Lilly. I love you. Always have. Always will."

She heard the plea in his voice, recognized the vulnerability in its tone.

Deep lines formed on his handsome face and his body seemed as tight as a bow string. "I bought land in Cripple Creek for a store, but if you want to continue with your investigation business, I'll not stop you. As much as I dislike the danger you put yourself in, I can adjust to it. Please say yes, Lilly. I can't live without you."

Her emotions rioting, she opened her mouth, but nothing came out.

Shunned by her family, she had borne a child all alone, raised, then buried her and started life over, all because of this man.

And her own unwise choices.

She was as much to blame as he, for she had let it happen.

And now she had fallen in love with the man all over again. Could she trust her instincts a second time?

As the seconds passed, Nick's shoulders slumped. "When I first saw you at the saloon, I hoped…." Nick sighed and shook his head. "Forget it. I shouldn't—"

"Hoped what?" she prodded, her breath catching as she found her voice.

"That there would be a future for us."

Her chest squeezed.

She found his hand. "For many years I dreamed you would find me and Celia and sweep us away to a place that was safe and wonderful and beautiful."

Widened eyes met her gaze.

"I wasn't going to trap you in a marriage you didn't want. And when it became clear you weren't coming for me, I gave up my dream. I was devastated. But I had a child to raise, and I grabbed hold of whatever I could find to keep going—mostly, the anger I held against you."

Sorrow entered the blue pools staring at her now.

"I used that emotion to provide direction and motivation to make a life for my ...for our daughter. I clung to it like a crutch, leaning on it for strength and comfort when I had nothing else to hold me up. Anger was my replacement for the hope I lost. I think it's time I abandon that support, don't you?"

She combed his face for a reaction. Anything.

A burst of sunshine sprang from the storm clouds in his eyes, the dazzling brightness almost blinding as a wide smile broke across his face. He had heard her message. Joy flooded her heart.

"I'm assuming that means yes?"

Lilly nodded, too caught up with emotion to speak.

"I bought two lots in Cripple Creek, Lilly," Nick blurted, his excitement bubbling over. "One on Bennett Avenue large enough for a clothing store. Another for a house. For you and me. For our children. You can operate your business from an office in the store, if you like."

Air failed to inflate her lungs.

Caught by a moonbeam streaming through the window, the shimmer of moisture in his eyes sparkled like diamonds. His strong hand tilted her head up, and he swept her face with a visual caress. One she felt as though he'd touched every part of her with the magic of his lips.

"There's one more thing you should know, Nick."

~~~~

His heart pounding, Nick held his breath. His future was on the line.

The half-smile on Lilly's face suddenly widened. And the pulsing in his veins eased.

"You don't have to worry about my being in danger anymore. I'm closing my business." Her eyes sparked like dew kissed emeralds.

Stunned into silence, he stared at her, his mouth open like a newly hatched bird. Closing? Giving up an enterprise she struggled seven years to build?

Why?

Certainly not because of him. A heaviness enveloped his heart, a cruel emotion he was most familiar with—guilt.

In the next breath the question slid out. "Why?"

Lilly stepped within a hair's breadth of his chest and cupped his cheek. "I'm doing this for me, Nick. Continuing my previous life is no longer practical, nor desirable. Too many bad things have happened recently. I …I discovered there are other things I want more than my work—respectability, peace, a house full of children and…and you."

She said this last in a whisper, a silky thread of sound that stirred his insides.

"Then I didn't unduly influence your decision."

"No. After I turned you down, I didn't expect you to come back. I arranged my life accordingly."

He placed his hand over hers on his cheek. "Aw, Lilly. I can't live without you. I would do whatever it took to have you by my side. Don't you know that?"

"I do now."

Drawing his head down, she took his mouth in a possessive kiss that sent fire speeding through his body. Her tongue forged in and danced with his, touching everywhere, telling him in no uncertain terms she was his, and he hers.

Her arms twined around his neck, and she tugged him closer, her turgid nipples digging into his chest like brass buttons on an overcoat.

Something shifted inside Nick. He delved into her offered heat and took what he wanted, what he craved. He meant to be sweet and tender, but his longing could no longer be denied. Hell, he was as hard as granite, and he needed to plunge into her wet heat.

Now.

Releasing her mouth, he asked, "Lilly?"

Her eyes were dark with passion, her pupils large and black, the green nearly obliterated. "Love me, Nick."

Her invitation. The words the same as seven years ago. Those nights on the sand, waves rolling to shore, moonbeams reflecting on the water. Desire spread like wildfire to the ends of his body.

With trembling hands, he cupped her face and pressed his lips to hers. Far from the one he ached to give her, this kiss was gentle, intended to distract rather than inflame. Tucking an arm under her knees, he carried her upstairs to the only room with an open door and placed her on the rumpled bed covers.

He stood back, unable to take his eyes off the woman he loved. She looked so tiny in the big bed, her night rail billowing around her like an extra sheet, her eyes warm and sensuous.

"Are you just going to stand there, or are you planning on joining me?"

Nick laughed. The pragmatic question could only have come from his practical Lilly, the voluptuous siren with the coy, beckoning smile. The owner of a mind equally capable of quick thinking and logical reasoning.

Oh, he intended to comply with his seductress's wishes, but not the way she might think. No, tonight he planned to push his control to the edge, to see to her pleasure first before giving in to his own wild urges. The passionate kisses they had shared in the kitchen would have to last him a little while longer.

Slowly, carefully, he slipped off the first item of clothing—his black string tie—and placed it on the dresser, lining the ends up precisely. His fingers lingered on each button of his shirt, worked it through the opening as slowly as he could manage. His hands moved lower and lower among the fastenings, lingering here, fumbling there while his heart pounded a rather unsteady rhythm against the inside of his rib cage.

Something akin to a frustrated sigh sounded from the vicinity of the bed.

Chuckling, Nick gauged Lilly's reaction through lowered lashes.

She gawked at him, her mouth opening slightly. Her pink tongue darted across kiss-swollen lips. Her full breasts rose and fell beneath her gown with fast, shallow breaths.

His arousal grew painful.

Item by item, the rest of his clothing came off in painstakingly slow fashion. His pulse tripped faster, his breath more erratic.

Damn if this wasn't hard as hell!

As he removed his trousers, Nick's fingers brushed the lump of his brother's toy soldier in his pocket. Bemused, he realized he had not sought its comfort in a long time. Hadn't needed to.

His undergarments came last. Trembling fingers fumbled the maneuver like an anxious child learning to undress.

Finally, naked and laboring to breathe, he faced Lilly head on, his stiffened rod advertising how much he wanted her. A desert formed in his throat.

She scrutinized him with unbridled hunger, her gaze settling like a caress on his jutting erection.

Which instantly lengthened.

Twin spots of color brightening her face, she reached for the buttons of her gown.

"Leave them. That's my job," he growled.

Lilly's head flew up. "Oh, it is, is it?"

The huskiness of her drawl sent blood pulsing to his groin. Her hands left the closure and slid to her creamy soft thighs. Thighs made for his attention. For his loving.

"Yes, ma'am. It is." Nick climbed on the bed, rolled to his side against her, and attacked the demure neck of the gauzy garment. First one button, then the next, then several more slipped through the openings. Unable to help himself, he caressed her exposed flesh as he worked, lingering a moment here, brushing lightly there.

Lilly's gaze on his face burned like a flying ember, yet he kept his head down, intent upon his mission, his breathing difficult, his hunger intense. As he opened the last button and spread the two sides apart, Lilly gasped.

"You are lovely, do you know that?"

Her voluptuous mounds rose and fell at a quickened pace, the nipples puckered and waiting, her skin soft and inviting. Like a star shining in the darkness, the amber locket lay between her breasts, a symbol of his love.

A love that, by the pendant's very presence, existed for Lilly as well.

Her back arched in a silent plea, a blatant bid to be touched, to be taken.

He didn't wait.

His control pushed to its limit, he cupped one breast and brushed his thumb across its hardened tip. The hiss of her gasp pierced his flesh and settled deep within his groin. Wanting to hear it again, he circled her nipple with his tongue, then suckled, the pleasure sweeping like lightning to his tightened balls.

Lilly's labored breathing spurred him on, her arched back telegraphing her desire. He switched to the other, his fingers glancing off the gemstone she still wore close to her heart.

But it was her moan, the soft expulsion of sound not far from his ear, that shattered his control.

Chapter 30

GOOD LORD, WHAT PLEASURE!

Lilly cupped Nick's head tighter as he suckled her breast, the warm, moist pressure of his mouth on her flesh sending spirals of sensation to her core. To the place she needed him the most. She couldn't help but writhe beneath him, her body demanding fulfillment. A moan slipped out.

Nick changed then, turned more feral, less controlled. His body trembled. His breathing grew more labored as his huffs of breath feathered irregularly across her goose-bumped flesh.

Teeth claimed her hardened tip and a sharp spike of near pain brought a dizzying wave of intense pleasure.

What was that?

Whatever it was, she desired more of it. Like a wanton, she thrust her torso up and begged.

She wanted it all.

Wanted the wildness she detected simmering beneath the surface, the raw passion about to explode, the uncontrolled essence of maleness exuding from behind his veneer.

Tugging on Nick's head until his mouth was even with hers, she whispered, "You are mine, and I am yours. Always, and forever. Whatever your emotions are, don't hold back."

"But Lilly ...."

Midnight blue eyes pleaded with her. An emotion she couldn't quite decipher inhabited the darkened pools. Fear?

What was he afraid of? Hurting her?

"I trust you."

And she did.

Implicitly.

Sudden tears welled in his eyes. His lips covered hers in a tender kiss so loving and giving she almost wept herself.

His flesh was soft and pliable, his taste of peppermint invigorating, his scent of mountain air, train soot and male musk captivating. Surrendering to the intoxicating heat of his tender caress, Lilly sifted her hands through his silky, blond hair, letting the sensual haze of awe and wonder flow through her.

What had she done to elicit this exquisite reaction?

She thought back.

I trust you.

Trust. Was that what he sought?

For *her* to affirm his worthiness.

In that instant she knew he would never intentionally hurt her again, would never leave her as he had done before. Peace and contentment seeped through her veins like a fine wine, and she knew the future would be filled with great joy and happiness.

As tender as he had been before, his kiss changed to one of demand and possession. His hands tightening on her head, he took control of her mouth in a fevered exploration that left no surface untouched.

Lost in his passion, he lay siege to her breasts, nibbling and biting and kissing and suckling. She clung to him as though drowning, for sinking into a sweet pool of pleasure was the only way to describe what his tongue moving down her body created. They were two helpless people drawn to a whirlpool of passion, the rhythmic motion of her torso increasing as she arched against him, yearning for completion.

"Please, Nick. I can't take much more." Her muscles curled into knots, her breasts turned hard and swollen, her belly tightened. Liquid seeped to her nether lips which pulsed with violent need.

Eager to press her body to his nakedness, she tugged the opened night rail over her head and flung it to the floor.

His knee fell between her thighs and a prayer of thanks worked its way out of her chest. Of their own accord, her hips rose, seeking his hardness. She needed him deep inside her, filling her, stretching her, spending within her.

Sweet William, more than anything, she wanted his child!

~~~~

"Show some mercy, Lilly."

Nick pushed her legs wide and gazed at her. Her swollen woman's tissues glistened with dew, beckoning the unleashed wildness raging inside him.

She was ready. Slick and warm, and he yearned to plunge into her and drive them both to oblivion. He wanted her so bad he was afraid he would spill.

Struggling against his own frenzied needs, he bent and licked across the hard nubbin at the top of her opening.

Lilly's pelvis jerked up, her moan music to his ears.

Blood roared through his veins and pulsed its way to the tip of his rod. Her sweet and salty flavor teased him, encouraged him, focused his energy on giving his beloved what she wanted, what she needed.

Without breaking his rhythm, he slid a finger within her. Her body arched, meeting his thrust with one of her own.

"Nicky!" she shrieked.

His childhood nickname on her lips startled him at first, but then a warmth stole over him that was as familiar and as comfortable as a well-worn pair of boots. Only his siblings had ever called him Nicky, a brother and sister he loved and who loved him unconditionally.

That Lilly should shout it out in the throes of her pleasure, a mindless expression of unconditional love, thrilled him to no end.

Her moans and other mewling sounds driving him on, he slipped two fingers inside and worked them until he felt her insides clench tightly.

She was close.

Nick pulled out and moved up her writhing body.

God, she was beautiful. Sweat glistened across her full breasts, her labored breathing making her pillowy mounds dance before his eyes. Her chestnut hair lay in sensual disarray across the pillow. Her cheeks were aglow with inflamed desire. The scent of her arousal rose about them, a perfume of seduction that drew him like a bee to a flower.

Heart pounding with unspent passion, Nick positioned himself for entry and rubbed the tip of his shaft through Lilly's gleaming wetness. The light brush of air from her gasp fell across his throat, and an urgent need to be inside her raced through him.

Her arms twined around his back and a husky demand flowed like manna to his ears. "Now, Nick."

He kissed her softly, let her taste herself on his tongue. In one forceful thrust, he seated himself within her scalding heat, the contraction of her tight sheath welcoming.

And humbling.

She opened to him without pause, without reflection.

"Ah Lilly, you feel so good."

Then she moved, and the world disappeared, leaving the two locked in a timeless communication. Desire, gratitude, and longing burst into an inferno that blazed through his veins. There was nowhere else he would rather be than inside this glorious woman.

Raw emotion took over, and he let the tempest he held at bay reign free.

He withdrew. Lilly's moan of disapproval sped straight to his heart. He thrust in again hard, pulled out, and moved his hand between them, seeking the nubbin he knew would draw her greatest response. Finding it, he stroked, and she bucked against his fingers, asking for more.

"Look at me, Lilly."

Her closed eyes opened, her heavy-lidded gaze filled with arousal. A moan escaped her lips.

With an animal-like growl, he lifted her hips and thrust into her repeatedly. Body parts shifted against each other, passionate cries urged him on, erratic breaths whispered words of love, and roving fingernails spoke of frenzy.

Whatever vestige of control he commanded over his long-bottled emotions evaporated. The raw anger shaping his behavior since childhood broke free, its wild powerful force seeking violence and retribution. But it quickly abated within the sweet, hot confines of Lilly's body. She was his salvation, his sanctuary. He couldn't live without her.

Lilly tensed as she neared her release.

As did he, the insistent tingling along the bottom of his spine signaling the start of his climax. His body quaking with impending fulfillment, Nick thrust hard several more times. A primal shout worked its way up his throat. *Not yet, not yet.* He clamped his jaw tight.

Beneath him, Lilly convulsed, and a loud mewling wail erupted from her mouth as she reached her peak. Blood thrummed through his veins. His heartbeat raced like a steam engine. Muscles at the base of his erection squeezed hard. Capturing her lips, he poured his seed deep within, his shaft contracting in pulsing waves of unrelenting pleasure.

And joy.

Inside his beloved Lilly.

Wave upon wave of blinding sensation.

Finally spent, Nick fell upon her chest and felt her pull him close. Her breathing shuddered in his ear. He imagined his sounded similar. He lay quiet, relishing the intimacy, the feeling of belonging, the love that flowed between them swift and true.

When her arms loosened, he slid to his side, drawing her with him. She'd closed her eyes, the slight curve of her swollen lips that of a thoroughly pleasured woman. Male satisfaction socked him in the chest.

Maybe they conceived a child, one he would be able to nurture and love until the end of his days. One he would play with and comfort, read to and teach, guide and support. His heart swelled at the thought.

Nick shifted his arm around Lilly's shoulders and tucked her head under his chin.

As her fingers played along the cleft, Lilly chuckled.

He claimed her hand. "What is so funny?"

"Do you realize this is the first time we've ever made love in a bed?" She threaded her hand with his and drew both toward her lips.

Nick thought back to the times they had spent together. The last time they were intimate, they had lain on a nest of buffalo robes on a cabin floor. And seven years before, the sand on Lake Michigan's marshy shore provided the soft mattress for their passion-filled nights.

"You're right, but far be it our last." He raised up onto his elbow and tenderly pushed a stray curl behind her ear. "Would you like to hear about the plans for Cripple Creek?"

Would she approve? Would she want to share in his dream? The muscles in his throat constricted as he swallowed.

"Yes, I want to know all about them." The curiosity in her voice loosened a band circling his chest.

Nick smiled. "I'd like to open a clothing store for the millionaire miners who strike it rich. Currently, they're going to Denver for their apparel, but I see no reason why they can't buy the latest Paris fashions in town. There's a need I think we can fill."

"We?" A spark ignited in Lilly's eyes.

"Lilly, you're a great salesperson. I know you have your own business interests now, but if you help me, we could sell almost anything. Including those fancy hats women like so much. We could call it The Chicago Store. I bought a whole block, but we'll start with a smaller store at first."

She pushed up on one arm and tucked a hand under her chin. Her magnificent eyes were aglow with interest. "Well then, if I'm to help manage this store with you, I'll sell my interests here and join you up there."

"So, you like my idea?"

"I love it, and I love you. Oh, this is going to be a grand new adventure, Nick. We'll make it elegant, with crystal chandeliers and velvet chairs, and plush carpets, and piano music. Maybe even a harp—"

He slammed his mouth down on Lilly's and crushed her to the mattress.

Grand, indeed!

All he needed was her.

And he had her.

Now and forever.

Epilogue

June, 1895
Cripple Creek, Colorado

Leaning over the mezzanine railing as far as her swollen belly would allow, Lilly brought the crystal glass of water to her lips, barely able to contain her joy. Three days of free champagne, hors d'oeuvres and deep discounts had filled their store to overflowing for its first annual thank you sale. The extravaganza was a significant financial risk, but the return far exceeded their expectations.

From the day the expensive apparel shop opened, a brisk business kept the cash register ringing, but nothing prepared them for the wall-to-wall crowds attracted by free drink, food, and low prices. The store offered a varied selection of the practical and the fribble, the tailored and the whimsical. Even ladies' chapeaus, with their feathers and birds and tulle netting, were selling better than expected.

By far the tallest and most handsome man on the floor, Nick's blond head stood out in a sea of dark bowlers and feathered hats.

Lilly marveled at the turn her life had taken since the man she once despised first walked into her saloon. No longer ostracized for consorting with fallen women, Lilly's benevolence in this direction was now more private. Betty had purchased Sally's Silver Spoon in Colorado City and, with Lilly's fund to underwrite wages, former working girls had a legitimate way to bring in money besides on their backs.

Similarly, Thad bought out her share of the boarding house for Jenny whom he married shortly after. Jenny now offered the women a decent place to stay just as Lilly had. No soiled dove who wanted to leave her former profession would want for some place to sleep and a way to earn a respectable dollar.

With another new member of her growing family on the way, could her future get any better?

"Mrs. Shield?" a familiar voice broke into her musings from behind.

Lilly straightened and turned toward her main floor manager, a young man not yet out of his teens who would someday grow into his exquisitely tailored suit. His normally sunny expression had given way to a furrowed brow and tight lips, not a positive sign in the least.

"What is it, Thomas?"

"I think you might be needed downstairs. Some customer is driving the boss apoplectic. His face is beet red, and there may be a fight if someone doesn't put a stop to it."

"Oh, dear." She turned back to the railing and scanned the scene below once more. Nick, whose face was indeed crimson, had cornered a man she couldn't identify between two racks of men's suits, and was gesticulating wildly.

Heart pounding, she swung past Thomas, handing him the glass as she went, and descended the mezzanine stairs as fast as her child-laden body would allow. Plowing through the crowd in Nick's direction as politely as possible, she neared him.

What were they arguing about? Nearby customers were beginning to take note.

~~~~

Nick grabbed his father by the arm and hauled him to his office at the back of the store. Years of hurt and disappointment exploded in a loud stream of expletives.

Yanking on the light chain, he slammed the door behind him and turned to the one man whose regard he had sought for so many years. "You weren't on the guest list. What the hell are you doing here?"

The man had the audacity to shrug. "Curiosity, mostly. Saw a small item in the newspapers back East. The Chicago Store. The description sounded like Shield's." A rude sound flew from his mouth. "I would never have opened a store like this in such a hell-hole. What were you thinking?"

Never a good word.

Never an acknowledgment of success.

As the thought rolled in his head, he realized the usual grinding pain of his father's disparagement was absent.

The only emotion he could accurately identify was anger.

Old anger, harbored deep.

Layer upon layer of childhood hopes and disappointments fomenting, and churning, and bubbling upward.

"There was a time that remark would have bothered me. Seared me to my soul. But not now. I no longer give a damn what you think. When I was little, I would have done anything for a kind word from you, for a bit of encouragement, or a comment as simple as 'nice work, boy.' But it never came. You only cared about yourself and your damn mistress parked in the house behind us."

His father's jaw dropped. "You knew about her?"

His control at a low point, Nick curled his hands into fists. "How like you, Father. I tell you about a little boy, your youngest son, who was hurt repeatedly by your benign indifference, and you ask me about your mistress. Damn you to hell."

"Now, Nick. . ." His father grabbed Nick's shoulder.

He shoved it off. "Don't! As a father, you were a dismal failure."

The man's complexion paled.

Nick wanted to punch his father, give in to the violence cursing through his veins. But Lilly would never condone such conduct. Instead, he used every ounce of his failing control to keep his fists at his side.

"Well, good afternoon, Mr. Shield. Nice to see you again."

Nick started. Lilly stood in the doorway, her sweet words having been delivered in a syrupy voice dripping with sarcasm. When had she entered the office?

His father scrutinized her as if they had never met, his gaze landing on her very ripe belly. Didn't the man even remember her? She was his employee.

And he had sent more than his share of derogatory remarks her way, damn him.

Lilly lifted her chin.

"And who are you?" he said, his tone cold and brittle.

Straightening her spine, Lilly's gaze swept over his tall, thickening form. Her face remained amiable, but her eyes blazed green fire. "You know me quite well, I believe. I used to work in your store. My name is Lilly Kane. Now it's Lilly Shield."

Recognition seeped into his father's blue eyes, identical to his own. His face paled. "You!"

Nick threaded his fingers through Lilly's and pulled her closer. "Yes, Father. Lilly Kane, my wife."

Spots of color bloomed on his father's cheeks. "Filled with another Jew brat, I see. Divorce her, son, and come home. I'll make you manager of the store."

Nick's fist flew up.

Lilly caught it mid-air. "Don't, Nick. This man is your father, and you just can't assault him. The comment hurt, but not as before. It came from a pathetic, small-minded bigot, a nobody, and it signified nothing."

"Now see here," his father retorted, purple billowing up from his starched collar.

"Mr. Shield, eight years ago I bore you a beautiful granddaughter. She was the image of your son. She died of the fever when she was four." Some unfathomable emotion flickered through his father's eyes and disappeared. "You have a grandson now and another grandchild on the way. I'm as married to Nick as any woman could ever hope to be."

Nick relaxed, his arm circling his wife's shoulders. "I will never divorce Lilly, Father. I don't need you and your store to be happy. Nor do I need your approval of anything I choose to do. My life is perfect as it is. I'll never let you interfere again. Nor will I let your callous comments bother me. Nor will Rina."

Drawing strength from Lilly, he glared at his father, "As for the future, if you want to visit your grandchildren, mine or Rina's, I suggest you change what you do and how you think. I will not subject Lilly to your hateful slurs ever again. Nor will I allow you to harass Rina about her marriage. Am I clear?"

Gripping the brim of his expensive bowler, Nick's father stared at him dumb struck. "Well, well. A backbone. I didn't think you had it in you. However, I'm not going to apologize for anything I did or didn't do." With a smile that failed to reach his eyes, he placed his hat on his head. "Since I don't seem to be welcome here, I guess I'll be returning to Chicago now. Good day to you."

Then the man whose favor he once sought turned to Lilly, his face a mask of civility that belied the anger Nick sensed beneath. "And to you."

With that, he left.

Taking deep gulps of air to calm his pounding heart, Nick counted to twenty before pulling Lilly closer. "Well, that went well."

Lilly scanned his face for a moment before answering. "Did it?" But there was a twinkle in her eyes.

"What do you think?" The beginnings of a grin were already tugging at his mouth.

Abruptly, they burst out laughing. The confrontation had, indeed, gone well. Better than well. Nick had finally expressed his feelings regarding his father's failure to be a father. And it felt good.

The burden had been lifted off his back.

And if the man wanted to know his grandchildren, he would be the picture of politeness when next he returned, or he'd be put on the first train back to Chicago.

Nick hauled his wife against his chest, or as close as an eight-month pregnancy would allow. Seductive and tempting, her lilac scent wafted to his nostrils. Hardened nipples aroused his raging lust, the evidence of which rose against her expanding belly. "Well, Mrs. Shield. Had enough excitement for the day?"

She raised herself to her tiptoes and brushed something off his suit jacket. "Of this nonsense, I have indeed, but I long for a different kind of excitement, husband mine. But alas, the doctor said we have to wait."

He eyed her speculatively. "A little kissing won't hurt. In fact, it may be just what the man ordered."

"Man? Or one man in particular?"

"Guess."

Lilly passed her tongue along her bottom lip. Nick found the movement fascinating. "Now, where, oh where shall we go, dear husband?"

"I know the perfect place." He grabbed her hand and swept her deftly out of the office and through the throng of shoppers to the other side of the store.

To a dark stockroom not unlike the one in which their love began all those years ago.

Where he kissed her thoroughly until her whole body trembled in his arms.

<<<<THE END>>>>

Thanks for reading *Memories and Moonbeams*. I hope you enjoyed it as much as I did researching and writing it.

If you liked Lilly and Nick's story, come on down to Natchez, Mississippi, for the story of Birdie and Jack in *Promises and Passions*, Book 3 of The Chessmen series, as Birdie goes looking for her runaway husband. Discover what mess she gets herself into in this elegant Mississippi river town still clinging to the southern code of honor way of life. To give you a peak, I've included an excerpt at the end of this book. Check my website (below) to find out when Birdie's story will become available.

Website: http://www.averilreismanauthor.com

REVIEWS ARE THE LIFEBLOOD of author success. They let us know what you like and don't like. They guide other prospective readers in their purchasing decisions. And they are often qualifiers for promotional opportunities. I regularly troll my book pages at on-line book retailers to see what readers thought of my book. I would love to hear what you think if you would be so kind as to write a review about *Memories and Moonbeams* and post it on the book page at your favorite online retail bookstore.

And I'd love a posted comment about the book on Facebook, Twitter, or Goodreads.

Website: http://www.averilreismanauthor.com
Facebook: http://www.facebook.com/averilreismanauthor
Twitter: https://www.twitter.com/avreisman
Goodreads: http://bit.ly/1xKSxo0

Other Books by Averil Reisman

Print books and E-books are available at most online retail book stores.

The Chessmen Series
Shadows and Masks, Book 1

Stand Alone
The Captain's Temptress (formerly *To Cuba With Love*)

Author's Notes

Several topics in this book require more explanation. Two of them are the white slave trade and the existence of female investigators in the 1890s.

Let's take the first, the white slave trade. My initial view, gleaned from research into Chicago's 1893 Columbian Exposition for my last book *Shadows and Masks*, was that the term *white slavery* meant the enslavement of white women for nefarious reasons, primarily sex. Posters all over Chicago and ads in newspapers at the time of the Exposition and later warned unsuspecting young women of unscrupulous men who might lure them into a life of sexual slavery through promises of nice clothes, money, and entry into wealthy society. The term *white slavery* was prominent in these posters and ads.

However, when I read Margit Stange's book *Personal Property— Wives, White Slaves, and the Market in Women* as background research for this book, I learned the definition of white slavery is a virtual hornet's nest of interrelated concepts including racism, sexism, immigration, and colonialism.

According to Stange, the word white, as applied to this term, leans on the fact that color white as a symbol of purity and good, rather than anything having to do with race. The term *white slavery* was originally coined during the eighteenth century in early industrial Britain. The word *slavery* indicated the coercive power industry illegally wielded over free wage workers. The word *white* referred to *privileged* males entitled to a race privilege that might have been eliminated by economic oppression.

During the nineteenth century, the term gradually became associated with prostitutes. British social purity reformers referred to prostitutes as *white slaves*. Over time *white slavery* came to mean sexual slavery to differentiate from slaves considered chattel. White slavery has no reference to a racial identity. In the US, more Native American, Chinese, Mexican, and African American women were victims of *white slavery* than Caucasians.

During the early 1900s, anti-immigration and racist beliefs seeped into the sensationalized reports, books, pamphlets on the subject, leading to outraged public opinion that "white woman" were being exploited and needed to be saved. In recent times, some scholars claim the literature itself was racist, as it implied that other races weren't worthy of "being saved."

Because public opinion at the time saw those who profited from *white slavery* as being immigrants, the Senate passed legislation "extending the government's power to bar and deport aliens suspected of trafficking in white slaves." In 1910, the White Slave Traffic Act, also known as the Mann Act, was passed by Congress making it a felony to aid, entice or force a woman to cross state lines for the purpose of prostitution or debauchery, or any other immoral purpose. The Mann Act is still in force today after being amended several times.

Since *Memories and Moonbeams* is an historical novel taking place nearly two decades prior to this legislation, I used the prevailing concept of *white slavery* of the time, meaning enslavement of Caucasian women, and not one that might be more relevant today. If that offends some of my readers, I apologize. That was not my intent. To be historically accurate, I had no choice but to represent what I thought had been the prevailing opinion of the era. Where I have taken creative license is in claiming the government had any interest in prosecuting sex slave traffickers at all. It's what I would have wished they had done rather than what they might have done.

The next question is—were there female investigators in the 1890s? The Pinkerton Agency hired Kate Warne as their first female investigator in 1856. Warne was an expert in disguise and was able to transform not only her appearance, but her accent as well, and was an extraordinarily successful sleuth. The Agency went on to hire numerous other female agents to ferret out information male agents were less likely to obtain.

Which draws us to the next question—were female detectives given dangerous jobs? Pinkerton placed Warne as head of the Union Intelligence Service, the forerunner to the Secret Service, charged with gathering information about the Confederate army. Many of Pinkerton's female agents worked in this service as Union spies behind enemy lines, donning disguises and false identities to ferret out military plans. One even stole submarine plans, sewed them into her hem and walked 200 miles past Confederate lines to present them directly to Union war officials. Warne herself was assigned to help secret president-elect Abraham Lincoln from Illinois to Washington for his inauguration after an assassination plot had been uncovered.

Prior to the formation of the (Federal) Bureau of Investigation in 1908, the U.S. Justice Department used borrowed federal agents and marshals, and detectives from the Pinkerton Agency and other private investigating firms to fight the growing federal crime rate. In 1893, the Anti-Pinkerton Act limited the Justice Department's ability to hire investigators and mercenaries employed by private firms. The plan was to bring the job in-house. Today, the U.S. still uses private security firms and military contractors.

Colorado's last great gold rush occurred on the southwestern slope of Pike's Peak in the Cripple Creek Mining District, a caldera on the top of a deep volcano measuring roughly 24 square miles. Gold was discovered there in 1891 and shortly thereafter, hastily thrown up tents turned to camps and camps turned to towns. Mines and mills sprang up. By 1893, 150 mines had dug $2,025,518 of gold out of mountains, worth over $60 million in today's dollars. By 1900, the boom had peaked. By 1951 only 30 mines were still open and $432,974,848 in gold had been produced over 61 years of mining, nearly $13 billion by today's standards.

With all the new millionaires, business catering to their needs, including clothes, sprang up, and Cripple Creek became known as the Paris of the West, including a store called The Chicago Bazaar. Telephones, telegraph, and electricity came to Cripple Creek in 1892. After mining petered out because of the high cost of deep rock mining, the district dwindled to ghost town status. In 1966, the town was listed on the National Register of Historic Places

The first time my husband and I traveled there, Victor, known as the City of Mines, had a population of only 25. Burros, the descendants of those who had worked in the mines, were more numerous than humans. Cripple Creek had a few hundred more people. Today, the district is a popular vacation destination (if you can handle the 9,400 ft altitude) for gambling and tourism. The Cripple Creek and Victor Mining Company purchased Battle Mountain above Victor and operates the Cresson Mine, an open strip mine. The Molly Kathleen Mine operates as a tourist attraction.

Colorado City, known today as Old Colorado City, was founded in 1859 on two square miles of land near Ute Pass, the westward route around Pike's Peak used by gold miners. It served farmers, ranchers, freighters, prospectors, and the mining industry. Because nearby Colorado Springs was dry, Colorado City catered to a wild lifestyle of opium dens, saloons, dance halls and bordellos. Tunnels were dug from legitimate businesses on one street to bordellos and saloons on the street behind so respectable gents could enter without being seen. Colorado City was incorporated into Colorado Springs in 1917 and the neighborhood now caters to tourists with boutiques, art galleries and restaurants.

Prior to the development of the tetanus vaccine in 1924, untreated lockjaw, or tetanus, had a mortality rate of 85%. Various serums were developed and experimented with from 1898 and later, however it wasn't until World War I that serious military efforts were brought to the development of a safe and effect vaccine. The disease is caused by bacteria present in the environment usually introduced in the body through a cut or a deep wound. Symptoms include intense painful muscle spasms, especially in the jaw, trouble swallowing, sweating, and fever. Symptoms generally occur after an incubation period of eight days but may range from three days to three weeks. For the sake of my story, I used the three-day incubation.

Acknowledgements

There are loads of people I wish to thank for helping me bring this story to life. First off is my husband Art who let me do my thing in peace, reminding me when I needed to come up for air (and meals), and for being my sounding board and alpha reader. Having a retired high school English teacher on your team is a huge plus. Without him, my stories would have more stomach churning, more references to soul, and more supercharged emotions erupting out of nowhere.

Another big thank you goes to my critique partner, author Kathleen Bitner Roth, who plugged through my chapters regularly even though she's half-way around the world. You are my inspiration, and my friend. And I love you dearly.

I want to thank my editor, Ann Leslie Tuttle, who shortened my tendency toward verbosity, red-lined my frequent bouts of purple prose, pointed out what needed to be reworked, and made suggestions for overall story improvement. I am in awe of your insight.

And I want to thank Kim Killion of The Killion Group Inc., for creating this cover in less than twenty-four hours after I inquired as to her services. You are a sweetheart.

When I got stuck during my research of white slavery, my daughter Julie, who has a degree in Women's Studies, put me in touch with one of her professors who suggested several books to read. Thank you, Julie.

I also want to give a shout-out to the ladies of the Boulder Ridge Book Club who have been my supporters all these years, and my children (Lisa, Marla and Julie and their spouses Jason and Miranda) for their encouragement. Jason has graciously volunteered himself as a model for one of my book covers, and I must say, he'd make a dandy one.

A big thank you goes to the people at the Cripple Creek Museum, the Cripple Creek Library, the Colorado Springs Historical Library and the Denver Historical Society who dragged out microfiche rolls, 100-year-old photos, and old newspapers when I did research for a book I'd thought I'd write about ten years ago. I never let a research trip go to waste.

And lastly, I want to thank the Sassy Scribes Sisterhood for answering several writer's conundrum questions, the members of Chicago-North chapter of Romance Writers of America for their critiques of my rough draft opening chapters, and the national Romance Writers of America organization and other chapters for holding workshops, conferences and contests I found invaluable.

Excerpt

Promises and Passions
Book 3 of the Chessmen series

Chapter 1

Late Sept. 1893
Natchez, MS

BIRDIE Devereaux watched in fascination as heavy, elongated, drops of dark red slid slowly down her arm and dripped off her hand onto her new moss green dress. She lowered her fog-shrouded head and gazed curiously at the widening stain advancing thread by thread across her lap like a marauding army.

Surely this can't be real.

Of course not. It was a dream. Or she hoped it was anyway.

Yet, her heart pounded in her ears and sweat rolled between her breasts. The rest of her felt cold and clammy. The breeze from an open window created a chill that pebbled across her moist flesh

Real, or a bad dream?

She glanced at her hand again. Was this blood even hers? Her muddled brain took stock of her body. Nothing seemed to hurt. No wounds, no sores, no broken bones.

No, the blood belonged to someone else.

But who?

Peering impassively around the study, her gaze landed on a body in front of her knees.

On Antoine, her husband.

Dead.

The blood must be his.

Why was she on her knees? And why was he dead?

His open eyes were still startling blue, though in death he looked surprised. He'd always been a handsome man, even with the heavy beard he'd worn. Yet today, his jaw was bare, revealing an even more handsome face, one Birdie had not seen before. His high cheek bones contained not an ounce of extra flesh, their chiseled structure giving him the appearance of strength and command.

But no more.

His full lips, markers of his selfish passion, were twisted into the unpleasant sneer that had been forever a part of his face.

Birdie squeezed her eyes shut.

Her husband was dead.

She should be crying.

Should be feeling something.

Anything.

But the truth was, she felt nothing.

Because she wouldn't miss him.

Then a shallow and wild thought careened through her head. Now she would never be able to buy out his half of their gold mine. Her reason for traveling all the way from Colorado now lay on the floor of his study covered in blood.

She stared at the knife protruding from his chest. How had this happened?

Sitting back on her heels, she reflected on the question. But clear thinking was impossible. A thickening white fog floating through her brain smothered her ability to recall the immediate past.

Somewhere in the distance a dog barked. A child called out. Male voices drifted on the air.

The sound of heavy footsteps lumbering down the long hallway and stopping at the study door broke through the murkiness clouding her mind.

She barely noticed the intrusion until the door swung open with a bang.

"Put your arms above your head, ma'am." The slow cadence of a bass voice came from behind her, commanding but not unkind.

She twisted toward the sound.

And came face to face with the muzzle of a gun pointed directly at her.

Birdie's breath hitched. She froze in place, and stared at the officer, an older man wearing a badge on his burly chest. What had he said?

"I'll repeat. Raise your hands. I'm arresting you for the murder of Antoine Devereaux."

The fog shrouding Birdie's mind instantly lifted, leaving her dizzy and feeling faint. Her gaze skittered over her husband's body, settling on the knife protruding at an awkward angle.

"I didn't do this. I found him this way."

"Tell that to the judge, lady." Stepping forward, the man bent to help her stand. Startled, Birdie shrugged him off and rose on her own power.

As a sudden bout of lightheadedness caused her knees to buckle, she felt the rugged strength of the man's arm circle her waist.

She flinched and tried to pull away.

His eyes narrowed. "No, you don't. We don't allow faintin' in Natchez. Leastwise in my company. You're walking out of here on your own power, missy."

Mumbling a few choice words in her native language, Birdie gave in to his assistance.

"You ain't from around here, I see. Well, you should know there's a mighty concerned little girl out on the veranda who says her mama's in here. That be you?" His voice softened, sounding almost fatherly.

Willow! How could she have forgotten leaving her eight-year-old daughter and Dog on the porch? She nodded, grateful her child hadn't seen her father dead and covered with blood.

Gritting her teeth, Birdie reluctantly leaned into the lawman's strength, and stumbled down the long hallway to the front door of her husband's house without fainting.

As she stepped outside, Willow barreled into her, flinging her arms tight about Birdie's waist in a hard grip. The familiar, clean scent of lemons drifted up from the child's hair. Two years of separation had torn their worlds apart. And now that they had been reunited and had vowed to never let anything part them again, she was being arrested, torn away yet another time from the only person left in the world who mattered to her.

"Caleb, take this little girl to Rev. Grafton. He'll know someone who'll see to her comfort."

Noooo!

On instinct, she gripped Willow's shoulders and dragged her backward.

The other man, much younger than the first, stepped forward and reached for Willow. "Come on, little missy. You'll be safe with me." His smile seemed genuine, yet her daughter sank back into Birdie's arms with a soft whimper of protest.

"She stays with me," Birdie bit out. Nobody was going to split them again.

The man paled. "She can't. Sheriff Cameron, here, is putting you in jail and that is no place for her."

"Then arrest us both because I won't be parted from her."

The Sheriff frowned and his jaw tightened. "All right, then. We'll do just that. Take 'em, Caleb. And the dog, too. No sense leaving that wolf-beast loose. He'll scare the bejeebers out of the whole town."

Caleb's face screwed up. "Aw Chuck, you can't do that. This one's only a child."

"I know, but you heard what her mother said. My prime suspect for Devereaux's murder is not going anywhere without that girl. Put 'em both in the wagon."

Wagon?

Sharp-edged talons of panic ripped into Birdie's chest and choked off her air supply. A black enclosed coach with barred windows and doors sat on the curved driveway, its team of horses stomping impatiently.

In an instant she was back in Colorado, chained to a wagon bed, servicing miners who'd lined up six deep to relieve their needs in her body. Nearby, a man with a heavy French accent drummed up business for his three captive females.

Birdie's vision grayed at the edges.

From a great distance she heard someone yell *shock*.

Then everything went black.

~~~~

Lifting the full glass of amber forgetfulness to the sunlight daring to stream through his office window, Jack Mason admired its sparkling translucence.

Four of these ought to do it.

They always did.

Four bourbons to silence the screams. The cries. The wailing.

Four bourbons to muffle the helplessness. The guilt.

Four bourbons to blessed oblivion.

Bringing the cut Waterford to his lips, he drained the contents in one fast gulp. Fire raced down his throat and his whole body shuddered with the onslaught.

He plunked his glass on the massive wooden desk a few inches from where he had propped his feet. Picking the top card off the well-worn deck, he eyed the battered top hat on the floor and pitched.

The card landed on the silk hat's brim and teetered for a second before falling in.

A winner!

He poured himself another glass and polished it off.

It wasn't enough.

The screams still reverberated through his head. Still clawed at his belly. Still gnawed at what was left of his sanity.

Emptying the decanter sooner rather than later might be a better idea. Before he could act, however, the office door flew open with an ear-splitting jangle of bells.

"Workin' hard, I see." Caleb Dolman, Natchez's deputy sheriff, and as close a friend as Jack ever had, shuffled in. He parked his ass on the cluttered desktop, and eyeing the empty glass, lifted it to the light.

Jack slid his crossed feet two inches away to accommodate the nearness of his friend's butt and flipped another card toward the top hat.

"As hard as I care to." The card sank into the hat's black depths.

Another winner! He was on a streak.

"Well, I gotta lawyerin' case for you. A right juicy one." Caleb studied Jack warily from under the wide brim of his sweat-stained, four-dents uniform hat.

"At the moment, I'm working on reaching the bottom of this decanter of Harper bourbon. Won first place at the Chicago fair, mind you. My reward for getting cards in that ole hat."

He grabbed the glass from Caleb's hand and refilled it. The spirits' pungent fumes tickled his nose.

His friend rose and faced him square on.

Which was why Jack liked him so much. Always honest. Always straightforward.

"This case is different. Sheriff brought this woman in for murderin' Antoine Devereaux. Claims to be his wife."

"That snake? He earned his demise." Jack guzzled his third drink and picked another card. Things were quieting down in his head somewhat.

"Yes, but the lady says she didn't do it. My gut agrees. Quite a looker, she is, by the way. Somethin' fragile about her makes ya want to protect her. She ain't like no other woman I seen behind them bars. If I weren't already married, I'd. . .." Caleb shook his head as though shaking away the thought. "She needs an expert like you to defend her, Jack."

"Nope. She doesn't. Go find someone better than me. I haven't been lawyering for two years." The next card slid across the black brim and landed on the floor behind. Damn!

Caleb pulled his hat from his head in one swift movement. "Not that you were lookin' for any cases lately. Come on, Jack. Maggie and Anna have been gone two whole years now. You gotta join the rest of us sometime. Hell man, this woman asked for you specifically."

Now that drew Jack's attention. He glanced up at his friend's earnest face. "How would she know to ask for me? Did you suggest she hire me?"

"No. She gave me this." Caleb handed him a badly crinkled slip of paper.

Jack's name was scrawled in the loopy handwriting of what appeared to be that of a woman writing in a hurry.

He passed it back. "This proves nothing. She could have picked my name from the town directory."

"She could have, but I doubt it. She was adamant about having you help her. So was her young daughter."

A pang darted through his chest. He frowned. "Daughter? How

old?"

"Can't be much more than eight or nine, as far as I can tell."

"The child isn't with her in the cell, is she?"

Something swept into Caleb's eyes and disappeared, something that looked like the gleam of victory. "Yep. Sheriff brought them both in because they refused to be separated. They are behind them bars as we speak. That little girl is as beautiful as her mother, but such a sad little thing."

Jack dropped his feet to the floor with a soft thud. "Well, I don't do *lawyering* anymore and you know it. Just investigating."

But his interest had been piqued.

"Jail's no place for a child," he muttered, his jaw tightening.

"Nor for a woman either. Leastwise this woman. She's a real lady, Jack. She needs a smart lawyer, and you're the best around. I wouldn't be asking ya if I thought you couldn't help her."

Jack studied the plea in his friend's serious brown eyes. The man's solid instincts made him an excellent officer of the law, and an even better friend. Over the years, he had come to trust in Caleb's talent of reading people accurately.

Jack flipped another card into the hat. He *was* a good lawyer. A *damn fine* one at that.

Awe hell. What would it hurt to just talk to the woman?

He replaced the decanter stopper and rose. "You know, this could be the biggest mistake you ever made, Caleb." He turned his head toward the back room where his latest protégé had holed up with a pile of law books. "Sammy?"

His young assistant, the fourteen-year-old grandson of his housekeeper, poked his head into the front office. "Yes, Mr. Jack?"

"Run home and ask your grandmama to prepare a pot of strong coffee." Jack brushed his hand over the three-day beard gracing his cheeks. "Better tell her to lay out a clean shirt as well. I'll be right home."

"Yes, sir." The boy grinned, ran through the room, and slammed the door behind him. The bells jangled, the sound shooting through Jack's skull like a cannon.

Caleb shot his hand out and clasped Jack's with the strength of twenty men. "Glad to see you're finally joining the world of the living."

"I'm not there yet, my friend. I'll interview this woman, but I'm not promising anything else."

Two hours later, Jack halted at the entrance to the jail's cell block and took a quick survey of its guests.

Thomas Green, the town drunk, snored one off on the right. The left cell was empty. The center hold, however, was crowded with a child, a pacing woman, and a wolfdog watching him intently.

As his eyes returned to the girl, his heart stuttered. Dressed in a fashionable pink and white dress, she looked like Anna. Same age Anna was, same dark hair, same ladylike demeanor—hands folded as though waiting for lemonade in the front parlor.

But Anna was dead. And so was her mother.

This girl was alive.

She looked up, and her large brown eyes bored deep into Jack's soul, neither accusing nor judging. Just sad, and achingly wise for someone so young. The father in him wanted to hug her, tell her everything would be just fine. The man he had become stood there, paralyzed by emotions spinning beneath the surface.

This child didn't belong here. She should be outside, laughing and playing.

As Anna would have been.

Jack straightened and glanced at the woman pacing the small space like a caged lion—the child's mother. Hair as black as night, thick and straight, braided and knotted at her neck. Tall and thin, with the hint of curves beneath her clothing, she paced with purpose, her stride long and unfettered despite her voluminous skirts. If he had to put one word to her bearing, he would say regal.

A queen.

The woman turned then, and he sucked in a breath. Blood, dark and dried, covered the front of her green gown from bosom to knees—the source of the peculiar odor he had smelled when first entering the room.

Did she really kill the bastard?

Then his gaze rose to her face. She was beautiful. Everything Caleb said had been true. Her skin was smooth and dark, almost olive colored, her cheekbones high, her nose prominent but no more than her face could carry. A widow's peak marked her forehead dead center of her symmetrical features. The rest of her was all woman——a generous bosom, tiny waist, and what had to be long legs, judging by her height.

Those legs turned and strode toward the back wall again.

This was no ordinary woman.

He studied her movements. The longer she paced, the more tense she became. Her mouth had tightened into a straight, firm line, and deep furrows notched above her eyebrows in the few minutes of his observation. Once, when she lifted her head without seeing him, fear had flashed in her eyes. Or was the emotion terror?

How had she gotten herself into this mess?

And how could she have married that snake oil salesman, Devereaux? The man never told the truth. About anything.

He crossed the threshold. "Mrs. Devereaux?"

~~~~

Six paces to the bricks.

This place is suffocating!

Six paces back.

Can't breathe.

Need to get out of here.

One, two, three, four, five, six. The wall was too close.

Let me out!

"Mrs. Devereaux?"

A man's voice, deep and rich. Its slow, melodic rhythm drifted across the room on a breath.

Soothing.

Calming.

Inviting.

Birdie lifted her gaze from the wooden floor of the cramped enclosure and peered into gray eyes so light they seemed colorless. Embedded in one of the most handsome faces she had seen, the silver pools were startling in their clarity.

And in the emotions they conveyed.

She read them clearly—curiosity, reluctance, sadness.

They captured her attention, held her spellbound.

Or had it been his voice?

The man filled the doorway. His head nearly reached the top of the frame, his shoulders nearly to the sides. His body tapered to a narrow waist, while long legs, planted on the threshold, appeared as solid as oak.

The cell, the deputy, even her daughter, disappeared from her vision. An invisible thread seemed to wind between her and this man, binding them together as though tethered by rope.

She didn't trust men as a rule. Too much had happened to her to ever trust a man again.

But for some reason, she sensed he was her destiny. For good or for bad.

Birdie straightened. "Yes?" she answered, aware of the hope filling her voice.

The mountain of a man moved closer. Surprisingly for his size, he walked with the easy, loose-limbed gait of endless time. Close up, she noticed a jagged scar running from his temple to his cheekbone, the only feature marring his striking beauty. His gaze was made all the more intense by the ring of black circling the iris of his silvery eyes.

The man's face may speak of danger, yet gentleness lurked beneath its features.

Her head yelled, *beware*. Her heart remained silent.

"I'm Jack Mason. You asked for me?"

Startled, she stared at him. Then smiled. A tentative one, as hope continued to grow. This was the man Lilly Kane, the woman who had rescued her in Colorado, had recommended. A man Lilly said could be trusted.

When she'd awakened behind these bars, groggy and confused, she found Willow eating a cookie and talking with the younger officer named Caleb. Before Birdie had her wits about her, her daughter had given the man their names and the reason for their visit, along with the slip of paper with Jack Mason's name. Birdie had confirmed the information during a short interview after she had awakened.

And he had come.

She had been arrested for killing Antoine. Only she hadn't killed anyone. Maybe this man could help her find out who had.

She grabbed the bars with both hands. "I've been looking for you to help me with something else. But now I find I need a lawyer. The deputy told me you were smart, Mr. Mason. I didn't kill Antoine, no matter how much evidence the Sheriff might think he has."

Mr. Mason's hand flew to the back of his neck where his fingers fiddled with his longer, black hair, hair she knew would be silky to the touch. "Mrs. Devereaux, I haven't practiced in a while. You need someone else who isn't as rusty with the law. Your life is in the balance."

Caleb shifted against the back wall. "Jack, you're a damn good lawyer even if it's been a while, and you know it. Take her case."

Mr. Mason's eyes never strayed from hers, however a new emotion flashed in them.

Fear?

What was he afraid of?

Think fast, Birdie. Don't lose his interest. He's the one who can help us.

"Please. My daughter shouldn't be in here, but there is nobody I can trust to care for her and her pet."

The man's gaze jumped to Willow as though just remembering she was there. His eyes softened. And for a moment she thought she saw a haze of tears. "Azalea Hall has many unused bedrooms. I can take your daughter with me if you'd like. My housekeeper has a granddaughter about her age who could use a friend."

Birdie paused. As much as she hated parting from Willow yet again, a jail cell was no place for a child.

No place for any female, for that matter. But if it kept Mr. Mason interested in her plight, she'd do it.

"Thank you," she breathed out, hoping she could endure yet another separation from her beloved daughter. Hoping Miss Kane's regard for this man wasn't misplaced.

Mr. Mason nodded his approval. "Unlock the cell, Caleb."

Shadows and Masks

Book 1 of The Chessmen series

Booksellers Best Finalist

**A desperate woman...a man with a secret...
an undeniable passion.**

Scientist Emmeline Griffith needs a husband--just long enough to prevent the loss of her inheritance to a hated cousin. The arrangement will be all business--no intimacy, no love, no passion. What she didn't count on was her attraction to the virile detective who steps into the role.

Private investigator Bartholomew Turner thought he had his secret demons under control. But when a marriage in name only turns into something far more enduring, he must confront his past and the danger that's stalking Emmie in order to claim the woman he has grown to love.

Available now at most online retail bookstores.

Excerpt:

*Chicago, Illinois
May, 1893*

"I need a husband in a week's time. Can you help me secure one?"

Emmeline Griffith's request crackled about the investigator's office like heat lightning on a hot summer day, its effect bold and intense. She scrutinized the man sitting opposite her, thankful a veil hid her heated cheeks.

Lordy! To be reduced to needing help to find a husband. She clamped her jaw tight, afraid she would utter a blasphemy as colorful as the ones her father once spouted and spoil the only course of action she had left. However, she doubted even a curse would have mattered to the man sitting opposite her.

Bartholomew Turner, the professional her uncle had recommended eons ago, might have been a statue for all the response he gave. Not a word. Not an expression. Not even a blink of his penetrating brown eyes that matched the walls of his office.

Well, fine. Two could play at this game of silence, embarrassment be damned. She would just wait him out, make him speak first. Patience was not only a virtue, but the key to the art of negotiating. As president of Chicagoland Electric, she understood negotiating—both winning and losing. In this, she would not lose. Too many people's livelihoods depended upon her success.

She surveyed the brownstone home office in the hopes of obtaining some measure of the man she planned to hire. Definitely a male domain. In fact, more like a lion's den—dark and foreboding, remarkably akin to the man himself. Three tall bay windows overlooking Eugenie Street were covered with heavy swag and cascade drapery. Shrouds, really. Walls of carved mahogany paneling added to the gloom. The office occupied the front parlor of a three-story rowhouse in a fashionable but not quite tony residential neighborhood.

Emmie straightened, tucked her crossed feet tight to the davenport, and stared at the investigator. His silence was deafening, his gaze intense. It was as if he saw right through to her soul where her darkest desires and most shameful secrets were buried. And that made her uncomfortable. Extremely uncomfortable.

He reminded her of a lion she had seen in one of her father's safari photographs, the animal lying in wait to strike its stalked prey. Even the way he had moved when greeting her—graceful and fluid—bore a strong resemblance to the big cat at the zoo. Unruly curls drifted about his handsome face as though each strand had a mind of its own. A mane. Brown instead of golden. One coil dangled over his eye, begging to be tucked behind his ear if not for the aura of aggression about him. The man's height, width of his shoulders, length of his arms, even the size of his hands spoke of power and command.

A shiver tracked up her spine. He was danger personified. And absolutely fascinating.

Author Biography

Averil Reisman loves to write steamy American-set historical romances of the late Victorian period during which America's aristocracy, created by the Industrial Revolution, lived like lords and ladies of England. A closet feminist, she greatly admires the brave women of the era who fought for equal voting rights, and who often broke society's strict rules to bring about social change and women's equality.

Averil lives with her own hero, Art, in a far suburb of Chicago where the corn still grows down the road. They see their three grown daughters, respective beloved spouses, and four very bright grandchildren as often as possible.

Printed in the USA
CPSIA information can be obtained
at www.ICGtesting.com
CBHW021037240324
5780CB00009B/189